Barbara CARTLAND

Three Complete Novels of Courtly Love

Barbara Cartland

Three Complete Novels of
Courtly Love

The Prude and
the Prodigal

Lies
for Love

From Hate
to Love

WINGS BOOKS
New York • Avenel, New Jersey

This edition contains the complete and unabridged texts of the original editions. They have been completely reset for this volume.

This omnibus was originally published in separate volumes under the titles:

The Prude and the Prodigal, copyright © 1980 by Barbara Cartland.
Lies for Love, copyright © 1982 by Barbara Cartland.
From Hate to Love, copyright © 1982 by Barbara Cartland.

This 1996 edition is published by Wings Books,
a division of Random House Value Publishing, Inc.,
40 Engelhard Avenue, Avenel, New Jersey 07001,
by arrangement with the author.

Random House
New York • Toronto • London • Sydney • Auckland

Printed and bound in the United States of America

Library of Congress Cataloging-in-Publication Data

Cartland, Barbara, 1902–
    [Novels. Selections]
    Three complete novels of courtly love / Barbara Cartland.
       p.   cm.
    Contents: The prude and the prodigal—Lies for love—From hate to love.
    ISBN 0-517-18238-6
1. Love stories, English.   2. Historical fiction, English.   3. Courts and courtiers—Fiction. I. Title.
PR6005.A765A6   1996c
823'.912—dc20   96-7361
                                                         CIP

8   7   6   5   4   3   2   1

CONTENTS

———————— ❧ ————————

THE PRUDE AND THE PRODIGAL
1

LIES FOR LOVE
153

FROM HATE TO LOVE
301

THE PRUDE AND THE PRODIGAL

Author's Note

Inigo Jones, 1573–1652, was the founder of the English classical school of Architecture. He visited Italy and attracted the patronage of Christian IV of Denmark, whose sister was married to James I of England.

Jones's greatest surviving buildings are the Banqueting Hall in Whitehall, the Queen's House at Greenwich, the Queen's Chapel in St. James's Palace, and the restoration of St. Paul's Cathedral.

Sir Anthony Van Dyke, 1599–1641, was, after Rubens, the most prominent Flemish painter of the Seventeenth Century. His enduring fame is for his portraits. He idolized his models without sacrificing any of their individuality. Their beautiful hands are characteristic of a genius.

CHAPTER ONE

❧

1817

*P*runella awoke and instantly began to think about Nanette.

Usually in the time between waking and being called she said her prayers, but this morning it was as if the problem which had been in her mind when she went to sleep was waiting for her like a ghoul sitting on the end of her bed.

"What am I to do?" she asked herself, feeling that she had tried everything already.

It had seemed such a good idea that Nanette, who was so pretty and so intelligent, should be presented at Court when she was seventeen.

Many of the girls in Society made their debut at that age, and as the mourning for their father had ended in March, it seemed almost like fate when Lady Carnworth, who was Nanette's Godmother, wrote and suggested that she should present her god-daughter to the Queen at Buckingham Palace at the end of April.

That gave them time, Prunella had calculated quickly, for Nanette to buy the elegant gowns that were essential for the London Season and to gain a few weeks' sophisticated poise before she actually made her curtsey.

Therefore, with complete confidence, Prunella had

5

accepted Lady Carnworth's kind invitation and had sent Nanette to London with a lady's-maid and an experienced Courier.

"I cannot think why you do not take me yourself," Nanette had said.

Actually the idea had never occurred to Prunella, but when Nanette suggested it she knew that Lady Carnworth would not want to chaperone two girls, and besides, Prunella had missed her chance years earlier.

"I am much too old," she had replied, her smile taking the sting from the words.

"Of course you are not!" Nanette had said loyally.

But she had not referred to it again, and Prunella knew she was a little embarrassed when she thought of how dull and dreary her elder sister's life had been these past three years.

Prunella, however, was not thinking of herself at the moment but of Nanette.

She had returned home the second week in June, after the Regent had left Carlton House for Brighton and the Season had to all intents and purposes come to an end.

"You must tell me everything, dearest," Prunella had said the first evening of her return.

Although Nanette had chattered away, she knew her sister well enough to suspect that something was being kept back.

It was soon obvious what that was, because even before Nanette had confessed—if that was the right word—Lady Carnworth wrote to Prunella:

There is no need for me to tell you that Nanette has been an unqualified success. Everybody was delighted with her looks, her gowns, for which I am prepared to take full credit, and of course for her sweet nature and exquisite good manners.

I am not going to pretend to you, Prunella, that the fact that she is an heiress did not smooth the way and open the doors for her to receive many invitations she might otherwise not have received. But of course, a young woman with money is bound to encounter difficulties, and the one I am going to tell you about, of course in confidence, is called Pascoe Lowes. He is the son of Lord Lowestoft and has been spoilt all his life by a doting mother and the fact that he is far too good-looking for any young girl's peace of mind.

When he attached himself to Nanette, my heart sank and I did everything in my power to put him off and to make her understand that he is well known as a "fortune-hunter" and therefore is a most undesirable parti in every way.

I am only hoping that now Nanette has left London and returned to the country, he will forget about her, and I thought it my duty to warn you that he has been very attentive and Nanette has, I am afraid, in consequence turned a cold shoulder on two quite suitable gentlemen who would, I am certain, had they been encouraged, have offered for her.

You must forgive me, dear Prunella, for not having somehow prevented this situation from arising, although I do not know what else I could have done to keep them apart once they had met.

I feel sure when you talk to Nanette you will make her see sense and that she can do far better for herself than to waste her time with Pascoe Lowes.

Prunella read the letter over and over again, and then wisely, because she loved her sister, waited until Nanette was ready to confide in her.

It was something she was eventually obliged to do, when a Post-Chaise arrived from London containing a huge bouquet of flowers and a letter.

Naturally Nanette had been excited by such an extravagant and flamboyant gesture.

"Can you imagine him sending flowers such a long way?" she had asked.

7

"Your admirer must be very rich!" Prunella had remarked.

Then, of course, the story came out.

"Godmama says that Pascoe is a fortune-hunter," Nanette related, "but it is untrue. He told me quite frankly he has no money, and he would have loved me even if I had not a penny to my name."

"But, dearest, you are in fact very rich," Prunella said, "and I cannot help thinking it would be a great mistake to marry a man without money."

"He will be able to spend mine," Nanette replied.

"If he was a decent man he would feel embarrassed at being in such a position," Prunella said firmly.

She talked quietly and eloquently on the subject, until she realised that Nanette was not listening but was looking with glowing eyes at the huge bouquet of flowers and touching the letter that had come with them, which was tucked into the sash of her gown.

A week later the Honourable Pascoe Lowes arrived to stay in a house about five miles away.

Prunella was surprised that he knew people in the area, until she suddenly remembered that his mother was the elder daughter of the late Earl of Winslow.

"I took no notice of his name," she said to herself, "but now I recall that Lady Anne married Lord Lowestoft, whose family name is Lowes. It was stupid of me not to remember it."

When she thought back she remembered hearing the Earl, who had been a great friend of her father's, say how boring he found his son-in-law, with the result that Lord and Lady Lowestoft seldom stayed at the Hall.

Prunella supposed they must have done so when she was a child, but later she had heard that Lord Lowestoft was bed-ridden, and of course during the war the Earl seldom entertained and her father appeared to be his only guest.

'It is a pity the Earl is not alive today,' Prunella

thought when she learnt about Nanette's interest in his grandson.

She was quite certain that the old Earl, a fierce and rather terrifying old man, would not have allowed his grandson to behave in any way which was unbecoming to a gentleman. And what, indeed, could be worse than to be branded as a "fortune-hunter"?

When Pascoe Lowes was announced, Prunella saw at first glance that it was going to be difficult to persuade Nanette that he was only an extremely handsome, if overdressed, young man.

Prunella had never visited London and had therefore no idea of what the Bucks, Beaux, and Dandies actually looked like, but here was a man who was undoubtedly all three, walking towards her and to her eyes looking so fantastic that she felt she must be gaping at him with her mouth open like a goldfish.

"I am so delighted to make your acquaintance, Miss Broughton," this vision of elegance was saying. "Your sister has extolled your beauty and your virtues until I found it hard to believe that such a paragon really existed, and yet I see she has not exaggerated."

'He certainly puts on an excellent performance,' Prunella thought.

But at the same time the Honourable Pascoe spoke with such apparent sincerity and undoubted charm that despite herself she found she was smiling at his compliment.

He obviously was not listening to what she said, but was watching Nanette, and there was no doubt that he was looking at her in a meaningful and ardent manner which Prunella felt would turn the head of any girl, especially one as inexperienced as her sister.

By the time the visit was over, and the Honourable Pascoe was clever enough to make it short, Prunella was really alarmed.

He was, she was quite certain, everything that she

would dislike in a brother-in-law and she felt that he would make Nanette extremely unhappy.

How could any girl who was country-bred tolerate a husband who must spend hours having his cravat tied in such a difficult, intricate fashion just to make all the other Dandies envious?

The points of his collar reached exactly the prescribed position above his chin, and his hair was arranged in the wind-swept style set by the Prince Regent.

His Hessian boots owed their fine polish, if Nanette was to be believed, to champagne.

"Champagne!" Prunella wanted to cry out loud, when he had no money and was doubtless accumulating a pile of debts!

When he left, after paying more extravagant compliments to Prunella and holding Nanette's hand far longer than was necessary, there was no doubt that he had left an impression that was not easy to erase.

Nanette was starry-eyed the whole evening and Prunella knew that whatever she might say to disparage Pascoe Lowes, it would fall on deaf ears.

"What am I to do?" she asked herself when she went to bed that night, and it was a question she had been repeating over and over again all through the week.

She heard her bedroom door open and knew that it was Charity, the maid who had looked after her ever since she was a child, who was carefully crossing the room towards the window.

Charity, who had been inflicted with such a cruel name by the Orphanage in which she had been brought up, was getting on in years.

But because she had been well trained she still moved as silently as when she had come to the Manor first as an under under-housemaid, then as a Nurserymaid, and finally, soon after Nanette had been born, she had been promoted to Nanny.

Now she was lady's-maid, Housekeeper, and self-appointed Chaperone to Prunella and Nanette since Sir Roderick had died.

Prunella had toyed with the idea of having an elderly lady to live with them, but she did not know anyone suitable, and also she knew that it would be depressing and a restriction that she would find intolerable.

"We live very quietly," she told herself, "and anyway there is little more the County can say about us that has not been said already."

At this there was a hardness in her eyes and a bitter twist to her lips, before deliberately she turned her thoughts elsewhere, and that inevitably was to Nanette.

Charity pulled back the curtains and the sunshine flooded in through the windows. Then she turned towards the bed, and Prunella knew before she spoke that she had something to relate.

"What is it, Charity?" she asked, instinctively feeling that it would not be good news.

"Another letter came for Miss Nanette this morning," Charity replied, "and it was almost as if she knew clairvoyantly it was a-coming. She was down the stairs and at the front door before Bates could get there!"

"Was she already dressed?" Prunella asked.

"In her dressing-gown she was! I says to her: 'Really, Miss Nanette, you ought to be ashamed of yourself,' coming down the stairs in a way no lady would!' "

"What did she answer?" Prunella enquired.

"I might as well have been talking to the wall!" Charity replied. "She just rushes past me, hugging the letter to her chest, goes into her bedroom, and I hears the key turn in the lock."

Prunella sighed.

"Oh, Charity, what are we to do about her?"

"I haven't the least idea what we can do, Miss Prunella, and that's the truth!" Charity replied. "I don't know what your father would have said if he could have seen her, going to the front door in her bed-attire, with the men-servants about!"

It was obvious that Charity was extremely shocked by it and in fact so was Prunella.

Not that Bates really mattered, for he had been with them almost as long as Charity had, and the only footman they had at the moment was Bates's grandson, who was rather simple and not likely to notice what anyone was wearing.

It was the principle of the thing that mattered, and Prunella told herself that it was her duty to rebuke Nanette and to make her promise it would not happen again.

Charity had gone to the bedroom door to bring in a tray on which were a pot of the finest China tea, a slice of very thin bread, and butter.

She set it down on the table beside Prunella, saying as she did so:

"Mrs. Goodwin brought surprising news this morning!"

Prunella, pouring her tea, waited without much interest to hear what it was.

Mrs. Goodwin was one of the women on the Estate who came in to help with the scrubbing, but she spent more time talking than she did keeping the passages clean.

"She says, Miss Prunella," Charity went on, "that Mr. Gerald came back last night!"

Prunella put down the tea-pot.

"Mr. Gerald?" she repeated with a questioning note in her voice.

"I suppose I should say 'His Lordship' but somehow it comes strangely to the tongue."

Prunella's eyes were suddenly very wide.

"You are not saying . . . you cannot mean . . ."

"Yes, Miss Prunella, the new Earl of Winslow's home, if Mrs. Goodwin's to be believed. And after fourteen years!"

"It cannot be true!" Prunella gasped. "I had begun to think he would never come back."

"Well, he's here now," Charity said, "and if you asks me, he's only come to see what he can sell!"

"Oh, no!"

Prunella only breathed the words, but they seemed to come from the very depths of her being.

As Charity moved across the room to the wardrobe, Prunella said, almost as if she spoke to herself:

"The Earl is a relative of Pascoe Lowes, and . . ."

Her voice trailed away, but Charity heard what she had said.

"If you're thinking he'll be any help in stopping that overdressed young gentleman from pursuing Miss Nanette, Miss, I think you're mistaken. He's as bad, if not worse, than his nephew!"

There was no need to elaborate, because Prunella had heard all her life of the indiscretions and the raffish behaviour of the Earl's only son, Gerald.

When he had been living at home, the Estate, the village, and the County had talked of nothing else but his escapades, his wild parties, his fashionable friends, and the beautiful, alluring women whom he pursued and, if rumour was to be believed, who pursued him.

Then in 1803 during the Armistice between France and England things came to a climax.

Prunella was only seven and at the time was quite unaware of what was going on, but the tale had been related to her so often all through her life that she knew it as well as she knew her Catechism.

By this time it had been varied and embellished until she would have found it hard, if she had been hearing it for the first time, to believe it could possibly be true.

Knowing the old Earl as well as she did, there was no doubt that he, like all autocrats, was determined to have his own way, and apparently his son was the same.

They were both obstinate, self-willed, and undoubtedly overbearing, and the Earl had told Gerald that his philanderings were to cease, that he was to stop spending so much money, and that the best thing he could do would be to marry and settle down.

But Gerald had replied that he had no intention of doing any such thing.

"Like two fighting cocks they was!" one of the old retainers had said to Prunella. "Neither of 'em would give in, and when His Lordship knew he was being defied he loses his temper!"

Prunella had seen the old Earl in a temper many times and knew it was an extremely awesome sight, but she had learnt that Mr. Gerald had a temper too.

They had therefore been evenly matched, but the outcome had been that the old Earl had threatened to cut his son off without a penny and had loaded the threat with many insults.

Gerald had told his father exactly what he could do with his money.

"Fine words!" the old Earl had sneered. "But you will soon find yourself in 'Queer Street' without it and come running back to ask for my help!"

"I would rather die than do that!" Gerald had replied. "So you can keep your damned money, your advice, and your everlasting disapproval of everything I do. As for my inheritance and this Estate by which you set so much store, it can rot for all I care and the house can fall to the ground before I would raise a finger to stop it!"

He could not have said anything which would have infuriated the Earl more, but before he could think of a suitable reply Gerald had gone.

The next thing they learnt was that "young Mr. Gerald" had left England, taking with him the pretty young wife of one of their neighbours, and her elderly husband was threatening to "shoot him down like a dog"!

From that moment there had been silence.

A month later war had started again with France,

and all that was known was that Gerald had left England, and if he had gone to Paris, as seemed likely, the lady who had left with him had not returned.

There were a few people who escaped from the prisons in which Napoleon had confined all the British tourists, but Gerald was not amongst them.

It was five years before it was learnt quite casually that the lady who had left England with him had died of cholera in the East.

Whether or not Gerald had died with her was not known at the time, but Prunella remembered that four years ago the Earl had told her father that he had received a letter from a friend informing him that Gerald had been seen in India.

There was no question of his coming home, and it would have been difficult unless he travelled in a troop-ship, for although Britain "ruled the waves" it was a long passage from India and a dangerous one.

The only ships that made the six-month voyage were those taking soldiers out or bringing them home.

A year before Prunella's father died, the Earl of Winslow had a stroke.

He had got into one of his rages, and when he dropped unconscious to the floor, it was impossible to save him, and although he lingered for two or three months he finally died.

It was partly the loss of his old friend, Prunella thought, that had made her father relinquish his already frail hold upon life.

She had nursed him day and night because he disliked having strangers about him, and he clung to her in a manner which made it almost impossible for her to do anything else.

If she was not there in his bedroom in the daytime he called her, and even at night he would send for her two or three times for no reason except that he wanted to see her.

This did not prevent him from being querulous,

irritable, and difficult as only an invalid can be, and when finally he died Prunella herself was exhausted to the point of collapse.

It was Charity who had put her to bed, and she had slept without waking for forty-eight hours.

"I must get up," she had said weakly when she realised that she had lost two days out of her life.

"You'll stay where you are, Miss Prunella!" Charity had said firmly.

"But . . ."

"Miss Nanette and I can cope. Go back to sleep, Miss Prunella, and I'll wake you when we needs you."

Because she felt so tired and so weak, Prunella had done as she was told.

She knew afterwards that Charity's treatment had really saved her from a breakdown from sheer fatigue.

At first she could hardly believe that she was free to live a life of her own without hearing her father call her, without finding herself thinking of his comfort every second of the day.

Then she found that there were a great many things to be done which only she could do.

Now as she got up and dressed, she found herself wondering whether the new Earl would behave like his father.

Surely, after being away so long, he would want to make reparation for the past and take up his position as head of the family.

The old Earl had always looked and behaved rather like a Biblical character, and although Prunella could hardly remember his son, she felt sure that he would want to follow the long succession of Winslows who had lived at the Hall and made it a place of importance not only to the Winn family but in the surrounding countryside.

Then as she buttoned her gown she suddenly remembered, almost as if someone had struck her, what Charity had said.

"He's come back looking for money, I suppose."

The words seemed to echo and re-echo round her bedroom and she knew that the new Earl of Winslow was going to have a shock which would doubtless be a very unpleasant one.

Two hours later Prunella stepped into the old-fashioned but well-sprung carriage drawn by two well-bred horses and set off for the Hall.

The old coachman who was driving her was not surprised when she told him where she wished to go, and she wondered if he knew that the Earl had returned.

After all, news about him would run like wildfire through the Estate, and if Mrs. Goodwin knew, then so would everybody else by this time.

Prunella gave a little sigh.

It was not going to be an easy interview and she wished somebody could have gone with her to give her support.

She knew that Nanette would be worse than useless, especially after this morning when she had received the letter from Pascoe, and besides, what she had to say to the Earl when she had explained everything else was something her sister must not overhear.

She could have taken Charity, but she could not help thinking with a little smile that her stringent comments on "Mr. Gerald's" past behaviour would not help the situation.

It was difficult to anticipate what his attitude would be.

The carriage carried Prunella through the village, with its black-and-white Inn on the other side of the Green, the small pond on which there were always a few ducks, and the old Alms Houses that had been built by the previous Earl in more prosperous days.

The horses turned in through the gates to the Hall with their stone lodges on either side. They were occupied by gate-keepers who by now were so old and decrepit that they were no longer capable of attending to the gates; which were therefore left open permanently.

There was a long drive which wanted gravelling, bordered by oak trees which needed attention, then there was the lake with its banks overgrown with irises, and beyond it was the Hall.

It was beautiful architecturally, in that it was designed by Inigo Jones, but the bricks needed pointing and there were a number of panes missing from the top-floor windows.

Yet Prunella could see that the first and second floor were not only in good repair but shining because they had recently been cleaned.

The carriage stopped at the steps leading up to the front door, which she noticed was open.

Dawson, the coachman, was too old to get down to assist Prunella to alight, but she managed it herself and stepped out.

"Shall I wait here for ye, Miss Prunella," he asked, "or go round to the back?"

She hesitated a moment, then replied:

"I think you should go round to the back, Dawson, and find out what is happening, and if the Carters are all right. They may be upset by His Lordship's unexpected return."

"I'll do that, Miss Prunella."

She did not wait to say any more but hurried up the steps and walked in through the open door.

As she had expected, there was nobody in the main Hall, and although she was feeling a little nervous she walked resolutely towards the Library, which she felt was where the Earl would be.

But the Library was empty, and so was the large Salon where the shutters had not been opened and the furniture was still covered with Holland dust-sheets.

She thought for a moment, then walked up the staircase, with its exquisite Seventeenth Century iron-work, towards the Picture-Gallery.

She had a feeling almost like a pain in her heart that she knew she would find the Earl there and why he was there.

She was not mistaken. In the Gallery which ran the whole length of the central block was a man.

He had his back to her and for a moment she did not notice that he was tall and very broad-shoul-dered, but she saw that he was staring at a picture which had been painted by Van Dyke.

Prunella's lips tightened. Then as she walked slowly down the Gallery he must have heard her footsteps, for he turned his head and she saw that Gerald, the sixth Earl of Winslow, did not look in the least what she had expected.

Somehow, because she had always heard so much about his wild, raffish behaviour, she had expected him to look dandified and perhaps to bear some re-semblance to his nephew Pascoe.

The man who turned to watch her approach, with what she thought was an expression of surprise in his dark eyes, was so casually dressed that it told her more surely than anything else that Charity was right: he had come back to find something to sell.

His coat was cut on the right lines but was some-what loose-fitting, there was nothing special about his pantaloons, and his boots definitely needed polishing.

As for his cravat, Prunella was sure that Pascoe would view it with horror, and even to her eyes it looked loose and comfortable rather than elegant and restricting.

What was strange was that his skin was so brown, and it took Prunella a second to remember that he had been in India and was therefore sunburnt.

While she was scrutinising the Earl, he was doing

the same to her. In fact, he was wondering who this woman could be and trying to recall if he had ever seen her before.

Then as she drew nearer he was aware that she was too young for him ever to have met her.

He had at first been deceived, by the plain grey of her gown and her bonnet trimmed with grey ribbons, into thinking she was perhaps middle-aged.

Then he saw that her oval face, which was dominated by two very large grey eyes, was that of a young woman and that she was looking at him critically and with, understandably, an expression of disapproval.

As she reached him he asked:

"May I enquire if you have called to see me, which seems unlikely? Or have you another reason for being here in the Hall?"

Prunella dropped him a little curtsey.

"I am Prunella Broughton, My Lord. My father, Sir Roderick, who unfortunately died a year ago, was a very close friend of your father."

"I remember Sir Roderick," the Earl replied, "and I fancy I can now recall a small, pretty child who used to accompany him when he came here, who undoubtedly was yourself."

"I am gratified that Your Lordship should remember me," Prunella answered, "for I have something to tell you which I think you should know."

"I shall of course be delighted to listen, Miss Broughton," the Earl answered. "As you are doubtless aware, I arrived here only last night, and I was just now reacquainting myself with my ancestors."

As he spoke he indicated a portrait for the second Earl, and despite her resolution to remain calm Prunella gave a little cry.

"Oh, please," she said, "if you are going to sell any of the paintings, do not sell that one. It is the very best of them all, and your father used to relate that when Van Dyke had finished it, he said to your forebear: 'I shall never do a better portrait and this actually is the moment I should die!' "

As her voice died away there was silence. Then the Earl said:

"You are implying that I am intending to sell some of these paintings?"

"I was afraid that was in your mind, My Lord," Prunella answered, "and if you will permit me to do so, I will show you a list I have made of things in the house which would fetch quite a considerable sum but which would not be so cruelly missed by the future generations as the paintings in this Gallery."

"I do not understand," the Earl said, and his voice was dry, "why you should concern yourself, Miss Broughton, so closely with my private affairs."

Prunella drew in her breath.

"That is what I have come to . . . explain to Your Lordship."

The Earl looked round as if he was going to suggest that they sit down, but the chairs in the Gallery were all covered to prevent them from fading, and as if it was obviously what was in his thoughts, Prunella said:

"It would be best, I think, if we went down to the Library. I have always kept that room open."

"*You* have kept it open?" the Earl questioned.

He saw a faint flush come into her cheeks as she said:

"That is another thing I am going to . . . explain to you."

"And I shall be very interested to hear your explanation," he replied.

She thought there was an edge to his voice, as if already he resented her.

They walked in silence back along the Gallery, down the staircase, and into the Hall.

When they reached it a man appeared who Prunella guessed was a valet.

"So there y'are, M'Lord!" he said in what she privately thought was a slightly familiar tone. "I was

21

thinking, as there's nothing to eat in the house I'd best pop down to the village and buy something."

"All right—do that," the Earl agreed.

The valet would have turned away but Prunella said quickly:

"I am afraid there is not much to buy in Little Stodbury, but if you go to the Home Farm you will find that Mrs. Gabriel will let you have an excellent ham that she has cured herself, and you could ask, when they are slaughtering their sheep, if they would keep a leg for His Lordship."

"Thank ye, Ma'am," the valet said.

"And of course, as Mrs. Carter should have told you, the Home Farm will provide eggs, milk, and butter, but I am afraid you will have to pay for them."

She looked a little anxiously at the Earl as she said:

"The arrangements they had with your father have lapsed since his death, and as they have to struggle to make two ends meet, they could not provide you with food for nothing."

"I did not intend to ask them to do so," the Earl replied sharply.

He turned to his valet.

"Pay for everything as you go, Jim."

"Very good, M'Lord."

As the valet disappeared Prunella could not help wondering where the money was coming from.

It seemed strange that the valet did not ask his master for any, and she thought it might be his own he was using until the Earl could sell something in the house and pay him back.

Once again she felt that pain within herself at the thought of parting with the treasures she had known and admired ever since she was a child.

At first, when they had been so isolated during the war, with the horses commandeered by the Army and with the younger men either away fighting under Wellington or enjoying themselves in the world of gaiety created by the Regent, the old Earl had been very lonely.

He used to encourage Prunella to borrow books from his Library because, he said, it was good for her education, but really it was because he liked talking to her and otherwise nobody except the servants came to the big house.

He would tell her tales about the paintings and the furniture, but because he was obsessed by the family and what it meant to him, his stories were nearly always about his ancestors, who had been soldiers, Statesmen, explorers, gamblers, and Rakes.

And now, she thought, another Rake had come home to diminish a treasure-chest which to her was part of history and which, because she too lived a very quiet life, was somehow part of herself.

They reached the Library and the Earl stood back for her to enter first.

She did not know why, but she felt he did it almost mockingly, and then as they walked into the room Prunella was suddenly acutely conscious of how shabby it looked.

She had never noticed it before, but now, as if she were seeing it with a newcomer's eyes, she realised that parts of the carpet were threadbare, the covers on the chairs had faded, and the linings of the curtains were in such rags that it was impossible for them to be mended any more.

She wondered if the Earl was thinking that things had been neglected since he had gone away.

She seated herself in an arm-chair at the side of the fireplace while he stood with his back to it, his hands deep in the pockets of his breeches, looking at her in an uncompromising manner.

"Well, what is all this about?"

Ever since she had arrived at the Hall Prunella had been holding in her hand a notebook, which she now placed on her lap as she said:

"I . . . I suppose it would be polite of me first to

. . . welcome you home and say that . . . although
your return is unexpected, it is . . . better late than
never!"

"Do I detect a note of condemnation in your voice,
Miss Broughton?" the Earl enquired.

"You must realise, My Lord, that since your father
died things have been very . . . difficult."

"Why?"

"To begin with, no-one had any idea where you
were, and secondly there was nobody to look after the
Estate."

"What happened to Andrews? I always understood
that he was a perfectly capable man."

"Fourteen years ago he was," Prunella answered,
"but, as it happens, Mr. Andrews has been bedridden
for the last eighteen months, and for some years before that he was really incapable of getting round the
Estate, even when somebody could drive him."

The Earl appeared to digest this information for a
moment before he said, with a slight curl of his lips:

"Surely somebody has been engaged to take his
place?"

"And how would he be paid?" Prunella enquired.

There was silence. Then the Earl asked:

"Are you telling me there is no money?"

"If I speak frankly and truthfully, My Lord, the
answer is 'yes.' "

"But why? I understood—I always believed my father was a rich man."

"And so he was when you left home. But I think
perhaps he had not as much captital as you thought,
or else it was badly invested. Anyway, My Lord, many
people's fortunes dwindled during the war, and Estates like this ceased to be profitable."

"Why? Why?" the Earl asked sharply.

"The tenants grew old and became incapable of
farming their land properly, and they could not afford to employ enough men, even if they could have

got them. Most able-bodied men were in the Army or the Navy, and gradually things deteriorated."

This news obviously shook the Earl, and she saw by the expression on his face that it was something he had not expected, and it made him knit his brows and set his lips in a tight line. Then he asked:

"I am quite prepared to believe what you tell me, but I want to know how you come into this."

Prunella looked down at the book on her lap as if it gave her some comfort. Then she said:

"When my father was alive, he . . . helped yours in . . . one way or another."

"Are you telling me that my father borrowed money from yours?"

Prunella nodded her head.

"I would like to be informed of how much, and I expect, of course, to repay you."

"There is no need for that. It was not a loan but a gift."

"I shall look upon it as a debt!" the Earl said in an uncompromising voice.

Prunella did not speak, and as if he thought he had sounded rude he said quickly:

"But of course I am extremely grateful. I am only astonished that my father should have needed help of that sort."

"What worries me," Prunella said, "is what will . . . happen now."

"What do you mean by that?"

"There are certain pensioners who, if they are not paid, will starve because . . . they are old . . . past work . . . and there is nowhere else they can . . . go."

"Who has been paying these pensioners?"

There was silence until he said, even more sharply:

"I want to know the truth, Miss Broughton!"

"Since my father's death . . . I have," she replied.

She raised her eyes to his as she added:

"I was not interfering . . . it is just that they are

25

people I have known all my life, and so the ones who were active worked here in the house for very little, but it kept them from starvation and I could not bear to see everything going to rack and ruin and covered in dust."

"So you paid *my* employees to keep *my* house in order?"

"It sounds a strange thing to do," Prunella said, "but because I came here so often when your . . . father was alive . . . and because I have always . . . known and loved the Hall, it meant almost as much to me as my . . . own house."

"And what else did you do?"

"I have put it all down in this little . . . notebook," Prunella replied. "Those who are receiving small pensions every week . . . so that they can keep alive . . . those who can work and earn a little money . . . although it often has to be supplemented . . . and the rents that are coming in more or less regularly."

She gave a quick glance at the Earl's face and was afraid of what she was seeing, before she added:

"In some cases . . . I cancelled the farmers' rents . . . altogether."

"Why did you do that?"

"You do not . . . understand," Prunella answered, and now her voice rose a little. "Since the war ended, the farmers have found that the prices for their produce have fallen disastrously. What is more, this year many of the County Banks have closed their doors and people have lost their savings of a lifetime."

The Earl did not speak and she went on:

"It is bad enough having thousands of men pouring out of the Army and the Navy without being given pensions, without any recompense for their injuries. The cost of living has gone up and for most of them there is no work. I had to take care of the people on this Estate . . . there was nobody else."

The Earl walked across to the window to stare out onto the lake and the Park beyond it.

"You must of course accept my gratitude, Miss Broughton," he said. "I am only surprised that you should have been so generous."

He did not sound very grateful and she felt that the way he praised her was not exactly a compliment, but she replied:

"If you are really grateful . . . then I want to ask you to do . . . something for me."

The Earl turned from the window and now there was a smile on his lips.

"So you are human after all!" he said. "I began to think you were some strange philanthropist who was doing good if not for your soul then perhaps for mine—and now, if you have a human frailty, I shall believe after all that you are real."

Prunella stared at him in sheer astonishment. Then she said sharply:

"I assure you I am real, My Lord, and the favour I have to . . . ask you is a very real trouble to me."

"I am waiting to hear it," the Earl said.

Now she felt, and she could not think why, that he was definitely mocking her.

CHAPTER TWO

*T*he Earl sat down in a chair on the other side of the hearth-rug.

He crossed his legs, sat back at his ease, and regarded her with what she thought was a slight smile on his lips.

Because she had felt slightly embarrassed ever since coming to call on the Earl, she had not looked at him very closely. Now she thought that his eyes in his suntanned face were definitely penetrating, although his eye-lids drooped a little lazily, as if he regarded life cynically.

There was something about his whole attitude that she resented.

She thought it was what she might have expected to feel about a man who, having left his home in such a reprehensible manner, had returned to be critical of everything that had been done in his absence.

There was a distinct silence before the Earl said, again with a mocking note in his voice:

"I am waiting, Miss Broughton, and of course, being deeply in your debt, I am prepared to be very sympathetic towards anything you require of me."

Prunella felt she wished to challenge this statement, but there was no excuse for doing so, and after a moment she said:

"What I am asking you to do, My Lord, is to

prevent your nephew from paying attention to my sister."

The Earl raised his eye-brows and she knew this was something he had not been expecting.

"My nephew?" he asked.

"Pascoe Lowes, the eldest son of your sister, Lady Lowestoft."

The Earl smiled.

"I suppose I had forgotten his existence," he said, "because, as you may be aware, since I have been abroad my relations have not communicated with me. But it would interest me to know why my nephew should not pay his addresses, if that is what he intends to do, to your sister."

Prunella's back was stiff and her voice was hard as she replied:

"I will be frank with you, My Lord. Pascoe Lowes has a reputation, which I understand is fully justified, of being a fortune-hunter. He is also a Dandy."

Her tone was contemptuous and to her surprise the Earl laughed.

"He has certainly got on the wrong side of you, Miss Broughton. In fact, I feel quite sorry for him."

"There is no need for you to do that," Prunella said sharply. "But as my sister is only seventeen, she is young and impressionable."

"Then where did she meet my nephew?"

"In London. My father died a year ago and we were out of mourning in March. I therefore arranged for Nanette to be presented at Court."

"*You* arranged it?" the Earl remarked. "I see you lead a very busy life, Miss Broughton. You not only arrange my affairs but also those of your sister. Surely you have some assistance?"

"Since my father's death we have been living alone at the Manor," Prunella explained, "and as we live very quietly, there has been no need to have anybody living with us."

"You refer to your quiet life," the Earl said. "It

surprises me. This used to be a lively place and there were many large houses with very hospitable owners."

He spoke almost as if he was reminiscing to himself, and therefore he was surprised when Prunella said in a repressed voice:

"I am sure, now that the war is over, that you, at any rate, will find quite a number of people ready to entertain you, My Lord."

As she spoke she thought that because he was the Earl of Winslow and unmarried, their neighbours would be too curious not to wish to meet him, even if he could not return their hospitality.

"So, while I can be entertained, you have not been so fortunate," the Earl remarked.

Prunella felt he was being uncomfortably perceptive and there was a distinct pause before she said:

"I have been in mourning for a year."

"And before that?"

"May I point out that my life is none of your business, My Lord?"

"That seems extraordinary!" the Earl remarked. "You have made my life your business. You have taken over control of my household and apparently my Estate, and yet now, because I am interested in you as a person, you are closing the door on me."

Prunella had the feeling that he was deliberately pursuing the subject simply because he was aware that she did not wish to talk about herself.

Then she said desperately:

"I wish to speak to Your Lordship about your nephew."

"That is what I understood. At the same time, I am trying to get a picture of what is happening, and unaccountably, Miss Broughton, you are refusing to assist me."

"What I was thinking," Prunella said quickly, "is that now that you are home, I am quite certain your nephew will ask you for financial help."

"Why do you imagine he will do that?" the Earl asked.

"For one thing, I presume he is your heir, and also . . ."

"And for another?"

She did not reply and the Earl said:

"It would be a mistake not to finish that sentence and keep anything from me."

"Very well," Prunella said. "I learnt yesterday that a week ago, when he was staying in the County, Mr. Lowes visited your father's Solicitors to find out if it would be possible to take steps to prove that you were dead, in which case he wished to put forward a claim for the house and its contents."

The Earl said nothing and Prunella went on:

"Surely you understand that would mean he would sell it. He would have no wish to live here, because he obviously prefers London, and anyway he could not afford to do so . . . and . . . and the Van Dykes would go first."

She spoke with a passionate note in her voice, and the Earl said, almost drawling the words:

"I can see that my paintings mean a great deal to you, Miss Broughton, but after all they are only paintings!"

"How can you say that when they have been handed down from father to son for two hundred years? When so many of them are of your ancestors and Inigo Jones designed the Gallery especially for them?"

"You are certainly very well informed, Miss Broughton."

He was being sarcastic but Prunella did not care.

"I consider them, as your father did, a sacred trust to be handed on to your children and their children, and not to be disposed of by any 'n'er-do-well' who wants money to throw away at the gaming-tables or on women!"

Her voice seemed to ring out and again the Earl laughed.

"Well done, Miss Broughton! And of course I understand only too well what you are saying, having heard such tirades a thousand times, until I could stand them no longer and left England to prevent myself from having to do so again."

Prunella felt her spirits drop and the fire went out of her.

What was the point of talking?

Everything that had been said against him in the past must be true, and he was no better now than he had been when he ran away from his father, taking with him the wife of another man.

She thought that the best thing she could do was to leave with dignity and let the Earl, as he apparently wished to do, manage his own life in his own way.

Then she remembered how many people depended on her.

There were the old people in the two Lodges, who were so frail that in the winter she usually took them what food they required because they were incapable of walking even the short distance to the shop on the Green.

Then there were the farmers who could only just manage to produce the food they themselves needed and could not afford to do necessary repairs to their farm-houses, nor to the barns which had fallen down.

There were so many others. Even the Carters were long past retirement age, but there had been no cottage available, and they might just as well stay at the Hall and do what they could to keep it clean.

Her thoughts seemed to race through her mind, and all the time she was aware that the Earl was watching her, the mocking smile she disliked twisting his lips.

"Suppose we continue," he said after a moment. "You were telling me about my nephew and making it quite clear that you would not tolerate him as a brother-in-law."

"I will do anything to prevent it, My Lord!"

"Even come to me for assistance, although you are well aware it is asking the 'pot to call the kettle black'?"

Prunella thought this was only too true, and, as she could not think of a reply, she merely waited, her eyes on the Earl's face.

As if his thoughts were once again on her, he said:

"I assume, from what you have said, that your sister is an heiress, in which case I presume you are also one."

"No, My Lord."

"No?"

"My sister was left a considerable amount of money by . . .

She hesitated before she ended:

". . . My mother."

"I believe I remember your mother," the Earl said reflectively. "Yes, I do remember her, and she was very beautiful. I am sorry to hear that she is dead."

Prunella did not reply, and when he looked at her he saw that she had dropped her eyes so that her lashes were dark against her cheeks and her lips were pressed together in what he thought was a hard line.

"I said I am sorry your mother is dead!"

"I heard you, My Lord."

"Where did she die?"

"I have no idea."

"You must be aware that you are making me curious?" the Earl remarked.

"I do not wish to speak of it, My Lord. I want to talk to you about Nanette."

"Nanette can wait," the Earl answered. "What is this mystery about your mother?"

Prunella rose from the chair in which she was sitting to walk to the window, even as he had done earlier in their conversation.

She stood looking out, and now that her figure was silhouetted against the light, the Earl could see that she was very slender and graceful, and it was only her grey gown, which he thought had nothing to commend it, that concealed the fact.

After a moment, as if she had made up her mind, she said, still with her back to him:

"I expect sooner or later you will be told what occurred, so it might as well be now."

The Earl was aware that she drew in a deep breath before she said:

"My mother . . . ran away . . . six years . . . ago!"

"It seems a somewhat prevalent exercise in this part of the world," the Earl remarked.

"It is not something I can laugh about, My Lord, and now that I have told you, will you please not speak of it again? My mother's name was never mentioned in my father's house from the time she left."

There was silence. Then with a very obvious effort Prunella walked back from the window to the chair in which she had been sitting.

"It is obvious that, like myself, your mother could stand things no longer," the Earl remarked. "Did you miss her?"

"I have no wish to talk about my mother, My Lord."

"But I am interested," he insisted. "Now that I remember how beautiful your mother was, I think I am right in saying that your father was very much older than she was. In fact, he was a contemporary of my father, who was getting on for fifty when I was born."

Prunella did not reply, and the Earl, with a distinct twinkle in his eyes, continued:

"So the beautiful Lady Broughton followed my example and left a deadly existence of respectability and psalm-singing for what is popularly termed 'a life of sin'!"

He saw Prunella shudder, and finished:

"The punishment for which, of course, is fire and brimstone, hell and damnation, which is, I can assure you, far more pleasant and on the whole more enjoyable than what we left behind."

"I do not have to listen to this, My Lord."

"But you will do so because I want you to," the Earl replied. "I can see all too clearly, Miss Broughton, that you are condemning your mother to damnation as you condemn me and my nephew. I would be interested to know by what right you sit in judgement upon us."

"I am not judging, My Lord," Prunella protested, "I am only asking you to understand the position in which you find yourself now that you have come home, and I am trying to explain why, after your father died, I tried to save those who were suffering through no fault of their own."

"Very commendable!" the Earl remarked, but it did not sound like a compliment.

"Your private life is no concern of mine."

"But you are shocked by what you think I have been doing," the Earl insisted, "just as you were shocked by your mother."

As if he goaded her into a reply, Prunella said:

"Of course I was shocked . . . shocked, horrified, and disgusted! How could any woman leave her husband and her . . . family?"

"Her family!" the Earl replied softly. "That is the operative word, is it not? You minded her leaving you!"

For a fleeting second he saw the pain in Prunella's eyes as she looked at him, and he said in a different tone:

"When you are as old as I am, Miss Broughton, you will understand that for every human action there are always extenuating circumstances, and if one has a kind heart and a perceptive mind, one can find them and understand."

Now it was her turn to be surprised, and her eyes

were very large in her face as she looked at him before she said slowly:

"Perhaps you are . . . right. Perhaps I have not . . . looked further than what seemed to me to be a . . . wicked act of selfishness!"

"Did your mother leave alone?"

Again Prunella shuddered, and he felt as if it vibrated through her and came from the very depths of her being as she said, her voice barely above a whisper:

"N-no!"

"Then I imagine she was in love," the Earl said, "and love, my dear Miss Broughton, is something that is irresistible at the time, even if one is disappointed later."

The way he spoke made Prunella remember that he had been in love with the woman he had taken away with him when he had left.

She remembered the story had been that she was very pretty and they had met at first clandestinely while out riding, before finally they had disappeared together, leaving everybody shocked and horrified by their outrageous behaviour.

It was, Prunella thought now, not only a hatred for his father that had made Gerald storm out of the Hall swearing he would not return, but also that he had heard the irresistible call of love for a woman who was perhaps as unhappy in her environment as he was in his.

Then she realised that this was what had happened to her mother.

Of course it was true that she was very much younger than the man she had married straight from the School-Room.

Prunella's father had loved her in his own way, but she supposed that none of them had realised how unhappy and frustrated her mother had been before she had met . . .

Prunella stopped her thoughts.

She had sworn never again to think of the man she had utterly condemned for seducing her mother and taking her from them.

Because he had always been so charming to her she had, in an adolescent way, been in love with him herself.

She had thought he looked exactly as a gentleman should look. She admired the way he rode, and because he paid her the first compliments she had ever received she had cherished them and had taken more trouble over her appearance whenever she knew he was coming to the house.

That he should have betrayed not only her father but herself, by running away with her mother, had seemed a final act of treachery.

It had been so horrible, so unforgivable, that Prunella had told herself she loathed not only him but also her mother with a violence that made her feel murderous towards them.

"It was Mama who killed Papa!" she had said when her father died.

But she knew he had been ailing long before her mother had left, although perhaps it was because his wife had gone that he made no effort to get well or keep himself alive.

She had known when her father had clung to her that he was in a way making her a substitute for the wife who had deserted him.

Because she wanted to erase her mother's crime from his mind, her devotion to him had astonished everybody including the Doctors.

Yet she had known that deep in her heart it was not only love for her father but hatred for her mother which activated her.

Now the Earl, whose own life had been so reprehensible, was asking her to forgive, or rather, far more difficult, to understand her mother's motives and his own.

Because she felt at the moment as if he had created

a chaos in her mind and she could not think clearly, she said:

"I would like, My Lord, to talk of your nephew. You said you would listen sympathetically to my request, and I am deeply perturbed by his pursuit of Nanette."

"I am prepared to talk about Pascoe," the Earl said, "but I want to get one thing quite clear: your mother left her money—and I am assuming she had a considerable fortune—to your sister and nothing to you?"

"I cannot see how that is of any importance to you, My Lord," Prunella replied, "but as it happens she divided it equally between us, and we were to have it when we became twenty-one."

She paused and the Earl interposed by saying:

"So when you reached that age you gave your share to your sister?"

"Yes."

"But you still have enough money of your own to spend on my Estate and my servants?"

"I have enough, My Lord, but Nanette is only seventeen and a fortune at that age is not only a responsibility but can also be a liability."

"You mean when a young man like my nephew is interested in her?"

"Exactly, My Lord!"

"I presume the money is in trust?"

"The Trustees are my father, who is dead, and the Solicitors who are also the Solicitors for your Estate. But the moment Nanette marries, the money of course will legally be administered by her husband."

"And she would wish that man to be my nephew?"

"I have already told you," Prunella said, a little edge to her voice, "that she is very young and very inexperienced. Your nephew is considered extremely handsome, and he behaves in an exaggerated manner, sending a Post-Chaise here from London with flowers and letters and paying her compliments which in my opinion are too glib and too suave to be sincere."

"And of course you are an authority on how a man would behave when he is in love?"

The Earl was mocking her again and Prunella told herself that she hated him.

Yet, because there was so much more at stake than her personal feelings for the Earl, she said:

"Please, My Lord, look at this sensibly and help me if you can."

"I think it is far more important that I look at it from your sister's point of view," the Earl said. "What I am going to suggest, Miss Broughton, is that I should have the privilege of calling on you in the near future, to meet your sister and to discuss not only her problems but my own."

He held out his hand and asked:

"Will you give me your notebook in which you say you have written everything that concerns my Estate? I will go into it at my leisure and see if I can under-stand what you have transcribed, although I daresay I shall need some explanations later."

Prunella could have handed him the book across the hearth-rug, but instead she rose to her feet and walked to his side.

He did not rise but took the book from her, open-ing it and seeing that she had set down in her neat, upright handwriting the names of all the pensioners, where they lived, their ages, and in what capacities they had been employed before being retired.

There were also the amounts of money they had received and the dates on which it had been paid to them.

As she turned over the pages without speaking, Prunella said:

"I am afraid it will amount to rather . . . a lot, My Lord. That is why I have made out a list of the things that can be . . . sold."

"Yet you regret that they must leave the Hall?"

"Yes, of course, but I realise that the house needs a great many repairs done to it, and that too will be expensive."

"I thought that what I have seen so far seems in surprisingly good condition."

"We had to have a great number of the windows repaired after the winter gales," Prunella replied, "and one of the ceilings on the second floor fell down last month."

"I wish to have an account of the things you paid for, Miss Broughton."

"Yes, of course, but what is more important is that the pensions should continue."

The Earl was staring down at the notebook and Prunella said a little hesitatingly:

"Most of these will be . . . due next week . . . and I thought if you . . . could not find the money so . . . quickly, I could . . . lend it to you."

The Earl glanced up at her and she did not dare to look at the expression on his face.

"I can see, Miss Broughton, that you are quite certain I cannot manage my own affairs," he said.

She did not reply and after a moment he went on:

"As you quite obviously disapprove of me—I can feel it vibrating from you—I wonder that you do not leave me to go to hell in my own way."

Again Prunella felt he was peering at her, and almost despite herself she retorted:

"I am not preventing you from going to hell, My Lord, or anywhere else you fancy, but I cannot stand by and see you taking a lot of innocent people with you!"

The Earl shut the notebook with a slap.

"I must say," he remarked, rising to his feet, "that when I returned home last night I did not expect to find myself facing the Day of Judgement! It is almost, Miss Broughton, as if my father is still here, still determined that nothing I do is right."

Prunella sighed.

"I do not mean to make you feel like that, My Lord. But I was afraid that if you ever did return home you would misunderstand my motives in doing what seemed to me best."

"So you expected me?"

"Your father heard five years ago that you were alive and had been seen in India."

"And what was his reaction?"

"I think, although I cannot be sure," Prunella answered, "that he was glad. He was very lonely in the last years of the war, when my father was too ill to visit him and no-one ever seemed to come to the Hall."

"What you are saying is that there would have been a welcome even for me!"

"I think that is true, and I think he would have liked to make up your quarrel before he died."

She paused for a moment, then said:

"When I used to come here to see him, we often walked round the house together, and he would talk about you when you were very young. We even went up to the Nursery once and looked at your toys."

"I suppose you are telling me to make me feel contrite and ashamed."

Prunella did not answer, and after a moment he said:

"Perhaps if there had not been a war I would have come home earlier—I am not sure. But, as it was, the journey was almost impossible unless I had been a soldier."

"I can understand that."

"Well, there is nothing I can do about it now," the Earl said, "except to read your notebook, Miss Broughton, and of course to thank you for all you have done."

"I am not looking for your gratitude, My Lord. What I did was for your father and in a way for my own satisfaction. I love the Hall and I love all the people on the Estate, most of whom I have known ever since I was a child."

"How old are you?" the Earl asked unexpectedly.

"I am nearly twenty-two years of age."

"And yet you talk as if you had dedicated your life to the service of other people," the Earl said. "Why did you not go to London as your sister did, and why, which is more important, are you not married?"

"Quite simply, because I have not had the opportunity, My Lord."

"I am expected to believe that?" the Earl asked.

"It happens to be the truth. You see . . ."

She stopped, telling herself that it was none of his business what she did or did not do.

"I suppose," the Earl said, "what you are preventing yourself from telling me is that as your mother created such a scandal you have suffered for it."

It was the truth, but Prunella was angry with him for having guessed it.

"I had my father to look after for the last three years," she replied evasively. "He was very ill."

"You would not have been so important to him if your mother had been there," the Earl remarked.

"I have been perfectly content."

"That is untrue—and you know it!"

"I am not interested in myself but in Nanette, My Lord. I am finding it very difficult to make you keep to the point, which is that I have asked you a favour, and I beg you to concentrate on that and on nothing else."

"When I see your sister Nanette," the Earl replied, "I shall doubtless find myself involved in her problems whether I like it or not. For the moment, Miss Broughton, I am interested in yours, which seem to me to be very urgent."

"Urgent?" Prunella asked almost despite herself. "I do not . . . quite understand what you are saying."

"That is obvious," he replied. "We must find you a husband before your philanthropy gains such a hold that you are more interested in your soul than in your heart."

Three days later, Charity, when she called Prunella in the morning, had obviously some news to impart.

Although she was feeling somewhat heavy-eyed, Prunella forced herself to listen.

"Mrs. Goodwin says," Charity announced, "that there's ever so much activity going on up at the Hall and there's pictures being taken off the walls and stacked on the floors."

Prunella sat bolt upright in bed.

"From the Gallery? Oh, Charity, not from the Gallery?"

"Mrs. Goodwin didn't say where," Charity replied, "but there's more pictures in the Gallery than anywhere else."

"Yes, I know," Prunella sighed, "but I did ask him not to sell those."

She spoke the words almost beneath her breath, but Charity was not listening.

"Mrs. Goodwin also said as His Lordship sent for people from London and some of them arrived yesterday to see him. Tradesmen, they was, of some sort."

"Picture-Dealers!" Prunella murmured beneath her breath.

She had hoped that the Earl would come to see her yesterday, being sure that he would not do so the day after her visit. But although she had waited expectantly there had been no sign of him and now she knew the reason why.

Despite all she had said to him, despite the fact that she had left the list of what she thought could be sold without damage to the collection, he was selling the Van Dykes.

Of course they were likely to fetch more money

than anything else, but how could he be so insensitive and part with them after all she had told him?

She was worrying too about the pensioners and the tenant-farmers.

Suppose he insisted on rent from the Jacksons? They would not be able to afford it and they would have to go. But Mrs. Jackson had been so ill during the winter and two of her children were always ailing.

"Why does he not come to see me?" Prunella asked herself not once but a dozen times.

Yesterday afternoon it had been extremely hard not to order the carriage and drive to the Hall to see for herself what was going on.

"I am sure Pascoe will want to visit his uncle," Nanette had said yesterday afternoon.

"Why should he know that he is here?" Prunella asked stiffly.

"Because I wrote and told him the very first day he arrived," Nanette answered.

"Well, if Mr. Lowes has expectations in that direction, he is going to be disappointed," Prunella said sharply.

"You never think of anything but money, Prunella," Nanette complained. "Poor Pascoe cannot help it if his father's Estate is impoverished, just like that of the Winslows."

"I agree he cannot help it personally," Prunella replied, "but he need not be so extravagant. You should tell him, Nanette, that he is not to send you flowers and letters by Post-Chaise."

"Of course I could not do that," Nanette replied. "I think it is very kind of him and very, very romantic."

She gave a deep sigh.

"Oh, Prunella, I am so bored with being here and having nothing to do except wait for Pascoe's letters. Do you think you could write and ask Godmama if she would have me to stay with her just for a few days?"

"It would be useless for me to do so, and you only

wish to go to London so that you can see Mr. Lowes. Your Godmother has already told me that she disapproves of the manner in which he is pursuing you, and she has made it quite clear, Nanette, as I have, that she thinks he is after your fortune and really has no interest in you apart from that."

"That is not true!" Nanette replied. "In fact it is a lie, and I believe Pascoe when he says he would love me had I not a penny in the world!"

"He might love you," Prunella said, "but if he did, he certainly would not propose that he should marry you."

"How do you know? How can you be so unkind, so cruel about him?"

As she spoke Nanette jumped up from the chair in which she was sitting, and there were tears in her eyes.

She walked quickly to the door and only when she had reached it did she say:

"The trouble is, Prunella, that no man has ever looked at you, so you know nothing about love. When you die an old maid you will be sorry, very sorry for what you have missed!"

As she finished speaking Nanette went from the Drawing-Room, slamming the door behind her.

Prunella sat thinking miserably that she had made a mistake in saying what she had and wishing that she had been more tactful. But it had been difficult not to express her feelings.

Nanette had been walking about looking bored and unhappy except when she received letters from London, and, because there were no distractions locally, Prunella was racking her brains as to how she could turn her sister's yearning for Pascoe Lowes in another direction.

She remembered reading that the only antidote for one love-affair was another one, but how could she find a young man who would interest Nanette when they were isolated here at the Manor?

They were never invited to anything more exciting than tea at the Vicarage or to take part in the village Bazaar.

The Earl had been right in guessing that because of the scandal caused by her mother when she had run away, her daughters had suffered.

But it was only this year that the whole consequence of this had been revealed to Nanette.

While she was in the School-Room she not only had a Governess but teachers had come from the nearest towns to instruct her, because Sir Roderick believed that his daughters should have a good education and was quite prepared to pay for it.

When their father died, Prunella, knowing that the years of mourning would be a gloomy period, had sent Nanette to a fashionable Seminary at Cheltenham.

Therefore, it was only when she had returned from London that Nanette had found the quietness of the Manor and the fact that they never saw anyone but themselves almost insufferable.

Prunella had grown used to it, although sometimes she missed her father's voice calling her from his sick-bed and the bustle of the Doctors arriving and leaving.

There had been medicines and luxuries to be fetched by the grooms and hundreds of other things which were required in the sick-room, which always resulted in the household being kept on its toes.

Now there was just the monotony of one day being exactly like another, except, of course, for the Earl's arrival at the Hall.

He had not called yesterday and Prunella felt that if he was busy selling his paintings, and doubtless also the tapestries and the silver, he would have no time left in which to be social.

She went downstairs to find her sister in the Breakfast-Room.

Nanette looked at her a little uncertainly, then,

because she had a warm, impulsive nature, she ran to Prunella and flung her arms round her.

"Forgive me! Forgive me, dearest!" she cried. "I am sorry I was such a beast last night!"

Prunella put her cheek against Nanette's.

"Of course I forgive you," she said, "and really there is nothing to forgive. We have always understood each other, you and I."

"Until now."

She kissed Prunella again before she said:

"Dearest Prunella, you must try to help me. I cannot help being in love with Pascoe, and every day without him seems to pass like a century of time."

"It is only because you have not enough to do," Prunella said. "I have been thinking that perhaps I should write to our cousins who live in Bath. You might find it amusing to go there for a holiday, and I believe they have an excellent Theatre."

"I want to go to London!" Nanette said with a petulant note in her voice.

"I do not think we can possibly ask your Godmother to have you again so soon," Prunella said. "Surely you made some other friends when you were there?"

She was determined that Nanette should not go to London, knowing that she would do anything to see Pascoe Lowes. But she thought it would be diplomatic to pretend to agree and in that manner play for time.

Anyway, it might stop Nanette from moping, Prunella thought.

"I cannot think of anyone, but I will try," Nanette answered. "Most of Godmama's friends were either very smart and obviously did not wish to be bothered with a débutante, or else they had girls of their own and regarded me as a potential rival."

She thought Prunella looked surprised, and she laughed.

"Do not be so foolish, dearest Prunella! I am beautiful—at least Pascoe thinks so—and I am rich!

The other girls had very little chance when I was round."

"What about the other gentlemen you met?" Prunella asked. "Your Godmother said there were two who would have proposed to you if you had given them any encouragement."

Nanette laughed scornfully.

"You should have seen them! One was a Baronet, old and rather fat, and the other was a Marquis, but the girls called him 'the Chinless Wonder' behind his back, because he was so stupid. How could I have a husband like either of them?"

"No, of course not," Prunella agreed.

"When I marry," Nanette said in a soft little voice, "I want to be in love, and I *am* in love!"

The conversation always came back to the same point, Prunella thought as she helped herself to bacon and eggs.

She was determined not to antagonise Nanette as she had done last night, so she listened to her sister eulogising over the looks, cleverness, and charm of Pascoe Lowes, and wondered what she could do about it.

When breakfast was finished Prunella said:

"I was thinking that we might go riding this morning. I notice you did not exercise your horse yesterday, and you know it is bad for them not to be taken out regularly."

"All right, we will go riding," Nanette agreed without much enthusiasm.

Then as an idea struck her she asked:

"Could we not go in the Park?"

She was, of course, referring to the Park belonging to Winslow Hall, where they had always ridden in the past because it was so much bigger than their own and also because there was a long, flat stretch in one part of it that was a perfect place for a gallop.

The present Earl's grandfather had trained his race-horses there, and Prunella enjoyed the exhilaration of galloping when she knew there was no need to watch the ground for rabbit-holes or to be apprehensive about not being able to pull in her mount at the end of it.

She made up her mind.

"We will go to the gallop," she said.

If the Earl was busy selling his possessions he would not know what was happening in another part of the Estate, and, what was more, he would not be interested.

It was so painful to think of what he was doing that Prunella thought anything would be better than to sit at home, as she had done yesterday, expecting him, only to realise late in the afternoon that she had waited in vain.

Half-an-hour later, having changed into their riding-habits, the two girls set off on the horses which had always been their own.

"Pascoe says I should buy myself some horses at Tattersall's," Nanette confided conversationally as they rode down the drive, "and I think Dragonfly is getting too old and too staid for what I require."

Prunella knew it was only another excuse to go to London, so she said nothing.

Dragonfly was an excellent horse in every way and had cost a considerable sum of money when she had told their Head Groom to buy him eighteen months ago.

"Pascoe is very knowledgeable about horses," Nanette went on. "He wants to become a Corinthian, but I think he already drives better than anyone I have ever seen."

"You went driving with him when you were in London?" Prunella asked. "I hope you were chaperoned."

Nanette laughed.

"There is only room for two people in a Phaeton, and I cannot see Godmama perched up behind on the rear seat! All the girls were allowed to go driving in Hyde Park, but Pascoe's Phaeton was the smartest there! I could see everybody envying me when I drove with him."

There was nothing Prunella could do but listen, and she was glad when they rode across the top of Winslow Park towards the gallop.

When they reached it, there was no need to touch their horses with the whip, for they had been there far too often before not to know what was expected of them.

It was a wild, exciting gallop and Prunella felt as if it swept away some of her apprehension and the heaviness which had been with her when she had awakened because she was so worried.

She knew that Nanette was trying to beat her and she pressed her own horse, but eventually as they reached the end of the gallop they did so side by side.

Then as they drew in their horses, both laughing a little at the speed at which they had travelled, a man on horseback appeared through the trees and rode towards them.

It was the Earl, and Prunella looked at him, thinking he was riding exceedingly well.

Then she saw that he was astride a large black stallion which she had never seen before, and she knew it had certainly not come from the empty stables at the Hall.

CHAPTER THREE

The Earl rode up to them and took off his hat.

"Good-morning, Miss Broughton," he said, then looked at Nanette.

Before Prunella could introduce her sister, Nanette exclaimed:

"You must be the new Earl! I have been so looking forward to meeting you!"

"I am flattered!" the Earl replied. "And I have heard a lot about you, Miss Nanette!"

Nanette gave him a mischievous glance as she said:

"None of it, I am sure, to my advantage!"

The Earl laughed.

"I hope, My Lord," Prunella said, "you do not mind us using the gallop?"

"As a matter of fact," Nanette said irrepressibly, before the Earl could speak, "we thought you would be too busy to know that we were here."

"I always used the gallop when I was a boy," the Earl said, "and I thought it would do Caesar good to exercise his legs."

"If that is Caesar," Nanette exclaimed, "I think he is the finest horse I have ever seen!"

"That is what I thought when I first saw him," the Earl replied.

Because it was difficult to restrain her curiosity, Prunella enquired:

"Where did you find him? I can hardly believe you brought him with you from India!"

"Jim must have the credit for discovering him," the Earl replied. "When we arrived at Southampton he heard there was a Horse-Fair in the vicinity and insisted on seeing if there was anything for sale that would enable us to arrive at the Hall quicker than if we came by carriage."

"And he found Caesar," Prunella remarked.

She thought it was strange that a valet should be a good judge of a horse, especially one as superlative as the stallion which the Earl was riding.

"Jim is very knowledgeable where horses are concerned," the Earl explained, "and he is anxious to fill the stables, which I find most depressingly bare."

With difficulty Prunella stopped the words that rose to her lips.

She could understand only too well what was happening.

The Earl had sold some of the paintings, and instead of spending the money on repairs that were necessary to the house, on the farms, and on the pensioners, he had chosen to spend it on horses and doubtless on women.

In her mind the two went together.

She thought of all the stories she had heard of the horses and carriages that the Bucks bought for enormous sums to give to the "Cyprians" and other ladies of easy virtue who took their fancy.

It had always shocked her that women who were what Charity described as being "no better than they should be!" should have so much money spent on them, when there were children starving in the slums and men who had served their country during the war now begging by the roadside.

As if her disapproval vibrated from her and the Earl was aware of it, he looked at her and after a moment he said:

"You apparently do not think Jim's idea, and of course mine, is to be commended, Miss Broughton."

"Your ideas on horse-flesh are not my concern, My Lord," Prunella replied.

"I think it is a wonderful idea!" Nanette exclaimed "And I cannot think why Prunella should disparage it. After all, she loves horses."

"I can see that from the very fine, well-bred animals you are both riding," the Earl replied.

"I was just saying that I want to go to Tattersall's to buy myself a new horse," Nanette chattered on. "Dragonfly is too slow and not half as spirited as I can see Caesar is."

"I think you would find Caesar too much for you," the Earl replied, "but of course when there are more horses in my stables I should be delighted for you to ride them, Miss Nanette."

Nanette gave a cry of joy.

"Thank you, thank you, and do please hurry and buy lots of horses so that I can avail myself of your kindness!"

"You will have to come and speak to Jim," the Earl said, "and I hope too that you will visit me."

Nanette gave a little laugh.

"You must be aware that I am longing to do so. I am so curious about you, and Prunella and I were both so disappointed when you did not call on us yesterday."

"You were expecting me?" the Earl enquired.

He looked at Prunella as he spoke, but she deliberately turned her head away so that he could not see her face.

"Prunella thought you would want to see her about a lot of things concerning the Estate," Nanette said. "After all, she has been fussing over it like an anxious hen ever since your father died, and she spends all her money on repairing your house and feeding your pensioners, so you ought to be very grateful to her."

Prunella's fingers tightened on the reins.

She was intensely embarrassed by what her sister was saying. At the same time, she did not know how to stop her.

While Nanette was talking she had turned her horse and now she and the Earl were both riding beside Prunella.

"I am of course extremely grateful," the Earl said, "and it is very remiss of me not to have called on you yesterday as I intended, but unfortunately I was detained by some people who arrived from London to see me."

'Picture-Dealers . . . silversmiths . . . and sharks,' Prunella thought to herself, but she forced herself to say nothing aloud, and Nanette went on:

"You must find it fascinating to come back, after being away for so long, to find everything just as you left it."

"Not quite," the Earl said. "The gardens are overgrown and the peach- and grape-houses are almost falling down."

Prunella stiffened, and, as if he was aware of the anger she was feeling, her horse fidgeted a little.

'How dare he!' Prunella thought to herself. 'How dare he complain? The gardens overgrown indeed! If I had not paid poor old Ives, he and his family would have starved to death, and as for the peaches and grapes . . . !'

If she had been speaking, words would have failed her.

As it was, only by keeping her lips tightly closed did she prevent herself from telling the Earl exactly what she thought of him.

"What I have been wondering," he was saying, "is if, in order to make up for my impoliteness, I could invite you and your sister to dine with me tomorrow evening!"

"We would love to!" Nanette said. "Would we not, Prunella?"

"I am not . . . sure we can manage it," Prunella answered in a cold voice.

"But of course we can!" Nanette insisted. "You well know we have no other engagement, and it is years and years since I had a meal at the Hall. It would be great fun to be back there again with you."

She gave the Earl a flirtatious little look which she had learnt in London was very effective where older men were concerned.

"Then I shall look forward very much to entertaining you, Miss Nanette," he said, "and I feel that as we have known each other's families for so long—and unless I am mistaken we were introduced when you were in your cradle—I should be allowed to call you Nanette."

"But of course!" Nanette agreed. "And I would like to say that you are much, much nicer than I thought you would be."

"Thank you," the Earl said with a smile.

Because she could listen no longer to this exchange of pleasantries, Prunella touched her horse with her heel, and as he trotted ahead, Nanette turned towards the Earl.

"I want to talk to you," she said in a low voice.

"About my nephew?" the Earl enquired.

"Yes," Nanette said. "How did you guess?"

Before he could reply, she added:

"I suppose Prunella told you and has put you against him—a most sneaky, underhanded thing to do!"

"Let me say, before you work yourself up unnecessarily against your sister," the Earl said, "that I always rely on my own judgement where people are concerned."

"I know you will like Pascoe."

She smiled at him and he thought that Prunella had been right when she had said how lovely she was.

With her fair hair, blue eyes, and pink-and-white complexion, she was exactly the type of English girl

55

that embodied the dreams of every young man when he was abroad and far away from home.

The Earl also appreciated the picture she made in her leaf-green riding-habit and her high-crowned hat encircled by a gauze veil.

Because Nanette did not wish her sister to know she had spoken to the Earl about Pascoe, she trotted after her, and as she did so the Earl turned and rode back through the trees in the direction of the Hall.

"It will be exciting to dine with him!" Nanette said as she caught up with Prunella. "I cannot think why you had to be so snooty about it."

"He will only be spending money he can ill afford."

"Oh, good heavens, Prunella!" Nanette exclaimed. "You cannot begrudge him a little amusement when he has been away for so long. Anyway, I want to see him again and talk to him."

"About his nephew?"

"Why not?" Nanette asked defiantly. "If he is as poverty-stricken as Pascoe, he might be sympathetic and all the more grateful to us."

"That is not the sort of thing you should say," Prunella said quickly.

"Why not?" Nanette asked again. "The Earl should be down on his knees thanking you for all you have done for the Winslow Estate, and I would like Pascoe to be grateful to me. As far as I am concerned, he can spend every penny I possess, and I will enjoy watching him do so!"

"Nanette, you are not to say such things!" Prunella said crossly. "Any man who had a vestige of pride would be ashamed to live on his wife's money."

"Papa never complained because Mama was rich," Nanette said with unanswerable logic.

"Papa had a great deal of money of his own," Prunella replied.

"Not really enough for you to spend all you want on the Winslow Estate. I suppose you told the Earl how you had to buy a new range for his kitchen and repaint the large Salon after it was spoilt by flooding?"

"I prefer not to talk about it."

"Oh, well, if you like spending your money in such a boring way, who is going to stop you?" Nanette asked. "But I can tell you one thing, Prunella, you must wear something pretty if you are going to dine with the earl."

"The gowns I have are quite good enough."

Nanette laughed.

"You must be crazy! I have been thinking ever since I came back from London how old-fashioned and out-of-date you look, but I did not like to say so for fear of hurting your feelings."

Prunella looked in a startled manner at her young sister, then as she would have hotly denied the accusation she knew it was the truth.

She had in fact hardly thought about her appearance since her father had been so ill, except that when he died she had bought herself several black gowns from the nearest town.

Then, after six months, when she was in half-mourning she had augmented them with two gowns in grey and one in mauve.

She realised that while they were the best the country dressmaker could supply, they certainly bore little resemblance to the copious collection of elegant gowns which Nanette had brought back with her from London.

It was true, Prunella realised now, that with the end of the war fashions had changed. The very straight, plain, Grecian-type gowns, which had been the vogue at the beginning of the century and which were said to have been modelled on those introduced by Napoleon's wife Josephine, had given way to a much more elaborate style.

Now the gowns widened out at the hem, and although the waist remained high, both the bodice and the skirt of the gowns were amply decorated with lace or embroidery, frills or fringes.

Nanette's gowns were far more feminine and very much more attractive than anything Prunella had seen before.

And she learnt that older women in the evening wore turbans trimmed with feathers and jewels, while their day-dresses were embellished with gold braid, buttons, and even epaulettes until they appeared almost as dashing as a Dragoon on parade.

"Perhaps I do look a little dowdy," Prunella admitted humbly. "When I have time we must go shopping and you can help me choose some clothes that are more up-to-date. But tomorrow evening I shall have the choice of a black gown or one in grey."

"Then I absolutely refuse to go with you!" Nanette said. "From all I have heard, the Earl has an eye for beautiful women. And I rather like his raffish air. I can almost imagine him as a pirate or a buccaneer of some sort."

"I certainly do not think of him like that!" Prunella snapped.

"Whatever he is, he is still a man," Nanette said, "and although you often forget it, Prunella, you are a woman!"

"We can solve this problem quite easily by not dining at the Hall," Prunella said, "and I will send a message this afternoon to say so."

"If you do that, I shall go alone," Nanette threatened. "I want to dine with the Earl, and you cannot be so silly and prudish as to try to stop me."

Prunella did not reply and Nanette said:

"I know exactly why you are being so disagreeable to him. It is because he ran away centuries ago with that pretty Lady 'What's-Her-Name?' and you still hold it against him."

"I am surprised that you know about such things!" Prunella exclaimed.

"Know?" Nanette repeated. "When everyone has

talked about the 'goings on of Master Gerald' ever
since I can remember? There was not one woman but
dozens of them!"

She gave a little laugh.

"I think that instead of being told fairy-stories
when I was a child, I was told of the exploits of the
young heir at the Hall, and quite frankly, until I met
Pascoe I thought Master Gerald was the Prince
Charming I sought in my dreams."

"Really, Nanette, I am sure that is not true!" Prunella protested.

"It is! So we are both going to dress up and look
our best. And as we are nearly the same size, you are
going to wear one of my gowns until we can buy you
something decent of your own."

Prunella laughed as if she could not help herself.

"You are the débutante, Nanette, not I."

"At the moment you are making me feel like an
elderly Chaperone trying to launch a 'Country Miss'
into the *Beau Monde!*" Nanette teased. "And goodness
knows if you will sink or swim!"

"I have never heard such an outrageous . . ." Prunella began, only to realise that, laughing at her own
audacity, Nanette was already galloping away.

The only thing Prunella could do was to follow her.

That afternoon when Nanette was busy writing a
letter which Prunella guessed was to Pascoe and had
no idea how she could prevent her sister from sending it, she decided to visit an old woman who had
been Nurse to the Earl when he was a child.

She had wanted to explain to him that Nanny Gray
was one of the people whom it was most important
for him to see, because she was not only very old but
had been praying ever since he had gone away that
he would come home.

She had intended to tell the Earl this if, as she had expected, he called the previous day.

But as she had had no chance to talk to him since that first visit to the Hall, she knew that she must go and visit Nanny Gray herself.

If she had heard that the Earl was home she would be in a fever of anxiety to see "her baby," as she always called him.

It took longer than usual to get to Nanny's cottage, situated as it was on the other side of the Earl's Estate, because Prunella deliberately told old Dawson not to drive through the Park.

She felt that as she and Nanette had been caught trespassing once today, she did not wish the Earl to feel they were taking advantage of what had happened in the past or of the Manor's proximity to the Hall.

Accordingly, the horses drove her along the dusty country lanes until they reached another small village, which was known as "Lower Stodbury" to distinguish it from the villages which were known as "Little Stodbury" and "Greater Stodbury."

It consisted of only a dozen cottages, all occupied by those who either worked on or were pensioners of the Winslow Estate, an Inn, a Church, and a very small shop.

Outside the village were various houses belonging to those who were slightly better off, besides a larger one, now closed and in a dilapidated state, which was the Dower House of the Winslow family.

As the last two Countesses had died before their husbands there had been no particular use for it, and Prunella had often thought it was a pity it could not be redecorated and perhaps let to people who would be an asset to the neighborhood.

'It is the sort of idea,' she thought bitterly, 'that would be of no interest to the Earl, even if he had the money to spend on it.'

She sighed and continued in her mind:

'If he has sold the Van Dykes, he will doubtless go to London, and once there, like his nephew, he will find it easy to become a fortune-hunter.'

She was certain, as her thoughts continued, that there would be plenty of women ready to surrender everything they possessed to wear the coronet of a Countess at the Opening of Parliament.

When that happened, the Earl would have plenty of money to spend on restoring the Hall, but it would be too late to save the Van Dykes.

Her thoughts about the Earl made her for the moment forget her surrounds, and with a start Prunella realised that Dawson had brought the horses to a stop outside Nanny Gray's cottage.

It was a little way outside the village and had been chosen for Nanny by the last Earl when she retired because it was better built and had a larger garden than those of his other pensioners.

Nanny had at first been proud of her new home, even though she missed being at the Hall, and when Prunella went to see her she found everything spotless, and Nanny, although she was often lonely, apparently was quite content.

Then as Nanny had grown older it had become more difficult for her to walk even as far as the small shop, and Prunella found that the old woman dwelt almost entirely in the past, saying: "Master Gerald did this" and "Master Gerald did that."

There were tales about "my baby" from when he was born to the moment when, with tears in her eyes, she had seen him off to School.

Nanny had also found, after being waited on and catered for most of her life, that it was difficult to adjust herself to doing her own housekeeping and cooking her own food.

Prunella had travelled almost daily to the small cottage last winter because she knew it would be impossible for Nanny to cook food for herself, much less to go out and buy what she needed.

Now she alighted at the cottage gate and walked up the garden-path noting that while it was colorful with flowers there was also a profusion of weeds and nettles.

She knocked on the door but did not wait for a reply and walked in. She knew it would be difficult for Nanny to move out of her chair.

"Is that you, Miss Prunella?" Nanny asked in a quavering voice.

"Yes, Nanny. How are you today?"

Prunella put down on the kitchen-table the basket she was carrying. It contained a pie which only needed heating, a sponge pudding, a newly baked loaf, a large pat of butter, and a pot of home-made strawberry jam.

"Is it true, Miss Prunella? Really true that His Lordship's come back?"

"Yes, Nanny, and I am sure he will be coming to see you."

"My baby! My baby's home after all these years!" Nanny cried.

She was very old and frail and her eyesight was failing, but for the moment there was in her voice a youthful excitement that Prunella had not heard for years.

"You'll tell him I'm still here, Miss Prunella? You won't let him think I've passed on?"

"No, of course not, Nanny," Prunella replied.

"He'll have to come soon," Nanny said. "Last night I dreamt I was being took, and it was an omen. I well knows that I'll not live thro' another winter."

"Now, Nanny, you must not talk like that," Prunella said. "You know how much we would miss you."

"I don't mind dying if I can see my baby again," Nanny replied. "It's the thought of him that's kept me going all these years."

"His Lordship would certainly not wish you to die as soon as he comes home, now would he, Nanny?"

"Is he wed?"

"No."

"I'm not surprised. I never thought he'd get round to marrying that lady who went off with him."

"I believe she is dead," Prunella said in a cold voice.

"A good thing too, if you ask me," Nanny observed. "She'd no right leaving her husband and running away with a boy not old enough to know his own mind."

"I always thought he knew that only too well," Prunella observed tartly. "After all, no-one made him run away."

"That's as may be, Miss Prunella, but I think His Lordship was to blame, always finding fault with Master Gerald. If Her Ladyship had been alive she'd have understood him, and I've often said to him myself: 'Take no notice what His Lordship says.' But he was never one to take things lying down."

Prunella thought this was doubtless true. At the same time, what had been the point of making himself an exile, doubtless in very uncomfortable circumstances, when he might have stayed at home and looked after his Estate?

Nanny began to ramble on about the old days and Prunella found her thoughts slipping away to think of the Earl and the woman he had run off with.

She wondered what his life had been like when he was living on the other side of the world.

Suddenly the door opened behind her, which made her start, for she had not heard the sound of carriage-wheels. Then Nanny's cry of happiness made her realise who had come into the cottage.

"Master Gerald! My baby! Is it really you?"

"Yes, I am here, Nanny," the Earl replied.

He seemed very large and almost overpowering in the small kitchen, and he moved across it to bend and kiss his old Nurse on the cheek.

"I knew you'd come!" Nanny Gray was saying ecstatically. "I felt in my bones that you were alive, even

when they said you were dead, and as I was just telling Miss Prunella, now that I've seen you I don't
mind dying."

"Why should you be talking about dying, Nanny,"
the Earl asked, "when I have only just come home? I
want to talk to you. I need your advice."

"You need me, Master Gerald? I suppose I should
say 'M'Lord' now that you father's dead, God rest his
soul."

"I shall answer to 'Master Gerald' as I have," the
Earl said with a smile, "and of course I want your
advice, Nanny. I expect Miss Prunella has been telling you how ignorant I am of what has been going on
here while I have been away for so long."

As he spoke he gave Prunella a glance which she
thought was deliberately provocative, and she rose to
her feet.

"Now that His Lordship has arrived, Nanny, I will
say good-bye."

She put out her hand but the old woman held on
to it.

"Now you stay where you are, Miss Prunella," she
said. "I want to talk to His Lordship about you and
tell him all you've done for us when there was no-one
else after the old Master died. There would have
been many more in the Church-yard if it hadn't been
for you."

"Oh, please, do not say such things," Prunella said
quickly. "His Lordship does not want to hear them."

"They have to be said," Nanny contradicted, keeping a tight hold on Prunella's hand. "It's an Angel of
Mercy you've been, bringing us old ones food in the
winter and paying the Doctor when he wouldn't call
without it. One day, you mark my words, you'll get
your reward."

"I am sure that is a long time away," Prunella said.
"But now, Nanny, I must go. Dawson does not like
the horses being kept waiting."

"That is the oldest excuse in the world!" the Earl

remarked drily. "But I would like a word with you, so perhaps the horses can contain themselves for a little while longer?"

Prunella wanted to reply that it was not the horses who were fidgety but herself.

But because she thought it would be uncomfortable to argue in front of Nanny, she managed to release her hand, and instead of sitting down again she walked to the small diamond-paned window to look out onto the road outside.

The Earl was sitting close to Nanny and she heard him say:

"What I want you to tell me, Nanny, is what you need done to your cottage. Those I have visited so far seem to require a lot of renovation."

"I'm all right, Master Gerald, Miss Prunella's seen to that. The roof leaks a little in the top room when it rains, but it's not the one I use, so it doesn't matter that much."

"Nevertheless, it should be seen to," the Earl said.

He drew a small notebook from the pocket of his coat and wrote in it. Then he said:

"I have brought your pension, and in the future it will be trebled, but this week there is a little more in the packet than usual."

"That's very kind of you, Master Gerald, very kind indeed," Nanny said, "but then you always were a generous one. You're like your dear mother, who, as I've often told you, was the 'giving' sort, and it came from her heart."

"That is what is important, is it not, Nanny?" the Earl said. "And it was you who taught me that to give a present with love counts a dozen times more than if it is given with disapproval and contempt."

Although she did not turn her head, Prunella was aware that he glanced in her direction, and she knew that what he was saying was directed at her personally.

"I *have* given with my heart," she wanted to say.

But she knew that in a way he was right. She loved the people she had helped, but she hated him for his indifference and because he had neglected them by remaining abroad when he should have been at home.

Her small chin went a little higher as she listened to the Earl saying good-bye in an affectionate tone to his old Nurse, and she told herself he was only putting on an act for her benefit.

'He is trying to show me that he is sympathetic and understanding,' she thought.

She told herself that however much money he gave away, it was only to placate his conscience, but to do so he had sold the treasures that should have been preserved for the generations which would come after him.

"I will come and see you again soon, Nanny," the Earl said, "and if there is anything you want particularly, send someone to the Hall to let me know."

"I'm happy that you're here," Nanny answered, "and it's like old times to think of you where you were born."

"I am enjoying being home," the Earl said simply.

Then when he would have left she held his hand in both of hers, saying:

"Before I do die, Master Gerald, what I'd like is to hold your son in my arms and know that he was like you—and what a bonny boy you were, too!"

"But first I have to find myself a wife," the Earl said with a note of amusement in his voice.

"That shouldn't be difficult," Nanny replied. "You always had a way with the ladies, and I don't suppose you've lost it now that you've got older!"

The Earl laughed.

"You still remember my reputation, Nanny!"

"Nobody round here's likely to forget it," Nanny retorted, and the Earl laughed again.

"Good-bye, Nanny," Prunella said.

The old woman replied, but Prunella was sure that

once they had gone, it was only the Earl of whom she would be thinking.

The Earl followed Prunella onto the paving-stones which ran from the door to the gate.

"May I drive home with you?" he enquired.

"What about your horse?" Prunella enquired, looking to where Jim, astride another fine animal, was holding Caesar's reins.

"Jim can bring him along behind," the Earl said.

"Very well, My Lord."

She wondered what he had to say to her, and when they were seated in the carriage and Dawson started to drive back the way they had come, the Earl said:

"I have heard your praises extolled everywhere I have been. I realise more every moment how deeply I am in your debt, and I do not mean only financially."

"Country people always exaggerate," Prunella said, "and I do not want your gratitude. I am only glad that you remembered Nanny Gray."

"Of course I remembered her," the Earl replied, "even without the entries in your little black book. It is very helpful, but there are a number of omissions."

"Omissions?" Prunella asked sharply.

"Nanny mentioned two of them this morning."

"Oh . . . that!"

"Yes, that," the Earl agreed, "and of course the Carters were very voluble about what you have done to the house! I am getting the uncomfortable feeling that it is more yours than mine."

"What you are saying only upsets me," Prunella said sharply. "I explained to you exactly why I did some repairs at the Hall, and there is really no point in going over and over it again. Have you seen the farmers?"

"Some of them," the Earl replied, "and I am appalled by the conditions on the farms."

"Please do not throw them out . . . not the Jacksons . . . at any rate. They really have tried . . . and I know it would cost a fortune to put their farms

67

back into working order . . . but I do beg you to let them stay where they are."

The Earl turned sideways in the carriage-seat to look at Prunella.

"I wonder where you get your impression of me and what you fancy is likely to be my behaviour?" he asked.

"Must one pretend to be ignorant of the fact that you have returned with no money to find that your inheritance is impoverished?" Prunella asked sharply.

"You sound almost as if you are blaming me personally for that."

"Perhaps in a way I am," she said. "I cannot help feeling, although I may be wrong, that if you had been here, you might have been able to prevent everything from getting to its present state."

"My father did not want my help, as he always thought Andrews was completely competent. And even though he was a close friend of your father, I doubt if he ever confided in him."

"I am quite certain he would have done nothing of the sort. When your father was ill everything went from bad to worse, and when he died it was the Solicitors who told me there was no money. So I did what I could, but you should have been here yourself."

"You speak very frankly, Prunella," the Earl remarked in a dry voice.

She noticed the way he addressed her and thought it was rather an impertinence on his part. Then she remembered that if he called Nanette by her name without a prefix, it was obvious that he would do the same to her, although she had not expected it.

They drove along in silence. Then, because she could not bear the suspense, Prunella said in a very different voice from the one she had used before:

"It may be . . . wrong of me . . . to ask you . . . but . . . I have to know . . . have you . . . sold the Van Dykes . . . and if so . . . how many?"

Once again the Earl turned to look at her, and

because she was embarrassed she would not meet his eyes, but stared ahead at the faded cushions in the carriage.

"I am not going to answer that question," he said after a perceptible pause. "I shall leave you guessing, or perhaps we might discuss it tomorrow night when you dine with me."

"I cannot think why you should be so mysterious about it," Prunella said crossly.

She had the feeling that he was teasing her, and she told herself that the sale of the Van Dykes was not something that should be treated lightly or as a joke.

"There are other things I want to talk to you about," the Earl said, "but perhaps the most important is what you intend to do about yourself now that you are free of the responsibility of Winslow Hall. And of course, what you intend to do about Nanette. She will moulder away at the Manor without any amusement or local entertainments except that, I am told, you occasionally have the riotous gaiety of tea at the Vicarage."

"Who has been talking to you? Who has been telling you these things?" Prunella asked sharply.

The Earl made a gesture with his hands.

"The world and his wife, or rather everybody I have talked to since I came home."

"Then I wish you would mind your own business!" Prunella ejaculated. "What Nanette and I do is not your affair, My Lord, and we are perfectly happy."

"Then you must be a fat cow, chewing the cud, and I do not need to be told that that is untrue, while what you are saying is!"

He saw Prunella purse her lips together, and he smiled as he continued:

"I am quite sure that Nanette will find Little Stodbury a very poor substitute for London, and if you are content as you say, then it is certainly time you were shaken out of your dream-world, which has nothing to offer except perhaps a soporific against suicide!"

"You are certainly very eloquent on the subject, My Lord," Prunella said scathingly.

"As for it not being my business, you have already asked for my help," the Earl continued. "I am quite certain that my nephew, whatever he is like, would seem to Nanette like all the heroes of mythology and the Prince Charming of every fairy-tale, after a few lonely weeks in the gloom of the Manor."

"I will not have you talking like this about my home!" Prunella objected.

"What I am saying is the truth and you know it! What you and I have to decide, Prunella, is how we can bring life and laughter into the lives of two forlorn maidens."

"I should think Your Lordship had plenty to occupy you at the moment without troubling yourself about us," Prunella answered. "You will soon forget Little Stodbury when you return to London."

"Who said I was going to London?"

"I cannot believe that, after the way you have described my home, you will find yours any more enlivening."

"On the contrary, I find the Hall absorbing," the Earl said. "But then, as you have discovered for yourself, there is a great deal to do both in the house and on the Estate."

By this time they were passing through the village and the Manor was not far ahead.

"Are you going to help me, as you suggested before," the Earl asked, "or fight me?"

"The place is yours."

"I am getting rather tired of being continually engaged in a pitched battle."

Prunella turned to look at him in surprise.

"A pitched battle?" she questioned.

"I am not so obtuse as not to be aware that you dislike and despise me," he said. "You are merely waiting for me to commit some unforgivable sin so that you can vent your righteous wrath upon me."

"That is not true!" Prunella exclaimed. "And talking in that exaggerated manner does not help our relationship."

"So we have one! That really does surprise me!" the Earl remarked.

She felt as if they were duelling and she had given him an opening which he had not failed to take.

"I think, My Lord," she said, "that you are making far more out of this than is necessary. I want to help you to do what is right as regards the people on your Estate, and I want you to help me be rid of your nephew Pascoe. Surely we can do these two things together without fighting?"

"What you mean is being permanently at each other's throats," the Earl said, "and that, my prudish little Prunella, is something you have been doing ever since I returned."

She would have spoken, but he held up his hand to interrupt her.

"All right, what I did when you were too young to know what I was doing has shocked you, and I think, if you are honest, you will admit that you have added my sins to your mother's, which I consider extremely unfair."

As he spoke Prunella had bent her head, and he went on in a very much quieter and more gentle tone:

"Suppose for the moment, Prunella, we bury the hatchet? I need your help and I will try to help you. That is, at least, a basis for a relationship that need not be so acrimonious as it has been up to this moment. Do you agree?"

He held out his hand as he spoke, and almost despite herself and because she could not find words in which to answer him, Prunella put hers in it.

She had taken off her gloves when she was talking to Nanny, and, because she had been so agitated by the Earl's visit and by his request to drive home with her, she had not replaced them.

Now as his fingers closed over hers, she felt the hard strength of them and it gave her a very strange feeling.

She could not explain it except that she supposed she had never been touched in such an intimate way by a man before, and it was different from what she had expected.

"I am . . . sorry if I . . . have been . . . disagreeable, My Lord."

As the words came from her lips she thought that she sounded like Nanette, and she was sure that if she looked up at the Earl she would see him smiling, thinking he had won a small victory.

Instead he said very quietly:

"If you are sorry, then I too am sorry that I am not what you expected."

Just then they turned in at the drive to the Manor.

As they did so, the Earl raised Prunella's hand to his lips and kissed it.

CHAPTER FOUR

*D*riving beside Nanette towards the Hall, Prunella had an unaccountable feeling in her breast which she could not explain.

She supposed it was because she felt embarrassed at seeing the Earl after their conversation of yesterday, but she was aware that it was also due to her appearance.

Although she had protested violently, Nanette had insisted on her trying on a number of her gowns to see which was the most becoming.

"I will not go anywhere dressed in white like a débutante!" Prunella had said firmly. "I am nearly twenty-two, and, as you pointed out when you were angry with me, I am well on the way to being an old maid."

"I only said that because you upset me," Nanette answered. "You may be older in years, Prunella, but sometimes I feel that you are younger than I. But then I went away to School, and I have also been to London."

Prunella thought that was very near the truth.

Nanette sometimes talked in a worldly-wise, sophisticated manner which left her gasping.

Then she would remember humbly how little she knew of the world outside Little Stodbury.

Nanette's new gowns were lovely, elegant, and had cost what seemed to Prunella to be an astronomical amount of money.

"I thought you would be shocked at my extravagance," she said, "but Godmama said firmly that first appearances are very important and she would not take me anywhere until I was dressed in a way she considered suitable for an heiress."

"I think that is rather an unladylike way of talking," Prunella said. "Mama always said that ladies and gentlemen never spoke of money."

Nanette laughed scornfully.

"If that was true they certainly did not live in Little Stodbury!"

She smiled before she went on:

"You know as well as I do, Prunella, that ever since I have been home, conversation has been everlastingly about the lack of money at the Hall! While in London, although they talk of it in low voices, people are continually telling each other what somebody else is worth."

"I prefer to think about people's characters," Prunella said airily.

Nanette gave a little cry and clapped her hands.

"That is exactly what I have been asking you to do where Pascoe is concerned. He has an adorable character—kind, gentle, considerate, and you forget all that simply because he has not a lot of guineas to jingle in his pocket."

Prunella thought a little ruefully that she had certainly fallen into that trap! It was almost as if she were duelling with the Earl in words rather than with her own sister.

She had the feeling that the authority which she had always had over Nanette was slipping away, and it made her more determined than ever that she would not wear white, because she did not wish to appear the same age as her sister.

"Would you consider white and silver?" Nanette asked, looking into a wardrobe that was packed with gowns, each of which was prettier than the last.

Prunella shook her head.

"I will wear my black gown, and as a concession to the occasion I will wear Mama's diamond necklace."

"You will look like a crow!" Nanette said rudely.

Then she gave an exclamation.

"I have it! I have exactly the right gown for you!"

She opened another cupboard where Charity had put the gowns that could not be squeezed into her big wardrobe.

Prunella waited, but very expectantly.

Being a woman, she naturally longed to have lovely clothes to wear as Nanette did, but the truth was that she had spent more than she could afford on restoring the Salon at the Hall.

'I suppose I could always draw on my capital,' she had thought, and could not help knowing how horrified her father would have been at the idea.

Nanette came back from the cupboard with a gown that was even more elaborate than the ones at which they had been looking, but instead of being white it was a pale, misty blue.

"Godmama and I chose this in an artificial light," she said, "and when I put it on it did not suit me, so I have never worn it."

Prunella knew, however, that it was exactly what she wanted! The blue was very soft and at night it deepened a little so that it looked like the sky on a misty day.

When she put it on it fitted her almost exactly, and made her look not only different from what she had ever looked before but very much lovelier.

While Nanette had golden hair that was the colour of ripening corn, Prunella's was fair but with a touch of brown in it, and her eyes instead of being blue were cloudy grey.

Yet her skin, like Nanette's, was dazzlingly white and had a translucence which, although she was unaware of it, made it glow almost like a pearl.

The blacks and greys she had worn for over a year had seemed to take the sparkle from her eyes, and the way her gowns were made had prevented anyone from being aware of the grace of her figure.

Now the close-fitting bodice, the sweeping line from the high breast to the hem, gave her an elegance and at the same time something classical which was almost Grecian.

"You look lovely!" Nanette exclaimed when Prunella went into her room to see if she was ready.

She looked her sister up and down, then added:

"Do you know, Prunella, if the London dressmakers saw you, they would say you 'paid with dressing,' and that is the truth."

"I think you are speaking metaphorically," Prunella replied, "but what I am wondering is how much it would cost in hard cash."

Nanette laughed.

"Whatever it costs, I am going to see that in the future you are properly gowned, and you know, dearest, that I will pay for anything you cannot afford, considering you gave me all the money Mama left you."

Prunella stiffened and did not reply.

Nanette looked at her. Then she said:

"People in London talk about Mama without looking shocked. All the old Dowagers told me how beautiful she was, and although I think it is unlikely if she were alive that they would invite her to their parties, they never said anything unpleasant in my hearing."

Prunella was determined not to discuss her mother, so she said quickly:

"We must hurry and finish dressing or we will be late. And you know as well as I do that Mrs. Carter is not a very good cook, and if she gets agitated the dinner will be inedible."

"I am ready," Nanette said. "Do you think I look nice?"

"Nice" was not the word to describe her.

In her white gown trimmed round the shoulders and hem with shadow lace, she looked like a Princess in a fairy-story. To add to the illusion, she wore a little wreath of blue forget-me-nots in her hair and a necklace of small turquoises to match.

Prunella was certain that the forget-me-nots had a special meaning but she did not comment on them, and she told her sister the truth, that she did indeed look lovely.

As she turned away, Nanette enquired:

"What are you going to wear over your gown to drive to the Hall?"

"I have my velvet cloak downstairs."

"That old thing!" Nanette exclaimed scornfully. "You must have one of my scarves. There is a very pretty one here trimmed with maribou which will keep you warm."

She wrapped it round Prunella's shoulders as she spoke, when she gave a little sigh.

"I wish we were going to dine with the Earl in London, then on to a Ball where I could dance with Pascoe."

Prunella thought it was a mistake to answer this and she moved towards the stairs. Because her gown was so elegant and made of such expensive material she felt as if she were floating rather than walking.

Dawson was waiting for them outside with the closed carriage and they drove away. The sun was sinking, the shadows had grown longer and darker on the lawn, and the rooks were going to roost in the oak trees in the Park.

"Are you excited, Prunella?" Nanette asked. "After all, although you disapprove of the Earl, he is a man, and surely it must be thrilling for you to talk to him rather than to the Vicar, who is the only man we ever see in Little Stodbury."

As it happened, Prunella was thinking very much the same thing, and when they arrived at the Hall she thought that for Nanette's sake she would try to be more pleasant to the Earl than she had been on previous occasions when they met.

They alighted, then as Prunella walked up the old stone steps that she had climbed for so many years of her life, she looked with astonishment at the figure standing at the top of them.

She had expected to see Carter, who was very old and rheumaticky and, because his feet hurt him, always shuffled about in bedroom slippers.

But the servant waiting for them at the open door was extremely impressive-looking. He was bearded and wore a turban on his head.

Prunella recognised him as a Sikh. As he salaamed to them politely, Nanette stared at him in astonishment and whispered:

"The Earl must have brought him back from India."

"Yes, of course," Prunella replied. "But he looks very strange at the Hall."

The Indian servant walked ahead and to Prunella's surprise opened the door of the Salon.

She had expected that, as the Earl was alone, he would be using the Library, where they had talked the first day that she had come to the Hall to find him.

Now as she walked into what had always been known as the Gold Salon she saw that the Holland covers had gone, the curtains were drawn, the chandeliers were lit, and the walls, which she had restored, were revealed in all their glory.

This was the most important room in the whole house and had been designed by Inigo Jones with the help of his pupil John Webb, and it was in Prunella's mind the most beautiful room she had ever imagined.

After a burst water-pipe from the floor above had damaged it, she had searched through all the old designs and found the actual sketches which Inigo Jones had made for the room.

Following them, she had had the walls painted white and had regilded the huge swags of fruit, flowers, and foliage in different shades of gold.

Fortunately, the paintings had not been damaged, nor the console tables with porphyry tops designed by William Kent. The curtains of crimson velvet matched the furniture and it now looked exactly, Prunella thought, as it had when it had first been completed.

She was so intent on looking at the room itself, and glancing up at the painted ceiling with its gods and goddesses depicted against a blue sky, that it was difficult for a moment to focus her eyes on the Earl.

Then as she saw him moving across the room to greet them she was aware that behind him there was another man and with a start she recognised Pascoe Lowes.

Even if she had not done so, she would have been

made aware that he was there by the sudden exclamation of sheer delight which came from Nanette's lips.

"Pascoe!" she murmured rapturously.

Then Prunella heard the Earl saying:

"Let me welcome you, Prunella, and tell you what a pleasure it is that you and Nanette, together with my nephew Pascoe, should be my first guests on my return home."

With an effort Prunella remembered to curtsey.

Then before she could speak she heard Nanette say to the Earl:

"Thank you, thank you! I knew this would be an exciting evening!"

She was looking at him as if he had given her a present of inestimable worth.

Then, as if she could not wait, she ran from his side towards Pascoe and her hands were in his.

The Earl's eyes were on Prunella's face and he said in a low voice that only she could hear:

"Before you start finding fault, let me say quickly that I have a reason for including my nephew in this particular party."

"I hope it is a good one!" Prunella said repressively.

"It is," the Earl replied, "but first may I tell you how attractive you look? It is the first time I have seen you fashionably gowned, and as we are always so frank with each other, let me add that it is a very great improvement!"

Prunella looked at him angrily, thinking that what he was saying was an impertinence.

Then as she saw the twinkle in his eyes and knew that he was teasing her, she thought that if she allowed herself to be provoked by what he was saying, it would seem childish.

"Nanette has already made me humbly conscious that I am a country mouse, My Lord."

"If that is true, it is a mouse with very extravagant taste," the Earl said.

Prunella looked at him in surprise, thinking that he was referring to her gown, but he added quietly:

"I thought it appropriate that we should be in this room tonight, considering how much it owes to you."

Because it was something she had not expected him to say, she merely looked round, wondering if he was rebuking her for spending so much on just one room when it was unlikely that he would ever be able to repay her.

Then, struggling to find the right words, she answered:

"I think this room . . . is one of the finest Inigo Jones ever designed . . . it belongs . . . not only to the Hall . . . My Lord, but to posterity."

"I am sure you are right, Prunella, but at the moment I am very grateful that it belongs to me."

There was an undoubted note of sincerity in the Earl's voice, to which Prunella was unable to reply, for at that moment Pascoe had detached himself from Nanette who had been talking to him eagerly, to say:

"Forgive me, Miss Broughton. It is a very great pleasure to see you again."

"Thank you," Prunella answered, but she had stiffened at his approach and her tone was cold.

"Because this is a house-warming," the Earl said, "I insist that we celebrate with champagne and that you drink my health."

As he spoke, the Indian servant came into the room with a silver tray on which reposed a bottle of champagne in a silver wine-cooler.

He set it down on the table and when they each had a glass in their hands the Earl raised his.

"To Winslow Hall!" he said. "And to its Guardian Angel, who has preserved it for my home-coming and to whom I am overwhelmingly grateful."

His toast took Prunella by surprise and she felt the colour flooding into her face as they drank to her.

Then Nanette said:

"You see, Prunella, all the time and effort you put into the Hall is really appreciated! Is that not so, My Lord?"

"I am indeed very grateful," the Earl replied, "and every day I find new instances of your sister's generosity."

Because she was afraid he was resenting that she had done so much, Prunella blushed again, and to change the subject she said to Pascoe in a more pleasant way than she would have done otherwise:

"Did you remember your uncle after not seeing him for so many years?"

"Of course I remembered him!" Pascoe replied. "How could I forget anyone who always seemed to me to be a dashing hero and was made all the more so as everybody spoke of him with bated breath?"

"On the contrary, Prunella will tell you that I was talked about with horror!" the Earl remarked.

"Only because they had nothing else to talk about!" Nanette said quickly. "And now you are home it will be quite easy for you to earn yourself a halo, and then the past will be forgotten."

The Earl laughed.

"You are very encouraging, Nanette, and I shall look to you to help me on the upward path which I have a feeling is going to be a somewhat wearisome climb from the Prodigal son."

"We will help you," Nanette said with a smile, "will we not, Pascoe?"

She held out her hand as she spoke and he took it in both of his.

Prunella turned away with a little flounce of her skirt. She walked to the table that stood between two of the windows and looked down at its contents.

It contained a collection of snuff-boxes which had belonged to the Earl's father and grandfather. She had arranged them against a background of new blue velvet which replaced one which had become faded and dusty.

The Earl went to her side to ask:

"Are you counting to see if I have already disposed of my most valuable possessions?"

Prunella started as she remembered that they were on her list of things which she had thought were the most saleable.

She knew it would be a great pity to part with them. At the same time, they were not so old or so unique as many of the other treasures in the house.

"Actually I was thinking how attractive they look," she replied.

"At the same time, you were ready to let them go," he said, almost as if he wanted to force her into an admission.

"Everything is precious when it means something personal," she answered, "and therefore I know how difficult it must be for you to make a choice."

"Are you really considering my feelings in the matter?"

"Of course I am!" Prunella replied. "These are your possessions and you have known them all your life. Naturally it will be hard for you to part with even one of them."

"I am glad that you think of me like that," the Earl said. "I had the feeling that you thought I was ready to sell anything and everything to raise enough money to provide me with the amusements that I must obviously crave after being in exile for so many years."

Because this was so near the truth as to be uncomfortable, Prunella walked to the window.

"I see you have started work on the garden," she said. "Have you been able to find somebody to help old Ives?"

"Ives tells me he wishes to retire," the Earl replied, "and I do not think he is capable of working more than an hour or so a day."

"That is true," Prunella agreed, "but he has done his best."

"I appreciate that," the Earl said, "and I have found a cottage for him."

"Found a cottage?" Prunella questioned. "What is wrong with the house in which he is now living? He has been there for twenty years, since he became Head Gardener, and he would not wish to leave."

"I have spoken to Ives," the Earl answered, "and he quite understands that I should require his house for the man who is to replace him. I am sure Ives will be quite comfortable as soon as I have done up the cottage I have chosen for him."

With great difficulty Prunella prevented herself from asking which one.

She had an uneasy feeling that the Earl was deliberately tantalising her by telling her of the innovations he was making without being exactly explicit.

'He wants to make me curious,' she thought. 'He wants me to appear to interfere so that he can tell me he intends to do what he wants without my assistance.'

She turned round from the window to look to where Nanette was talking intimately with Pascoe.

They were close to each other, and any onlooker would have realised as they looked at each other that they were in love.

"My nephew arrived today," the Earl said quietly at Prunella's side. "As you told me to expect, he is a handsome and attractive young man."

"Superficially," Prunella replied.

"He has told me quite frankly of his circumstances," the Earl said, "and I find it difficult to understand how my brother-in-law could have made such a mess of his affairs. I always believed him to be a rich man."

"Your father believed the same thing."

"Which is unfortunate for me, as it is for my nephew."

"I asked your help," Prunella said in a low voice.

"Which I am prepared to give you," the Earl answered, "if you can prove to me that it is for your sister's happiness that they should be parted, and of course for my nephew's."

Prunella looked at him indignantly.

"Are you suggesting for one moment," she asked, "that you will encourage that dressed-up Dandy to marry my sister for her money?"

"Certainly not, if that is what he is doing," the Earl replied firmly.

"Then tell him he is to leave her alone."

"Is there any other man in her life?"

"No, not at the moment. But if your nephew is not there, I will make sure that she finds one."

"How can you do that?"

"By letting her go back to London, and even taking her there if necessary."

The Earl smiled.

"I have a feeling that is an original idea where you are concerned, and why not? It would do you good to go to London, and I think it might widen your horizons quite considerably."

"I am not concerned with myself, My Lord," Prunella snapped. "I am thinking of Nanette."

"While I," the Earl replied, "although you may not believe me, am thinking of you as well as of Nanette and Pascoe."

The dinner was a more enjoyable meal than Prunella had expected, and certainly it was a surprising one.

To begin with, there were two Indian servants to wait on them, and as soon as the food was brought to the table she knew that it had not been cooked by Mrs. Carter.

Not only was it delicious, but the wines that accompanied it were superb, some of which Prunella had never tasted before.

The Earl set out to make the dinner stimulating mentally as well as physically.

Prunella had already realised that he was cleverer and more intelligent than she had expected him to be, and now he made them laugh with his stories of India and of the long, rather dismal voyage home.

Because he was talking animatedly, Pascoe forgot to drawl in what was the fashionable manner amongst the Bucks of St. James's Street, and tried to cap his uncle's stories in a way which entranced Nanette and even made Prunella laugh despite herself.

Time seemed to speed past, and when Prunella rose to leave the gentlemen to their port, Nanette, as soon as they were outside the Dining-Room, slipped her hand into hers.

"Oh, Prunella, what fun it is, and I have never known Pascoe to be so amusing. Even you had to laugh at his jokes."

They reached the Hall, and when Nanette would have gone towards the Salon, Prunella said:

"I want to go upstairs. You need not come with me if you do not want to."

"Of course I will come with you," Nanette replied.

They walked up the staircase, but when Nanette expected her sister to move towards one of the State Bedrooms she went in the opposite direction and a moment or two later they entered the Picture-Gallery.

Prunella stood still in the doorway.

Then as she looked down the length of the Gallery she felt a constriction in her heart, as if somebody had stabbed her.

Mrs. Goodwin had been right!

The paintings had been taken down from the walls and she could see some of them, she could not count how many, stacked on the floor, and there was not one Van Dyke hanging in its place.

She did not say anything, she only turned and walked back down the stairs and into the Salon, feeling as if the house itself had fallen down and was lying in ruins at her feet.

"I know you are upset!" Nanette cried. "But you know as well as I do, Prunella, he had to sell something to pay for his horses, those funny-looking servants, and the repairs he is doing to the cottages."

She paused before she added:

"You should be pleased about that, at any rate. You have always worried yourself silly about the old people and you have spent all your own money on them."

Prunella found it impossible to answer.

She was only feeling that in some way the Earl had deceived her by being so pleasant in asking for her advice and promising to help her about Pascoe.

She had thought, perhaps foolishly, that he intended to do what she wished and sell some of the treasures but not the Van Dykes.

"They are his paintings," she tried to tell herself, "and it is for him to make the decision . . . not me."

But somehow she still felt betrayed and cheated, and once again she was hating him.

"Oh, Prunella, do stop looking so upset," Nanette pleaded. "You will spoil the whole evening. I am enjoying myself, and it is so wonderful to have Pascoe here. I have been thinking about him all day and how miserable I am without him."

"I will tell you what we will do," Prunella said.

She had found her voice at last and it seemed somehow unlike her own.

"What is that?" Nanette asked.

"We will go to London! There is not much of the Season left. In fact, most people are leaving. But you want to buy me new clothes, you want to see your friends, and I am sure some of them will still be there! At least we can get away from here."

Nanette looked at her in astonishment.

Prunella knew she was running away from

something which hurt her unbearably, but she could not stand by and see it happening without protesting!

And that she had no right to do.

When they left for London the next morning Nanette was complaining volubly.

"I cannot understand why you are in such a hurry, Prunella," she had said. "Pascoe is staying with his uncle until tomorrow, and I wanted to see him."

"We are leaving!" Prunella said firmly. "And because I cannot leave you alone in the house, you will have to come with me."

"Of course I am prepared to come with you, and I want to go to London," Nanette replied, "but not in such a hurry!"

Charity said the same thing.

"Good gracious me, Miss Prunella, you've sat here year after year without a word passing your lips, and now you're leaving before I've even got me breath!"

Prunella was adamant, and because she had so little packing to do it was easy for everybody in the house to push Nanette's gowns into several trunks, and they were on their way before noon.

When they had reached home the night before, Prunella had been unable to sleep.

All she could think of was the long Gallery with its bare walls, the shadows in the corners seeming as dark and dismal as the misery within her heart.

The loss of the paintings made her feel again, and even more strongly, that the Earl had deceived her in being so pleasant, thanking her for what she had done for the Hall, when all the time he was doing the one thing that she had begged him not to do.

She felt as if the portraits of his ancestors had called out to her to save them, and she had failed, while treasures which were far less important were still in their places.

'I expect they too will soon go,' she thought bitterly. 'They will be sold to pay for servants, to buy horses, and doubtless for the repairs to the peach- and grape-houses.'

"How can he be so stupid," she raged in the darkness of the night, "not to know what is part of history and what are unessential luxuries?"

When the Earl and Pascoe had joined them in the Salon she had felt an irresistible impulse to rage at him; to tell him in front of the two young people how his successors in the future would look back and curse him for despoiling what should have become theirs.

Then she told herself that that would only be to behave just as his father had behaved, which had driven "Master Gerald" away in the first place.

She knew that neither Nanette nor Pascoe would understand how much she minded, and they would be shocked if she behaved in an uncontrolled manner or in any way like her usual self.

She therefore sat stiff and unsmiling while the others laughed and talked, and long before Nanette was ready to leave, she rose to say they should go home.

"Oh, not yet, Prunella! What is the hurry?"

"Old Dawson is not used to being kept out late," Prunella replied with the first excuse that came to her mind.

"I thought of that," the Earl said. "Actually I told him to go home before dinner and I have arranged to send you back in my carriage."

"In your carriage?" Prunella echoed.

"I was surprised to find that my father had anything so comfortable," the Earl answered, "but of course later I must buy a Cabriolet, which is more up-to-date and better sprung. Tonight Jim will drive you home and I promise he will get you there safely."

"How wonderful of you to think of it!" Nanette cried. "I promised I would show Pascoe the Library. We will not be long."

They disappeared together before Prunella could

expostulate, and as soon as they had gone the Earl said:

"What has upset you?"

"Nothing," she answered untruthfully. "I am just anxious, as you well know, that Nanette should not become more involved and enamoured of your nephew than she is already."

"She is a very lovely girl," the Earl said reflectively.

"In which case you will realise that I do not wish her to throw herself away on a man who is not worthy of her."

The Earl's lips twisted in a rather cynical smile.

"If marriage was always based on worthiness, there would be very few weddings."

"That may be your idea," Prunella said scathingly, "but you must understand that as Nanette has no parents I am her Guardian."

"You have a propensity for taking on other people's burdens," the Earl said, but he did not make it sound a virtue, and Prunella replied:

"I have to do what I believe to be my duty."

The Earl laughed.

"Duty! How I loathe that word! It was drummed into me when I was a child that it was my 'duty' to do this and my 'duty' to do that. It was a word my father was very fond of, and so, I am certain, was yours."

"A lot of people, My Lord, are very conscious of their responsibilities in life."

"And some are not," the Earl replied. "Oh, well, happiness is where you find it. I may be wrong, but I have a feeling that is something you have not yet discovered."

Prunella looked at him in a startled fashion.

"Why should you think I am unhappy?"

"Are you?"

"That is not a question I want to answer."

"I should like you to answer it—not to me, but to yourself—because real happiness, Prunella, and remember this, is enjoying life to the full, and that is something that I have a feeling you have not begun to do and have no idea how to start."

Prunella lifted her chin a little higher.

"I think, My Lord, you are trying to make me dissatisfied with my life as it is," she said, "and I cannot quite understand your motives for doing so."

"Perhaps I am merely opening the door to new interests, new adventures," the Earl said. "I would like, Prunella, to show you a very different world from the one in which you have incarcerated yourself like a small snail carrying its house upon its back."

"I cannot imagine what you are trying to say," Prunella said crushingly, "and now, My Lord, I think it is definitely time for Nanette and me to go home."

She rose to her feet as she spoke, and as she did so Nanette and Pascoe came back into the room.

There was a rapt look on their faces which aroused in Prunella an uneasy suspicion that Nanette had been kissed.

She could hardly believe that her sister would behave in such a reprehensible fashion, yet the suspicion persisted all the way home.

Nanette sat very quietly in the corner of the carriage, not talking, as she usually did, her eyes shining, a smile on her lips, and her hands clasped together as if in a kind of ecstasy.

Only when Prunella told her that they were leaving for London the next morning did she rouse herself to protest and argue, but it was to no avail.

When they reached London, Prunella drove to a quiet, old-fashioned Hotel where their father had occasionally stayed when obliged to visit London for a Regimental dinner or some reason connected with his official duties in the County.

When Prunella explained who they were, the Manager greeted them effusively and offered his deepest condolences on Sir Roderick's death.

They had been shown into a large, gloomy Suite

furnished with heavy mahogany and with two impersonal, rather cheerless bedrooms opening out of it.

Nanette threw herself down in a chair to say:

"Well, we have come to London when I never expected it. At the same time, I cannot think what you
are up to, Prunella."

"Why should I be 'up to' anything?" Prunella enquired. "It is an expression I do not care for."

"Because I know you so well," Nanette replied.
"You hate London and like being at the Manor, boss-
ing everybody about . . ."

She stopped suddenly.

"Now I know why you have come away!" she exclaimed. "It is because you are piqued with the Earl
for taking over your position as 'Lady Bountiful'!"

"That is not true," Prunella objected.

"But of course it is!" Nanette replied. "You have
had everything your own way for so long, running
the Hall as well as the Manor, having everybody on
the Estate saying you were an 'Angel of Mercy.' Now
they are all fawning on the Earl. Oh, poor Prunella,
of course you mind!"

"I do not! I do not mind in the slightest! And what
you are saying is quite untrue!"

Then as Prunella spoke she knew that her protest
was half-hearted and that Nanette had unerringly
put her finger on the real reason for their departure.

CHAPTER FIVE

*P*ascoe walked into the Breakfast-Room and as the Earl looked up from the table he knew something was wrong.

"What has happened?" he enquired.

"They are leaving for London this morning!"

"How do you know?"

"I have just had a note which Nanette sent me by a groom. She says her sister is determined to go to London, and of course it is to be rid of me."

The Earl smiled.

"I think I must also take some of the blame."

"You?" his nephew enquired.

"I told Prunella last night that it would be good for her to widen her horizons."

"I am not concerned with what Miss Prunella does, but with her sister."

"That is obvious."

Pascoe walked to the sideboard where a whole array of silver dishes were waiting for him to make a choice of what he would eat.

He took the heavy crested lids off them, one after another, then in a petulant manner helped himself to a slice of cold ham and sat down at the table.

He looked at his uncle and asked:

"What is to stop us from going to London too?"

"Nothing, as far as I am concerned," the Earl replied.

Pascoe's expression lightened.

"Then we will leave immediately," he said, "and the first thing we will do is to buy you some new clothes."

The Earl laughed.

"I am well aware that I need them."

"You most certainly do! If you are playing the part of the Prodigal Son, you are not eating husks—you are wearing them!"

The Earl laughed again.

"What I have is the best that Calcutta could provide."

"Then I am sorry for those who have to live in India," his nephew retorted.

"I am not as clothes-conscious as you, my dear boy, but I agree with you that I need a new wardrobe, and I do not wish my old friends to be ashamed of me."

Pascoe glanced at him slyly.

"If you are speaking of your erstwhile ladyfriends, they will be a bit long in the tooth by this time."

"I can always look at their daughters," the Earl replied.

There was silence as Pascoe ate a few mouthfuls of the ham, then pushed aside his plate.

"I have not had a chance to talk to you, Uncle Gerald, but you know that I wish to marry Nanette?"

"I certainly had that impression," the Earl remarked drily.

"The difficulty is that her sister, who I gather is in the position of being her Guardian, is violently opposed to me. I have done my best, but I doubt if I made the slightest impression on her conviction that I am a fortune-hunter."

The Earl sat back in his chair.

"Is that what you are?"

"Of course I am—or I was," Pascoe replied frankly. "It has been drummed into me by father and mother ever since I left Eton that if I am to keep the Estate going and live in a Castle, I have to marry money."

"And that is what you wish to do now?"

"I want to marry Nanette, which is a very different thing," Pascoe answered. "No-one will believe me, least of all her sister, but I would still want to marry her if she had not a penny. I love her! She is the most adorable person I have ever met in my whole life."

The Earl thought for a moment. Then he said:

"If it is true, then it looks as if you will have to wait until she is twenty-one."

"I am prepared to do that, even though it will be hell for both of us," Pascoe answered, "and especially for me, knowing that her mind is being poisoned against me by her sister, and doubtless also by you."

"I have not condemned you," the Earl replied mildly. "After all, why should I? You are very much like what I was at your age."

"Am I really?" Pascoe asked eagerly. "You certainly had a reputation for being very wild and doing outrageous things, but I never heard you referred to as a 'fortune-hunter.' "

"I suppose I always considered my father rich enough for me to avoid that stigma," the Earl said, "but I certainly sowed my wild oats and enjoyed doing so."

"Which resulted in your being more or less exiled for fourteen years," Pascoe said. "That is something I do not wish to happen to me."

"You might enjoy India."

"No! I wish to live in England, in London part of the time, and in the country if I can afford horses to hunt and to race, and to entertain."

Pascoe gave an exasperated exclamation as he added:

"But what is the use? I am in debt and I have nothing to offer Nanette except my heart, which will certainly not fetch much on the open market."

"I should have thought that its value was what she put on it," the Earl said quietly.

Pascoe rose from the table and walked across the room.

"If I could persuade that damned sister of hers to give me a chance, we could be married by Christmas, and I swear to you I would make her a very good husband."

The Earl was watching his nephew and thinking that he could understand any young woman of Nanette's age being fascinated by him.

He was undoubtedly very handsome, but, what was more important, his expression was open and frank and when he smiled it reached his eyes.

The Earl was a good judge of men and he thought to himself that his nephew, while undoubtedly spoilt by too much adulation from the fair sex, had certain qualities that were important in a man.

"I suppose what I should say to you," he said aloud, "is that if you really care for Nanette you should be prepared to fight for her. If not, drop her, and look elsewhere."

"I have no wish to do that."

"Then as I say—you must fight!"

"But how? How can I manage to marry her when that dragon stands between us?"

He sat down again at the table and leant towards his uncle.

"Help me, Uncle Gerald. Heaven knows you have had enough experience with women! Convince Miss Prunella that I am not as black as I am painted. Surely that is not too much to ask you?"

"I thought when you arrived here," the Earl answered, "that you intended to ask me for a loan."

Pascoe gave him a somewhat rueful smile.

"I thought of it when I heard you had returned from India," he said. "But when I saw you wearing those rusy old clothes and heard of the condition of the Winslow Estate, I knew there was no hope of any financial assistance."

He bent forward again.

"But you can help me in a very different and much more fundamental way. Will you try?"

"I must point out to you that the lady in question has an aversion to me which is deep-rooted," the Earl replied. "All her life she has been shocked by knowing that when I left this country I did not travel alone. She also berates me for allowing the Estate to fall into disrepair, and now for selling the Van Dykes."

"Have you sold them?" Pascoe asked. "Well, I do not blame you. Those old jossers on the walls had their good time when they were alive, and there is no reason why they should not contribute to your enjoyment now that they are dead!"

The Earl laughed.

"I think if you said that to Prunella she would have a stroke!"

"Let her!" Pascoe said. "I only wish I had a few Van Dykes of my own, but doubtless you remember that the paintings at the Castle were a pretty mouldy lot."

"Thinking of your father's Estate," the Earl said, "I cannot help feeling that if it was properly managed it might do well. After all, the soil in Huntingdonshire is good."

"I know nothing about it."

"Then why not learn?"

His nephew looked at the Earl in astonishment.

"Are you suggesting that I should manage the Estate myself?"

"Why not? Your father, as you told me yesterday, is now incapable of exercising any control over it, and I am quite certain that you mother would welcome any interest you showed in what after all is your inheritance."

Pascoe digested this with a frown between his eyes.

"Now that I think of it," he said, "I have often

thought that everything was done in a very old-fashioned way, and there was no possibility of introducing new ideas, which of course my father would never consider."

"When he dies, the responsibility will be yours," the Earl said. "Think it over, Pascoe. I cannot help feeling that there are things which you and I have not yet discovered about the countryside, and which should receive our attention."

"I will tell you what I have discovered," Pascoe replied grimly, "and that is crumbling farms, broken-down cottages, pensioners too old to work, and of course no money to take on extra labourers."

"All in all, a depressingly dismal picture," the Earl remarked.

"I would not know where to begin, unless I had the money to put things right," Pascoe said.

"Which brings us back to Nanette."

"Dammit all, I will marry her, however her sister tries to stop me!" Pascoe exclaimed. "And what is more, if she does marry me, we will make a go of the old place together. It has always meant something to me, I suppose, because it is my home."

"I wish you luck."

"And you will help me with Miss Prunella?"

"I will think about it," the Earl answered. "In the meantime, if we are going to London I had best order my Phaeton. I presume you would wish to drive there as swiftly as my new team will carry us?"

"But of course," Pascoe agreed, his eyes lighting up.

Prunella was sitting in the dark and rather dreary Sitting-Room of their Hotel Suite when Nanette came into it from her bedroom.

"I feel so mean, dearest Prunella," she said, "leaving you alone, but I did not like to ask Godmama to invite you a second time. You know how she dislikes too many unattached women."

"Of course I understand," Prunella replied, "and

your friends have been very kind to me. I had a delightful luncheon yesterday with that nice Lady Dobson, and I enjoyed the other evening with our cousins."

"That is more than I did," Nanette replied. "I thought they were a stuffy lot, and all they wanted to talk about, if you had let them, was Mama."

"I realised that," Prunella said, "and I thought it was very tactless of Cousin Cecilia to keep referring to her."

"I think she is too old to know any better," Nanette said. "But it was certainly an evening we need not repeat."

Prunella gave a little sigh.

Ever since they had come to London she had been scouring her memory to recall not only their relations but friends of their father's with whom he had kept in touch.

Fortunately Nanette had found quite a number of the acquaintances she had made in the Season who had still not left for the country. They had welcomed her effusively and invited her to dinner and to parties.

The only difficulty was that they did not want two unattached girls, and Prunella was very anxious not to make Nanette feel that she was an encumbrance.

The first thing they had done immediately on arrival was to search Bond Street for new gowns. Nanette was determined that her sister should be as well dressed as she was herself, and she swept aside all Prunella's protests and chose so many different garments for her that she lost count.

"I am not going to be ashamed of you," Nanette said fiercely, "and that means it is going to cost money! It does not matter who pays; whether it is you or I, you still have to look right, and that is all that matters."

Prunella certainly looked right at the moment,

wearing an evening-gown of pale green which seemed somehow to be reflected in her eyes.

It made her skin look even more dazzlingly white than usual, and Nanette said penitently:

"I ought not to leave you behind, but, dearest, what can I do?"

"I shall be all right," Prunella said. "I only put on this gown because Charity wanted to be sure it fitted me in case I wanted to wear it on a more important occasion."

"You look far too lovely to dine alone," Nanette said, "but tomorrow we will do something exciting together, that I promise you."

She dropped a kiss on Prunella's cheek, who asked:

"Surely somebody is calling for you?"

"Yes, of course," Nanette answered, "but God-mama said they would wait downstairs, and I am late as it is."

She hurried from the room before Prunella could formulate any other questions.

Then with a little sigh she rose from the chair on which she had been sitting and walked to the table on which there was a vase of flowers.

They made her think of home, and there was an ache in her heart when she thought of the flowers in the garden, the green lawns sloping down to a small stream, and her horse waiting for her in the stables.

'That is where I want to be,' she thought.

She found herself wondering whether the Earl was riding every morning on the gallop and if she would ever own a horse swift enough to beat Caesar.

It seemed absurd, in fact she told herself it was sheer imagination, but she missed the Earl, her fights with him, and even the feeling of disapproval which he aroused in her whenever they met.

What was he doing now? How many paintings had he sold? When she went back, would there be nothing left in the Gallery?

It was agonising to think of what had been lost, and

yet instead of seeing the treasures she loved she had a different vision in her mind.

It was of the Earl himself, the mocking look in his eyes, the twist to his lips, the manner in which he was entirely at his ease in his untidy, rather disreputable clothes.

Wherever he was, he seemed to dominate everything, even the Gold Salon and herself.

'I hate him!' she thought.

At the same time, she wanted to see him. She wanted to spar with him, to hear his deep voice, to try to get the better of him in an argument.

"He is destroying everything I love, everything I have cared for," she told herself.

Then she had the uncomfortable feeling that it was more pleasant to be with him, and to be shocked and angry, than to be alone as she was now in a dismal Hotel in a city she disliked.

Prunella wondered why anyone found London alluring.

It might be all right for Nanette, surrounded as she was by young people, but to Prunella the streets were narrow and dirty, and she missed the freshness of the air, and the horses she could ride at home.

Most of all she missed everything that was familiar at home and in which she was personally involved.

She knew now how much she enjoyed owning the Manor, having people in the village turning to her for advice and help, and, most of all, looking after the Winslow Estate and the Hall.

Last year, after her father had died, there had hardly been a day when she had not gone to the great house to see if there was anything that needed doing.

Most of all, to wander through it, enjoying the beauty of the Salons, the ceilings, the paintings, the State-Rooms, and to know with a feeling of pride that she had prevented many of them from deteriorating or suffering irreparable damage through neglect.

"I want to go home," she said suddenly beneath

her breath, but she was thinking of the Hall, not the Manor.

To her dismay, she was suddenly aware that there were tears in her eyes, and even as she tried to blink them away, ashamed at her own weakness, the door opened and a servant announced:

"A gentleman to see you, Miss."

Prunella looked up through her tears, but for a moment she was not certain that it was the Earl.

He looked so different, but it did not immediately strike her what the difference was, until she realised that he was wearing evening-dress, which was very different in every way from what he had worn when she and Nanette had dined with him at the Hall.

Now his long-tailed coat, with its silk revers, fitted as if it were a second skin, his cravat was as intricately tied in a complicated style as anything she had seen on his nephew, and the points of his collar reached above his sunburnt chin at exactly the right angle.

"Good-evening, Prunella!"

After a little hesitation from sheer surprise, Prunella remembered to curtsey.

"Good-evening . . . My Lord."

"I see you are alone. I was half-afraid you would either be at some amusing party or entertaining."

"Nanette is dining with her Godmother, Lady Carnworth."

"And you were not invited?"

"Her Ladyship was kind enough to have me to dinner three nights ago."

"So tonight Cinderella is left at home. Well, I am prepared to offer you an evening that will be more interesting than moping here."

"That is very kind of Your Lordship . . . but I am quite . . . happy, thank . . . you."

"I think that is untrue," the Earl said, "and, as you are so hospitable, I would enjoy a glass of sherry."

Prunella gave a little start.

"I am sorry," she said, "I should have offered you

101

some refreshment, but I was in fact so surprised to see you."

"You were thinking of me as being at the Hall?" the Earl enquired.

"Yes, of course! I thought you would have too much to do to wish to come to London."

"I found my work considerably impeded because you were not there to help me."

He noticed that for a moment there was a glint in Prunella's eyes before she replied:

"I doubt that is . . . true."

"But I assure you I am speaking the truth. I missed you, Prunella, and I am perceptive enough to think you missed me—or rather my house."

Prunella turned away and rang the bell, and before it was answered she seated herself in a chair and with her hand indicated one near it.

"Will you not sit down, My Lord?"

"Thank you."

As she leant back and crossed her legs, she thought that he seemed very relaxed, while she felt tense and, for no reason she could understand, a little nervous.

A servant answered the bell, and she ordered sherry for the Earl and a glass of Madeira for herself.

"Are you brave enough to defy the conventions and have supper with me?" the Earl asked.

"Would that not be . . . wrong?" Prunella enquired.

He realised that she really did not know the answer, and he said:

"Not exactly wrong, though perhaps a little indiscreet. Unfortunately, as I know no-one I can ask to join us at this late hour in the evening, I suggest we go first to the Theatre Royal, Drury Lane, where I have already ordered a Box, then to some quiet, discreet place for supper, where we can talk."

It sounded to Prunella so exciting, after the dull evening she had expected for herself, that she wanted to answer that there was nothing she would enjoy more.

Instead she said in a prim little voice:

"It is very kind of Your Lordship to think of me when there must be so many old friends longing to see you, since your return to England after being away for so . . . long."

"Are you gunning for me, Prunella?"

"No, of course not!"

"I can hear that little sting in your voice when you refer to my long absence abroad, and I am tired of excusing myself by pointing out that there was a war taking place, or perhaps it would be better to be honest and say I had rather more important things to do than crawl humbly home and be, as Pascoe has suggested, the 'Prodigal Son.' "

"At least he had the fatted calf killed for him," Prunella said, without really considering her words.

Then she wished she had not spoken, as the Earl laughed.

"You are quite right, Prunella, there was no-one to kill a calf, fatted or otherwise, except yourself."

There was silence, then Prunella said:

"I do not mean, My Lord, to sound as if I am continually . . . reproaching you. We promised to help each other, but I am not certain you are keeping to your part of the bargain."

"Only time will tell you that," the Earl replied, and Prunella was not certain what he meant.

She noticed when the sherry arrived that the Earl took only a sip from his glass, and she had the feeling that he had asked for it merely to put her in the wrong by making her appear inhospitable.

At the same time, she had no wish to quarrel, and despite her conviction that she ought to refuse his invitation, she went eagerly to her bedroom to collect a wrap to wear over her green gown.

Nanette had fortunately been most insistent that every evening-gown should have a scarf to match it, and a number of them were trimmed with maribou or fur.

It was a warm night and Prunella's long scarf was of soft chiffon, which she wrapped round her. Although she was not aware of it, it made her look like the embodiment of spring just coming into bud.

She took a swift glance at herself in the mirror, seeing that the new style in which her hair was dressed was neat and becoming. Then, with an irrepressible light in her eyes and a smile on her lips, she joined the Earl in the Sitting-Room.

Outside the Hotel, Prunella found that the Earl had waiting for him a very smart closed carriage drawn by two horses.

There was a coachman and a footman on the box and she supposed that he had hired them and wondered what it must have cost.

The carriage she and Nanette had hired while they were in London was drawn by only one horse and had only one coachman, but it had still seemed to Prunella to be extremely expensive.

As they drove along Piccadilly she found herself remembering excitedly that the Theatre Royal, Drury Lane, which had been burnt down for the second time in 1809, had been rebuilt three years later.

She had read about it in the newspapers and had been so interested because her father had met and often talked about Samuel Whitbread, who had raised four hundred thousand pounds for the rebuilding of the Theatre.

Prunella had read that it was magnificent and she knew it was something she wished to see, and, what was even more exciting this year, the *Morning Post* had told her that they had installed gas in the Theatre as an illuminant.

She was so deep in her thoughts as to what lay ahead that she felt quite surprised when the Earl, sitting beside her, asked:

"What are you thinking about? One thing is quite obvious—it is not your host!"

Prunella blushed.

"I am sorry," she said. "Am I being rude? I was thinking about the Theatre Royal and how exciting it will be to see it. Will Edmund Kean be playing to-night?"

"He will," the Earl answered, "and after everything that has been said about him as the greatest actor of our time, I think you would like to see him play Othello."

He knew by the way Prunella drew in her breath and clasped her hands together that she was excited, and when they sat in the Box in what was undoubtedly the finest Theatre London had ever seen, the look in her eyes was that of a child seeing a lighted Christmas-tree for the first time.

Edmund Kean was born to smoulder, to glow, and to blaze with such an intensity of glory that he consumed himself in the white-hot fire of his genius.

When he had first elected to play Othello, the prophets of gloom had forecast failure.

But his dramatic prowess knew no bounds and his Othello was acclaimed as the most perfect of all the portrayals of the Moor of Venice. Kean surpassed all he had done before, and Lord Byron had cried:

"By God, he is a soul!"

To Prunella, *Othello* was a revelation and she felt herself carried away by Kean's brilliant acting and by the magic of the Theatre itself.

She had never had an opportunity of visiting a Play-House since she was grown up and had seen only performances given by amateurs in the nearest town to Little Stodbury.

Now she felt as if she herself were part of Shakespeare's drama. She suffered the agonies of Desdemona and the wild grief of Othello until their tragedy was hers and she had been transported out of herself.

Only as the curtain finally fell did she come back to

the real world from the magical one where she had been emotionally moved in a manner which she had never experienced in her whole life.

She had not been aware that while she was watching the stage, the Earl had been watching her and understanding what she was feeling.

Somehow it was impossible to utter commonplaces or even to thank him for an unforgettable experience. She could only move in silence through the Theatre to where the Earl's carriage was waiting outside.

Only as they drove away did Prunella say in a very small voice:

"I did not . . . know I could . . . feel like that."

There was no need to explain what she meant, and the Earl said quietly:

"I knew that you could, but I wanted to have evidence of it."

She was too bemused to ask him for an explanation, and only when she found herself sitting in a small Restaurant not far from the Theatre Royal did she say, as the Earl asked her what she would like:

"I feel as if I . . . could never eat . . . or drink again."

"You will," the Earl replied with confidence. "I am therefore going to order what I think you will enjoy."

Prunella had no wish to argue with him, and when the waiter poured out a glass of champagne she sipped it absently, her ears still seeming to hear Kean's vibrant voice.

Then when the food came, she found, surprisingly, that she was hungry, and after she had eaten a few mouthfuls she gave a little laugh and said to the Earl:

"Forgive me, but I have never known anything so . . . moving and in a way so . . . marvellous!"

He did not reply, and she added:

"I told you I was a country mouse."

"I am actually congratulating myself," he said, "in having taken you to see something which I knew, unless I was a bad judge of character, would move you as the story of Othello has always moved me."

"It is very sad."

"Like all women, you would like a love-story to end happily."

"How could he not have realised that she . . . loved him?"

"Do you feel, after that, that you now know a little more about love than you knew previously?" the Earl enquired.

The way he spoke made Prunella look at him quickly. Then she said:

"I think perhaps . . . one has to . . . be in love . . . oneself, to know . . . anything about it."

"And you have never been in love?"

"No . . . of course not!"

"Why so vehement? If there were any justice in the world you should have been in love a dozen times already at your age."

Unexpectedly Prunella found herself thinking of the man her mother had run away with.

That had not been love, not real love, and yet she knew there had been a reflection of it in that he had meant something in her mother's life, and when he betrayed her something precious had been shattered.

"Who was he, Prunella?" the Earl asked.

The question startled her and she looked at him, then looked away again.

"There was . . . no-one."

"That is not true! For a moment I could see you living again what you felt, and suffered."

"You are talking nonsense," she said quickly.

"On the contrary, you are denying the truth, which I always find rather tiresome, and yet it is the inevitable habit of most women."

"I always tell the truth!" Prunella asserted angrily.

"Then tell me whom you loved and what happened."

Almost as if he compelled her, she said:

"It was . . . not like . . . that . . . I just . . . admired someone . . . and because he said charming . . . and flattering things to me . . . I found myself . . . thinking about him . . . and perhaps . . . d-dreaming of him too. . . ."

She stopped speaking and the Earl said quietly:

"Then you were disillusioned? In what way?"

"I have . . . no wish to . . . explain what . . . h-happened . . . but I . . . s-suppose it made me feel suspicious of men and everything . . . they . . . do."

"It is time you grew up, Prunella," the Earl said. "That was a childish dream and children are often disappointed. Now that you are older, you will have to realise that no-one is perfect, any more than you are yourself."

She looked at him without speaking, and he went on:

"If you think that women are unsure and uncertain of themselves, men are too. They do valiant deeds to pretend they are braver than they really are. They even attempt the impossible, to satisfy some imperfection in themselves."

"I did not . . . think of . . . men as ever feeling like . . . that," Prunella said.

"I think you thought they were all strong, omnipotent, imperious, as a child believes her father to be," the Earl smiled, "but you will find they are weak, sometimes afraid, and very much in need of tenderness."

The way he spoke was so astonishing that Prunella stared at him wide-eyed, and he said:

"Think back and you will find I am right. Your father was a dominating man, as mine was, and I fought wildly, frantically, against being made subservient, against being manipulated and forced to obey orders that were given to me without explanation."

There was that twisted smile on his lips that was somehow very intriguing as he went on:

"Now I am beginning to realise that my father was just a man who in many ways was disappointed with life and who, to placate his own conscience, wished to appear the conquering hero he never was in reality."

"I never thought that he, or Papa, was like that," Prunella said.

Then she began to wonder if the Earl was not right.

His father had, in his subtle way, always tried to prove he was right, and he directed and even dominated the lives of all those round him.

The Earl watched the expression on her face and after a little while he said:

"I see you begin to understand. Now think about yourself and your own reactions."

Being taken off her guard, Prunella had a sudden vision of her mother, very beautiful with her fair hair and blue eyes, laughing as she played in the sunshine with Nanette and herself.

Then, as she chased them between the trees and over the grass towards the lily-pool, her father had unexpectedly appeared walking towards them, leaning on his cane.

Prunella could remember all too clearly now how there had seemed to be a sudden silence as she and her mother had stopped running, while Nanette, who could barely toddle, sat down on the grass.

Her mother had walked towards her father.

"I was playing with the children," she said, her voice a little breathless, her hands trying to tidy her hair.

"So I see," Sir Roderick had remarked briefly. "I want you, Lucia. Kindly come back to the house with me."

"Yes, of course, Roderick."

Her mother's voice had been meek and she had turned to Prunella.

"Run to Charity, dearest," she had said, "and take Nanette with you."

"But, Mama, you promised to play with us," Prunella protested.

"Your father wants me, darling. I will come and see you later in the Nursery."

Her mother had gone walking sedately beside her father, who was very slow.

Because that moment of time had come back so vividly, Prunella said almost angrily to the Earl:

"We are being introspective and what is the point of it? It cannot undo what has happened."

"Of course not," he answered, "but what we can avoid is allowing it to remain in the shadows of the past instead of leaving it behind to come out into the sunshine."

"Is that what you are asking me to do?"

"Yes," the Earl said, "and with me, Prunella!"

Her eyes widened.

She looked at him for an explanation and the expression she saw in his eyes made her stiffen.

She did not know why, but she felt her heart beating strangely in her breast and a feeling she did not understand crept over her.

It was what she felt when she listened to Edmund Kean as Othello making love, and yet because it was within herself it was more intense.

"I do not . . . understand . . . what you are . . . s-saying," she faltered.

"I think you do," the Earl said quietly. "You see, Prunella, I have been looking for you for a very long time."

"I . . . I do not . . . understand."

Prunella forced her eyes away from his, and now she was staring across the room, conscious as she did so that although he had not moved, the Earl was somehow closer to her and she was acutely conscious of him.

He was overwhelming and overpowering and she wanted to run away and yet she wanted to stay.

Then as if from far away she saw two people come into the Restaurant.

The waiter was leading them to a secluded table and as they followed him there was no mistaking who they were.

It was Nanette and with her was Pascoe!

CHAPTER SIX

"*H*ow could she? How could she lie to me?" Prunella said over and over again as they drove from the Restaurant back towards the Hotel.

Nanette and Pascoe had not been aware that she and the Earl were in the same Restaurant and had seen them, and although in her first fury at having been deceived Prunella had wished to go and confront them, the Earl had prevented her.

She had half-risen to her feet when she felt his hand on her wrist.

"No!" he said firmly. "You cannot make a scene here!"

"I only want her to know I have seen her and am aware of her lies and deception," Prunella replied.

"And what good will that do?"

Because the Earl's hand held her prisoner and she felt him drawing her back into her seat, she sat down again.

"I trusted her when she said she was going out with her Godmother," Prunella said almost as if she spoke to herself, "and I suppose on all the other evenings when I thought I was not invited with her, she was in fact with your nephew."

"Is that so very reprehensible when she has seen him so many times before?" the Earl enquired.

"She . . . lied to . . . me."

"I imagine she did so because she knew the fuss you would make if she wished to see the man she loves and who loves her."

"Are you condoning their behaviour?" Prunella asked incredulously.

"Not condoning it," the Earl replied, "but trying to understand why Nanette has behaved as she has. You are a very formidable person, Prunella, when you are being aggressive."

She looked at him and he saw a sudden bewilderment in her eyes, as if she had not expected him to attack her.

"I do not . . . mean to be," she said after a moment. "I am only trying to do what is . . . right."

"What is right for one person is not necessarily right for another, and who can decide what is right or wrong where love is concerned?"

"I do not believe Nanette is really in love with your nephew," Prunella said sharply. "She is too young to know anything about real love, which lasts for a lifetime."

"While you, of course, know a great deal about it," the Earl said mockingly.

Prunella did not answer but he saw her lips tighten, and after a moment he said:

"Stop being so unnecessarily upset. I assure you, although it is perhaps reprehensible of Nanette to have supper alone with Pascoe, she will come to no harm. He loves her."

As if Prunella understood the meaning behind the

112

words, he saw the colour rise in her cheeks, and after a moment she said a little incoherently:

"I was . . . not thinking . . . of anything like . . . that."

"I thought, from the way you were behaving, that that was in your mind."

"No, of course not!" she said in a shocked voice. "But I am very annoyed and hurt that Nanette should lie to me so . . . blatantly."

"I can understand that," the Earl said, "but you have to learn, Prunella, that when one is in love, nobody else, not even one's nearest and dearest, has any importance beside the man or the woman who has captured one's heart."

"What am I to do?" Prunella asked desperately. "How can I stop Nanette from seeing your nephew and endangering her reputation by having supper in public with him?"

"If you really think her reputation will be ruined, what about your own?"

Again the colour rose in Prunella's cheeks, but she answered:

"I am older and completely unknown in London, and you are . . . different."

"In what way?"

Prunella had not expected the question and she found it hard to find an answer.

In fact, as she tried in her confusion to find words, he said mockingly:

"Perhaps you are accusing me also of being a fortune-hunter?"

"No, of course not," Prunella said quickly.

"Are you sure? After all, even if you are not as rich as your sister, you still own the Manor and its grounds and have a considerable income, much of which has already been expended on my property."

"I do not wish to . . . talk about myself," Prunella said after a moment's hesitation, "but you promised me you would try to help me to prevent your nephew from paying so much attention to Nanette. Instead of which, I think you have made the situation worse."

"I asked him to stay with me so that I could judge for myself if the things you told me about him are true."

"And now you know they are?"

"I believe he is not the danger you consider him to be."

"Of course he is a danger!" Prunella said crossly. "He is trying to marry Nanette and she is infatuated with him! And how can she help it, when he is so good-looking and has what Charity calls, 'a honeyed tongue'?"

She did not mean to be funny but when the Earl laughed a faint smile touched the corners of her lips.

"It is exactly what he has," she said helplessly, "and of course Nanette is mesmerised by him like a stupid little rabbit."

"I think your metaphors are a little mixed," the Earl said. "At the same time, I know what you are saying and I too find my nephew has 'a honeyed tongue.' "

"He pulled the wool over your eyes, and you still believe he loves Nanette and not her money?"

"I think it would be difficult for anyone, even you, Prunella, to blind me to the truth," the Earl said, "and the truth is, whether you like it or not, Pascoe loves your sister as much as he is capable of loving anybody, and I think she feels the same about him."

"If that is what you feel, then there is nothing more for me to say on the subject," Prunella said stiffly, "and I would like to go home."

"Of course," the Earl agreed.

He called for the bill and when it was paid he rose to his feet and said to Prunella:

"I want you to leave without attracting your sister's attention."

The Earl thought she was about to argue with him, but instead she gave a little toss of her head and, pulling her chiffon scarf round her shoulders, walked straight out of the Restaurant, looking neither to right nor to left.

The Earl followed her and when they had stepped into his carriage, which was waiting outside, they drove for some way in silence until, as if she knew she was being rude, Prunella said:

"I must thank Your Lordship for taking me to *Othello*. I enjoyed it more than I can say, and my evening was only spoilt by . . . what happened . . . afterwards."

"I should have thought the play might have taught you, if nothing else, that it is a mistake to jump to hasty conclusions."

"You can hardly compare what Othello thought about Desdemona with what I feel about your nephew."

"I think if you look for it you will find a similarity," the Earl said drily.

Prunella thought he was being rather stupid in his defence of both Pascoe's and Nanette's behaviour and she planned in her mind exactly what she was going to say to her sister.

Nanette was ignorant of the fact that she had been seen, her deception discovered, and her lies exposed.

Because Prunella loved Nanette it was an agony to think she had lied to her not once but probably several times since they came to London.

Where had she been on Wednesday night when she had said she was dining with some friends she had met on her previous visit?

And Prunella remembered another day when she had said she had been asked out to luncheon and she had looked very pretty, in fact radiant, before she left the Hotel.

Of course she had been going to meet Pascoe, but why had she not told her the truth?

Prunella knew the answer to that question, but she kept telling herself that if she had been told, she would have been reasonable about it and would even have acquiesced and allowed her sister to meet Pascoe Lowes.

She thought now that she had been very foolish in not realising that if he was in London it was obvious that he would call to see Nanette at the Hotel, if he had not been meeting her elsewhere.

'I should have suspected they were doing something behind my back,' Prunella thought bitterly, and was surprised to find that they had arrived at the Hotel.

Deep in her thoughts, she stepped out and went up the stairs towards her Suite, hardly aware that the Earl was accompanying her.

They went into the Sitting-Room, which still looked gloomy even though it was lit by candles in the sconces on the walls and a small brass chandelier hanging from the ceiling.

Prunella, still resenting how she had been treated by Nanette, threw her gloves and her scarf down on a chair, then walked towards the fireplace to turn as she reached it and say to the Earl:

"You have to help me! I will talk to Nanette, but you must speak to your nephew."

"What about?"

"Leaving Nanette alone. We could suggest that they do not see each other for a year, in which case I could have the chance, as I intended when I came to London, to find her a new interest."

"What you mean is another man," the Earl said. "Do you really believe she could fall out of love so quickly or that you, even with your extensive acquaintance with presentable young men, could find someone as handsome as Pascoe?"

He was being sarcastic and mocking her, but Prunella was past caring.

"You have to help me, you have to!" she insisted. "I will not allow my sister to make a disastrous marriage just because she has money."

"Are you quite certain it would be disastrous?"

"Of course I am certain!" Prunella snapped. "Your nephew has chased after a number of heiresses who have managed to elude his greedy, grasping hands, and, as I have said until I am tired of saying it, it is only because Nanette is so young that she cannot see what he is really like beneath his dandified appearance."

"You are very vehement, Prunella," the Earl said, "but what I find so pathetic is that you are railing against something that is bigger than yourself."

She looked at him questioningly and he said quietly:

"Love! Something about which you, Prunella, know nothing, and which is, as I have told you once before, irresistible and, as we saw tonight at the Theatre, overwhelming and uncontrollable."

"What is depicted on a stage is very different from real life."

"How do you know?"

"Of course it is," she argued. "What we were watching was very skilfully portrayed, but by cardboard characters. They suffered agonies because of their emotions, but that sort of thing does not happen in real life."

"How do you know that?"

"Because it does not."

"If you had ever been in love, Prunella, you would know that your body becomes a battleground of conflicting sensations, and love can carry you high into a rapturous Heaven or cast you into the darkest depths of Hell."

Prunella gave a little laugh that had no humour in it.

"Now you are being dramatic," she said, "and not as skilfully as Edmund Kean!"

"I think, Prunella," the Earl said slowly, "you are offering me a challenge to make you feel dramatic too."

"A . . . challenge?"

She looked at the Earl as she spoke and realised he was standing very close to her.

Because she had been concentrating on Nanette, she had not really looked at him since they had left the Restaurant, and in the Theatre she had been intent on watching the play.

Now she realised how different he looked in his new clothes, and how, in a way, magnificent.

He was not as handsome as his nephew, but he had, as Nanette had seen the first time she met him, the raffish look of a pirate or a buccaneer, which was in fact very noticeable at the moment.

His eyes seemed dark and penetrating as they looked into hers, and because they were standing close to each other Prunella was suddenly very conscious of how tall and broad-shouldered he was, and how very masculine.

She had never been close to an attractive man in the same way before, and it gave her a strange feeling which she could not understand and which she instinctively thought she should avoid.

She would have taken a step backwards but the mantelpiece behind her prevented her from doing so, and she could only stand with her eyes held by the Earl's and feel that for the moment everything she had been saying was swept away from her mind and there was no other problem except him.

"I wanted you, Prunella, to come to London," he said, "and broaden your horizons. But I suppose it is too soon to know if London by itself can do this for you, so perhaps we should find a different way of achieving the same thing."

"I do not . . . know what you are . . . talking about."

"I am talking about love," the Earl said, "and of course your ignorance of it."

"I am not ashamed of being ignorant, My Lord, if

love makes people behave in a deceitful, under-handed manner."

"And how would you behave in the same circum-stances?"

"I would always do what is right."

The Earl laughed softly.

"You are so very positive and still so aggressive, and yet I find it attractive because you are so different from anyone I have ever met before."

"By that I understand you to mean that you have met some very . . . strange people."

"Of course they have been that, but they were none of them as lovely as you, Prunella, or as prudish."

He had not appeared to move, and yet Prunella had the uncomfortable feeling that he was nearer to her than he had been a moment earlier.

"I think, My Lord . . ." she began.

Then to her astonishment the Earl's arms were round her, he pulled her against him, and his lips were on hers.

For a moment she was too surprised to do anything but freeze into immobility.

Then as she began to struggle, his arms tightened and his lips against hers were demanding.

She felt that he held her completely captive, and as he held her close against him, his mouth made her his prisoner in a way that she had never imagined was possible through a kiss.

Even as she told herself that what he was doing was outrageous and she hated him for it, she felt a strange sensation she had never known before rise within her, move through her body, up to her throat, and into her lips.

It was like a warm wave flowing relentlessly through her and at the same time filling her mind with a radiance and a light that seemed to shine from her heart.

It was so strange, so utterly inexpressible, and yet in a way it was so wonderful that, despite herself, she

felt her resistance cease as she surrendered her lips
and her whole body to what he asked of her.

She knew that his mouth was fierce and demanding, passionate and insistent, and yet when it should
have disgusted and frightened her, she found instead
that she was subservient to his demands.

Then when she felt as if time and place had ceased
to exist, that her feet were no longer on the ground,
and that he was carrying her up into a cloudless sky,
he twisted her lips with his.

The sudden pain was so intense that it was almost
like lightning streaking through her, to be succeeded
by a feeling of rapture and wonder that was inde-
scribable.

She only knew that for the moment she felt as if she
had touched the stars and held them to her breast.

Then when the ecstasy of it was almost too intense
to bear, the Earl raised his head.

Because for the moment Prunella could think of
nothing but what he had made her feel, she gave a
little murmur that came from the depths of her heart
and hid her face against his shoulder.

He did not speak but only held her closer with a
strength which made her feel as if he prevented her
from falling, and his lips were against her hair.

How long they stood there Prunella could afterwards never remember.

She only knew that her whole being was struggling
with the feelings he had aroused in her.

She felt as if her heart were singing; her eyes were
still blinded by a light that came from themselves or
perhaps from the stars to which they had journeyed.

Then as she tried to come back to earth she heard
the Earl say:

"Now do you understand, my sweet, what I have
been saying to you?"

He kissed her forehead before he went on:

"How soon will you marry me so that I can continue to teach you about love?"

Prunella drew in her breath.

For a moment she thought she could not have heard what he had said and must have imagined it.

Then, with what was almost a superhuman effort, because she needed the strength of his arms to hold her, she forced herself away from him.

"What . . . did you . . . say?" she asked in a very small voice.

"I asked you to marry me," he replied. "After all, if you think about it, my darling, what could be more suitable? You have already made the Hall part of yourself."

"D-do you really . . . think I would . . . marry you?" Prunella enquired.

"Can you think of any reason why you should not do so?" the Earl asked.

He did not move but she put out her hands as if she felt he was encroaching on her.

"Of course I could not . . . do such . . . a thing!"

"Why not?"

"How could I do anything that would give Nanette grounds for thinking I must approve of the way in which she is . . . behaving?"

"I am not concerned with Nanette," the Earl replied, "but with us—you and me, Prunella. Although you may not agree with me at the moment, we would be very happy together."

As if she thought her legs were too weak to carry her, Prunella sat down in a chair.

"Please," she pleaded. "I cannot . . . talk about this . . . now."

The Earl stood looking at her and he knew she had no idea how lovely she looked in her green gown with her eyes wide and still a little ecstatic from the emotions he had aroused in her, a flush on her cheeks, her lips red and soft from his lips.

"We will talk about it tomorrow," he said quietly.

"Go to bed and dream of what I made you feel just now."

He moved to her side, took her hand, and raised it to his lips.

He kissed the back of it and then turned it over to kiss the softness of her palm.

He felt a little quiver go through her, and as her eyes met his he said quietly in his deep voice:

"I love you! Do not worry about anything else, just remember what this was like."

He released her hand and walked to the door without looking back, and when he had gone Prunella gave a little cry and put her hands up to her face.

It was dawn before Prunella fell asleep, and when she awoke it was far later than her usual time of being awakened and she knew that Charity had let her sleep.

Everything she had thought and felt the night before came flooding over her and once again she told herself, as she had done in the hours of darkness, that what had happened to her with the Earl was inconceivable, incredible, and must have been part of her imagination!

And yet it actually had happened.

He had kissed her and aroused in her feelings which she had no idea existed and which she had to admit were wonderful and beyond the bounds of her imagination.

It was, she told herself, something which must never occur again, and that the Earl had asked her to marry him was too amazing to be credible.

He had known what she felt about him before they came to London!

He had known that she was shocked by his behaviour in the past and by his staying away from home for fourteen years, and if he was not aware that she despised him for selling the Van Dykes, then he must be far more obtuse than he appeared to be.

No, he knew, and perhaps he had deliberately de-fied her because she had asked him not to sell them.

But all this which concerned only herself was im-material compared with the fact that if she married the Earl, then there would be no possibility of her preventing Nanette from throwing herself away on his fortune-hunting nephew and ruining her life for all time.

"I must not see him again," Prunella told herself, and wondered how she could ever prevent herself from remembering what he had made her feel.

It has been an ecstasy that was not of this world, and instinctively she tried to arm herself against the feelings he had aroused in her.

"I will have to leave with Nanette," she whispered to herself in the darkness, and wondered why it was difficult to speak with lips that had been kissed.

Now with a dull light coming through the sides of the curtains she told herself that she had to be strong.

First she would remonstrate with Nanette for her behaviour of last night and for the lies she had told her, and then she must think of some way by which she could not only prevent Nanette from seeing Pas-coe but prevent herself from seeing the Earl.

There was no time to lose and she got quickly out of bed. Putting on a very attractive robe which Nanette had made her buy, of heavy silk trimmed with lace and velvet ribbons, she crossed the room to pull back the curtains.

It was raining outside and she thought the grey sky was symbolic of the task which lay ahead of her.

She combed her hair, put on her bedroom slippers, and went into Nanette's room.

Her sister was sitting up in bed, finishing her breakfast, which had been brought to her on a tray.

"Good-morning, Prunella!" she said. "Charity told

me that you were not awake. It is unlike you to sleep so late. You are not ill?"

"I am not ill," Prunella replied, "but upset."

Nanette raised her eye-brows and Prunella asked:

"Where were you last night . . . and with whom?"

"I told you . . ." Nanette began; then she saw the expression on her sister's face and exclaimed: "Oh—you know!"

"I saw you!"

"Saw me? How?"

"I happened to be having supper in the same Restaurant as you were."

"Good Heavens!" Nanette exclaimed. "I did not see you. Whom were you with?"

"I was with the Earl, and I could hardly believe my eyes, Nanette, when I saw you come in with his nephew and realised how you had deceived me and lied to me."

"I am sorry—dearest," Nanette said lightly, "but you know what a fuss you would have made if I had told you I was going out with Pascoe, and I *had* to see him! Besides, I have had enough of those dreary dinner-parties with our boring relations and even listening to Godmama gossipping always in the same way about the same people. Her conversation never varies."

"What we were talking about," Prunella said scathingly, "is your behaviour in deceiving me."

"I know you are angry," Nanette answered, "but do try to understand, Prunella, that I love Pascoe and I intend to marry him."

"Over my dead body!" Prunella said firmly. "Let me make this clear once and for all, Nanette. You will not marry Pascoe, or if you do, it will not be until you are twenty-one, which means you will have to wait three years."

She saw her sister go very pale and she went on:

"I very much doubt if *he* will wait for you as long as

that, for there will doubtless be other heiresses for him to chase long before you are available."

"How can you be so—cruel and so—unkind to—me?" Nanette asked.

"Although you will not believe it, I am thinking entirely of your happiness," Prunella said. "Both Pascoe and his uncle are ne'er-do-wells and I intend that we shall have nothing more to do with either of them."

"How do you propose to manage that?" Nanette asked scornfully. "How can you avoid seeing the Earl when he lives next door, or Pascoe, if he is staying with him?"

"We will avoid them because we are not going home!"

"Not going home?" Nanette exclaimed.

"No. I have made up my mind," Prunella replied. "I am taking you to Bath, where quite a number of people go at this time of the year, so there is a good chance you will meet a man there who will prove much more suitable as a husband than the one you have chosen for yourself."

"That is impossible!" Nanette cried, but Prunella continued as if she had not spoken:

"If Bath proves disappointing, then we might consider going to France . . . to Paris."

Nanette looked at her sister incredulously.

"I think you have gone mad!" she said. "Why should you drag me round the world simply because you think I will forget Pascoe? I shall never forget him! Never! I love him, and I intend to marry him whatever you may say or do."

"A great deal can happen in three years," Prunella said.

Feeling that there was nothing more to say, she walked out of Nanette's bedroom, closing the door sharply behind her.

When she was dressed she sent Charity downstairs to ask the Manager of the Hotel to come and speak to her in the Sitting-Room.

When he arrived he bowed politely at the door as Prunella said:

"I wish to talk to you, Mr. Mayhew."

"I'm honoured, Miss Broughton," the Manager replied. "I'm only hoping you've not any complaints to make as to the comfort of your rooms or the service you've received."

"No, indeed, Mr. Mayhew, you have done everything possible for me and my sister," Prunella answered. "What I want you to arrange is a Courier and a conveyance to take us to Bath."

"To Bath, Miss Broughton?" Mr. Mayhew exclaimed in surprise.

"We have decided to go there for a short visit," Prunella said. "I have had no chance to make arrangements, and I want your Courier to take us to a quiet, respectable Hotel and see that we have the same accommodation that we have had here."

"Of course, Miss Broughton. It'll be a great pleasure to make this arrangement for you."

Mr. Mayhew paused for a moment before he said:

"I hope it'll be possible to find a Courier who is suitable and of course a carriage and horses at such short notice. But I'll try to perform miracles, and I hope that you and Miss Nanette Broughton will be able to leave here at perhaps ten o'clock tomorrow morning."

"Thank you very much, Mr. Mayhew," Prunella said briskly. "It is extremely obliging of you, and I know if my father were alive he would thank you for the care you have taken of us."

"I'm deeply touched by the kind things you say," Mr. Mayhew replied.

Then he bowed himself from the room and Prunella went in search of Charity, whom she found in her bedroom.

As she told the old woman what she was about to do, Charity threw up her hands in dismay.

"Mercy on us, Miss Prunella!" she exclaimed.

"What's come over you? This rush, rush, tear, tear—leaves me not knowing if I'm standing on my head or my heels. Bath indeed! What's wrong with going home?"

"You know the answer to that," Prunella replied crossly. "Miss Nanette will see Mr. Lowes, and that is something I am determined to prevent."

She thought Charity was going to argue with her, but instead she went away muttering beneath her breath, and Prunella went to the wardrobe to find one of her new bonnets and to search for her gloves and sunshade.

Some of her new gowns had not yet been delivered, and she knew that she must have them sent today if they were to travel with her tomorrow.

She thought that by this time Nanette would be dressed, and she went into her room to find that only Charity was there.

"Where is Miss Nanette?" she asked.

"She's downstairs."

Prunella's lips tightened.

"That means she is sending a note to Mr. Lowes," she said. "Why did you not stop her, Charity? You know it is something I will not allow!"

"Miss Nanette's grown up," Charity replied, "and there's no use, Miss Prunella, treating her as if she were a child. She's a will of her own, and if you drive her too hard you'll regret it."

"Do not be so ridiculous, Charity!" Prunella snapped. "Miss Nanette is behaving extremely badly and that is something I will not tolerate."

At the same time, she wondered, with a little sinking of her heart, what she would do if now that Pascoe knew where they were going he followed them to Bath. In that case, they would have run away for nothing.

Then she had a clever idea and wondered why she had not thought of it before.

She had told Nanette and Charity, and the Hotel

Manager, for that matter, that they were going to Bath.

At the last moment she would change her plans and instead of Bath they would go to Cheltenham.

She had read in the newspapers that at this time of the year a great number of people congregated in Cheltenham both for the races and to drink the waters of the Spa.

But that was not to say that the visitors were mostly invalids, and, if the newspapers were to be believed, the Balls in the Assembly-Rooms which the Duke of Wellington himself had attended and the Theatre Royal where Mrs. Siddons had performed were equal to anything to be seen in London.

'We will go to Cheltenham,' Prunella thought with a little smile of triumph, 'and it will be a very long time before Pascoe finds out where we have gone, especially if I manage to prevent any of Nanette's letters from reaching him.'

The Earl had talked of a challenge. Very well, Prunella thought, this was a challenge in which she would prove the victor.

Just for a moment she found herself remembering the wonder and rapture of his kiss and the strange sensations he had given her which she still thought were not of this world.

Then she told herself firmly that what she felt or did not feel was of no importance in relation to her duty, which was to save Nanette.

Very well, she would save her sister without the Earl's help, and she had the feeling that Cheltenham would solve her problems because the idea had come to her almost like an inspiration.

"I will show the Earl I am cleverer than he is," Prunella murmured.

Then she found herself wondering how many of the Van Dykes he had sold to pay for his new clothes in which he looked so magnificent.

Prunella and Nanette had been invited to luncheon by an elderly Judge who had been a friend of their father.

Prunella had remembered his name and had written, when they first arrived in London, to ask Sir Simeon Hunt if he would call on them at their Hotel.

He had replied, as she had expected, that he would be delighted to entertain them at his house in Park Street.

Although Nanette was pale and rather silent, she did not make any comment when Prunella had returned to the Hotel after visiting several shops in Bond Street.

"I am afraid, dearest, you will not remember Sir Simeon Hunt," Prunella said as they drove towards Park Street, "but he was a very distinguished-looking man when I last saw him, and Papa always said he had one of the finest brains there had ever been at the Bar."

"How interesting!" Nanette remarked in a tone that implied that as far as she was concerned it was nothing of the sort.

But the party was not as dull as Nanette had anticipated, for Sir Simeon had invited to meet them not only his son and his daughter-in-law but also his three grandsons, who were young, unmarried, and only a few years older than Nanette.

She therefore laughed and flirted with them while Prunella listened to the old Judge reminiscing about her father and how much they had enjoyed themselves when they had been undergraduates at Oxford together.

There was more shopping to do in the afternoon, and when it was nearly time to dress for dinner, Prunella expected Nanette to tell her some lie to enable her to meet Pascoe.

Instead she said:

"I have a headache, Prunella, and I am going to bed early. Can we have dinner at seven o'clock?"

"Of course, dearest, and it would be wise for us all, including Charity, to have an early night, as we have a long drive in front of us tomorrow."

After a light meal in their Sitting-Room, Nanette said to Prunella:

"I am sorry if you are angry with me and I have disappointed you. I know that you have always loved me and tried in a way to take Mama's place, and I am grateful, I am really!"

Prunella was so touched that she felt the tears come into her eyes.

"I love you, Nanette," she said, "and everything I do is because I want you to be happy."

"I know that," Nanette answered, "and I love you too."

She kissed Prunella and went to her own bedroom.

Prunella went to hers and when she was undressed and in bed she told herself that she had been right in thinking that Nanette had communicated with Pascoe.

She would have told him she was going to Bath and he had doubtless replied that he would follow her.

"That fortune-hunting young man will get a surprise when he cannot find her," Prunella told herself.

Then she wondered what the Earl would think.

Had he really asked her to marry him? She could hardly believe it was true, and yet he had actually said the words.

It suddenly struck her that perhaps being married to the Earl would be as wonderful as his kiss had been.

Then she forced herself not to think of the strange streak of pain which had swept through her and which had changed to an ecstasy that had carried her towards the stars.

"I have to . . . think only of Nanette . . .
Nanette . . . Nanette!"

She thought the words were being repeated over
and over again in her mind as finally she fell into a
restless, disturbed sleep in which she dreamt she was
running away from the Earl but could not escape
him.

CHAPTER SEVEN

𝒫runella pulled back the curtains from her bedroom
window before Charity came to call her.

It was a sunny morning and she had the feeling
that she was taking a momentous step into the unknown and she had no idea what would happen in
the future.

How could she and Nanette wander about the
world simply with the object of avoiding two men?

Then she told herself sharply that she had to do
what was right, and that was to prevent Nanette from
marrying a fortune-hunter.

She dressed quickly, expecting every moment to
hear Charity knock on the door.

She thought perhaps her clock was wrong and remembered that it had been erratic for some time.

When she was dressed she did not stop to admire
her new gown in the mirror, but walked briskly
through the Sitting-Room towards Nanette's room on
the other side of it.

She entered and found the curtains drawn, and to her surprise Charity was sitting in a chair crying.

"What is the matter? What has happened?" Prunella asked as she looked towards the bed to see that it was empty.

"She's gone—Miss Prunella," Charity sobbed, "and I'll never—forgive myself—never!"

"What are you talking about?" Prunella asked.

Then she saw that lying on the pillow on the bed there was a note.

She opened it, anticipating almost exactly what she would read.

Dearest Prunella,

Forgive me, and I know you will be angry, but Pascoe and I have run away to be married. We are going to France, where Pascoe says there will be no uncomfortable questions asked as to whether I have my Guardian's permission, and we will honeymoon in Paris.

When we return, please, please, forgive me, because I love you.

Nanette

When she had finished reading Prunella stood as if turned to stone. Then she turned towards Charity, saying:

"You knew about this!"

"I should have told you, Miss Prunella, but she'd have gone anyway, and how could you have stopped her with you only in your nightgown?"

Prunella drew in her breath and asked in a quite calm voice:

"At what time did she leave?"

"About seven-o'clock. I heard her moving and came into the room to find her dressed in a travelling-gown ordering a porter to carry down her baggage."

"Seven-o'clock!" Prunella repeated to herself.

She was calculating in her mind how long it would take Nanette and Pascoe to reach Dover.

Then she knew there was only one person who could help her, and that was the Earl.

'He could catch them up,' she thought.

Then, as if she had received a painful blow, she remembered that she did not know where he was.

"Have you any idea, Charity," she asked, "where His Lordship is staying in London?"

"He's at Winslow House, Miss Prunella."

"Winslow House!" Prunella exclaimed incredulously. "How can he be? And how do you know?"

"The footman told me when he brought a note for Miss Nanette every morning. Oh, Miss! You'll never forgive me! I should have told you, but it made her so happy."

Charity's voice was almost incoherent and the tears were streaming down her old face.

Prunella walked from the room back to her own bedroom.

Hastily she put on her bonnet and, picking up her reticule, hurried down the stairs to the vestibule.

"I want a hackney-carriage," she said to the porter, "and tell him to drive me to Winslow House in Berkeley Square."

"Very good, Miss."

There was a hackney-carriage waiting outside and a few minutes later Prunella was on her way.

She found it hard to believe that the Earl was staying in Winslow House, which had been closed ever since the late Earl had felt he was too ill and too old to visit London.

The Earl's Town-House was one thing she had not made her responsibility, and she wondered if there were old servants there who had not been paid, or if the place had become very dilapidated with anyone being aware of it.

Then she told herself sharply that the only person who need concern her now was Nanette.

It was only a short distance to Berkeley Square and when she stepped out of the carriage and rang the bell, the door was opened by a servant who looked surprised at anyone calling so early.

"I wish to see His Lordship!"

"Is His Lordship expecting you, Madam?"

"No, but please tell him Miss Broughton is here and that it is very urgent."

"Will you come this way, Miss?"

She was led across a marble Hall, and servants who, she noted with surprise, were dressed in the Winslow livery, opened the door of what was obviously a Morning-Room.

The furniture was impressive and obviously valuable, and the walls were hung with old masters in gold frames, although the curtains looked faded, as did the brocade on the chairs and the sofa.

'There must be many treasures worth a great deal of money here!' Prunella thought to herself, and wondered if the Earl would sell these as well.

Then the door opened and when he came into the room she could not help a sudden feeling that her heart had turned a somersault.

He looked very smart and impressive and there was that buccaneering, raffish look in his eyes which made her remember, although she tried not to do so, what she had felt when he had kissed her.

"Good-morning, Prunella! You are an early visitor," he remarked.

Prunella forced her voice to sound cold and accusing as she held out Nanette's letter.

"This is your fault!"

The Earl took the letter from her, read it, and said with a smile:

"At least Pascoe is putting up a fight for what he wants!"

"If that is your only comment," Prunella said, "I consider it extremely reprehensible!"

"I knew you would feel angry," the Earl replied, "but they have taken things into their own hands and there is nothing we can do about it."

"There is certainly something I can do!" Prunella retorted, "but I need your help."

"In what way?"

"I am sure it will take them, with the sort of horses Pascoe is likely to be able to afford, at least six hours if not more to reach Dover. I believe, and I think I am not mistaken, that there are usually only two ships to France every day, one in the morning and one in the afternoon."

"So you intend to try to prevent them from catching the afternoon ship?"

"I do!"

"And you wish me to drive you to Dover?"

"I think you could do so far quicker than I could manage with a Post-Chaise, however expensive."

"Very well," the Earl said. "I will order my Phaeton to come to your Hotel in an hour's time."

"Why must I wait an hour?"

"I have certain arrangements to make before I can leave London," the Earl replied. "I also have not yet had my breakfast."

Prunella made an exasperated little sound, but she knew from the way he had spoken that she would gain nothing by arguing with him.

Instead of which she said:

"Very well, I will return to the Hotel and will bring with me a small bag in case Nanette and I have to stay the night."

The Earl's lips curled in a faint smile, but he merely crossed the room to open the door. Only as they reached the Hall did he ask:

"You would not like to wait while I send for my carriage?"

"I shall be waiting impatiently at the Hotel, My

Lord," Prunella answered. "As you are well aware, we have to reach Dover before the afternoon ship sails."

"I will not forget," the Earl replied.

The footman fetched a hackney-carriage, and standing on the doorstep, the Earl watched Prunella drive away.

Sitting stiffly upright, she did not bow to him but looked straight ahead, and when she was out of sight the Earl turned back into the Hall and started to give orders.

It was an hour and ten minutes later when the Earl's Phaeton, with a team of perfectly matched chestnuts, drew up outside the Hotel.

On any other occasion Prunella would not only have admired the horses but would also have wondered how he managed to afford them.

But because he was late she was too agitated to think of anything but that they should be on their way and she must reach Dover before Nanette was spirited away to France.

Then there would be no possibility of her preventing her sister from becoming the wife of the man she despised.

Her small case, which had been packed by Charity, was placed at the back of the Phaeton, and Prunella was helped by one of the porters into the seat beside the Earl.

Standing forlornly in the doorway, Charity waved good-bye but received no response from her mistress.

"What am I to do with myself? Where am I to go, Miss Prunella?" she had asked.

"You will wait here with my luggage until I return, Charity," Prunella replied.

She had said nothing more, and although she longed to reproach Charity for having helped

Nanette in being so deceitful, she did not want to upset the old woman.

The Earl drove superbly and she knew it was what
she might have expected of him. The horses were
fresh and they moved quickly out of London and
were soon in the open countryside.

They had driven for quite a long way in silence
before Prunella remarked:

"There is certainly not as much traffic as I expected."

"When one is in a hurry it is always wise to avoid
the main highways," the Earl replied.

Prunella said no more, for it was difficult to speak
when they were moving so fast. She also had no wish
to divert the Earl's attention from his horses when
time was of such importance.

It was noon when the Earl drew into the yard of a
small but attractive Posting-Inn.

"Why are we stopping?" Prunella asked.

"I am hungry," the Earl replied, "and I am sure
you are too. Also this is where we change horses."

"You have your own horses here?" Prunella asked
in surprise.

"Yes," the Earl replied.

He did not sound as if he wished to be any more
communicative, but it flashed through Prunella's
mind that it was yet another unnecessary extravagance.

Yet she was well aware that Gentlemen of Fashion
kept their own horses at Posting-Inns on all the main
roads.

Prunella was taken upstairs to a low oak-beamed
bedroom to wash and she took off her bonnet to
smooth her hair.

Downstairs again, she was shown into a small private parlour where the Earl was waiting and luncheon, an unexpectedly good one, was served almost
immediately.

Because she was so intent on hurrying, Prunella

did not argue when the Earl insisted on her having a glass of wine with her meal.

They had eaten for a short while in silence before he said:

"Perhaps I have been remiss in not telling you sooner that you look very lovely today."

She looked at him in surprise because it was a compliment she had not expected, then when her eyes met his, she felt herself blush.

"I have no . . . time to think about . . . myself," she said after a moment.

Her reply was meant to sound cold and impersonal but instead it was low and shy, and she was unable to go on looking at the Earl.

"But I have had time to think about you," he said, "and later, when you are not so agitated, I would like to talk about us—you and me."

"N-no . . . please . . ." Prunella pleaded.

"Why not?" he asked. "After all, although I should like your sister to be happy, I am not really concerned with her but with you."

"It is . . . something you . . . must not be."

"Why?"

"Because I have to look after Nanette . . . and that means that we cannot . . . stay at the Manor . . ."

She broke off what she was saying and gave an exasperated little sound.

"All this has happened because I told her yesterday we were going to Bath and then perhaps to Paris. She must have written to Pascoe immediately, and they plotted together to elope."

"That is exactly what happened."

Prunella looked at the Earl and gave a little cry.

"You knew . . . this was what they were . . . going to . . . do?"

"Shall I say I had a good idea of it?"

"Why did you not prevent them? Why did you not tell me?"

"Because, Prunella," the Earl said, "Pascoe is a man. He must make his own decisions in life, and I would also point out that he is my nephew, not my son."

"At the same time . . . you might have thought . . . of me."

"I did think of you, as it happens, and later I will tell you how much, but now we ought to be on our way."

"Yes, of course," Prunella agreed.

She put on her bonnet and tied it under her chin. As she did so, she told herself that she was very angry with the Earl for not having taken a more positive attitude towards the run-aways.

But somehow the hatred she had been able to feel about him in the past was no longer there.

Instead she could only think of the expression in his eyes and the faint smile on his lips—lips which had kissed hers.

The Earl's fresh team of the fittest bays seemed to move as quickly as, if not quicker than, the chestnuts.

'How can he possess such marvellous animals?' Prunella wondered.

They were moving too quickly to ask questions, and time passed before, driving down a narrow, empty road, the Earl suddenly drew the bays to a standstill under the shade of a great chestnut tree.

Prunella looked at him in surprise.

"Why are we stopping?"

"There is something I want to tell you."

There was a note in the Earl's voice that made her look up at him apprehensively.

He transferred the reins to his right hand and turned in his seat so that he was facing her.

"You think we are on our way to Dover," he said quietly, "but actually we have less than two hours' driving before we reach home."

For a moment Prunella felt that she could not have heard him aright.

"H-home?" she faltered.

"Your home and mine," the Earl said. "The Hall!"

"But I want to go to Dover . . . and Nanette! How dare you not . . . take me there as you . . . promised!"

"I did not promise anything," the Earl replied. "You gave me your orders and you assumed I was obeying you."

"I have to stop Nanette!" Prunella cried almost wildly.

"If you were able to do so, it would be, I think, a great mistake."

"How can you say such a thing?"

"I am saying it because I believe in all sincerity that Nanette and my nephew Pascoe are well suited to each other. They will have to struggle to put Pascoe's Estate in order, just as they have had to struggle to get married, and I think it will be very good for both of them."

"You do not know what you are . . . saying!"

"I do know," the Earl answered. "Just as I know what is best for you, my darling, even though you may not agree with me."

Despite her bewilderment, because of the depth of feeling in his voice she felt a little quiver go through her.

"What is more," the Earl went on, "we are on our way home, but as I cannot take you to the Hall without a Chaperone, I have decided that we must first be married."

"Married. . . . ?"

Prunella could barely say the word.

"Half-a-mile from here," the Earl continued, "there is a Church where a Parson is waiting for us. It is no use raging at me, Prunella. I love you, and although you may deny it, I know you love me. I have a Special Licence and we are going to be married at once."

For a moment Prunella was speechless, but then as the Earl waited she found her voice.

"Of course I . . . will not . . . marry you! How can you . . . think of . . . such . . . a thing?"

The Earl reached out his left hand and put his fingers under Prunella's chin to turn her face up to his.

"Look at me, my sweet, look me in the eyes and tell me, by everything you hold sacred, that you do not love me and that when I kissed you it meant nothing to you except to increase the dislike and contempt you have expressed so often before."

Prunella wanted to struggle against him but somehow it was impossible to do so.

His fingers held her chin firmly, and despite herself her eyes met his.

Then she could not look away or struggle any more.

Instead, she felt as if the whole world vanished and there was nothing but his eyes and a strange, unaccountable ecstasy rising within her as it had done the night he had kissed her.

For a long, long moment neither of them could move. Then the Earl said very quietly:

"You are mine, my precious, as I always meant you to be!"

He released her and drove on.

Utterly bemused and feeling as if the whole world had turned upside-down, Prunella could not move until she saw just ahead of them a small grey-stone Church, and standing at the lych-gate was a man she recognised as Jim.

As the Earl drew up his horses he ran to their heads.

Prunella sat still until the Earl reached her side of the Phaeton and helped her to the ground.

Then, although she did not intend it to happen, her fingers held on to his as if he gave her the strength she needed.

"You . . . really . . . mean to do . . . this?" she asked in a whisper.

"I mean to make you my wife," he replied.

He put her hand on his arm, then covered it with his.

She found that her will had left her, and, no longer able to think what she should or should not do, she felt utterly subservient to him.

He led her down the small path and in through the door of the Church.

It was very old and quiet and their footsteps seemed to ring out on the flagged floor as they walked up the aisle to where at the Chancel steps a Parson, wearing a white surplice, was waiting for them.

Afterwards Prunella could only think that a stranger had taken possession of her body, a stranger had spoken her responses in the Marriage Service, a stranger had knelt beside the Earl after the Parson had declared them man and wife and blessed them.

Then, without speaking to each other, without saying a word, they walked back through the sunlit Church-yard. Jim released the horses' heads and they were driving on.

It was after a short while that Prunella began to recognise the countryside and wonder how she had been so foolish as to be deceived into thinking they were going to Dover instead of . . . home.

She felt the word meant something different from what it had ever meant before, because it was not to the Manor the Earl was taking her, but to the Hall.

She thought too that she must have all her life dreamt, although she had never put it into words, that it would one day be hers, and she would love it and tend it and somehow, in a way which seemed impossible, she would restore it to its former glory.

Although she was thinking of the Earl's house, at the same time she was acutely conscious that he was beside her; that he was a man whose name she now bore, that he had kissed her and had said he loved her.

She knew he had been right when he had claimed she loved him too, even though she had tried to fight against it.

He had taken her heart from between her lips and made it his, and even before that she had loved him, although she would rather have died than admit it.

It was her love that made her hate London and miss being with him in the country; and it was love that had made her want to hear his voice and see the smile on his lips and that strange glint in his eyes when he looked at her.

"I love him!" she told herself. "But he had no . . . right to . . . marry me like . . . this!"

It was, however, only her mind that was protesting, because it was conventional to do so.

She knew there was a strange singing in her heart and a feeling of rapture that increased every time she glanced at him out of the corner of her eye.

Then at last, far quicker than she had expected, there were the familiar woods, the undulating countryside, and the small hamlets which she knew were only a few miles from Little Stodbury.

They passed the village Green, then the lane which led to the Manor, and were driving through the stone lodges with the open gates. The great house lay ahead, its windows glittering in the afternoon sun, which was turning to gold.

The Earl drew up his horses with a flourish outside the wide stone steps.

As if they had been waiting for him, two Indian servants stood in the doorway. The Earl handed his reins to a groom, then went round to the other side of the Phaeton.

Prunella put out her hand so that he could help

her alight, but to her surprise he lifted her down; then, carrying her in his arms, he walked up the steps and in through the front door.

Then as he set her down on her feet in the great Hall with its curving staircase he said quietly:

"Welcome home, my darling!"

The way he spoke made her feel almost as if he had kissed her, and because she was shy she turned towards the staircase.

"You will find the Queen's Bedroom has been prepared for you," the Earl said.

Prunella's eyes widened in astonishment.

She wanted to ask him how it could be prepared, how they knew she was to be married. But the servants were listening, so instead she went up the stairs, feeling as if she were moving in a dream from which it was impossible to awaken.

She knew the Queen's Bedroom well, and she loved it. It was one of the State-Rooms she had kept clean and open because it was so beautiful.

It adjoined what was always known as the Master Suite and the windows overlooked both the lake and the rose-garden.

She opened the door and saw to her astonishment that the room, with its huge four-poster bed carved with cupids and draped with blue silk, was not empty.

Charity was there, unpacking her trunks, which lay open on the floor.

"Charity!" Prunella exclaimed.

The old woman rose from the ground to say:

"You're surprised to see me, Miss Prunella? Or rather I should say 'My Lady'!"

Prunella looked at her in bewilderment.

"You . . . know. . . . ? How did . . . you know?"

"As soon as you left, His Lordship's servants arrived with a travelling-carriage drawn by six horses. Think of that, M'Lady! Never in m' life have I travelled with six horses, until now!"

"Charity . . . Charity! I do not know what to say," Prunella said.

"There's no point in talking when you should be changing," Charity said sharply in the tone she had used to Prunella when she was a small girl. "Come along now and get out of that dusty gown and into one of your pretty ones, or we'll have His Lordship wishing he had married someone else!"

Prunella gave a weak little laugh that was somehow not very far from tears.

How could this be happening to her? How could she be here in the Queen's Bedroom, with Charity calling her "My Lady"?

They had arrived later than she had thought, and while Charity was helping her out of her gown, a message came from the Earl to say that she should rest until dinner, which would be at seven-thirty.

"Now that's what I call sensible!" Charity said with approval. "You can do with a rest, M'Lady, after having been up half last night a-worrying over Miss Nanette."

"I am still very worried about her," Prunella replied. "Oh, Charity, she ought never to have run away to France to marry Mr. Lowes!"

There was silence for a moment. Then Charity said:

"I know you'll not believe me, M'Lady, but if ever I saw two people truly in love with each other, it was Miss Nanette and His Lordship's nephew."

"She loves him, I grant you that," Prunella said.

"And he loves her. I'd stake my hope of Heaven on it, and that's the truth, Miss—I mean, M'Lady."

"Do you really think so, Charity?"

"Would I be telling you a lie, and would I not want the happiness of my baby?"

There was no answering this, and Prunella allowed herself to be helped into bed, and as Charity pulled the curtains she shut her eyes.

She had the feeling that when she awoke she would

find she really had been dreaming and she would not be at the Hall but in her own ordinary little bed at the Manor.

But it was not the Hall or the Manor that she thought of as she fell asleep, but the Earl's eyes looking into hers. . . .

Dinner was finished and it had been a meal with strange, inexplicable silences, interspersed with laughter and moments of shyness when Prunella found it impossible to meet her husband's eyes.

She was vividly conscious of him looking raffish and at the same time extremely elegant in his new evening-clothes.

She was aware that the Indian servants had brought out the finest Winslow silver to decorate the Dining-Room table.

The candles illuminated them both with a golden glow and Prunella felt as if they were taking part in a play in which she was playing the lead part but was not certain how the third act ended.

The servants withdrew soft-footed from the room and Prunella asked:

"What did you do in India?"

It was after a pause which was so pregnant that she felt he must hear her heart beating.

"I worked."

"Worked?"

"I will tell you all about it sometime, but at the moment I can think only of you."

The way he spoke made Prunella blush, and he thought it the loveliest thing he had ever seen.

"You are so young, my darling," he said softly, "so sweet and untouched that I did not believe anyone like you existed today in this blasé, sophisticated world."

"That is the . . . world you . . . know and like,"

Prunella replied. "I am afraid you will find me . . . very boring."

"It will excite me more than I can tell you to teach you about the things which interest me."

He saw the question in Prunella's eyes and added: "Which, as far as you are concerned, my beautiful wife, is love."

As Prunella blushed again he rose to his feet.

"You do not wish me to leave you to your port?" she asked.

"I have no wish for any port, nor for you to leave me now or ever!" he replied. "Come, I have something to show you."

He put out his hand and when she took it he felt her fingers tremble in his.

He drew her from the Dining-Room along the corridor, through the Hall, and up the staircase.

The direction in which he turned when they reached the landing told Prunella where they were going, and she felt a sudden impulse to beg him not to spoil the enchantment of their first evening together.

She felt he was going to show her the Picture-Gallery and explain why he had sold the Van Dykes and ask her to forgive him for having done so.

'I shall have to say that I . . . understand . . . and it does not . . . matter,' she thought to herself.

Although she was unaware of it, her fingers stiffened in his and her whole body was tense.

The door of the Picture-Gallery was closed, and as the Earl put out his hand, Prunella wanted to shut her eyes and refuse to look.

Why must he do this to her on their first night together at the Hall?

Why must he spoil what she had known at dinner was a happiness that seemed to vibrate between them and which deepened until she knew it was the love she felt for him.

A love which she could not prevent from growing every second that she was with him.

"This is what I want to show you, my darling," the Earl said.

Reluctantly, wishing she could run away, Prunella forced herself to look.

For a moment she thought she must have come to the wrong place and that she was not seeing the Picture-Gallery but part of the house she had never been in before.

Then she gave an audible little gasp and knew that as she stared ahead the Earl was watching her face with a smile on his lips.

The three great chandeliers hanging from the ceiling were ablaze with lighted candles and they revealed that the walls which Prunella had last seen empty and dingy with the dust of years had been painted an exquisite shade of red, which was a perfect background for the Van Dykes in their gold frames.

It was the colour which had originally, Prunella knew from the sketches, been chosen by Inigo Jones himself.

The friezes, pediments, and cornices were white picked out in gold, and the curtains which draped the windows were of gold and white brocade.

The paintings in such a setting seemed each to glow like a precious jewel and she could only stand staring, feeling it was not real.

"This is one of my presents to you, my precious one," the Earl said softly.

She turned to look at him, and somehow, she was not certain how it happened, his arms were round her.

"I . . . I do not . . . understand . . . how could you have . . . done this? How could you have . . . made it so perfect?"

"It was done very quickly to please you," he said, "and together you and I will do the rest of the house and restore it to its former glory."

"But how can . . . you? How is . . . it possible?"
Prunella stammered.

"What you are really asking is how could I afford
it!"

He turned her face up to his.

"Why did you not trust me? Why were you so determined, from the very first moment you met me,
that I was a scallywag without a penny to my name?"

"I . . . I thought that you had . . . come to the
Hall . . . to find something to . . . s-sell," Prunella
whispered.

"And when you saw me looking at the Van Dykes
you jumped to the conclusion that I intended to dispose of them."

"You do not . . . have to do . . . so?"

The Earl smiled.

"I happen to be a very rich man, my darling, with
more than enough money for both of us without having to marry you for your fortune."

"I . . . I never suspected . . . you were doing
. . . that."

"Yes, I know," he said, "but you believed that I was
prepared to throw away my family heirlooms for the
horses and for the amusements I would find in London."

Prunella hid her face against his shoulder.

"Forgive . . . me," she whispered.

His arms tightened round her and he said:

"I will forgive you only if you promise not to berate
me for crimes I have not committed, or even for
those I have."

"I . . . promise . . ."

The words were barely audible but he heard them,
and he gave a little laugh before he said:

"I think now that you should thank me for my first
wedding-present. I have another for you in my bedroom, and several will be arriving from London
within the course of a few days, but perhaps this is the
most important."

Prunella raised her head slowly; then, almost before she expected it, the Earl's lips were on hers.

She felt the hard insistence of them, and although she did not try to oppose him or to struggle against him, she was not prepared for the manner in which, without even thinking about it, her mouth surrendered itself to his and her body seemed to melt into his body.

His lips became more passionate and more demanding, then the streak of pain that became a rapture seemed to flash between them, filling her with that wild, unaccountable ecstasy which made her feel that he carried her towards the stars.

"This is love!" she thought.

A love so powerful, so irresistible, so utterly and completely wonderful that nothing else in the whole world mattered or was of any consequence.

Just for one moment she thought that if he offered her a choice between such a wonder and happiness or the possession of every Van Dyke ever painted, she knew which she would take.

It was love she wanted, his love, and him, and no paintings, money, or anything else in the world were of any consequence.

"I love . . . you!" she said, first in her heart, then a little incoherently as the Earl raised his head.

"And I love you, my precious, darling little prude! You beguile me, you intrigue and entrance me, as you have done ever since I first saw you looking at me with such condemnation in your eyes."

"You must . . . have been . . . laughing at me."

"Not laughing, but loving you," he continued, "because you are everything I have sought all over the world but never expected to find."

"Is that . . . true?"

"How could I do anything else but love you, my lovely one, not only for your beauty but because in every way you are the opposite of what I have been myself."

"It does not . . . matter what . . . you have . . . been."

"Do you mean that?"

She looked up at him and he could see the truth shining in her eyes.

"I . . . love you . . . just as you are . . . and you are right . . . love is . . . irresistible and very . . . very wonderful!"

She saw the smile that came to his lips before he pulled her closer to him.

Then he was kissing her again; kissing her until the Picture-Gallery whirled round them and there was nothing but themselves and a starlit sky.

What they owned, precious and divine, was the treasure all men and women seek—the love which cannot be bought but only given by God.

LIES FOR LOVE

Author's Note

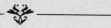

At the beginning of the Nineteenth Century the penalty for robbery of any sort was very severe. A person was hanged for "privately stealing in a shop, warehouse and coachhouse or stable to the amount of five shillings."

Poaching a hare or a pheasant meant, as a merciful sentence, transportation in a convict ship to New South Wales for seven years.

The prisons were filthy shambles, the police were inadequate, badly organised, and poorly paid, which meant they were often corrupt.

A boy arrested for minor pilfering could be sent to prison, flogged, then turned out without a penny in his pocket.

Select Committees set up in 1817 produced numerous petitions to Parliament, but the Reform Bill was many frustrating years ahead.

CHAPTER ONE

"*H*enry, stop kicking Lucy and eat up your porridge," Carmela said.

"I won't!"

Henry was a fat, ugly boy nearly seven years of age and in Carmela's opinion was quite uncontrollable.

To prove his defiance he gave his sister Lucy another kick, and she started to cry.

"Stop that at once, do you hear?" Carmela said sharply, thinking as she spoke that it would have little effect.

She was right.

Henry picked up his bowl of porridge and deliberately turned it upside-down on the table-cloth.

At the same time the baby in the cot, awakened by the noise Lucy was making, started to cry too.

Carmela thought helplessly that there was really nothing she could do about them.

It was almost to be expected, she thought, as she had thought many times since she came to the Vicarage, that the Vicar's children should be the worst behaved and most unmanageable of any in the village.

Because she felt she could do nothing with Henry, and Lucy would cry whatever happened, she went to the cot to pick up the baby and rock him in her arms.

As she was doing so the door opened and the Vicar's wife put her head round it to say:

"Can't you keep those children quiet? You know the Vicar's trying to write his sermon for tomorrow."

"I am sorry, Mrs. Cooper," Carmela apologised.

The Vicar's wife did not wait for her answer but merely shut the door so sharply that it sounded suspiciously like a slam.

Henry waited until his mother had gone, then shouted above the noise his sister was making:

"I want my egg!"

"You can have it after you have eaten your porridge," Carmela replied.

She knew as she spoke that she was fighting a losing battle.

Sure enough, while she was away from the table Henry seized the egg-cup next to the ones intended for his sister and Carmela, and after knocking off the top of the egg started to eat it eagerly.

Carmela felt desparingly that there was nothing she could do with him.

Ever since she had come to the Vicarage to look after the children she had known that however clever she might be, she could not control Henry.

His parents must have discovered how difficult he was almost as soon as he was born. They had given in to him on every occasion and allowed him to have his own way, with the result that like a cuckoo in the nest he pushed the other children aside and invariably got what he wanted.

Sometimes when she went to bed at night too tired to sleep, Carmela thought she could not face the years ahead spent in looking after children like Henry and knowing that she was capable of making little or no impact on them.

After her father died there had been the necessity of finding herself employment of some sort, and when Mrs. Cooper suggested that she come to the

Vicarage it had seemed the easy solution to her problem.

She told herself that at least she would be staying amongst people whom she knew and who did not make her afraid.

She faced her position bravely and admitted that she was afraid of being alone, afraid of going out into an alien, hostile world, and most of all, afraid of being incompetent.

That her father had always found her very intelligent was quite a different thing from being able to earn money by using her brain.

Her father had tried to do so by selling his pictures, which unfortunately had not proved at all saleable.

Just occasionally he received what seemed to Carmela and her mother a large sum for a portrait of some local dignitary, but the pictures he really enjoyed painting were on the whole "too beautiful to be sold."

That was how her mother had once described them, and they had all laughed, but Carmela had known exactly what she meant and why her father's pictures did not appeal to the ordinary purchaser.

But to her the manner in which he painted the mist rising over a stream at dawn, or a sunset behind distant hills, was so lovely that she felt as if when she looked at them they carried her into a mystical world which only she and her father realised existed.

It was the same world she had known as a child when he had told her stories of fairies and goblins, of elves and nymphs, and showed her the mushroom-rings in the fields where the "little people" had danced the night before.

It was a world of wonder and beauty and to Carmela it was very real, but it was not really something one could express on canvass. Peregrine Lyndon's beautiful pictures therefore stayed in the Art Dealer's shop until he sent them back as unsaleable.

Her mother had died first, and there was very little

money coming into the small house where they lived on the edge of the village.

This was because the only way Carmela's father could assuage his grief was by painting the pictures that appealed to him, and he gave up suggesting to the fat Aldermen in the market-town five miles away, and the local Squires, that they should have their portraits painted.

Because her father was so handsome and what in the village they called a "perfect gentleman," it was locally considered a compliment to be painted by him.

Unfortunately, however, few people in Huntingdon were willing to pay for such luxuries and therefore Peregrine Lyndon's commissions were few and far between.

The house became filled with the pictures he liked to paint, and after her mother's death Carmela would ask her father when the day was over what work he had done, to find as often as not that because it dissatisfied him he had cleaned off his canvass and started again.

"I always think of your mother," he would say, "when I see the sun rising above the horizon."

In consequence he expected each picture to be perfection, and he would paint the same scene over and over again but still not be satisfied with the result.

Only by taking the canvasses away from him after two or three attempts could Carmela keep the pictures she liked best from being destroyed. She had to hide them in her bedroom to look at them when she was alone.

When her father died last winter, having caught pneumonia through sitting out in the bitter cold and frost to paint the stars, as soon as she could take in what had happened she had discovered that all she possessed in the world were her father's pictures, which nobody wanted, and the few pounds which was all she could get by selling the contents of the house.

The house itself was only rented, and although what they paid was very little she knew that she could not find even that amount without earning it.

It was when she was in the depths of despair over losing her father, whom she had dearly loved, that Mrs. Cooper's suggestion that she might work at the Vicarage had seemed like a glimmer of light in the darkness.

It was only when she had moved in to the ugly house and was confronted by the Vicar's extremely plain children that she realised to what misery she had committed herself.

But she could think of nothing else she could do, and at least the Vicarage would provide a roof over her head and food to eat that she did not have to pay for.

With some embarrassment Mrs. Cooper had suggested she should pay her ten pounds a year for her labours, and as Carmela had no idea if that was generous or not, she had accepted the offer thankfully.

Now she thought, as she had a dozen times already, that she would rather starve than go on trying to cope with children whose only response to everything she said was to be rude and obstructive.

Carmela had always thought that anyone with any intelligence should be able to communicate with other human beings, however primitive or difficult they might be.

She had often talked with her father of the way Missionaries travelled in countries inhabited by savage tribes and somehow gained their confidence even though in many cases they could not speak their language.

"Men and women should be able to communicate with one another in the same way as animals do," Peregrine Lyndon had said.

He had therefore believed that there must be people somewhere in the world who would understand what he was trying to say on canvass because it was

161

something which came from both his mind and his heart.

"I think the truth is that you are in advance of your time, Papa," Carmela had told him. "Artists at the moment want to portray exactly what they see. In the past there have been men like Botticelli and Michelangelo, who painted with their imagination, and that is what you are trying to do."

"I am honoured by the company in which you include me," her father had said with a smile. "But you are right. I want to put down what I think and feel, rather than what I actually see with my eyes, and as long as you and I understand, why should we worry about anybody else?"

"Why indeed?" Carmela had replied.

However, imagination did not pay the butcher, the baker, or the grocer, and their Landlord would not accept "imaginary" money.

The baby stopped crying and fell asleep, and Carmela laid him down very gently in his cot. At the moment he was comparatively good, but she felt that he would soon grow up to be like his brother and sister.

As she turned towards the table, Lucy gave a little scream.

"Henry's eating my egg! Stop him, Miss Lyndon! He eating my egg!"

It was true, Carmela saw. Henry, having eaten his own egg, had now taken the brown one which was set on one side for Lucy.

This too he was eating as quickly as he could, defying her with his small pig-like eyes to stop him.

"Never mind, Lucy," Carmela said to the small girl, "you can have my egg."

"I want mine, it's brown!" Lucy expostulated fiercely. "I hate Henry, I hate him! He's always taking my things!"

Carmela looked at Henry and thought she hated him too.

In front of him on the table the porridge was

oozing out from the bowl, which had cracked when he turned it over.

The empty egg-shell from the first egg had fallen out of the egg-cup, and the yoke from the second egg was spilling onto the table-cloth because of the haste in which he was eating it.

It was also spattered on his white shirt, which Carmela had spent a long time yesterday washing and pressing.

She did not say anything but merely put her egg in front of Lucy, took the top off it, and put a clean spoon in her hand.

"I want a brown egg—a brown one!" Lucy shrieked. "I don't like white ones!"

"They taste exactly the same inside," Carmela tried to console her.

"You're a liar!" Henry said rudely.

"That's right! You're a liar!" Lucy echoed, forgetting her anger with her brother and glad to have an ally against a common enemy. "Brown eggs taste different from white ones! I want a brown egg!"

Carmela gave a sigh and sat down at the table.

She filled her cup with the cheap, rather unpleasant-tasting tea which was all that was provided at the Vicarage and cut herself a slice of bread from a loaf which had been stale yesterday.

Lucy was still screaming for a brown egg when suddenly, getting into a worse tantrum than she was in already, she hit the egg in front of her with the back of her hand.

It shot across the table and smashed against the teapot. The yoke spattered in all directions and Carmela received a large portion of it on her hand.

She opened her lips to reprove Lucy, then suddenly thought the whole thing was too much for her.

She felt the tears come into her eyes, and as she did so the door behind her opened.

She stiffened, expecting to hear Mrs. Cooper's querulous voice demanding that she should keep the children quiet, or else the Vicar shouting at them, which always made things worse.

Then when she was aware that somebody had come into the room but had not spoken, she turned her head.

Then she stared in astonishment.

Standing in the doorway, making the untidy room that was used as a Nursery look even more unpleasant than it usually did, was a Vision of loveliness.

The Vision wore a high-crowned bonnet trimmed with flowers and a high-waisted gown of sprigged muslin trimmed with bows of mauve ribbon, and had a very attractive face with two exceedingly large blue eyes and a red mouth, which was smiling at her.

"Hello, Carmela!"

"Felicity!"

Carmela jumped up from the table, wiping the egg-yolk from her hand as she did so, to run to the doorway and kiss the girl who had just appeared.

Lady Felicity Gale was her closest friend, and except when she was away staying with friends, they had been inseparable.

"When did you get back?" Carmela asked. "I have been . . . longing to . . . see you."

Her words seemed to fall over themselves, and Lady Felicity kissed her affectionately as she replied:

"I got back only last night. I could not believe it when I was told you had come to the Vicarage!"

"There was nowhere else I could go after Papa died."

"I had no idea he was dead. Oh, Carmela, I am sorry!"

Carmela did not speak, but she could not help the tears coming into her eyes.

She could be brave until anybody spoke of her father, but then, however hard she tried, it was impossible not to realise how terribly she missed him.

"Now I am back," Lady Felicity said, "and I want you. I want you at once, Carmela!"

"I . . . I am working . . . here."

Lady Felicity looked at the table and the children, who were gaping open-mouthed at her appearance.

"I have something better for you to do than look after these little horrors!" she said. "I remember Henry. He is the one who was always spitting and making faces in Church when his father was not looking."

Carmela laughed. She could not help it.

"Who are you?" Lucy asked, resenting that she was no longer the centre of attention.

"Somebody who is going to take this nice, kind Miss Lyndon away from you," Lady Felicity replied, "and I hope perhaps your father will find somebody horrid to take her place and give you the beating you all deserve!"

She did not sound very ferocious because she was laughing as she spoke. Then, taking Carmela by the hand, she said:

"Get your things. I have a carriage waiting outside."

"But I cannot . . . leave just like . . . that," Carmela protested.

"Yes, you can," Felicity replied, "and while you are packing I will explain to Mrs. Cooper that I need you and it is absolutely essential that you come with me at once."

"She will be furious," Carmela said, "and she will never employ me again!"

"She is not going to have the chance to do so," Felicity stated. "I will explain everything when we get away from here."

She looked round the room and added:

"Hurry, Carmela, I cannot bear to be in such a sordid place longer than a few minutes. I cannot think how you have endured it."

"It has been rather horrid," Carmela admitted, "but, Felicity, I must give my notice in the proper way."

"Leave everything to me," Felicity replied. "Just do as I tell you."

"I . . . I do not think I . . . should."

Even as she spoke Felicity gave her a little push with her kid-gloved hands.

"I need you, I need you desperately, Carmela, and you cannot refuse me."

"I suppose not," Carmela said doubtfully, "and you know I want to come with you, Felicity."

"Then pack your clothes—no, never mind—you will not need them. I have masses of things for you at the Castle."

Carmela looked at her in bewilderment as she went on:

"Just do as I say. Bring only the things you treasure. I expect that includes your father's pictures."

"They are downstairs in an outhouse. There was no room for them here."

"I will tell the footman to collect them," Felicity said, "and then to come upstairs for your trunk. I will go talk to Mrs. Cooper."

Before Carmela could say any more, she turned and left the room.

The children stared after her until Lucy asked:

"Are you going away with that lady?"

"Mama won't let you go," Henry said before Carmela could reply.

It was as if his rude, oafish voice made up her mind for her.

"Yes, I am going away," she said, and ran into the small room next door.

Because there was nowhere else to put her clothes except a small, rickety chest-of-drawers which she shared with Lucy, most of her things had been left packed in her trunk.

She hurriedly packed what she had been using, put the dressing-table set that had been her mother's on top, added a shawl that was on the bed because there were so few blankets, and did up the strap of her trunk.

As she was doing so a footman appeared in the doorway, resplendent in the Gale livery with its crested silver buttons and carrying his cockaded top-hat in his hand.

"Morning, Miss Carmela," he said with a grin.

"Good-morning, Ben."

"Her Ladyship says I were to fetch yer trunk."

"It is there," Carmela said, pointing to where it stood. "Can you manage it alone?"

"Course I can!" Ben replied.

He put his hat on his head, picked up the trunk, and carried it easily across the Nursery.

The children were still sitting at the table, watching what was occurring in astonishment.

As Carmela came from the bedroom wearing the cloak that had belonged to her mother and a plain chip bonnet trimmed with black ribbons, she thought that compared to Felicity she must look like a hedge-sparrow beside a bird-of-paradise.

At the same time, she felt nervous as to what Mrs. Cooper would say.

As she went down the stairs she was aware that the Vicar's wife would have every right to be annoyed and insulted by her precipitate departure.

Carmela had always done whatever Felicity wanted, and although she was in fact only a few months younger in age, at times her friend seemed almost to belong to a different generation.

She had always been the ring-leader in all their activities, and she was also very self-assured, having travelled and met people of importance. She was, Carmela had often said with a smile, in consequence grown-up before she was a child.

As Carmela reached the small dark Hall, she was aware that Felicity was in the Sitting-Room talking to Mrs. Cooper.

With her heart beating apprehensively, Carmela

walked into the room half-expecting to receive a torrent of abuse in the querulous voice that Mrs. Cooper could use most effectively when anything annoyed her.

Instead, to her surprise the Vicar's wife was smiling.

"Well, you're a lucky girl, and no mistake!" she said before Carmela could speak. "Her Ladyship's just been telling me that she's plans for you which'll be very much to your advantage."

"Mrs. Cooper is being so sweet and understanding in saying that she will not stand in your way," Felicity said.

Carmela had only to look at her friend to know that her eyes were twinkling, and she was speaking in the soft, dulcet tones she used when she was manipulating someone to her own ends.

"It . . . it is very . . . kind of you," Carmela managed to stammer.

"I'll miss you—I don't pretend I shan't," Mrs. Cooper replied. "But Her Ladyship has promised to send me one of the young girls from the kitchen of the Castle to straighten things out, and that'll be a help, it will indeed!"

"I will send her as soon as I get back," Felicity said, "and thank you once again, dear Mrs. Cooper, for being so kind. Please remember me to the Vicar. As I will not be able to attend Church this Sunday because Carmela and I are going away, perhaps you will be kind enough to place my small offering in the plate?"

As Felicity spoke she opened a pretty satin reticule that she carried over her arm and took out a little mesh purse from which she counted out five golden guineas into Mrs. Cooper's outstretched hand.

"That is really very kind of you," Mrs. Cooper said in gratified tones. "Very, very kind!"

She transferred the coins into her other hand so that she could say good-bye to Carmela.

Then, with Felicity moving ahead like a ship in full

sail and Carmela following almost as if she was mesmerised, they stepped into the carriage while Mrs.
Cooper waved from the doorway as they drove off.

Only as the horses turned out through the narrow
gate onto the roadway did Carmela say:

"Have you really . . . rescued me?"

"You certainly look as if you are in need of it," Felicity answered. "Dearest Carmela, how can all this
have happened to you in such a short time?"

"Papa died at the end of January," Carmela replied, "and I could not write to tell you, as I had no
idea where you were."

"I was in France staying first with one of Grandmama's friends, then another," Felicity replied, "so
even if you had written to me, I doubt if the letter
would have found me."

"You must miss her very, very much."

Felicity's grandmother with whom she had lived
ever since she was a child had been the Dowager
Countess of Galeston.

She had been a rather awe-inspiring lady and the
people in the village had been very much in awe of
her, but she had liked Carmela's mother and father
and had even encouraged the latter in his painting by
buying several of his pictures.

Because there were few children of Felicity's age in
the neighbourhood whom her grandmother would
allow her to know, Carmela was encouraged to visit
the Castle, and when the two girls became inseparable it was obviously with the Countess's approval.

It was only as Felicity grew older that she went
away often to stay with the Countess's friends, even
though her grandmother was not well enough to accompany her.

This meant that Felicity's knowledge of the world
was very different from Carmela's.

At the same time, as soon as she came home their
friendship continued as before, and Carmela was

content to be Felicity's confidante, listening to her adventures not with envy but with admiration.

"I was a success! A great success!" Felicity would boast after some interesting visit, and Carmela was only too ready to believe her.

It was just like old times, Carmela thought now, with Felicity telling her what to do and she being only too delighted and happy to oblige.

"What are your plans?" she asked as the carriage rolled on.

The horses turned through the imposing ironwork gates with their attractive stone lodges on either side, which was the entrance to the mile-long drive to the Castle.

"That is what I am going to tell you," Felicity said, "and it is also why I need your help."

"My help?" Carmela asked.

Felicity turned towards her and said in a tone of voice very different from the one she had used before:

"You will help me, Carmela? Promise that you will help me!"

"Of course I will, dearest," Carmela replied. "You know I will do anything you want me to."

"That is what I knew you would say," Felicity said. "What I am going to ask may seem a little strange, but I knew when I came to find you that you would never fail me."

"Why should I?" Carmela asked in a puzzled tone. "You have always been so very, very sweet to me."

She waited, wondering why her friend was looking so serious, and she knew without words that she was going to ask her something unusual and perhaps difficult.

Felicity was looking ahead to where the Castle stood on a high piece of ground, its towers silhouetted against the sky.

It was built on an ancient site but it was in fact quite a modern Castle, which the Countess had bought from its previous owner when she was looking for somewhere to live after she had shaken the dust of Galeston from her feet.

Carmela had heard the story often enough.

The Countess had been a great beauty and a social personality of her time, and sometime after her son had inherited she had quarrelled with him and the rest of the family and finally decided that she would have nothing further to do with them.

Although she had always been a very dominating person and determined to have her own way in everything, they had not at first believed her.

But after a series of bitter and prolonged arguments, and letters that sped back and forth between the Countess and the rest of the Gale family, she finally left the Dower House into which she had moved after her son had inherited.

Taking everything she possessed with her, the Countess told the Gales once and for all that she had no wish to see any of them again.

They found it hard to believe, especially as she had taken her son's young daughter with her.

This in fact had been one of the bones of contention between them, because Felicity's mother had died when she was born and the Countess had disapproved of the way in which she was being brought up.

Her son was more interested in his son and had allowed his mother to take charge of the upbringing of Felicity, thinking that the child might in fact sooner or later heal the breach between them.

The Countess, however, had moved to another part of England altogether and had no intention of being conciliatory.

As her son was nearly as obstinate as she was, the feud grew and grew until there ceased to be any communication between them.

Then the Countess had died, and when Felicity went to France to stay with some of her grandmother's friends, Carmela had wondered if she would turn towards the family she did not know.

This might be impossible, but it would obviously not be correct for her to live at the Castle alone without a Chaperone.

"We are going home," Felicity was saying, "and I will tell you the whole story as soon as we can be alone."

"You are making me very curious," Carmela said. "Is there anybody staying at the Castle?"

"No, not at the moment."

The way Felicity spoke sounded not quite natural, and Carmela could not help wondering what she had in store to tell her and how it concerned her personally.

At the same time, she was very thankful to leave the Vicarage.

She had always been deeply affected by her surroundings, and the ugliness of the Vicarage itself and the plainness of the children and their parents had been very hard to bear.

She had found it difficult to like either the Vicar or his wife, and although she knew she should be grateful to them, they were just not very pleasant people.

The Vicar particularly seemed to be lacking in Christian charity, and Mrs. Cooper was just a tiresome, neurotic woman who had too much to do and was not really fond of her children in spite of the fact that she had given them birth.

They were also comparative newcomers to the village, having lived there for only six years, while the previous Vicar had died after being the incumbent for over forty.

It was a joy for Carmela as she walked into the Castle to see again the perfect taste with which everything was arranged.

It was not only that the curtains were made of an expensive brocade, but they were exactly the right colour, just as the wall-coverings were restful and the pictures on them were a joy to look at.

There were also flowers arranged in large cut-glass vases that scented the atmosphere, and servants in smart uniforms smiling a welcome because they knew Carmela well and made her feel that, like Felicity, she had come home.

Felicity, handing her cloak to a footman and pulling off her bonnet, led the way into an attractive Sitting-Room that the two girls had always thought of as their own.

It had been furnished by the Countess with blue covers for the sofas and chairs which matched Felicity's eyes, and the pictures were in the Fragonard style, depicting ladies who Carmela thought had the same elegance as Felicity herself.

"Is there any refreshment you'd like, M'Lady?" the Butler asked from the door.

Felicity looked at Carmela, who shook her head.

"No, thank you, Bates."

The Butler closed the door and they were alone.

"You are sure you are not hungry?" Felicity asked. "You could not have eaten that filthy breakfast!"

"The very thought of it made me feel sick!" Carmela answered. "Oh, Felicity, I am hopeless at looking after children. At least—those children!"

"I am not surprised," Felicity answered. "But how could you do anything so stupid as to think that was where you would be happy?"

"What else could I do?" Carmela asked.

"You should have known I would have wanted you to come here," Felicity replied, "and do not pretend you were too proud, because I will not listen to you!"

They both laughed because it was an old joke about people being proud.

"When people talk about charity they always mean giving money," the Countess had said once. "But it is much more difficult and far more charitable to give one's self to people."

173

The two girls had thought this an amusing idea, and sometimes Felicity would go back to the Castle to say to her grandmother:

"I have been very charitable this afternoon, Grandmama. I talked for over ten minutes to that terrible old bore Miss Dobson, and I feel sure now I have moved up several places on the ladder to Heaven!"

"I am proud," Carmela said now, "but if you are thinking of being charitable to me, I am only too willing to accept."

"That is exactly what I want to do," Felicity said, "so now, dearest, listen to me."

"I am listening," Carmela answered, "and I have a strong feeling you are up to some mischief of some sort."

"I suppose that is what you might call it," Felicity agreed. "As it happens, I am going to be married!"

Carmela sat upright.

"Married? Oh, Felicity, how exciting! But . . . to whom?"

"To Jimmy—who else?"

Carmela was very still.

"Jimmy Salwick? But, Felicity, I did not know that his wife had died."

"She has not!"

Carmela looked at her friend wide-eyed.

"I . . . I do not . . . understand."

"She is dying, but she is not yet dead, and I am going away with Jimmy to France to stay there until we can be married."

There was silence. Then Carmela said:

"But, Felicity, you cannot do such a . . . thing! Think of your . . . reputation!"

"There are no arguments," Felicity said in a low voice. "This is something I must do, and, Carmela, you have to help me!"

Carmela looked worried.

She had known for over a year that Felicity was in love with Lord Salwick, who was a near neighbour.

He was an attractive, very charming young man who had inherited a large but dilapidated ancestral home and an impoverished Estate with no money to restore it.

Because Felicity had always known she would come into some money on her grandmother's death, they had been prepared to wait. She knew that if they approached the Countess she would make a great many difficulties because even if he were free she did not consider James Salwick, charming though he was, good enough for her granddaughter.

The Countess had always moved in the very highest of Society, and when she was young she had been a Lady of the Bed-Chamber to the Queen.

She had therefore set her heart on Felicity marrying one of the great noblemen who graced the Court, and she had compiled a list of the most eligible Dukes and Marquises whom she considered acceptable as her granddaughter's husband.

"It is no use arguing with Grandmama about Jimmy," Felicity had said often enough to Carmela. "You know how determined she is when she makes up her mind, and if I insist that I will marry no-one else, she will just make it impossible for us to see each other."

"I can understand that," Carmela replied, "but what will happen when she produces a man she considers an ideal husband for you?"

Fortunately that situation had not arisen, because the Countess became too ill and Felicity therefore was sent away to stay with her relatives, a number of whom, because the countess had French blood in her, lived in France.

As soon as the war was over and France began to settle down again, Felicity was sent to stay in a huge *Château* on the Loire with aristocrats who in some miraculous manner had survived not only the Revolution but the social changes effected by Napoleon Bonaparte.

175

But the Countess's connections were not only French.

Felicity had travelled to Northumberland to stay with a Duke, to Cornwall to visit some of the ancient Cornish families who had eligible sons, and once she went even as far north as Edinburgh.

Although she always returned with stories of the people she had met and the men who had made love to her, when she was alone with Carmela she admitted that the only man who really meant anything to her was Jimmy Salwick.

When he was very young his parents had arranged his marriage to a wife who gradually became more and more mentally deranged until finally she was placed in a private Asylum.

It was a cruel fate for the young man because there was no way he could ever be rid of his wife except by her death, and he was tied to a woman he never saw.

It was inevitable that he should lose his heart to what was to all intents and purposes the girl next door.

It was not surprising that he loved Felicity, because, as Carmela saw when they were together, love made her glow with a radiance that any man with eyes in his head would have found irresistible.

At the same time, for Felicity to go away with him was to Carmela inconceivable.

"What I do not understand, dearest," she said now, "is why you cannot wait. If Jimmy's wife is dying, then surely as you have waited so long already, another few months or perhaps even a year would not matter?"

As she spoke she thought it would matter even less now that Felicity did not have her grandmother trying to force her to marry somebody else.

"I thought that was what you would say," Felicity replied, "but it is far more complicated than that."

"Why?"

"Because I have only just learnt when I returned to

London from France that Grandmama has left me a huge fortune."

"A huge fortune?" Carmela repeated.

"It is enormous, really enormous!" Felicity said. "I never had the slightest idea that she had so much."

Carmela did not speak and after a moment Felicity went on:

"As you know, she quarrelled with Papa and all my other relatives. She said they were always battening on her, always expecting her to pay for everything, and it annoyed her."

"I always thought that living here she must be rich," Carmela said slowly.

"Yes, of course, rich by ordinary standards," Felicity agreed, "but not having a fortune that is so large that I cannot believe it! She kept it a secret."

"I suppose she did not wish your father to know about it."

"I realise that now," Felicity said, "but already it has begun to complicate things."

"Why?"

"Because as soon as the Solicitor came to see me," Felicity answered, "and he had been waiting for me to arrive back from France, I left London immediately and came here."

Carmela looked puzzled, and Felicity went on:

"I knew that I must go away with Jimmy before he heard of my fortune and before the Gales tried to get their hands on it."

Carmela looked bewildered.

"I . . . do not understand."

"It is quite simple," Felicity said. "First of all, if Jimmy knows how rich I am, he will not marry me."

"Why should you say that?" Carmela asked.

"Because he would be too proud," Felicity said, "and he will think that everybody will call him a for-tune-hunter. In consequence he will leave me, and it will break my heart!"

The way Felicity spoke was very positive, and

Carmela could not help agreeing that her reasoning was right.

James Salwick was a proud man. He disliked the fact that he could not repair his house or run his Estate the way he wished to do.

He was also in some ways almost ultra-sensitive about the tragedy of his wife, and Carmela was aware that he had at first fought against his feelings for Felicity because he had nothing to offer her.

It was Felicity who had fallen in love with him when they met out hunting and had made all the running.

Carmela knew how many excuses she had made to meet him when he was not expecting it, and that she had called at his house and had inveigled him under one pretext or another to come to the Castle.

When finally his feelings had been too much for him and he had confessed his love, Felicity had been frantic that she might lose him.

"He loves me, he loves me!" she had said to Carmela. "But he says he will never stand in my way, and if I want to marry somebody else, he will just disappear and I will never see him again!"

She gave a little cry of terror as she added:

"How can I lose him? Oh, Carmela, I cannot lose him!"

Thinking over what Felicity had said, Carmela understood now the danger if James Salwick knew how rich she was. Aloud she asked:

"Will he go away with you?"

"He will when he hears what next has happened."

"What is that?"

"I came back here from London the very moment I heard what the Solicitor had to tell me. And what do you think I found?"

"What?"

"A letter waiting here from Cousin Selwyn, the new Earl of Galeston."

"Why should he write to you?"

She knew that since Felicity's brother, who had

been the pride and joy of her father, had been killed just before Waterloo, the Earl when he died of a broken heart a year ago had no direct heir to follow him.

This meant that the title had gone to the son of his brother, who had married when he was very young.

Therefore, the present Earl of Galeston, Felicity's first cousin, was a considerably older man who had been a soldier without any prospects of inheriting the Earldom.

Carmela vaguely remembered hearing all this, but she had not been particularly interested because Felicity knew very little about her relatives, having never met them.

She had even learnt of her father's death only through the reports in the newspapers.

"Why should I care?" she had asked when Carmela pointed out the Obituary to her. "Grandmama hated him, and she told me often enough how much my father disliked me because I caused my mother's death when I was born."

"It seems wrong somehow not to like your relations," Carmela had said.

"Nanny always said that you choose your friends, but your relatives are wished onto you," Felicity had retorted.

Then Carmela thought it was obvious, since Felicity was now alone in the world, that her relatives would be interested in her, although it seemed rather late after there had been no communication from them since she was five.

"What did the new Earl have to say to you?" she asked.

Felicity's lips tightened and in a hard voice she said:

"He informed me that as Grandmama was dead he was now my Guardian, and he ordered me, as if I were one of his Troops, to come to Galeston immediately as he had plans for my future."

Carmela gasped.

"I cannot believe he wrote like that!"

"He did! You shall see the letter, and if he thinks I am going to obey him, he is very much mistaken."

"But . . . if he is your Guardian . . . ?"

"He is asserting himself as my Guardian now only because he has heard about the money Grandmama left me," Felicity interrupted. "I am not a fool. If it had been just a small amount on which I could live without any fuss, Cousin Selwyn would not have bothered about me or been interested as to whether I lived or died. But now that I am an heiress, it is a very different thing!"

"How can you be sure he is like that?" Carmela asked.

She hated the hard note in Felicity's voice and the hard expression that was in her eyes.

It somehow spoilt her beauty, and Carmela loved her too much to wish her ever to be bitter or cynical.

"Grandmama said they were a 'money-grubbing' lot, and she was right!" Felicity said. "I am quite certain that now that he has heard of the millions I own, Cousin Selwyn wants to get his grubby hands on it!"

"Oh, Felicity, that is going too far!" Carmela protested.

"Why are you sticking up for him?" Felicity asked. "Papa died a full ten months ago, but only now, after Grandmama's death, is the new Earl *ordering* me to come to Galeston. I would rather die!"

"You do not mean that!"

Felicity suddenly laughed.

"No, I do not mean it. I am going to live and marry Jimmy quickly, before he learns how rich I am. Once we are married, there will be nothing that either he or the Earl can do about it!"

"That is true enough," Carmela agreed. "But you cannot marry Jimmy until . . . his wife is . . . dead."

"She is dying! I told you that! Jimmy had a letter from the Surgeon who is looking after her, saying that she has a brain-tumour. I have asked a number of people about it, and a person with a brain-tumour never lives very long."

"I cannot pretend I am sorry," Carmela said, "but at the same time, please wait, Felicity. Please wait before you do anything . . . foolish."

"I am not taking any risks on that score!"

"But supposing the Earl finds you wherever you hide and brings you back?"

"That is the threat which I am going to use to Jimmy to make him take me away," Felicity said. "I shall show him Cousin Selwyn's letter, and he will know he means business."

She paused before she continued:

"He will guess there is an ulterior motive in his interest, but I shall not let him think it is money, but only that I am a Gale and therefore come under his jurisdiction because I am young, and of course—attractive!"

"Do you think Jimmy will believe you?"

"He will believe it because he will want to, and you know as well as I do, Carmela, that he really loves me."

Felicity's voice softened and Carmela said quickly:

"Yes, darling, I know he does, and you love him. At the same time, it is . . . wrong for you to be . . . together unless you are . . . man and wife."

As she spoke Carmela thought it was very shocking indeed, but she did not want to upset Felicity by saying so.

However, Felicity saw the expression on her face and gave a little laugh.

"I can see what you are thinking, Carmela. At the same time, I do not think you need worry about me. Jimmy himself is so protective that I am quite certain he will not do anything you think wrong until I am really his wife."

Her chin quivered as she went on:

"At the same time, if there is a question of Cousin Selwyn trying to annul the marriage because I am under-age, I shall make quite certain that I am having a baby!"

Carmela gave a cry of protest, but Felicity put out her hand to take hers.

"Please, dearest, I know what I am doing. Jimmy is everything that matters to me, and my whole happiness rests on our being together. That is why you have to help me."

"I . . . cannot see what I . . . can do," Carmela said.

"It is quite simple," Felicity answered. "You will go to Galeston in my place and stay there until I am married to Jimmy!"

CHAPTER TWO

"*I* cannot do it . . . it is impossible!" Carmela said over and over again.

But she knew her voice was beginning to weaken as she felt she would not be able to resist Felicity much longer.

It had always been the same ever since they were children.

When Felicity made up her mind to do something, she was so determined and so plausible that it was impossible to say "no."

"Of course they will know I am not you," Carmela protested.

"Why should they?" Felicity asked. "None of my

relatives have seen me since I was five, and until now, as you well know, they have not been interested in me."

She paused before she said bitterly:

"There was not a single letter from any of my cousins, my great-aunts, or my other relatives asking me to live with them after Grandmama died, until this one from Cousin Selwyn!"

She went on in a contemptuous tone:

"He is quite obviously interested only in my fortune. In fact, my Solicitor told me that he was the only person who knew about it!"

"How was your grandmother able to keep such a momentous secret from everybody?" Carmela asked.

"Apparently a great deal of her money is invested in Jamaica and has multiplied enormously in the last few years because of the demand for sugar. The Solicitor told me that her investments in England also have been very productive. They must have been, seeing the amount she has left me."

Carmela did not speak and after a moment Felicity sighed.

"This is a great responsibility and not really a blessing. I know that Jimmy will dislike my being so rich, and I shall never know whether people like me for myself or for what I possess."

"People will always love you because you are you," Carmela said impulsively, and Felicity smiled.

"That is what I want to hear," she said, "and I do not wish to become like Grandmama, who hated all the Gales because she felt they were after her money."

"Please do not let it spoil you," Carmela pleaded, "and I do understand how worrying it is to have so much and to have to hide it from Jimmy."

"If you understand that, you will help me," Felicity said quickly.

"But no-one will believe I am you," Carmela protested again.

"Why not?" Felicity enquired. "You are just as pretty as I am, and when you are dressed in my clothes we will not look unalike, in fact we might even be sisters."

There was some truth in this, for both girls were fair, both had blue eyes, and both had perfect pink-and-white complexions which were the admiration of the men and the envy of the women.

But while Felicity had a sophisticated elegance, Carmela looked like a simple country girl and lacked the polish which clothes and self-assurrance could give.

Felicity looked at Carmela now with a critical eye, then rose to her feet and took her by the hand.

"Come with me," she said, "we are going upstairs."

"What for?" Carmela asked.

"You are going to be made to look exactly like me," Felicity replied. "We will start by arranging your hair in a fashionable style, and I have already decided that you shall have all the gowns I have been wearing since Grandmama died."

Carmela thought that would be very appropriate because she was aware that Felicity was wearing mauve as half-mourning.

She herself had not been able to afford any new gowns after her father's death, in fact all she could do was to change the ribbons on her bonnet and wear a black sash.

As she walked beside Felicity she was acutely conscious of how threadbare was the gown she was wearing.

Also, as she had not changed before she left the Vicarage, there were not only some dirty marks on her skirt but there were also a few spots of egg which Lucy had splattered over her.

They went up the broad staircase to the beautiful bedroom where Felicity had always slept.

There were several trunks on the floor, but they

were not yet unpacked and there was no maid in the room.

"As I am going away tomorrow," Felicity explained before Carmela could question her, "I told them to unpack nothing. But these are the trunks you will be taking with you, and they contain all my latest clothes, which are either black or mauve."

"What are you going to wear?" Carmela asked with a little smile.

"I am going to make Jimmy take me to Paris and fit me out with an entire new wardrobe."

"Paris? Is that wise?"

"As it happens, Grandmama's French friends all live in other parts of France, so I am not likely to meet them. If I do, I shall just introduce Jimmy as my husband, and there is no reason why they should question it."

"You seem very sure that Jimmy will agree to this fantastic plan of yours."

As Carmela spoke she saw the expression of anxiety in Felicity's eyes before she replied:

"If Jimmy loves me as I know he does, he will not want me to go to Galeston to be pressured into marriage with somebody chosen for me by Cousin Selwyn."

"Do you really think that is what he intends?"

"I am sure of it!" Felicity said. "And I do not mind betting that it is a relation of some sort, so that they can keep the money in the family."

Carmela did not argue, as she felt there was nothing she could say.

At the same time, she could not believe that the Gales were quite as unpleasant as Felicity made them out to be.

Yet, she was well aware that a Guardian, like a parent, had complete control over a young girl until she was twenty-one.

If the present Earl wished Felicity to marry, then he could arrange it and there was nothing whatever she could do to prevent herself being taken up the aisle and married off to some man she did not love.

Because her own parents had been so happy, Carmela had always assumed that she and Felicity would someday be happy in the same way, and there was no doubt that Jimmy was the only man for Felicity.

"I still think what you are doing is . . . wrong," she said in a low voice, but even as she spoke she was aware that Felicity was not listening to her.

She had thrown open the lid of the trunk which had already been unstrapped and unlocked.

"I remember noticing what the maids in London put on top of this trunk," she said, "and just now I thought it is exactly what you need to travel in."

"I see you were not expecting me to refuse you," Carmela observed.

"How could you when it matters so much to me?" Felicity asked. "If it were the other way round, you know I would save you."

"As you have already done," Carmela said with a smile.

"From those ghastly children, and however ferocious Cousin Selwyn may be, he could not be worse than Henry Cooper!"

Carmela laughed. Then she said in a serious tone:

"I feel very . . . frightened at the thought of . . . going to Galeston expecting at any . . . moment to be . . . exposed."

"It cannot be for long," Felicity said soothingly. "The moment I am married to Jimmy, you will be able to leave."

"What am I to do then?"

"You are to go to Jimmy's house here and wait until we return from abroad. Then we will discuss your future, and I promise you, dearest, it will be a very happy, comfortable one."

"You know I cannot accept money from you . . ." Carmela began in an uncomfortable tone.

"If you talk like that, I shall slap you!" Felicity said.

"If you think I am going to listen to both you and Jimmy talking about my money as though it is contaminated, I shall put everything I possess in a bag and throw it into the sea!"

The way she spoke made Carmela laugh, but she said:

"I shall find something to do which will earn me enough to live on."

"What you will have to do is to get married," Felicity said. "We will find you a charming husband very nearly as nice as Jimmy, and you will live happily ever afterwards."

"I think that is unlikely . . ." Carmela began, but Felicity was pulling the gowns out of the trunk and the words died on her lips.

Never had she imagined that gowns in various shades of mauve could be so lovely and so alluring.

There was also a white gown embroidered with violets, with ribbons to match, and an evening-gown that glittered with embroidery which looked like amethysts and diamonds.

"Were you really . . . expecting to wear . . . those?" Carmela asked.

"Of course!" Felicity replied. "And to tell you the truth, dearest, I am sick to death of them! I miss Grandmama, I miss her terribly, but you know she always said that people who mourned someone for too long were bores, and if one were a Christian one believed anyway that they were not dead but alive in Heaven."

"Mama used to think the same thing," Carmela replied, "and anyway, I could not afford to buy any mourning for Papa."

"Then you can wear these clothes for another month or two, and if Jimmy's wife is not dead by then I will send you some coloured gowns from Paris."

"Will that not seem strange?" Carmela asked.

"With the money you are supposed to own, you

can be dressed from head to foot in gold and diamonds!"

"That is what I shall feel like in these dresses," Carmela answered.

"Then hurry and put them on," Felicity said. "And
I must do something about your hair."

An hour later, Carmela was staring at herself in the
mirror in a bemused fashion.

She was wearing a pale gown the colour of Parma
violets, and there was a large bunch of those flowers
at her waist.

Felicity's lady's-maid Martha had arranged her hair
in an exact copy of her mistress's, and when she had
added a little powder to Carmela's small straight nose
and a touch of salve to her lips, they might almost
have been twins.

Martha, who had been with Felicity for years and
knew Carmela well, was the only person to be let into
the secret of what the two girls were about to do.

"It's not that I approves of what Her Ladyship's up
to," Martha had said to Carmela, "but once she's set
her heart on something, it's no use arguing with her."

"That is true," Carmela had said, "but do you
think, Martha, that anybody will believe for one moment that I am really Her Ladyship?"

"You wait until I've finished with you, Miss,"
Martha had replied, and Carmela had to admit now
that she looked very unlike herself.

"Be very careful what you say downstairs, Martha,"
Felicity warned, "except that we are all leaving tomorrow."

"They knows that already," Martha said, "but they
didn't ask me any questions."

"That is a blessing."

Martha went from the room to fetch something,
and Carmela asked:

"How can you be sure of anything until Jimmy
agrees?"

"He will agree," Felicity said confidently, "and he should be arriving anytime now."

"Will you want to see him alone?" Carmela asked.

"Yes, of course," Felicity answered. "I am going to show him Cousin Selwyn's letter. I know then he will agree to all my plans."

Carmela hesitated for a moment. Then she said:

"Do you not think, Felicity dearest, that it would be more honest if you told him the truth? When after you have married him he finds out that you have been deceitful about your money, will it not make him angry and feel that he cannot trust you in the future?"

She knew by the way Felicity's lips tightened that she had thought about this already and knew the answer.

"That is a risk I have to take," she said, "but I cannot help feeling that when Jimmy is married to me, nothing will be of any importance except the fact that we are together."

That, Carmela was to think later, was the truth.

She had only to see Lord Salwick looking at Felicity to know that he loved her with all his heart and that his idea of perfect happiness was for her to be his wife.

He arrived just before luncheon, and Felicity had no time to tell him what was happening. So they ate first, a small but delicious meal cooked by a Chef who had been at the castle for ten years with the Countess.

Because Lord Salwick was obviously so pleased to see Felicity again, he could not take his eyes off her, and while they tried to talk sensibly of what they had each been doing while they were apart, there were moments when their words died away and they could only look at each other with love in their eyes.

Carmela had been amused when she first went down to the Drawing-Room before luncheon to find that for a moment Lord Salwick did not recognise her.

Then he had exclaimed:

"You have changed, Carmela! I thought you were one of Felicity's smart friends she had brought here from London."

"No, I am just myself," Carmela answered, "but 'fine feathers make fine birds'!"

"Oh, you have some new clothes," Lord Salwick said vaguely, "and you are doing your hair in a new way."

"It is like mine," Felicity said, "and I will tell you all about it, darling, after luncheon."

As soon as Felicity spoke, Carmela realised that Lord Salwick had forgotten her and had turned his attention to Felicity as if she filled his whole world.

As soon as the meal was over Carmela went upstairs.

"I will send for you when I have made Jimmy agree to everything," Felicity had said before he arrived.

"Be careful not to tell too many lies!"

"Yes of course," Felicity agreed.

Once Carmela was alone upstairs in Felicity's bedroom, she looked at the trunk which she knew contained more clothes than she had ever worn in her whole life, and the doubts as to whether she was doing the right thing, or something that was utterly and completely mad, came crowding back into her mind.

Then she told herself that the only thing that really mattered was that she should help Felicity because she loved her and should not think of herself.

At the same time, to go to a strange house and live with strange people, especially the Gales, who sounded terrifying, was almost as bad as returning to the Vicarage and being confronted by the obstreperous children again.

"I must be brave and adventurous," Carmela told herself, although she felt neither of those things, but just helpless, as she had felt when her father died.

Supposing she let Felicity down? Supposing the

moment she arrived one of the family whom Felicity had forgotten about denounced her as an impostor?

There were dozens of disasters that might happen, and because she had lived such a quiet, uneventful life she thought she would never be able to carry off an impersonation of Felicity, who was used to parties, dinners, Balls, and Receptions, and had often travelled abroad.

"Perhaps the Gales will not know that," Carmela tried to console herself, but she had the uncomfortable feeling that there would always be prying eyes and gossiping tongues!

Some kind friend would be only too willing to tittle-tattle about the Countess who had cut herself off from the rest of the family and brought up a very beautiful granddaughter without their help.

Because she felt perturbed and anxious, Carmela walked to the window and as she did so caught a glimpse of herself in the long mirror.

For a moment she could hardly believe she was seeing her own reflection. Then she told herself that whatever her inner fears might be, outwardly she really did look the part she was to play.

She would not have been human if she had not felt it a joy to wear a gown that was more beautiful and more elegant than anything she had ever worn before.

'I am sure if Papa could see me he would want to paint me,' she thought.

Then she knew that her father would be more likely to paint her as a nymph wearing something diaphanous that looked like the mist on the water or perhaps a sky sprinkled with stars if he was painting her at night.

'For the moment I am content with these real gowns,' Carmela thought with a smile.

She looked at those which Felicity had flung on the bed, thinking she had never imagined she would ever be able to wear anything that looked as if it had stepped straight out of a dream.

When there was a knock on the door and one of the servants asked her to go downstairs, she felt as if the sound jerked her back to reality.

She swallowed apprehensively as she entered the Drawing-Room, where Felicity and Lord Salwick were waiting.

They were both looking very happy, and Felicity, who was holding his hand, did not relinquish it as he rose to his feet.

"Come and talk to us, dearest Carmela," she said. "I have told Jimmy how kind you have promised to be and he is very grateful."

"I am indeed, Carmela!" Lord Salwick said. "But it seems we are asking a great deal of you."

"I . . . I want to . . . help," Carmela said quietly.

"And you will help us by staying at Galeston just until we are married," Felicity said.

"I only hope that I can . . . act the part skilfully."

"I can see now that you do look rather like Felicity," Lord Salwick said, "only . . ."

He stopped as if he realised that what he meant would sound rude, and Carmela finished the sentence for him.

". . . Only she is much, much lovelier than I could ever be."

"That is what I thought," Lord Salwick smiled, "but of course I am prejudiced."

"That is what I hope you will always be," Felicity said. "Otherwise, I warn you, Jimmy, I shall be very, very jealous!"

"Not half as jealous as I shall be about you," he said. "If you even look at another man I will murder him!"

Felicity laughed in delight, and taking his hand held it against her cheek.

"We are going to be very happy," she said, "and

there will be no time for anybody else in our lives except ourselves."

"You can be sure of that, my darling," Lord Salwick said. "But I wish it were easier and we could be married right away."

"I am sure it will not be long," Felicity said confidently, "and I cannot risk losing you."

"You will never do that," he said, "and although I think it is something I should not do, I cannot risk your obeying your cousin's summons and finding that he intends to marry you off to somebody else."

"I am sure that is what he intends," Felicity replied. "Otherwise, why should he have sent for me so suddenly when there have been no previous communications?"

"I agree, it is all very suspicious," Lord Salwick said, "and therefore we will do what you wish. I must go home now and make arrangements for the house and the horses to be looked after while I am away."

"Yes, of course!" Felicity said. "And you will not forget that I want one of your men to drive Carmela to London?"

Carmela looked surprised and Felicity explained:

"It would be a great mistake for old Gibbons to take you. We could not be sure he would not gossip with the servants at Galeston House, and another thing— he would forget to call you 'M'Lady.'"

"I can understand that," Carmela said, "but . . ."

"It is all arranged," Felicity interrupted. "Jimmy has a new coachman who has never seen you, and he is going to tell him to come here and drive a lady he will think is me to London in Grandmama's carriage, which, as you know, had the coat-of-arms on the door."

"And when I . . . get to . . . Galeston House in . . . London?" Carmela asked in a low voice.

"Cousin Selwyn had made arrangements for me to stay the night there and his horses will take you to Galeston the next day. He had it all 'cut and dried,' obviously not expecting me to be able to think for myself."

"Perhaps he is just being polite and considerate," Lord Salwick suggested quietly.

"To suit his own ends!" Felicity replied. "Do not forget, darling Jimmy, he never wrote to me when Grandmama died."

"I agree that was inexcusable."

"Now I am just wondering," Felicity said, "which of the impoverished, spendthrift Gales he is expecting me to marry."

Carmela looked at her warningly, fearing that Lord Salwick might suspect how rich she really was.

Then she remembered that even without the very large fortune she now had inherited, it would have been expected that Felicity should have some money left to her by her grandmother as well as the Castle and its contents.

As if Felicity realised what she was thinking, she said:

"I am keeping the Castle open for the time being until Jimmy can arrange everything for me and decide what we will move from here into his own house."

"Then would it not be better, when I know you are . . . married, for me to . . . come . . . here?" Carmela asked.

Felicity shook her head.

"You may have to run away, and if Cousin Selwyn tries to pursue you or wishes to make himself unpleasant, it would be better for you to be somewhere where he would not find you."

"Y-yes . . . of course," Carmela said hesitatingly, "but I hope he will not be very . . . very . . . angry when he knows he has been . . . deceived."

Felicity shrugged her shoulders.

"What does it matter if he is? I will be married by then, and we will look after you, will we not, darling Jimmy?"

"Of course," Lord Salwick agreed. "We will see that you do not have to go back to work at the Vicarage or anywhere else for that matter, and I am very sorry about your father. I did not know until Felicity told me that he had died."

Carmela felt the tears come into her eyes and for the moment she could not answer.

Felicity put her arms round her.

"It is all right, dearest," she said. "You are not alone any longer. You are with us! We love you and you will never again have to suffer as you have had to do by working for people like the Coopers."

"They . . . meant to be . . . kind," Carmela said with a little choke in her voice.

"No-one could be kind who possessed a son like that monster Henry!" Felicity answered.

Because it somehow sounded ridiculous, Carmela gave a choked little laugh.

"I really ought to go," Lord Salwick said. "Will you be ready if I fetch you in my travelling-carriage at nine o'clock?"

"Of course I will!" Felicity replied. "I shall have very little luggage because I am going to buy a whole trousseau in France in which you will think I look beautiful."

"How could you be anything else?" he said.

"Nobody knows anything except for Carmela and Martha," Felicity said. "I shall just tell the servants that I am going back to London."

"Are you going to stay there the night?" Carmela asked, knowing she also would be in London at Galeston House.

"Yes, but not in Grandmama's house, in case somebody should hear of it," Felicity replied. "I shall stay at an Hotel under an assumed name, and only when we get to France will Jimmy and I be known as Lord and Lady Salwick."

"Which you will be very, very soon," Lord Salwick said in a low voice.

"That is all I want, now and forever," Felicity replied.

They looked into each other's eyes and Carmela was forgotten.

Then, because she knew they wanted to say goodbye to each other, she slipped from the room and left them alone.

Because she had got her own way and everything appeared to be "plain sailing," Felicity was in sparkling spirits all the evening.

They laughed as she and Carmela reminisced about when they were children, and only when they went up to bed early did Felicity say in a more serious tone:

"I am very, very grateful to you, dearest! I cannot live without Jimmy, and this is the only way I can be sure of not losing him."

"I do not think you would ever do that," Carmela answered.

"I am giving you some money," Felicity went on. "I know how humiliating it must have been at the Vicarage to be without it."

They went into her bedroom and she took a sealed package from one of the drawers of the dressing-table, saying:

"There is one hundred pounds here, some in notes, some in sovereigns."

"One hundred pounds?" Carmela exclaimed. "I do not need as much as that!"

"Of course you do," Felicity said firmly, "and there is also a cheque for another hundred pounds, which you can cash anytime you want, from Coutts Bank in London."

"It is too much," Carmela protested.

"Remember, you are supposed to be well off, if not a millionairess," Felicity admonished. "You must tip generously and keep enough money with which to run away when the time comes. You may have to come back in a post-chaise. Anyway, it is fatal not to be able to pay one's way, and I am making sure you can do that."

"You are so . . . kind," Carmela said softly.

"Not in the least! You are being kind to me," Felicity answered, "and I have every intention of giving you all the money you need in the future, so there is no need to pinch and starve."

Carmela was about to say that her pride would not let her take it. Then the old joke about "pride and charity" occurred to them both and they laughed.

"Do not dare say it!" Felicity admonished. "You are my responsibility from now on, and let me say that because I am being married first, I already feel as if you are my debutante daughter and I have to launch you on the Social World."

They both laughed again because it sounded absurd, but when she was alone Carmela could not help feeling that it was almost true.

Because Felicity was so much more worldly-wise and sophisticated compared to herself, Carmela felt she was like an unfledged School-girl stepping into a world of which she knew nothing and would therefore appear gauche and unsure of herself.

At the same time, she could feel a sense of adventure seeping through her because it was so exciting to have such beautiful clothes and to get away from the Vicarage.

"God will look after me," she told herself before she fell asleep.

She felt quite sure too that her father and mother were near her and they would somehow protect her from any extreme consequences of the deception on which she was embarking to help Felicity.

"Whatever happens," Carmela said, "I will try not to have any regrets."

The Earl of Galeston was sitting in the Library at Galeston Park with a map of the Estate spread out in front of him.

"As I have not been here since I was a small boy," he said to the Manager standing beside him, "you must remind me of the names of the woods and the farms, and of course I shall want to know about the present tenants."

"I think Your Lordship will find I have set it all down in the memorandum I laid before you when you arrived."

"I have read it," the Earl replied, "but I did not find it as comprehensive as I would wish."

He knew as he spoke that the man beside him was anxious, and he thought that his suspicions were fully justified. It was quite obvious that the Manager was not only incompetent and lazy but very probably dishonest also.

The Earl had come to Galeston with an open mind, knowing that it would be a great mistake to make changes too quickly. In the words in which he would have advised a young Subaltern just joining the Regiment, he must "play himself in."

The Earl had never in his wildest dreams expected to inherit the title or any of the Estates.

As his father was a younger son he had always known that in the usual English tradition, the family money all belonged to the reigning Earl, while his brother and certainly his nephew could expect nothing.

He had therefore chosen the Army as his career and expected to stay in the Regiment until he retired.

Because he was a good soldier, he rose through sheer merit rather than by buying promotions, and he was actually a Colonel before, like being hit by a bombshell, he learnt that his uncle had died unexpectedly and he was the seventh Earl of Galeston.

Of course he had known that the direct heir, his

cousin, had been killed just before his twenty-first birthday.

But as his uncle was a comparatively young man who had been a widower for a long time, and if he thought about it at all, Selwyn Gale had assumed that the Earl would marry again and do his best to produce another son.

The thought indeed had just passed through his mind, then he forgot it, being too busy soldiering to have any other interests.

He had spent some years in India when he first joined the Regiment, then had come back with Sir Arthur Wellesley to join him in his campaigns against Napoleon in Portugal and Spain, and finally he had gone to France to defeat the French Emperor at the Battle of Waterloo.

Selwyn Gale had then been busy in the Army of Occupation, and it was only several months after succeeding to the title that he very reluctantly said goodbye to the Army and started a life that was very different from anything he had ever known before.

To begin with, he was overwhelmed by the amount of his possessions and the importance and authority that went with his new position.

He was also astonished to discover how rich he was.

Lack of money had always been a handicap in his life, and he now found it almost as difficult to accustom himself to being a rich man as to cope with the problems of being poor.

At the same time, he could not help thinking that the years of comparative poverty had taught him lessons that he would never forget, besides having given him an understanding and sympathy for those who had to pinch and save as he had been obliged to do.

However, there was one thing which infuriated him, and that was any form of dishonesty.

He had been quick to detect among those whom he commanded any who stole, cheated, or were deceitful in obtaining money they could not earn honestly.

When he inherited he was shrewdly aware that a rich man was considered "fair game" by those who knew how to profit from any blindness or carelessness on his part.

He therefore took things slowly, noting unnecessary extravagances here and there, but saying nothing.

He watched for any who were filling their own pockets at his expense and was waiting to strike at those who were definitely "fiddling the books" until they should have no defence against his accusations.

He looked at the map in front of him again before he said:

"I see you have sold a great deal of timber recently, Matthews. I would like an account of what the wood fetched and who bought it."

The Manager's eyes flickered, and the Earl was aware that this was another discrepancy in the accounts that had been handed to him.

"What is more," he said, "I have been unable to locate a number of farm implements which are listed here, but which have, I assume, been placed in some part of the Estate where I can inspect them!"

Now the Manager was tense, and the Earl knew without being told that the accounts had been falsified, and half the items that had been entered as having been bought had no substance in fact.

"Let me have all this information by tomorrow morning, Matthews," he said, "and when you bring it I would also like to see the Estate Accountant at the same time."

"That'll be Lane, M'Lord."

"I am aware of that," the Earl said, "and as I would not wish to waste more time than necessary, tell him to bring his books here within the hour so that I shall have a chance to peruse them."

The Manager's face now had an unhealthy pallor, and the Earl knew he had been right in suspecting

that he and the Accountant had been working together and the books were well and truly "cooked."

He rose to his feet.

"That will be all, Matthews," he said. "I will see you
at ten o'clock tomorrow morning."

"Very good, M'Lord."

The Manager walked towards the door.

He had almost reached it when he stopped, and
the Earl knew he was trying to make up his mind
whether to make a clean breast of what he had done
or to hand in his resignation.

Finally he decided to do neither but walked from
the room, and his footsteps going down the passage
seemed to get slower and slower as he went.

The Earl was certain that by tomorrow morning he
would either have packed up and left or would try to
make the Accountant the scapegoat, forcing him to
take the blame for what had occurred.

His lips were set in a hard line as he thought how
gullible his uncle had been in trusting such a man.

What was more, he suspected that he was just one
of many who would eventually have to leave the Estate to be replaced by men who were more honest.

It was depressing, to say the least of it, to find that
things were not as he had hoped and that he was not
being served by trustworthy servants who thought of
their positions as a privilege and revered the family to
which they owed their allegiance.

Then the Earl thought that he was being absurdly
idealistic to expect so much.

There were crooks in every walk of life, and even
amidst the beauty and grandeur of Galeston he must
expect them to show their heads like reptiles.

He had hoped—of course it was but a faint hope—
that because his inheritance was so fine and he was so
intensely proud of it, everything would be perfect.

But he was just a fool to think that anything in life
could be like that! Instead, he would have to work
and fight to attain the perfection he sought and must

expect to be disillusioned a dozen times in the process.

All the same, as he stood at a window which looked out over the lake to the great trees in the Park and thought of the ten thousand acres that surrounded him, a feeling of satisfaction seemed to well up in him almost like a paean of joy.

It was his—his for his lifetime and, if he was fortunate, for the sons who would follow him.

'I will not be such a fool as to have only one son,' the Earl thought to himself, remembering how his cousin had been killed in action. 'I want a dozen!'

Then he laughed because he knew he first had to find a wife.

That might not be so difficult now that he was in a position to be able to offer so much to the woman he married.

When he was a soldier he had thought it would be impossible for him ever to be able to afford to marry, unless he chose a rich wife. And that was unlikely not only because he disliked women who had more money than himself, but also because the women who attracted him would find it impossible to live on a soldier's pay.

In the course of his service in different lands there had been a number of lovely ladies with whom Selwyn Gale, being a very handsome and attractive man, had had fiery liaisons.

However, they had lasted only the short time he could spare between his varying duties.

But just as he had known that none of them was likely to become a permanent feature of his life, so the ladies in question, although they loved the strength of his arms, the fire of his kisses, and the sensations he aroused in them, had no intention of being "camp followers."

"I love you, Selwyn!" one of the most beautiful of his *affaires de coeur* had said to him one night. "Why, dearest, could you not be a rich Duke or a wealthy

Marquis, so that if Harry died, which is very likely from the way he is drinking at the moment, we could live happily ever after?"

Although it was a sentimental moment, Selwyn Gale had not been able to prevent himself from thinking a little cynically that the love which she had just demonstrated very effectively was not the sort that lasted.

In fact, he had been quite certain that by the time he returned to his Regiment, the lady now in his arms would be consoling herself very effectively with one of his brother-Officers.

What was more, he had known, if he was honest, that although he found her very alluring, he would seldom think of her once they had parted.

Marriage was something which had never entered into his plans, except perhaps for when he was about to retire and would want somebody to keep him company in the long winter evenings.

Now at thirty-three the future was very different, and he knew that marriage to somebody suitable who would be the mother of his children was certainly an important item on his programme.

"I shall have to think about it when I have got the Estate straight," he decided.

He admitted he had never been happier in his whole life than in reorganising and rearranging not only his house and Estates but also himself.

That was what he had always enjoyed doing, and although in the Regiment they used to laugh at him for wanting to change things and improve them, he had a taste for organisation that he could never lose.

Just as he planned his tactics in battle so that he invariably lost fewer men than any other Commander, so now he planned his improvements on the Estate and was ready to plan his own life down to the last detail.

"First things first!" he told himself as he looked out on the Park.

The door opened behind him and he heard his Butler say:

"His Royal Highness Prince Frederich has arrived, M'Lord! I have shown him into the Blue Salon."

"Thank you, Newman, I will join him there," the Earl replied.

He turned back for a moment to take another look at the sunshine outside.

Here was another problem to solve, but he thought with satisfaction that he had the answer to that.

Everything was under control, and the knowledge gave him a feeling of immense satisfaction.

Then, as if it was an effort, he turned away from the view and walked towards the door of the Library.

As he did so he forced himself to put his own problems to one side while he contemplated those of the Prince who was waiting for him in the Blue Salon.

He remembered that Napoleon had spoken of the "cupboards of the mind," and he thought it a good expression for the practice of keeping things in their own compartments, so that one closed one cupboard-door before opening another one.

The idea amused him, and there was a smile on his lips as he walked quickly down the long corridor furnished with treasures collected over the centuries by members of the Gale family to the Blue Salon, where Prince Frederich was waiting.

CHAPTER THREE

*A*s the Earl's carriage, drawn by four extremely fine horses, drew nearer to Galeston Park, Carmela felt more and more frightened.

It had been exciting to drive to London yesterday in the Countess's carriage, which she knew so well, and even when she arrived at Galeston House in Park Lane she did not feel overwhelmingly nervous.

This was because she was quite certain, from the letter which Felicity had shown her, that the Earl would not be there.

Instead there was his Secretary, an elderly man with delightful manners, who welcomed Carmela as if she were an old friend and spoke respectfully of the Countess, whom he had known in the past.

Because she was tired after the long journey, she was glad to have supper on a tray in her bedroom and then get into bed.

On Felicity's instructions, she had explained fulsomely but convincingly that the reason she had to travel alone was that her lady's-maid had unfortunately been taken ill at the last moment, and she had been obliged to leave her behind.

"I considered delaying my arrival," she said to the Earl's Secretary, "but I thought that might be inconvenient to His Lordship, and therefore I came alone."

"It is extremely unfortunate for you, M'Lady," the Secretary replied, "but I will make sure you are accompanied on the journey to Galeston tomorrow by one of our senior staff."

After a comparatively restful night Carmela was slightly amused to meet the elderly housemaid who was to chaperone her on the drive to the country.

With a beaded bonnet on her grey hair and a severe black cape over her plain dress, she looked a picture of propriety, and Carmela thought that nobody at Galeston could be anything but impressed by her arrival.

They talked on the journey, and Carmela learnt a lot that she wanted to know.

First, that the Earl had only in the last two months returned from the Continent.

That of course, she realised, explained why he had not known of the Countess's death and had not attended her Funeral or even sent a wreath.

He was also, she was informed by the housemaid, "a fine upstanding gentleman" but was used to commanding soldiers.

This information made Carmela certain that Felicity was right in saying that he was very autocratic and would not expect anyone to go against his wishes.

The housemaid went on talking about the old days, and Carmela sensed that the staff were nervous of the recent innovations, new ideas, and new duties that they had not had to undertake in the past.

All this seemed rather disturbing, and Carmela began to dislike the idea of meeting the Earl and being for even a short time under his jurisdiction.

If she had been doubtful whether Felicity had been wise in running away with Lord Salwick before they were married, she could not help feeling now that her friend might have risked her whole happiness if she had gone to Galeston as she had been ordered to do.

'I must be very careful not to be unmasked until Felicity and Jimmy are married,' Carmela thought.

She sent up a little prayer that Jimmy's mad wife would die soon and that Felicity, whom she loved, would be really happy with him.

The only thing that gave her any confidence was her new clothes.

The housemaids had been horrified that she should wear the same gown today as she had worn yesterday.

They had therefore unpacked a very attractive one of white muslin with a hem embroidered with mauve pansies and ribbons which matched her high-crowned bonnet.

Over it was a tight-fitting and very elegant coat of pale mauve silk with purple buttons and a velvet collar and cuffs in the same hue.

She thought it looked so fashionable that it might have come from Paris, and the maids thought the same.

"I wish you was stayin' here, M'Lady," they said, "so that we could see all your pretty clothes. It's a long time since we had any really smart ladies in the house."

"I expect the Earl will soon be giving parties," Carmela replied, for something to say.

"I hope so!" one of the housemaids exclaimed. "We finds it dismal being here with not much to do day after day, month after month. But as His Lordship's a young man, perhaps he'll be gettin' married."

As they spoke they looked at Carmela in a manner which made her think that they were visualising her as the Earl's bride.

Then she told herself that such an idea was ridiculous. After all, the Earl and Felicity were first cousins, and that was too close a relationship to be acceptable in most families.

"If he has a husband in mind for Felicity," Carmela told herself, "it will be another Gale who needs money, and I shall have to be very careful not to encourage anyone in case almost before I am aware of what is happening, I find myself married under false pretences!"

It was a frightening thought, but she was certain that she was upsetting herself unnecessarily even in considering it.

She knew it was fashionable to have long engagements, and in a month or two Jimmy's wife would be dead and then she would be free to disappear.

All the same, however calmly she tried to review the situation, however firmly she told herself there was no need to be agitated, her heart began to beat tumultuously as the housemaid exclaimed:

"We're here, M'Lady! Now you'll be able to see if you remember what a fine house Galeston is."

"As I was only five the last time I was here," Carmela replied, "I find it difficult to remember anything about it."

Nevertheless, when a few minutes later she saw that great house ahead of them, she thought that once they had seen it it would be impossible for anybody to forget such a magnificent building.

She had learnt from the Countess in the past that the house had originally been built on the site for a Cistercian Monastery, then altered, improved, and added to by every successive generation of Gales.

Felicity's grandfather in the last century had added a new facade to the house with high Corinthian columns and had bought statues and urns from Greece to ornament the top of the building.

The result was exceedingly impressive, and the house was so large that it made Carmela feel very small and insignificant and definitely apprehensive.

As if the horses which were pulling the very well-sprung carriage realised that they were home, they quickened their pace as they crossed the stone bridge over the lake with a swirl of wheels and drew up with a flourish outside the impressive front door.

There was a flight of steps leading up to it, and as the carriage arrived a red carpet was run down, and Carmela knew she was expected to walk on it to enter the house.

Feeling rather as if she were going to the guillotine, she stepped out of the carriage to see that the footmen in attendance wore powdered wigs with their elaborate livery, and each bowed to her politely as she passed them.

She smiled a little uncertainly in response, and on reaching the top of the steps she was greeted by the elderly Butler who looked like an Archbishop, and he said:

"Welcome home, M'Lady! It's a happy day for those of us who remember Your Ladyship to have you amongst us again."

"Thank you," Carmela replied. "I only wish my grandmother could be with me."

"That's what we all wishes, M'Lady, like it was in the good old days," the Butler said.

He led her through the great marble Hall with statues ornamenting it and some finely executed murals on the walls.

"His Lordship's expecting you, M'Lady. He'll join you in the Salon."

The Butler opened the door of a beautiful room hung with pictures, its windows looking out onto the garden filled with lilac and syringa.

"I will inform His Lordship of your arrival," the Butler said, then left her alone.

Carmela drew in her breath.

She found it difficult to take in much of the large room and instead walked to the window.

She had a sudden longing to be at home in the cottage with her father and to watch him paint one of his strange, mystical pictures. Nothing there would worry her except the problem of how to pay the bills they owed in the village.

Now that she was actually involved in this masquerade of deceiving the Earl into thinking she was Felicity, she thought that her position was not only perilous but exceedingly reprehensible.

How could she have agreed to act what was a lie when her mother had said a hundred times:

"Whoever we are, darling, it is a cowardly thing to evade the truth, and we should always be ready to face bravely whatever confronts us in life, however unpleasant."

"I am not lying for myself," Carmela protested to her conscience.

At the same time, she could not help feeling guilty, knowing that what she was doing, when it was exposed, would seem inexcusable.

She heard the door open and felt as if her heart had stopped beating. Then as she slowly turned round she saw the Earl walking towards her.

She was not quite certain how she had visualized him, but because Felicity hated him so violently and had described him in such venomous tones, she had expected someone grim and dark.

She was sure he would have a cruel face and in her mind he resembled the Roundheads whom she had always hated because they had beaten the Royalists.

Instead, the man advancing towards her was tall, slim, exceedingly handsome, and fashionably dressed.

At the same time, she was aware that he wore his clothes casually, as if they were not important, and she had the feeling that he would rather be attired in a uniform.

She could not think why she had such ideas, but as the Earl drew nearer and she saw him looking at her with what she thought were penetrating and critical eyes, she thought that after all he might be the ogre she had expected and Felicity had described.

"I am delighted to meet you, Cousin Felicity," the Earl said as he reached her side, and Carmela dropped him a curtsey.

210

She put out her hand as she did so, and as the Earl took it and she felt the strength of his fingers, she had the uncomfortable feeling that he was taking her captive and it would be difficult for her to escape from him.

"Have you had a good journey?" he asked.

"Yes, thank you," Carmela answered. "Your horses were very swift, and we did not linger on the way."

"Come and sit down," the Earl suggested, "and may I offer you some refreshment?"

"No, thank you."

"Luncheon will be ready in a short time. I am sure that you will wish to explore the place you have not seen for so many years."

"Yes, of course," Carmela agreed.

Because she was feeling shy, she was finding it difficult to look at the Earl.

But she was acutely conscious that his eyes were on her face and he seemed to be taking in not only her features but looking deep down inside her, as if already he suspected that she was not what she appeared to be.

Then she told herself she was being ridiculous.

She looked like Felicity, she was dressed like Felicity, and as none of the other Gales had seen her since she was five years old, why should they suspect for one moment that she was not who she said she was?

"I understand you are still in half-mourning for your grandmother," the Earl was saying. "I was not in England when she died, and it was only a month ago that I learnt you had been left alone."

Carmela did not speak. She merely inclined her head, thinking as she did so that that was when the Earl had learnt also of the vast fortune Felicity had been left.

Because he seemed to expect an answer, after a pause she replied in a low voice:

"I have been in France . . . staying with some of Grandmama's friends."

"In France?" the Earl questioned. "I learnt you were away from home, but I had not expected it to be abroad."

"Grandmama had French blood in her, and she had always wanted me to visit France, having very happy memories of it before the war."

"And what did you think of it now?" the Earl enquired.

"I loved the country and its people," Carmela answered evasively.

"They suffered greatly under Napoleon," he said. "We can only hope they will be able to reconstruct themselves as a nation and play their part in the restoration of Europe."

He spoke almost as if it mattered to him personally, and Carmela glanced at him, wanting to ask him a great deal more about France but feeling that it was a dangerous subject because she was actually so ignorant about it.

Instead she said:

"I have always heard how magnificent this house is, but it is even larger and more impressive than I expected."

The Earl smiled.

"That is what I felt too when I came back from Europe to take my place as head of the family."

He hesitated before he added:

"You realise that I am now your Guardian, Felicity, and as your Guardian I have plans for your future, which we will discuss later in the day. I am sure that now you would like to change before luncheon."

"Yes, of course," Carmela said, rising quickly to her feet.

The Earl walked beside her to the door and across the Hall to the foot of the stairs.

He glanced up and said:

"You will find the Housekeeper, Mrs. Humphries, who tells me she remembers your being born, waiting to show you to your room. I feel sure she will make you very comfortable."

"Thank you."

Carmela climbed the staircase, aware as she did so that she was glad to be leaving the Earl.

It was a comfort to be greeted effusively by Mrs. Humphries, who told her what a charming little girl she used to be and how much everybody on the Estate missed her grandmother.

"There's never been anybody like Her Ladyship," Mrs. Humphries said as she helped Carmela out of her travelling-clothes. "Like a Queen she looked, when there were parties here at Galeston. But there, I was only a young girl myself at the time and I thought the house itself was like a Palace."

"It is like one now!" Carmela said with a smile.

"We're only hoping His Lordship'll entertain and there'll be parties like there were in the old days," Mrs. Humphries said.

She went on to describe how sad and gloomy everything had been since the young Viscount had been killed in France, and her father had never recovered from the blow.

"His Lordship took it real bad, he did!" Mrs. Humphries said. "I used to wish you'd come back here to cheer him up. After all, M'Lady, you were his own flesh and blood, so to speak."

"I do not think it was ever suggested that I should come to him!" Carmela said.

She felt as if Mrs. Humphries was reproaching her for not being considerate towards her father. Then the Housekeeper replied:

"All this fighting amongst families is wrong, M'Lady, and that's a fact! It's bad enough when it's nation against nation, but when it's mother against son and the family is broken up, then it's not right, and nobody can tell me it is!"

"I quite agree with you," Carmela said.

"Well, now you're back, M'Lady, and although

your father is not here, God rest his soul, I feel sure you'll help His Lordship as no-one else can do."

Carmela was inclined to say that His Lordship seemed perfectly self-sufficient and would have no need of help from anybody.

The more she thought about him, the more she was convinced that he was a frightening man, although not exactly in the way that Felicity had led her to expect.

It was just that she knew she had to be on her guard with him, and she felt too that he was sizing her up.

She had to admit it was natural for him to be suspicious of somebody who had been isolated from the family for so many years, but she did not like it.

When she had changed into another of Felicity's lovely gowns, this one white, with the only touch of mourning being the little mauve slippers she wore with it and a mauve ribbon to match in her hair, Mrs. Humphries escorted her to the top of the stairs.

"You look a picture, M'Lady, that you do!" she said. "Now you make up your mind to enjoy yourself there as much as we'll all enjoy having you. Then everybody'll be happy!"

As she spoke Mrs. Humphries glanced over the bannisters down to the Hall below, and Carmela had the idea that she was looking down apprehensively in case the Earl was listening to her.

'Even the servants are afraid of him!' she thought, and wondered why.

Then she went down the stairs, conscious of the elegance of her gown, of her new hair-style, and of the slight dusting of powder on her small nose.

As a footman hurried across the Hall to open the door of the Salon for her, she heard voices and realised that the Earl was not alone.

It was something she had not expected, and instinctively she braced herself to meet more strangers, hoping that if they were relations she would not make any mistake or say something that would give her away.

Then as she entered the Salon she saw that standing at the far end of it and talking to the Earl was a young man, very gorgeously arrayed and looking exactly as she expected a Dandy would appear.

His cravat was dazzlingly white, tied in a complicated and tricky fashion, the points of his collar high above the line of his chin.

His coat fitted so tightly that it was almost as if he had been poured into it, and the same applied to his champagne-coloured pantaloons.

His Hessian boots with gold laces were dazzling, and as he moved his hand, the sunlight from the windows glittered on a jewelled ring.

As she walked down the length of the room she realised that the Earl and his companion had ceased speaking and were watching her approach.

She reached the Earl and he said:

"Let me present, Sir, my cousin Felicity Gale— Royal Highness Prince Frederich von Horngelstein!"

With a start Carmela remembered to curtsey, and the Prince bowed as he said in excellent English:

"I am delighted to make your acquaintance, My Lady!"

"My cousin has not been here at Galeston since she was a child," the Earl explained, "and she is finding the house as impressive as I do."

"It must certainly be a change after the dilapidated and uncomfortable billets you occupied during the war," the Prince remarked.

"That was certainly true of Portugal," the Earl replied, "but in your country, Sir, I was extremely comfortable."

"Which was more than I was!" the Prince said with a laugh.

Now that she was near him Carmela could see that there was a very foreign look about him which should have told her that he was not English the moment she saw him.

She wondered why he was there, then as the two men went on talking, she gathered that while the Earl was with the Army of Occupation after the cessation of hostilities he had been in the Prince's country.

She hurriedly tried to remember where Horngelstein was, and she thought it must be one of the small German Principalities overrun by Napoleon, which as far as she remembered were, under the Treaty of Vienna, being given back their Royal status.

However, she felt very ignorant about the situation and was thankful that for the moment the Earl and the Prince were content to talk to each other and were making little effort to include her in the conversation.

That was not to say that the Prince was prepared to ignore her.

All through the meal that followed Carmela was aware that his eyes were continually on her face. He seemed to be "sizing her up" just as the Earl had done and, as she said to herself, to be enumerating her good points.

She could not gather exactly why the Prince was in England, but it was evident that he was on very good terms with the Earl, and occasionally the Prince spoke to him in terms of admiration and, Carmela thought, of gratitude.

'The Earl has obviously helped the Prince to reinstate himself in his country,' she thought perceptively.

She decided that as soon as she had the opportunity she would find an Atlas to learn something about a country of which she knew nothing.

She thought the luncheon was excellent, and they were waited on by a large number of footmen.

The silver on the table was magnificent, and the Dining-Room itself was an extremely impressive room, hung with portraits of the Gale ancestors painted by famous artists.

'I wish Papa were with me,' Carmela thought to herself.

She knew he would be able not only to recognise most of the pictures but also to tell her amusing little anecdotes concerning the artists.

She remembered how he had once said to her when they were talking about pictures:

"What I would like to do is to take you with me to Florence or to Rome."

Carmela thought now she would be only too happy to have him here with her, as she knew from what the Countess had said that the Gales had a very fine collection of pictures not only by English but also by French and Dutch Masters.

She was thinking of her father when the Earl unexpectedly said:

"You look very serious, Felicity. Is anything worrying you?"

"No, indeed," Carmela replied. "I was thinking of your pictures."

"When I get back the collection stolen by Napoleon and taken to Paris," the Prince said before the Earl could speak, "I think you will find them not only beautiful but containing some very fine examples of mediaeval art that will be interesting to you."

"All pictures interest me," Carmela replied. "You say your collection was stolen . . . will there be any difficulty in getting it back now that the war is over?"

"That is what I am trying to find out," the Prince replied, "and I need His Lordship's help to make sure I am not cheated by the French Government."

"I have already spoken to the Duke of Wellington about your problem," the Earl said, "and he has promised me he will do everything in his power to see that justice is done."

"That is all I ask," the Prince replied, "and I think, My Lady, you will agree that justice is something we are all entitled to after the horrors and privations of war."

"Of course," Carmela agreed. "I hope Your Royal Highness will be fortunate in your quest."

"With your help I will make sure of it," the Prince replied.

Carmela looked at him wide-eyed. She felt she could not have heard him aright.

Then she supposed that he was in fact only expecting her to support her cousin in finding his treasures and having them returned to their rightful country.

When luncheon was ended they moved not to the Salon but to a large, impressive Library. The Prince made an excuse to leave, and the Earl and Carmela were left alone.

Carmela was not attending to what was being said but was looking round the Library with delight.

She felt there was so much here she wanted to read. The first book she needed was an Atlas, which she hoped would be quite easy to find.

Therefore, as the door closed behind the Prince, she said to the Earl:

"As I am lamentably ignorant as to where His Royal Highness's country is, do you think I could find an Atlas among this magnificent collection of books?"

"I am sure there is one," the Earl replied. "I will see if I can find the catalogue."

As he spoke he walked towards a table on which there were some books and papers, saying as he did so:

"I am delighted to learn that you are interested in Horngelstein."

"I am interested to know where it is and what sort of people live there. I presume from the name they speak German."

"Horngelstein is on the border of Germany and France, and the people are half-German and half-French," the Earl replied. "You will find them charming, anxious to be friendly, and very happy that the war has ended."

"Like a great many other people," Carmela remarked.

The Earl was turning over the papers on the table, then at last he exclaimed:

"Oh, here is the catalogue! I thought there must be one, although the last Curator has retired."

He looked up what he wanted in the catalogue, then handed Carmela a book covered in red leather. She set it down on the flat-topped writing-table which was almost in the centre of the room and opened it.

She turned over the pages until she came to a map depicting Europe, and the Earl pointed to a small country low down on the border of France and said:

"That is Horngelstein. Your future country!"

Carmela was very still. Then she asked after a moment:

"D-did you say . . . *my* country?"

"I thought you would have guessed by now why the Prince is here."

Carmela raised her eyes to the Earl's face as she said:

"I . . . I do not . . . understand what you are . . . saying to me."

"Then let me make it clear," the Earl replied. "As your Guardian I have arranged for you to marry—in fact a very brilliant match from your point of view— His Royal Highness Prince Frederich!"

Carmela felt her anger rising.

"You have arranged . . . this without . . . asking for my . . . permission to do so?"

"I cannot believe you would object."

She thought there was a note of genuine surprise in the Earl's voice, and she said quickly:

"But of course I object! Can you believe that I, or any other woman, would want to marry a man she had never met before and has talked to for only a few minutes?"

The Earl stared at her as if he could not believe what she was saying. Then he said:

"I never imagined you would not be delighted to be a reigning Princess."

"Why ever should you think that?" Carmela answered. "Although you may not be aware of it, women have feelings like everybody else!"

For a moment the Earl seemed to have difficulty in finding words in which to express himself. Then he said:

"I may have been mistaken, but I always understood that young girls had their marriages arranged for them by their parents, and that they accepted what was proposed without argument."

Carmela was uncomfortably aware that this was more or less the truth.

Jimmy Salwick had been pressured into marriage when he was young because his and the bride's parents had thought it advantageous for them both, and there had been no question of their being in love with each other.

She remembered too that Felicity had talked of her friends who had been married to men for whom they had a positive aversion, and they had not been able to avoid it.

Now she understood that Felicity had been afraid to come to Galeston just because this sort of thing could happen, and as the Earl was her Guardian, there would have been nothing she could do to prevent it.

Carmela knew she must fight not only because she was not the heiress the Earl believed her to be, but also because her father and mother had encouraged her to think for herself.

Even if the Prince had really wanted to marry Carmela Lyndon, a girl of no consequence, she would not accept him or any other man in such a high-handed manner.

She thought now that Felicity had been absolutely

right in saying that the Gales were ruthless and dominating.

Although it was not a Gale whom she was expected
to marry, she was certain from what had been said at
luncheon that the Prince needed money desperately
for his country, which had been ravaged by war.

That was why the Earl was arranging his marriage
to a very wealthy young woman.

Carmela knew that the Earl was staring at her in a
puzzled manner, and if she had not been in such an
uncomfortable situation it might almost have been
amusing.

"Perhaps," he conceded after a moment, "I should
have broken this to you more gently. But let me assure you that the Prince is a very charming man
whom I know well. He has suffered the humiliation
and misery of having his country overrun by the
French, his Palace pilfered, and other unpleasant in-
cidents such as always happen in wartime."

"I presume he is also in need of money!"

"Of course," the Earl agreed, "and I can imagine
no better way of spending your vast fortune, Felicity,
than by assisting this charming and able young man
and making his people happy."

Carmela did not speak for a moment and he
went on:

"The country needs Schools and Hospitals, and
Churches have to be rebuilt. I am certain you would
find it of absorbing interest."

"To be married to a man I do not know?" Carmela
enquired.

"I have told you he is charming."

"That may be your opinion," she said, "but you do
not have to live with him in a strange country surrounded by strangers."

"I am sure you will soon make friends with the
Prince and his countrymen," the Earl replied pa-
tiently.

"Perhaps, if I really wished to," Carmela retorted.

"But let me make it very clear, My Lord, that I have no intention of marrying at the moment, and certainly not a foreign Prince whom I met only an hour ago!"

The Earl put the catalogue down on the table with a slam and walked towards her.

"This is ridiculous, Felicity!" he said. "I consider it very wrong of you to take up this attitude. I have already apologised for being slightly precipitate, but you must be well aware that you have to be married sooner or later, and I have no wish to see you pursued by fortune-hunters."

"What else is the Prince?"

She was too angry at the moment to feel frightened.

She was thinking how fortunate it was that Felicity was on her way to France with Jimmy and was not here to fight frantically against the Earl, who she could see was growing angry too.

There was an expression in his eyes and a squareness of his chin that told her that he was as obstinate and determined as she had always been told the Gales were when opposed.

She and the Earl stood defying each other, and because he was so tall and broad-shouldered and towered above her, Carmela could not help feeling rather overwhelmed.

But because she knew she was in the fortunate position of being not Felicity but her poor, poverty-stricken self, she could fight for what she believed were the right principles in the whole argument, knowing that when it came to a real "show-down" the Prince would not wish to marry her because she actually had no money.

"It is, in my opinion," she said, "absolutely wrong that any woman should be sold over the counter as if she were a piece of merchandise. As I have already said, we have feelings, and I personally would not

222

marry any man, however important he might be, unless I . . . loved him and . . . he loved me."

"You astound me!" the Earl said. "And if it comes to that, how are you ever to know, with your fortune, whether a man loves you for yourself or for your money?"

Carmela was silent for a moment. Then she said:

"I think that love . . . real love . . . would be impossible to disguise or pretend! And unless one was very stupid one would not be taken in by compliments that were prompted only by greed, or loving words that were . . . insincere."

Because for the moment he could not think of an answer, the Earl walked away from her towards the window to stand looking out onto the Park.

After a long silence he said:

"I suppose that because I am very ignorant of young women, having never had much to do with them, I never anticipated for a moment that you would not accept my decision that this was in your best interests. In fact, I believed I was doing you a favour."

"A favour which is actually an insult to my intelligence!"

"I always believed that when they came out of the School-Room, girls were gauche and nit-witted," the Earl said, "but you are obviously neither of those things!"

"You never met my grandmother, but you must have heard of her," Carmela replied. "The old servants here have never forgotten her, and I can assure you that living with her was better than being educated at any of the finest Universities."

The Earl gave a short laugh.

"Now I begin to understand why the relations with whom I have been in contact since I inherited have always referred to the quarrel between your father and his mother as if it were a world-shattering epic."

"That is what it must have been to them. She left

here vowing she would never return, and she made a life for herself elsewhere."

"As you went with her, I presume you will grow up to be as awe-inspiring and determined as she was!" the Earl remarked.

"I sincerely hope so," Carmela replied.

As she spoke she thought how much she had admired and loved the Countess. It was the absolute truth to say that being with her was an education in itself, and both she and Felicity had been very lucky in knowing such a remarkable woman.

There was silence. Then the Earl said:

"You are only eighteen, Felicity. However well educated you may be, your grandmother is dead, and as I am now your Guardian you will have to obey me."

"And if I refuse to do so?"

"Then I shall have to find means, which I have no wish to do, to force you to acknowledge my authority."

Carmela smiled scornfully.

"What are you suggesting?" she asked. "Locking me up in the dungeon, if the house has one? Starving or beating me into submission? Or simply dragging me screaming to the altar?"

She spoke mockingly, and because her voice was very soft and musical it did not sound as aggressive as it might have done.

There was silence. Then the Earl said:

"I think it is rather easier than that. I believe that as your Guardian I have the use of your money and the spending of it until you are twenty-one."

Carmela thought frantically that if this was so, he might be able to prevent Felicity from drawing on her Bank Accounts, and it would be difficult to warn her that this might happen.

She tried to think of what she could do or what she could say, but she had the feeling that the Earl, having had the last word, was aware of her discomfiture and was gloating over it.

'I hate him!' she thought.

At the same time, she knew he had out-witted her for the moment and she must be very, very careful not to do Felicity any harm.

There was silence for a long time, then at last the Earl turned from the window and came back towards her.

"I think, Felicity," he said, "we are both being rather precipitate in drawing our daggers so quickly and fighting each other without a thought as to who might be injured in the process."

Carmela looked at him but did not speak, and he said:

"Shall we start again? I will apologise for acting too quickly and ask you instead to consider my proposition without committing yourself one way or the other."

Carmela was well aware that while he was conceding her a small victory, at the same time the battle was by no means over, and she was quite certain that he had every intention of being the victor in the end.

However, because it was an olive-branch which she thought it wise to accept, she said in a low voice:

"It is true that you took me by surprise, but if I can, as you suggest, consider this proposition and get to know the Prince a great deal better than I do at the moment . . . perhaps I shall come to think . . . differently."

As she finished speaking she thought that the Earl was smiling in a self-satisfied way.

"At the same time," she said quickly, "you will understand that as Grandmama has not been dead for very long and I am still in mourning for her, it would be impossible for me to think of being married for some months."

There was a frown on the Earl's forehead, and she realised that he had not thought of this before, any more than she had until this very minute.

"I cannot believe," he said after a second or so,

"that your grandmother would wish you to mourn unnecessarily long."

"I think how long one mourns depends more on what one's feelings are than on what is laid down in the social code," Carmela replied in a deceptively soft voice.

"I can understand that," the Earl agreed. "At the same time, Felicity, I want you to think of the good you can do with your fortune, the people who will benefit by your generosity, and what I genuinely believe will be the happiness you will find with a very remarkable and delightful young man."

"I will certainly think about it," Carmela answered.

The Earl held out his hand.

"That is all I want to hear," he said. "In the meantime, shall we try to be friends? We really cannot start another war amongst the Gales."

Because there was nothing else she could do, Carmela put her hand in his, and once again she was conscious of the strength of his fingers.

At the same time, she felt that he was drawing her, compelling her, and she would have to fight to resist him.

CHAPTER FOUR

Coming down the stairs for dinner dressed in a beautiful gown, Carmela thought that if she were not so frightened of doing something which might have repercussions on Felicity, the situation would actually be rather amusing.

Because the Earl had called a truce, he was going out of his way to be charming and to treat her like an intelligent woman instead of a brainless School-girl.

For the last two days she had realised the effort he was making, and she felt it was perhaps the first time in his life that he had had to consider a woman's feelings rather than his own.

Now he included her in any conversation he had with the Prince and asked her opinion and even listened to what she had to say.

She was quite certain that what he normally expected was to lay down the law and have everybody obey him.

However, protocol and good manners compelled him to defer to the Prince, although it was obvious that the younger man had so much admiration for him that it amounted almost to adoration.

Therefore, Carmela was left to balance the situation, and when she could be herself without being afraid of involving Felicity, she began to enjoy the cut and thrust of the dialogues she had with the Earl, which were almost as if they fenced with each other.

She knew that she surprised him with her knowledge of art, for in fact she knew more about pictures than he did.

What astonished him even more was that she also had a good grasp of the political situation in Europe.

This she owed not to her father, who of course had taught her about art, but to the Countess, who because of her long acquaintance with Statesmen and Politicians had always been interested in everything that was happening not only abroad but in Parliament at home.

Every day Carmela and Felicity had been made to read aloud the Members' speeches which were reported in *The Times* and *The Morning Post*.

The Countess would then explain to them what

they did not understand, and because she knew so many of the speakers, she would also give them a "thumb-nail sketch" of the Political Leaders on both sides of the House.

Felicity had found it rather boring, but to Carmela it was always extremely interesting, and she used her knowledge now to surprise and, she knew, bewilder the Earl.

"Why should he think all young girls are stupid?" she asked herself indignantly, and set out to prove that he had no grounds for thinking so.

Last night when they had had a spirited argument about the reforms that were sadly overdue to improve the lot of the farming community, the Earl had said:

"I may have been out of England for a long time, but I cannot believe that things are as bad as you say they are."

"Unfortunately, they are even worse," Carmela replied. "Cheap food from Europe is now beginning to flood the market, and it looks like the farmers in England are about to go bankrupt."

She saw by the expression on the Earl's face that he did not believe her, and she added:

"Ask how many Country Banks closed their doors last year, and if you talk to your tenant farmers rather than to those you employ, you will find they are fighting desperately to keep their heads above water."

The Earl was silent for a moment. Then he said:

"I thought young ladies like yourself were too busy dancing to know about the sufferings of the labouring class."

"We can still see with our eyes and hear with our ears," Carmela replied. "In the same way, Your Lordship might look at the condition of men who were crippled in the war and see how they are faring in a country that has given them no pension since they were dismissed from the Services and apparently expects them to live by begging in the streets."

Because she was angry at the sufferings she had seen even in Huntingdonshire and had read in reports in the newspapers, she spoke aggressively and her eyes flashed in a way which the Earl thought was extremely attractive.

He glanced at the Prince, hoping that he was not only listening to Carmela but admiring her, and realised he was looking down at his plate and crumbling a piece of bread absent-mindedly as he did so.

"What is worrying you, Sir?" the Earl asked.

The Prince started, as if his thoughts were far away. Then he replied after a pause:

"I was thinking that if these things are occurring in a rich, prosperous country like England, what must be happening in Horngelstein?"

There was silence and Carmela knew the Earl was thinking that the answer to this question was that soon he would have Lady Felicity's fortune to expend for the benefit of his subjects in need.

Because this was a dangerous topic, she said quickly:

"Let us talk of something more amusing for His Royal Highness. I am sure he should really be in London at this time of the year, attending the parties which the Prince Regent is giving at Carlton House."

"Have you ever been to one?" the Prince asked.

Carmela shook her head.

"I was to have been presented to the Queen this year at Buckingham Palace," she replied, "if my grandmother had not died."

"That must have been very disappointing for you."

"It was far more disastrous to lose my grandmother, who was a very remarkable person."

She glanced at the Earl from under her eye-lashes and said provocatively:

"She was clever, besides having too much personality for the Gale family! However, they will never know how much they missed in losing her for all those years after she left here."

"You can hardly blame me for that," the Earl said in an amused tone.

"Grandmama always said the Gales were obstinate, dogmatic, and very reluctant to see anybody else's point of view but their own."

The Earl laughed.

"Is that what you think of me?"

"I would not be so impolite to my host as to accuse him of any of those characteristics," Carmela said demurely. "But of course you are a Gale!"

"And so are you," he retorted.

"There is always a black sheep in every flock."

"Is that what you would call yourself?" he challenged. "I can think of much more flattering descriptions."

"And so can I," the Prince interposed. "You are very beautiful, Lady Felicity, as I expect dozens of men have told you."

His words sounded too smooth to be sincere, and Carmela looking at him knew that he admired her, but she was also sure that he was not in the least enamoured of her.

As she thought about it, she had the feeling that often when he appeared to be engrossed in the conversation and was even paying her compliments, some part of him was elsewhere, and she was determined to find out if she was right.

The opportunity came after dinner when the gentlemen joined her in the Salon, then almost immediately the Earl was called away.

The Butler had come and said something in his ear, whereupon he rose, murmured his apologies, and followed the servant from the room.

"I wonder what has happened," Carmela remarked.

"Does it matter?" the Prince asked.

Carrying a glass of brandy in his hand, he sat down beside her on the sofa and said:

"Now I can talk to you. I sometimes feel as if our

host, admirable though he is, is much too efficient a chaperone."

"Surely we have nothing to say to each other that the Earl could not overhear."

"That is not true," the Prince contradicted. "I would prefer to talk to you alone, Lady Felicity, and it is very difficult to make love to you in the presence of an audience."

Carmela quickly looked away from him.

"That is something I do not wish to hear," she said. "We have only . . . just met, Your Royal Highness . . . and as you are doubtless aware . . . although I would like to be your friend . . . there is no question of . . . anything else between us."

She spoke hesitatingly because she was choosing her words with care, and after a moment the Prince said:

"You know that your Guardian has agreed that you should marry me?"

"So he told me, and I informed him that I would not marry a man unless I was in love with him."

The Prince put his glass of brandy down on the small table by the side of the sofa, then bent forward to take Carmela's hand in his.

She stiffened because she did not like his touching her, and he said:

"Both I and my country need you as my wife."

"What you are really saying," Carmela replied, "is that you need my . . . fortune to repair the ravages of war."

She thought the Prince might be offended and went on quickly:

"It is a very great honour that Your Highness should wish to marry me . . . at the same time, because I am an ordinary English girl, I want to marry someone I love and who . . . loves me."

"And you do not think you would come to love me when we know each other better?" the Prince asked.

"That might possibly happen," Carmela agreed,

"but I cannot help feeling, and I know Your Highness will forgive me if I am wrong, that your heart is already given elsewhere."

It was a bold venture, but at the same time Carmela was almost certain she was right and that the Prince was often thinking wistfully of somebody who was not present.

At her words he started, and instead of dropping her hand his fingers tightened on them almost as if he needed her support.

"Why should you say that?" he asked.

"I just feel that you are thinking of somebody else," she replied, "and that she means a great deal to you."

The Prince gave a deep sigh.

"You are—how do you say?—clairvoyant!"

"Then it is true?"

He nodded.

"And it is impossible for you to marry her?" Carmela asked softly.

The Prince sighed again.

"That is what I want to do," he said, "but to tell the truth, I am a coward."

"A coward?" Carmela questioned.

Again his fingers seemed to grip her hand as if he drew strength from her, before he said:

"She means everything in the world to me! But she is—French!"

There was a little pause. Then Carmela said:

"I understand. After what your country has suffered from Napoleon Bonaparte, your people would not willingly accept a Princess who is of that nationality."

"I think perhaps they might do so in time," the Prince said, "and if there was no alternative."

Carmela felt that she understood.

"What Your Royal Highness is saying," she said, "is that when my cousin suggested that you needed a rich wife, you did not dare tell him you had any other ideas."

"You understand," the Prince murmured.

"Of course I understand," Carmela said, "and you must be brave and marry the woman you love and not be pressured into taking a wife who has been chosen for you by somebody else."

"It is difficult for me not to do what has been suggested first by your cousin, who was commanding the Army of Occupation in my country, and also by the Council of Ministers in Vienna," the Prince said.

"They may think they have the solution to your problems on paper," Carmela answered. "But for a country to be happy, it is necessary for the man who rules over it to be happy too."

"If only I could believe that," the Prince said.

"Will you tell me about this lady whom you love?" Carmela asked softly.

"Her father is a distinguished Frenchman who lived in France just at the border with Horngelstein. Until Napoleon became the Emperor and started to dominate the whole of Europe, we were happy with both the French and the other countries to the north and east of us."

"That is something which will happen again now that Napoleon is defeated and a prisoner on St. Helena," Carmela said.

"I am sure you are right," the Prince agreed, "but in the meantime your cousin, when he came to rescue us from the last pockets of opposition maintained by Napoleon's Troops, not only put me back on the throne but promised every help he could give me in reconstructing our industries and relieving the most poverty-stricken of my subjects."

Carmela thought how much the Earl would enjoy reorganising the whole country and setting it, as he thought, to rights, but aloud she said:

"I have always found that people who think they know what is best for us are somewhat overbearing, and if we have any character at all, we have to decide things for ourselves when they matter personally."

233

"That is what I have wanted to do," the Prince said in a low voice, "but Gabrielle told me I must think of Horngelstein and forget her."

"If she said that," Carmela said, "then I am sure she really loves you."

"Do you think so?" the Prince asked eagerly.

"But of course!" Carmela replied. "If a woman really loves a man with her whole heart, she tries to do what is right for him, whatever the sacrifice for herself."

As she spoke she was sure that for any woman, especially one who was French, a race always very conscious of rank and title, to give up a throne could mean only one thing—Gabrielle loved the Prince too much to hurt him.

"It is what I would feel myself," Carmela thought, and she went on:

"What you must do is to go back to the woman you love and ask her if she is brave enough to face those of your countrymen who will still be hostile to France, and help you to set things to rights in your own way."

"They will come to love her as I do," the Prince said. "I am sure of that."

"As some of your subjects have French blood in them," Carmela said, "I am sure it will not be as difficult as you think it will be!"

She paused before she continued:

"I have read in the newspapers that Europe is desperately short of all sorts of materials, implements, tools, and other necessities which were not manufactured during the war because every effort was directed to producing weapons."

"That is true," the Prince agreed.

"There must be many things that you could make in Horngelstein," Carmela suggested. "I am sure if you ask for a loan from England or from those who are trying to reorganise European affairs in Vienna, they would give you one to enable you at least to start the wheels turning and your people working."

The Prince lifted her hand to his lips.

"Thank you, thank you!" he said. "You have given me new heart, and now, thanks to you, I will try to behave like a man."

He gave a deep sigh as if a burden had fallen from his shoulders as he said:

"I am ashamed that I listened when your cousin tempted me with the suggestion that a very rich wife would solve all my problems. He said he would find one for me and made it sound so easy and so plausible that I thought I was doing the right thing in sacrificing myself and my own feelings for the good of my country. Now I realise I was just being weak, and what you would call—inefficient."

Carmela gave a little laugh.

She was thinking of how the Countess had always said that when the Gales were determined about something they let nothing and nobody stand in their way.

"What has really happened," she said, "is that you have been listening to the smooth talk of a salesman who is absolutely convinced that his goods are the best, but has not really given you the chance to express your own needs."

The Prince laughed.

"I think you are being unkind to your cousin. At the same time, he is rather overpowering."

"All the Gales are the same."

"Except you," the Prince said, "and I find you not only adorable but inspiring."

Once again he took Carmela's hand and kissed it and said:

"Thank you, thank you! I think you are very beautiful, one of the most attractive women I have ever met, and I want you to meet my Gabrielle."

"I shall be very delighted to do so," Carmela replied.

"We will reconstruct my country together," the Prince said with a light in his eyes and a note of joy in his voice that had not been there before, "and when you come to stay with us, Lady Felicity, you will be astounded at what we have achieved!"

"I am sure I shall," Carmela replied with a laugh.

Then as if the Prince suddenly remembered the Earl, he looked nervously towards the door before he said:

"What am I to say to your cousin? If I have to tell him that I have changed my mind, he will be very angry and perhaps insulted."

Carmela thought for a moment. Then she said:

"Can you not tell him you have received a communication from your Chancellor or your Prime Minister asking you to return immediately to Horngelstein because there is a crisis of some sort?"

The Prince did not speak, but he was listening and Carmela went on:

"You can tell him you will only be going away for a few days, perhaps a week. But in fact you must immediately go and see the lady you love and make arrangements for your wedding."

As she spoke Carmela gave a little cry and clasped her hands together.

"Do you not see," she said, "that a Royal wedding, whoever the bride may be, will excite and cheer up the people of your country when they are feeling low and depressed after the privations of wartime."

She smiled as she went on:

"The women will all want new gowns in which to celebrate such a romantic event, and if you tell them eloquently how much you love your future wife, I know that whatever her nationality they will want you to be happy."

As she spoke she thought that the mere fact that the Prince was in love would evoke a response in all the young people, especially the women. If he and Gabrielle handled the situation diplomatically, they would soon overcome any opposition there might be to their marriage.

"You are right, I am sure you are right!" the Prince said fervently.

He thought for a moment, then he said:

"As it happens I did receive some letters today. A courier brought them down from our Embassy in London, but they were not of any particular importance."

"The Earl is not to know that."

Carmela thought again before she said:

"You could say that you did not want to spoil the evening by telling him this earlier. And then, to prevent him from suspecting anything, you could go on to tell him that you have had an interesting conversation with me while we were alone, and I have promised that we will have a further talk on the position between us when you return."

It took a moment for the Prince to assimilate exactly what she was saying. Then he smiled and his eyes twinkled.

"That is very diplomatic, Lady Felicity," he said, "and will allay any suspicion the Earl may have as to why I am going back."

"Yes, of course," Carmela said. "It would be a mistake to let him think you are running away."

The Prince laughed, and it was a very young, boyish sound.

"You are magnificent! Perhaps after all I am making a great mistake in not insisting that you marry me and rule over my country in the manner of Catherine the Great!"

"There is nothing you would dislike more!" Carmela said. "And I am sure, without meaning to flatter Your Royal Highness, that you will be a very good and popular Monarch."

"Thank you," the Prince said, "thank you! It is difficult for me to tell you what you have done for me and how different I feel about the future."

"You will think I am being clairvoyant again when I tell you that you will be very happy with your

Gabrielle," Carmela said, "and that together you will make Horngelstein a very prosperous country."

"I hope so! I sincerely hope so!" the Prince replied. "I shall strive by every means in my power to make your words come true."

As he was speaking he was holding Carmela's hands in both of his and thanking her with a sincerity which she knew came from the very bottom of his heart.

She was smiling at him and he at her when the door opened and the Earl came in.

Because she was facing in that direction she saw him before the Prince did and was aware that he must have noticed their position on the sofa and that their hands were linked.

She was sure that he would put the wrong construction on it and she could see an expression of satisfaction on his face as he walked towards them.

The Prince released Carmela's hand and rose to his feet.

"I have just been telling Lady Felicity, My Lord," he said, "the disappointing news that I have to return to Horngelstein for a few days."

"You are leaving us?" the Earl asked.

"It is something that indeed I have no wish to do," the Prince went on, "but I have had a letter from my Prime Minister this morning, begging me to return to settle a small constitutional crisis which concerns the throne."

He sighed realistically before he added:

"It is something which necessitates my personal attention but will not take long. I hope to be back within a week."

There had been a frown on the Earl's forehead, but now it vanished as he said:

"I shall miss you, Sir, and I very much hope you will hurry back as quickly as possible."

"As I was telling the lovely Lady Felicity," the Prince said, "it is something I am very eager to do."

He smiled at Carmela in a flirtatious manner which made her want to laugh.

Instead, she said in a commiserative tone:

"It is so tiresome for Your Royal Highness, but from all I hear it is now much easier than it was to travel through France, especially at this time of the year."

"That is true," the Prince agreed, "and if I leave first thing tomorrow morning I shall hope to be back here at the end of next week."

"We will be looking forward to your return," Carmela said, "will we not, Cousin Selwyn?"

"Yes, indeed," the Earl replied. "I will arrange for my fastest horses to carry you to Dover, where my yacht will be ready to take you across the Channel. This will be far quicker than if you have to wait for the ordinary ships that now make the crossing, I believe, twice a day."

"You are very kind," the Prince said. "It is really impossible to express my gratitude for all you have done for me."

"Then please do not try," the Earl said hastily. "I will go and make arrangements for your journey, and as you suggest, it would be wise for you to leave early."

He walked towards the door as he spoke, and immediately he was out of earshot the Prince said to Carmela:

"It worked! It really worked!"

"Of course," she replied, "but be very careful not to arouse in any way his suspicions that you are not intending to return."

"No, of course not," the Prince agreed.

Then as if the thought struck him he asked:

"Will you tell him after I have gone that I will not be coming back?"

"Not unless I have to," Carmela replied. "I have no wish for his wrath to fall on my head until it is completely unavoidable."

"He has been very kind and helpful," the Prince said. "I dislike having to deceive him. At the same time . . ."

"Your future is yours, not his," Carmela interposed before he could finish the sentence.

As she spoke she thought it would do the Earl a lot of good for his plan to go awry.

"He is far too busy interfering in other people's affairs," she told herself.

She thought again how fortunate it was that she could lose nothing by defying the Earl and how very different it might have been for Felicity if, in ignorance that the Prince's heart was elsewhere, she had been forced into marrying him.

'It was lucky I guessed,' Carmela thought, and she knew that her perception, or her clairvoyance, as the Prince had called it, was something she had been born with. It was an instinct, or perhaps a talent, that Felicity did not have.

'Well, the Prince will be happy,' she thought, 'and I can play for time until Felicity is married.'

She and the Prince talked of other things until the Earl returned, and once again as he came in through the door and saw their heads together he was bound to think that his plans were going smoothly and they were becoming attached to each other.

Only when the Prince had said good-night and gone to his own room to make sure, as he said, that everything was packed to his satisfaction, were Carmela and the Earl alone together.

"It is extremely annoying," he remarked, "that Prince Frederich should have to leave us just when I thought you two were getting along so well together."

"He is a handsome young man," Carmela said, "and more intelligent than I suspected."

"That sounds a very pompous remark from a girl of your age," the Earl said scathingly.

"You have funny ideas about age," Carmela replied. "May I point out, as you do not seem to be aware of it, that there is no yard-stick by which one can measure people's intelligence, since year by year they develop in different ways."

"I am aware of that," the Earl said.

"Then you should also be aware that some women at thirty are nothing but frivolous, empty-headed fools, while a girl even of my age can sometimes have an intelligent thought in her head."

The Earl laughed.

"When you snarl at me like a small tiger-cat," he said, "your eyes flash sparks of fire and I am dazzled by your ferocity."

"I am sorry if it is something that disconcerts you."

"On the contrary, I find it intriguing," the Earl replied, "just as it obviously intrigues our Royal guest also. But now that he is leaving us, I have to make a decision as to what to do about you until he returns."

"There are horses to ride, and much of the Estate I have still not seen," Carmela said.

"I am in a similar position," the Earl answered, "but what I am really asking is if you wish to be entertained by members of the family, who will be only too eager and curious to make your acquaintance, or by my neighbours, who I believe have called on me but whom I have not yet met."

Because she thought that would be dangerous, Carmela said quickly and insistently:

"Oh, please let us be alone! I have no wish at the moment to be cross-questioned about Grandmama by other members of her family, and as the weather is so lovely you surely do not wish to sit indoors making polite chit-chat to folk who will be extremely curious about you."

"God forbid!" the Earl said fervently. "And now that I think about it, they might consider it very strange that you are staying here without being chaperoned by some elderly relative."

Carmela knew they would think it even stranger if

241

they were aware that she was not who she pretended to be.

Because she thought an elderly Chaperone would be a tremendous bore, she said quickly:

"Quite frankly, I imagine you are in the same position as if I were staying here with my father, and even the Gales could not object to that!"

The Earl laughed.

"The way you say 'even the Gales' tells me exactly what you think about them."

"I know what they thought about Grandmama," Carmela flashed.

"It was certainly no worse than what she thought about them," the Earl said. "I can only hope that you will not think the same."

"As you are the only Gale I have met so far, I will let you know my feelings when they become clarified in my mind."

"You are making me apprehensive!" the Earl said mockingly.

"I am not breaking our truce," Carmela said quickly.

"I should hope not," he replied. "Besides, I am content as things are, and very hopeful of what may be."

Carmela knew he was referring to the Prince, and because she thought it would lull him into a sense of security, she looked down in what she hoped was a coy, shy manner, her eye-lashes very dark against her pale cheeks.

There was silence, then while she was wondering what the Earl was thinking, he suddenly said:

"You are very beautiful, Felicity, and with the incredible fortune you possess, the Prince is a fool to leave now, without your promise in his pocket."

"It will not be for very long," Carmela said after a moment.

"I know," the Earl replied. "At the same time, I suppose I am afraid that the Archangel Gabriel may drop down out of the sky and carry you away, or there may be another even more advantageous offer for your hand, which I would find it hard to reject."

Carmela laughed.

"I think it is unlikely, My Lord, that the Archangel Gabriel will appear. But perhaps Apollo might offer me a seat in his chariot as he rides across the sky, and I would certainly find it hard to refuse him."

"Apollo's horses are no faster than mine," the Earl boasted, "and I will promise the Prince they will be waiting for him at Dover on his return, so that you will not have a chance to escape him."

"You sound as if you are certain I shall try."

"You are deliberately provoking me into saying I shall shut you up and keep you my prisoner," the Earl remarked.

"That would be an unusual experience," Carmela answered, "and will undoubtedly depend on who the gaoler might be."

She looked up at the Earl to see his reaction as they duelled once again with each other.

Then incredibly she was aware with a perception which could not be denied that he thought she was flirting with him.

The next morning, Carmela realised as she awoke that she was thinking of the Earl in the same way as she had when she had gone to sleep.

She had chuckled to herself then, because it had seemed to her absolutely absurd that the Earl should for one moment think that she was trying to attract him.

The idea had never been in her mind, but she supposed it was not an unreasonable one, considering that despite his overwhelming personality he was in fact a very presentable and attractive man.

"How could he think, how could he imagine for

one moment, that his cousin Felicity would think about him in such a way?" Carmela asked herself.

Then she told herself that if the Earl could imagine that she was considering him as a man, it would make him more eager than he was already to marry her off and get her out of the way.

She was well aware what sort of woman the Earl found attractive, and from all he had said it was quite obvious that it would not be a young girl.

When Carmela thought it over, she decided that it was really insulting that he should expect to find her a complacent nit-wit who would carry out his instructions immediately he gave them without having a thought in her head, or being able to express herself only by saying "yes" to everything he suggested.

When she thought back over the conversations of the last few days, she realised that he had been unable to hide his surprise whenever she said anything intelligent or argued with him in a manner which made him exert his own brain.

It would be a very good thing, she thought, if she could teach him a lesson in some way which would stop him from being so opinionated in the future.

As she thought it over, she knew that it would indeed be a lesson when he learnt that the Prince would not return and intended to marry the French-woman Gabrielle, about whom presumably the Earl had never heard.

'It will certainly surprise him, especially when I tell him that I knew the truth all along,' Carmela thought with satisfaction.

She wished she had not to wait for so long before she could score off the Earl and make him realise that he had been wrong in planning to marry her off to suit his own ends.

'I daresay he has been commended for his admirable powers of organisation when he was in the Army,' she thought scornfully, and wondered exactly what he had put in his reports to the Duke of Wellington.

"Well, he was wrong! Wrong! Wrong!" she told herself. "Just as he was wrong about Felicity! And he was not prepared to listen when I tried to argue with him about it."

Dressed in her riding-habit, she went downstairs, looking as she went at the portraits of the Gale ancestors on the wall, who seemed to be watching her defiantly, and lifting her chin she defied them in return.

She had arranged to ride with the Earl at ten o'clock. She had in fact been ready earlier, but she thought it would be a mistake if she was downstairs waiting for him rather than that he should wait for her.

However, he was not in the Hall, but she saw him outside patting the horses and talking to the groom who was holding a very fine animal which was intended for her.

The Lyndons had never been able to afford expensive or well-bred animals, no more than a hunter for her father and another horse which her mother rode.

But Carmela had been fortunate in that she could ride the horses at the Castle, and she had been taught by the same Riding-Master as Felicity and knew that her deportment on a horse was faultless.

She thought as she came down the steps that the Earl was pleased to see her, and it might have been because she had not kept him waiting.

She expected a groom to help her into the saddle, but the Earl lifted her up, his hands at each side of her waist, saying as he did so:

"You are so light that I find it hard to believe you can handle a horse as big and spirited as Flycatcher."

"He will not bolt with me, if that is what you are afraid of," Carmela replied.

"Actually I was paying you a compliment," the Earl said drily, "and it is too early in the day to spar with anybody!"

Carmela laughed.

"I am sorry. I think actually I was afraid you might

insist on my riding something docile, and I love Fly-catcher!"

"Then I promise I will not take him away from you," the Earl said, and mounted his own stallion.

They galloped until there were patches of pink in Carmela's cheeks and her eyes were shining with the excitement of it.

Then as they drew in their horses to a trot and moved side by side, the Earl said:

"You ride magnificently, and I will admit again, it is something I did not expect in a girl of your age."

"I would like to point out to you," Carmela said, "that my grandmother always said the Gales never admitted to being in the wrong."

"There are exceptions to every rule."

The Earl smiled at Carmela as he replied, and they rode on for a short while without speaking.

The sun was shining, the birds were singing in the trees, the butterflies were hovering over the blossoms, and the world was so beautiful that Carmela felt at peace within herself and had no wish to fight with anybody.

Only a short while ago she had been at the Vicarage, coping with the obstructive violence of Henry and the persistent, whining complaints of Lucy.

She remembered how she had felt that the misery of it would stretch on forever into a dark future in which there was no hope.

Now, as if at the touch of a magic wand, everything was changed.

She was wearing clothes that would grace a Princess, riding a horse that was far superior to any animal she had ever seen before, and sharpening her brain beside the most attractive man she had ever met.

She ticked off her blessings one by one and told herself that she should really be on her knees saying a prayer of gratitude.

Then as she reached the last item on her list she

found herself looking at the Earl and thinking that her description of him was very apt.

He was indeed most attractive when he was not being aggressive, and he was also very much a man.

Then insidiously, almost as if it intruded from a source outside her own mind, came the question:

Suppose, just suppose, she could go on riding beside him like this forever?

CHAPTER FIVE

"*T*his morning," the Earl said as they set off from the front door, "I want to ride to the top of Gale Hill. It is something that I can remember doing when I was a boy, and being very impressed by it."

Carmela thought for a moment and vaguely remembered hearing the Countess say something about it. But it was not clear in her mind and she therefore talked of other things when they were not moving too fast for conversation.

When finally they began to climb up through the thick wood, then emerged into an area of treeless ground which rose more steeply still, she was aware that when they reached the top there should be a fine view.

They had already ridden at least three miles from the house, and the horses had to move slowly along a path that was little more than a sheep-track.

When finally they reached the top, she saw she had

been right in thinking there would be a panoramic view, and there was also what looked like a stone monument.

As they dismounted she said:

"I expected a Folly. Why was that monument erected?"

"I will show you," the Earl said with a smile.

He walked ahead of her, holding his horse by the bridle, and Carmela followed, leading Flycatcher in the same way.

Then as they reached the monument she saw that it consisted of a large flat slab with the points of the compass carved on the stone. Then the meaning of what the Countess had once said came to her and she exclaimed:

"Now I remember hearing about this!"

The Earl looked at the view in front of him, then at the compass.

There was an inscription encircling it, and Carmela read:

" '*All the land you see from the top of this hill belongs to the Gale family, who have owned it since 1547.*' "

After she had read it aloud, the Earl said:

"I remember the first time I came here. I was so small that I found that sentence quite hard to read."

"I remember that Grandmama said it was untrue," Carmela replied, "and that on a clear day one can see into three other Counties where the land is not owned by the family."

The Earl stared at her. Then he asked:

"Is that true?"

"I am only repeating what Grandmama said to me. It was when she was reminiscing about the Estate and saying how much the Gales as a family liked to boast of their possessions."

She was teasing the Earl, and she thought he would

laugh. Instead there was a scowl on his face as he looked down at the compass. Then he said violently:

"I will have that inscription removed. If there is one thing I loathe and detest, it is lies and deception of any kind!"

He was obviously so angry that Carmela looked at him in surprise, wondering why something so unimportant should affect him so tremendously.

Because the Earl went on scowling at the compass, she said:

"I am . . . sorry. I did not . . . mean to make you . . . angry. Perhaps it would have been better if I had not repeated what Grandmama said, which may in fact not be . . . true."

There was silence for a moment. Then the Earl said:

"Perhaps it is I who should apologise, but I loathe being lied to and I have just had a very unpleasant example of it."

"What has . . . happened?" Carmela enquired.

For a moment she thought he would not answer and tell her what was perturbing him.

Then, almost as if he thought she had a right to know, he said:

"When I first came here I soon realised that your father had been lax in many ways, and those he employed had taken advantage of it."

"You mean they were stealing from him?" Carmela asked.

The Earl nodded.

"In quite a big way. In fact, thousands of pounds must have been lost annually, not just by petty pilfering but in well-organised theft over the whole Estate."

Carmela gave a little cry.

"How horrible! Galeston seems so perfect, which makes it doubly wrong that such things should occur beneath the beauty and peace of it."

"That is what I think," the Earl said in a hard voice,

"and I have sacked the worst malefactors, although I am convinced there are others."

"What positions did they hold?" Carmela enquired.

"The worst one was the Manager, a man called Matthews," the Earl replied, "and he was aided and abetted by the Accountant, Lane, which of course made it much easier for him to operate his thefts, which have taken place over a number of years."

Carmela sighed.

"It seems to me very sad."

"It makes me very angry."

"So you dismissed them?"

"Of course," he replied. "I gave them forty-eight hours to clear out, and I told them both that as far as I was concerned they would never get employment elsewhere."

"I suppose that was what they deserved," Carmela said.

"They could have gone to prison or even been hanged or at least transported," the Earl said briefly, "but I decided to spare them because I was protecting your father's name and of course the family from the scandal of a trial."

"That was kind of you."

The Earl's lips tightened.

"My kindness was rewarded when Matthews burnt his house down before he left! I am now deciding whether I should have him arrested."

Carmela did not reply.

She was thinking that she could understand in the circumstances how bitterly he disliked lies and deception, and she was wondering what he would feel when he learnt that she had committed both offences.

She knew that it would be impossible for her to face his wrath, and that once she learnt that Felicity was married, she must run away and hide somewhere where the Earl would not find her.

Even though he had been overbearing and it was certainly wrong of him to think that he could marry her off to the Prince without any consideration for her feelings, she had no wish to hurt him.

Then she told herself that she was being presumptuous in thinking that anything she did would hurt the Earl as she would be hurt in similar circumstances.

He was so self-sufficient and so sure of himself that the only thing he would dislike would be to be proved wrong in his estimation of her.

She was aware, since they had grown more friendly and he had talked to her as if she was an equal, that he had enjoyed their conversations and their rides together almost as much as she had.

"He likes me and I think he trusts me," she told herself.

She looked down again at the compass and knew now that she dreaded the moment when the Earl would be aware that she was not what she appeared to be and had been acting a lie from the very moment of her arrival.

Because she felt embarrassed by her own thoughts and was acutely conscious of the Earl standing beside her still with the shadow of a scowl between his eyes, she forced herself to look at the view.

It stretched out towards the horizon, and below and much nearer were the house, the lake, and the gardens, looking almost like a child's model, and a very beautiful one in the sunshine.

She could see the trees in the Park, the deer moving beneath them, the swans on the lake, and the flag flying on the roof above the statues and the urns.

The Earl followed the direction of her eyes and after a moment he said quietly in a very different voice:

"I want nothing to spoil that."

"Of course not," Carmela agreed, "and I am sure that with you to look after it, it will regain its perfection and remain so."

She was speaking her thoughts aloud, then she was aware that the Earl was no longer looking at the house but at her with a faintly mocking smile on his lips.

"Are you really paying me a compliment, Felicity?" he asked. "It is something I cannot remember you doing since you first arrived here."

"You must think me very . . . remiss . . . and of course very . . . ungrateful."

"There must be a 'sting in the tail' to this conversation somewhere!" he replied.

She laughed.

"I suppose I have not been eloquent on the subject of Galeston and of you, its owner, because I have been overwhelmed by the magnificence of you both, and also because I felt . . . shy."

"And now?" the Earl enquired, raising his eyebrows.

"You are trying to force me into saying that 'familiarity breeds contempt.'"

"I was hoping," he answered, "that familiarity would make you feel friendly and happy, because that is what I want you to be."

His voice was beguiling, and she was about to say that she was happy, then she thought of why he was being so pleasant.

"If you wish me to be happy here," she said aloud, "why are you sending me away from something I am beginning to love, to a strange country which I have the feeling will never . . . really seem like . . . home?"

As she spoke she thought that her logic was unanswerable and the Earl was really being crafty in getting his own way by more subtle methods than he had used before.

To her surprise, he did not reply but merely went on staring at the house below them, although she had the feeling that he did not see it.

Then abruptly and surprisingly he said:

"I think we should start back, and we must take the horses down slowly or we might have an accident."

As he spoke she knew that he did not want to go on talking to her, and she thought perhaps he was nervous of her using the Prince's absence as an opportunity to make him change his mind about their marriage.

Because she had no wish to annoy him, she replied: "Perhaps you would be kind enough to help me mount Flycatcher. I do not think I can manage alone."

"Yes, of course," the Earl agreed.

He slipped his horse's bridle over his arm and lifted her skilfully onto the saddle, then arranged her skirt over the stirrup.

"Thank you," Carmela said.

She was looking down at him and as she spoke he raised his head and looked up at her.

Their eyes met and she had a sudden strange feeling that he was saying something to her that he had not said before and that it was important.

But then the Earl looked away and busied himself mounting his own horse, and she thought she must have been mistaken.

Nevertheless, as she started down the hill she had the strange feeling that her heart was beating unaccountably fast.

They rode back through the wood, then returned towards the house, taking a different route back.

It was nearly noon when finally they rode through the Park and trotted towards the bridge which spanned the lake.

As soon as the front of the house came in sight they became aware of three carriages drawn up outside the front door.

Carmela gave a little gasp.

"You did not tell me you had friends coming to luncheon!"

"I invited nobody," the Earl answered briefly.

"Then who is here?"

"I may be wrong," he replied, "but I have a feeling you are going to meet a number of our relatives."

"Oh, no, I hope not!" Carmela exclaimed in dismay, but the Earl was right.

Afterwards, Carmela thought she might have expected that sooner or later the "grapevine," or the gossip which in the country was carried on the wind, would bring the Gale relatives flocking to the big house to make the acquaintance of the girl they supposed was Felicity.

As soon as Carmela had changed from her riding-habit into a pretty gown, she entered the Salon and saw by their resemblance to the portraits on the walls that the people gathered there were undoubtedly Gales.

A few of the women were attractive, though certainly they were not as pretty as Felicity. At the same time, most of them bore a vague resemblance to one another and they were on the whole a surprisingly good-looking family.

What was really surprising was that they had called not only because they had learnt that she was a guest in the house but because they also knew that the Countess had left her a huge fortune.

A short while after she had been introduced to each member of the family one by one, she learnt the truth of this from an elderly relative who drew her to a sofa and said:

"I have always been anxious to meet you again, Felicity, although I doubt if you will remember how often I used to see you as a child."

"I am afraid . . . not."

"You had great difficulty in pronouncing my name, which is Cousin Louise," the relative went on. "I was devoted to your grandmother, and hardly a week went by when we did not meet and gossip together."

"You must have missed her when she left," Carmela replied.

"I not only missed her but I was deeply hurt that she did not reply to the letters I wrote to her."

Carmela felt there was nothing she could say to this and therefore she remained silent.

"When I learnt that she had died and had not even left me a memento of what I believed was a deep affection we had for each other, I could hardly believe it!"

"I do not think Grandmama left mementoes to anybody," Carmela said consolingly.

"I know that!" came the response. "You have had everything! You must consider yourself very lucky to have such a fortune when all the rest of the family has been ignored and neglected."

Because the voice was now sharp, Carmela wondered how she had learnt of the Countess's Will, since Felicity and the Earl had said it was a secret.

"When I went to the Office of the family Solicitors," the cousin went on, "and demanded to hear the contents of your grandmother's Will, I could hardly believe my ears when he told me how wealthy she had become in the years after she left here."

Carmela thought it extremely pushy of the relative to have made such demands, and she wondered why the Solicitor had been so indiscreet.

Then, as if the Earl sensed her discomfiture, he came to her side to say:

"I think, Felicity, you must not allow the Duchess to monopolise you when your other relatives are longing to talk to you."

Carmela immediately rose to her feet, but the Earl had answered her question, and she now knew that the family Solicitor had been too over-awed by the Duchess to refuse to give her the information.

The other cousins were not quite so distinguished.

A number of the ladies had married important noblemen in the neighbourhood, although it was difficult for Carmela to understand who they were or where they fitted into Felicity's family-tree.

She was also to find that having arrived uninvited to call on the head of the family, they all expected to stay to luncheon and were quite surprised when he asked them if that was their intention.

"Of course, Selwyn!" she heard one Dowager say. "You can hardly expect us to make the journey home without first having some refreshment!"

They had all by this time been provided with champagne, and Carmela thought it quite a remarkable feat on the part of the Chef when only twenty minutes later than usual they sat down to an excellent meal which might have been planned several days previously.

The conversation she had had with the Duchess had made her realise that her supposed relatives were looking at her not only with curiosity but with envy and undoubtedly a certain amount of malice.

She could hear the sharpness in their voices when they asked her what were her plans for the future and where she intended to live.

"She can come to me if she wishes," the Duchess said on hearing this question.

Before Carmela could answer, someone said:

"You know you would find that an inconvenience, Louise. I was in fact thinking that Felicity would fit in very well with my household. After all, Mary is nearly the same age as she is, and the two girls could do things together."

This statement evoked a storm of argument, and soon it seemed to Carmela that they were all fighting over her as if she were a bone amongst a lot of hungry dogs.

She knew that all this concern was due entirely to Felicity's enormous fortune.

She could not help feeling what a bomb-shell it would be if she suddenly announced that she was quite penniless and would be delighted to have a

comfortable home to go to when she was no longer at
Galeston.

She was quite certain that there would be a sudden
silence and the offers of hospitality would die away on
the lips of those who had made them.

If anything was needed to convince her that Felicity
had been right in running away with Jimmy, it was
this.

She suddenly felt ashamed that people who were so
well born and comparatively wealthy in their own
right should sink to grubbing for more and in doing
so reveal their greed so obviously.

There came an end to this discussion only when the
Earl said, speaking in his most autocratic voice:

"I am sure you are all very generous in offering
Felicity a home, but as her Guardian I have made
quite extensive plans for her future and you will be
informed of them in due course."

"Plans?" the Duchess exclaimed. "But why, Selwyn,
should you concern yourself with Felicity?"

"Because Felicity is an orphan and I am head of the
family!" the Earl said curtly.

There was silence while obviously the Gales could
think of no answer to this. Because they looked so
discomfitted, Carmela said in her quiet, sweet voice:

"Thank you . . . very much all the same for being
so . . . kind. I am very . . . touched that you
should want me, and now I do not feel so alone as I
did . . . before."

"Oh, you sweet child, you need never feel alone!"
one of the relatives exclaimed. "After all, we are all
Gales and we must help one another and stick together."

"Of course," the Duchess said. "Did any of us even
think of doing anything else?"

The unspoken answer was that it was the Countess
who had cut herself off from them all and in doing so
had taken Felicity away from them too.

But as this was something they had no wish to

declare openly, there was a pause, and then the conversation started on a different subject and for the moment Felicity's future was forgotten.

It was only after luncheon when they were all leaving that one by one they drew Carmela aside, out of ear-shot of the others, to say:

"We have no wish to upset Selwyn's plans for you, dear child, but do let *me* know if you are not happy."

The Duchess, however, put it more bluntly.

"If you are being pushed into doing anything you do not wish to do," she said sharply, "I will look after you, if only for your father's sake."

"Thank you," Carmela said.

The Duchess then took her by the arm and drew her a little to one side.

"Now listen, child," she said. "Do not be in a hurry to get married to the first man who asks you. With a fortune like yours, you can pick and choose."

Carmela smiled but said nothing.

"And it would be common sense," the Duchess continued, "to ask my advice before you accept anyone."

"It is very kind of you to worry about me, Ma'am."

There was a pause, then the Duchess said:

"I hear there was a foreign Prince staying here. Is he a suitor for your hand?"

There seemed to be no reason why she should not tell the truth, and Carmela answered quietly:

"I think so."

The Duchess snorted.

"I might have guessed that when I learnt this morning that he had been here. You be careful of foreigners. They cannot be trusted, and when it comes to husbands there is no-one like an Englishman. You take my word for it."

"I will remember what you said, Ma'am," Carmela replied.

The Duchess glanced down the room to where the Earl was talking to another relative.

"Selwyn has been abroad for a long time," she said

as if she was speaking to herself. "He will settle down to our ways in a year or so—at least, that is what we can all hope."

The way the Duchess spoke seemed to Carmela so amusing that she almost laughed aloud.

Fortunately, before she could make any response, another relative interrupted them to say to Carmela:

"I live only four miles away, and I suggest, Felicity, that you come to luncheon with us next Sunday. I am very, very anxious for you to meet my two sons. They are both of them, although I say it, very charming, and it is a good thing for cousins to become friendly with each other."

"What you are hoping," the Duchess interposed tartly, "is that Felicity will marry one of them. If she does, she will need all her money to maintain them at the gaming-tables!"

"How can you say anything so unkind, Louise?" the affronted mother asked in plaintive tones.

"I always speak the truth, you know that," the Duchess replied, "and that is why Felicity should listen to me and not to all the 'soft soap' the rest of you are handing her. I am going now."

The Duchess walked away to say good-bye to the Earl, and the mother of the two sons said to Carmela:

"Do not listen to Cousin Louise. Although we all respect her, she is an embittered woman in many ways. Promise me you will accept my invitation."

"I will discuss it with His Lordship," Carmela replied. "As you realise, I shall have to have his permission."

"Yes, of course," was the answer. "At the same time, although Selwyn obviously takes his duties as head of the family very seriously, he is really too young to be an entirely suitable Guardian for a young girl."

"I think that is something I must decide for myself," the Earl interposed.

Both Carmela and the lady to whom she was speaking started, not having heard him approach.

"I have no wish to offend you!" the lady with the sons exclaimed quickly. "I was just thinking that dear Felicity might be happier in a family."

The Earl did not reply, but Carmela, seeing a twinkle in his eyes, realised that he was as amused as she was at the offers of hospitality that Felicity's fortune, rather than Felicity herself, was evoking.

When finally the last Gale relative had said her farewells, the Earl exclaimed:

"I hope you enjoyed that exhibition of blatant hypocrisy!"

Carmela laughed.

"I wonder," he went on, "if they would have pressed many invitations on you if you were penniless."

It was what Carmela had thought herself, but she replied:

"Perhaps they were really meaning to be kind."

"People are always kind to the rich."

"I think that is a very cynical remark!" Carmela said provocatively. "It may be true of some people, but not all."

"Where your relatives are concerned, I should take everything they say to you with a good 'pinch of salt'!"

"That might well include you," she answered.

"I might have guessed you would make that comment," he replied, "and when I suggested you should marry Prince Frederich, I was genuinely convinced that from a woman's point of view nothing could be more advantageous or more attractive."

He spoke with an unmistakable sincerity and Carmela knew that it was the truth.

However, to tease him she said:

"Well, at least now I have quite a considerable choice! I realise that all my relatives have at the back of their minds some aspirant for my hand . . . and of course for my pocket!"

"Who is being cynical now?" the Earl asked. "And

anyway, may I point out that you have to obtain my approval before you can marry anybody?"

"Are you saying that you might bar your own kith and kin from the competition?" Carmela asked. "I have a feeling they would consider that most unsporting, as you yourself have your money on another horse."

The Earl laughed and it was a sound of genuine amusement.

"You continue to surprise me, Felicity," he said. "I am sure most women would not look upon their marriage in such a frivolous manner."

"Would you prefer me to squint down my nose and look coy?" Carmela asked. "I certainly felt like that when my marriage was first mentioned, but now it seems to be a general topic of conversation and I find it hard to blush."

The Earl was silent for a moment. Then he said:

"I have the impression, Felicity, that you are not taking this subject, which should be an absorbing one for you, as seriously as I would wish."

He paused for a moment before he went on:

"I cannot explain quite what I mean. As I have said before, I am very ignorant where young girls are concerned, but there is something—I cannot put my finger on it, but it is nevertheless there—which tells me that you are playing with me."

Carmela thought he was more perceptive than she had expected.

Although he was finding it hard to put into words, some instinct was telling him that she was not really frightened of being swept up the aisle as the bride of the Prince and that, in a way which he could not determine, she would ultimately elude him.

She thought it was doubtless the first time he had been really puzzled by somebody who came under his command.

She knew too that it was his long experience of leadership when dealing with all sorts and conditions

of people which told him that she was not exactly
what she appeared to be, although he could find no
logical explanation for it.

Because she thought it was a mistake to let him
dwell too long on this aspect of her behaviour, she
said:

"I refuse to worry about it just now, and if you
remember, we had arranged this afternoon to see if
we could catch any fish in the lake as you used to do
when you were a boy."

"I had not forgotten, but I thought you had," the
Earl replied.

"Now you are fishing in a different sort of way,"
Carmela said with a smile, "and what are we waiting
for?"

The Earl laughed and they walked through the
front door and across the lawn in the direction of the
lake.

When Carmela went to bed that night, she thought
she had never enjoyed an evening more.

To be able to talk to the Earl alone, without his
continually deferring politely to the Prince, and to
argue with him over a dozen different subjects was an
enchantment that she could hardly put into words.

It had left her with a feeling of happiness that she
had not known since her father had died. They had
often sat at the Dining-Room table for hours after
their small meal was finished, simply because it was
easier to talk with what her father called "their elbows
on the table" than to move to the Sitting-Room.

But while their bodies were stationary their minds
had flown out over the whole Universe, covering
many countries, peoples, religions, and philoso-
phies. For Carmela it had meant finding new horizons or, as her father had sometimes said, exploring

"the mountains of the mind," of which she had not previously been aware.

She felt the same when talking with the Earl, and when at last they walked together towards the Salon he said:

"How can you be so intelligent when I expected you to be very different?"

"Gauche and nit-witted, I think, was the right description," Carmela said with a smile.

"I know now that I have not only to reassess you but to polish up my own knowledge and intelligence," the Earl said.

"That is certainly a confession, which I wish I could press like a flower and put in a scrap-book," Carmela teased.

They laughed, then talked seriously until finally and reluctantly Carmela felt that she should go to bed.

"You did suggest riding early tomorrow?" she asked.

"I thought we might go to the far end of the Estate," he said, "and as it will take several hours, if you could face bread and cheese at a wayside Inn, we could make an expedition of it."

"I would love that, and I like bread and cheese."

"Very well," the Earl replied. "That is what we will do, and I will order breakfast for eight o'clock, if you can be down by then."

"I shall not be late," Carmela promised. "Goodnight, Cousin Selwyn, I have enjoyed this evening."

"So have I," the Earl admitted.

She curtseyed to him, and to her surprise he took her hand in his.

"Good-night, Felicity," he said. "Please continue to surprise and perhaps I should say dazzle me, as it is something I enjoy."

He spoke quite seriously, then he lifted her hand to his lips and kissed it.

It was not what Carmela had expected, and as she

felt the pressure of his mouth on her skin it gave her a strange sensation she had never known before.

For a moment she was still, looking at the Earl a little questioningly.

Then because she was shy, she took away her hand and leaving the Salon hurried across the Hall and up the stairs without looking back.

She had the feeling that he was watching her, but she told herself she was probably imagining it.

In her bedroom an elderly housemaid helped her to undress, and when she got into bed she lay thinking of the Earl and of the way he had kissed her hand.

It was what she might have expected the Prince to do, but not the Earl. Yet, it had seemed to come quite naturally to him, and she knew that because he was so athletic he had a grace which made him never appear clumsy or ungainly in any way.

She looked back over the things they had said to each other and thought they might almost have been taking part in one of the witty Restoration Plays that she had sometimes read aloud to her father in the evenings.

'I suppose that because he has such a sharp brain and is so intelligent, he makes me intelligent too,' she thought.

She began to think of things she could say to him the next day that would sound witty or provocative.

She had almost fallen asleep when she heard her bedroom door open.

Then there was a light in the room and she realised it came from a candle held in somebody's hand.

"Wh-what . . . is it?" she asked.

As a figure approached her bed she saw that it was one of the younger maids who sometimes helped the elderly housemaid who usually looked after her.

"What is it, Suzy?" she asked again.

"I'm sorry to wake you, M'Lady," Suzy replied,

"but His Lordship asks if you'll go downstairs. There's been an accident and he wants your help."

"An accident?" Carmela exclaimed as she sat up in bed. "What sort of an accident?"

"I think it's one o' the dogs, M'Lady. His Lordship said as I were to fetch you."

Carmela got out of bed.

As she did so, she thought that there were several dogs that were kept in the stables and because they were not trained they were not allowed into the house.

"I want dogs of my own which will always be with me," the Earl had told her, "but I thought there were too many other things for me to do first before I could take on any others."

However, she had noticed that whenever he went to the stables he patted the dogs that were kept there in the kennels, and they would jump up and make a fuss over him.

She thought one of these must have been hurt in some way, and as she slipped on a pair of soft slippers she looked round for a dressing-gown.

The one she had been wearing was of very thin material trimmed with lace, but Suzy went to the wardrobe and brought out one of heavy satin with an inter-lining, which was really a winter garment and too warm for the spring.

Carmela thought as Suzy helped her into it that it was certainly more modest than anything lighter.

As she fastened the little pearl buttons that went all the way down the front, she thought that enveloping though it was, some of the Gale relatives who had called today would be shocked at her going downstairs in her night-attire.

However, she was not concerned with their feelings but only with the fact that the Earl needed her.

"Has His Lordship got bandages?" she asked.

"Yes, M'Lady," the maid replied. "He's everything like that, but he wants your help."

Carmela brushed her hair back quickly from her forehead and said:

"I am ready!"

"I'll lead the way, M'Lady."

Picking up the candle, Suzy went out the door and into the passage.

She shut the door behind her, then set off quickly along the corridor which led towards the top of the Grand Staircase, but she did not descend it.

Instead, she walked on towards the West Wing of the house until they came to a narrow staircase down which Suzy hurried.

In fact, she moved so quickly that they were now away from the light of candles in the main part of the building, and Carmela was afraid of being left behind in the dark.

They reached an unlit passage which she thought must be near the servants' part of the house, but Suzy went on and still on without looking back.

Carmela thought they were going in the direction of the stables and that was where the Earl must be with the injured dog. Then suddenly Suzy stopped and took a side-passage which led, Carmela could see, to an outer door.

Now she was eager to reach the Earl and find out exactly what was happening.

Suzy opened the door, which was unlocked, and walked outside into the darkness. Carmela followed her, then as she stepped out into the night, suddenly something thick, dark, and enveloping was thrown over her head.

She gave a cry of terror, but even as she did so she realised that her voice was stifled by the thickness of the covering.

At the same time, rough arms picked her up.

"What is . . . happening? Put me . . . down!" she tried to say.

But her voice lost, and the arms which were

encircling her held her so tightly that she felt as if the breath was squeezed out of her body.

Then roughly she was dumped inside what she realised was a carriage, because almost before she was seated, horses started to move and she could feel wheels revolving under her.

Then as the terror of what was happening swept over her, she knew she was being kidnapped!

CHAPTER SIX

The carriage was bumping very awkwardly over rough ground, perhaps even grass without a track, and she wondered frantically where she was being taken and who was beside her.

Even through the thickness of the cloth which covered her down to her knees, she was uncomfortably aware of a man sitting there.

He had taken his arms from her once he had thrown her down in the carriage, but the mere fact that he was close was frightening to the point where all she wanted to do was scream.

However, she realised that this was hopeless, first because she was sensible enough to know that nobody else would hear her, and secondly because it was difficult even to breathe through the thickness of the material in which she was enveloped.

She imagined it was some kind of felt, because

while it was pliable and seemed to cling to her face, it was unpleasantly rough.

She was not much worried about the discomfort but only about what was going to happen to her and why she was being kidnapped.

The motive for this, however, was not too difficult to determine.

Now that the extent of Felicity's fortune was known to all the Gales, it would also have been gossipped about in the country, and both the gentlefolk and their servants would be aware of it.

It seemed obvious that somebody was going to hold her for ransom, and she only hoped that the Earl would pay up without any delay.

Then she remembered that if he did so it would be impossible for her to repay him unless Felicity gave her the money.

The fact that she was absolutely penniless made everything more complicated, and she wondered what Felicity would have done in the circumstances if it was she who had been abducted as her captors intended.

'The one thing I must not do,' Carmela thought to herself, 'is to defy them in any way.'

She had read stories of people being tortured because they would not reveal where some treasure or their money was hidden, and she knew that she was a coward!

She thought that if she was threatened, she would be far too afraid to do anything but agree to what was demanded.

At the same time, it struck her that the Earl might have very different ideas.

She knew that nothing would infuriate him more than finding himself in the ignominious position of having to pay a ransom for her without being able to arrest the criminals who asked for it.

'Suppose he refuses to pay?' she thought frantically.

She felt herself shiver with fear lest those demanding the ransom might in that case punish her for his obstinacy.

She remembered stories of how in the East a victim in the same circumstances as herself could be mutilated in order to exact the payment of the price demanded.

First would be sent a finger, then an ear, and finally a nose to those who were refusing to pay the ransom.

The idea was so horrifying that Carmela wished she were unconscious so that she would not think of such things, but she knew that instinctively she would strive to the utmost to keep herself alive and to retain her ability to think.

On and on the carriage travelled.

Although she could move her hands underneath the heavy cloth, she was afraid to pull it up in case the man sitting next to her might stop her by force.

Suddenly she became aware that one of her feet was very cold and she realised that she had lost a slipper when being carried from the doorstep of the house into the carriage.

She rubbed her foot against her ankle very slowly and gently so as not to draw attention to herself, and then as she listened intently she thought she could hear the man breathing heavily.

He coughed once and moved restlessly, and with the sway of the carriage his shoulder knocked against hers and she cringed away from him as far as she could into the corner.

Now the horses were moving very slowly and she thought the ground beneath the wheels was rougher than ever.

She knew they had travelled quite a long way from the house, and she thought despairingly that even if the Earl searched for her thoroughly, he might never be able to find her.

The horses came to a halt, the man beside her

opened the carriage door, and for the first time she heard his voice.

"Can't you get any nearer, Arthur?"

It was not an educated voice, but it was certainly not as coarse as she had anticipated.

Then she heard another man answer:

"No, we'd get stuck in the trees."

"All right then," the first man said. "Tie up the horses and bring the lantern."

The word "trees" told Carmela that they must be in a wood of some sort.

The man got out of the carriage on his side, there was a pause, then he opened the door on her side and pulled her into his arms.

Again she wanted to scream but somehow prevented herself from doing so.

The man was obviously large and strong, for it seemed no effort for him to carry her with one arm round her body and the other under her knees.

Now she could hear dry twigs cracking under his feet and she was aware that he was not walking along a straight path but twisting, she presumed, between tree-trunks.

They walked for some way, then stopped.

"Open the door," he said.

"Mind your head," the other man warned.

He walked on a few steps more, and then Carmela was set down on a hard floor.

Now she steadied herself with her hands, and she found that she was touching not boards but ordinary earth which was dry and hard as if it had been trodden down.

She could hear the two men who had brought her there moving about, and fearing they might trip over her feet and hurt the one which was bare, she pulled them close to her body.

Then suddenly and so unexpectedly that it gave her a shock, the cloth that covered her was pulled away and she could see.

The first thing she was aware of was two men's faces staring at her in the light of a lantern.

One man was middle-aged. He was not as rough as Carmela had expected and was obviously not a labourer, and he had an intelligent face.

The other man was younger, thin and pale with a long nose, and was wearing spectacles.

Neither of them spoke, and Carmela drew in her breath and asked:

"Who . . . are you . . . and why have you . . . brought me . . . here?"

As she spoke she thought it was a foolish question.

At the same time, she was pleased that her voice did not tremble, although because she was breathless it was not very loud.

The older man smiled unpleasantly.

"I'll tell you why we've brought you here, Lady Felicity," he said. "We want money, and we want it quickly!"

"I doubt if His Lordship . . . my Guardian, will . . . give it to . . . you," Carmela replied.

The man laughed.

"You don't suppose we're going to ask him for it?"

He looked at the man with the glasses and said:

"Come on, Arthur, you tell her what she's got to do."

It was then that Carmela realised that the other man was standing by a large, roughly made wooden box and was taking some papers from his pocket to place them beside the lantern.

"All you've got to do, M'Lady," he said in a slightly high-pitched voice, "is to sign this cheque I've made out for you and also a letter I've written on your behalf."

Carmela did not speak and after a moment the other man said:

"We're only asking for our rights and what we're entitled to."

"What do you mean by that?" Carmela asked, since he seemed to expect her to reply.

"Your Guardian, as you call him, has after years of hard work thrown me out without a penny, and Lane here's in the same position."

It was then that Carmela knew who these men were.

They were the Manager and the Accountant who had made the Earl so angry because they had robbed the Estate, and it was Matthews who had burnt his house down before leaving.

It flashed through her mind that she should confront them by saying they were fortunate not to have been imprisoned or hanged.

Then she knew it would be a foolish thing to do and nothing she could say would change their intention of extracting money from her.

She also knew that if she told them she did not actually own any money, they would only laugh and not believe her.

They seemed to be waiting for her to say something, and after a moment she said:

"When I have signed the cheque as you have . . . asked me to do . . . what do you intend to . . . do with me?"

There was a tremor in her voice in the last three words, and she lifted her chin higher as if to refute it.

Matthews smiled again, unpleasantly.

"I expect you'll be found sooner or later," he said, "and if you feel a bit hungry while you're waiting, you can always remember that that's what your nice, kind Guardian intended us to be."

"You realise that if you are caught obtaining money by . . . blackmail," Carmela said, "it will be added to your other crimes and the . . . penalties will be very . . . severe?"

"We won't be caught," Matthews replied. "We're going abroad, aren't we, Arthur? But you might ask

His Lordship, if he's feeling generous, to look after our families for us."

He smirked before he added:

"There'll be plenty of women where we're going!"

"You are talking too much," Lane said. "Come on, let's get on with it."

As he spoke, Carmela was sure that Matthews had been drinking, perhaps to give himself "Dutch Courage."

As he moved to pull her to her feet, she could smell the drink on his breath and knew she was right.

Loathing the touch of his hand on her arm, she shook herself free of him and tried to walk with dignity to the wooden box, but she found it difficult with only one shoe, and the ground hurt her bare foot.

Then as she reached the box she saw there was a block of wood behind it to be used as a seat.

As Carmela seated herself, Lane took from a small leather bag an ink-well which he opened and two quill-pens.

He put them in front of her and she saw that the letter he had written was in the flowing script of a clerk.

She picked it up and read it.

To Messrs. Coutts:
Sirs, Will you kindly cash the enclosed cheque for the sum of ten thousand pounds made payable to F. J. Matthews.

Yours truly,

Carmela looked at the top of the letter and saw that it was embossed with the Earl's coronet over the words "Galeston Park," and knew that Lane had stolen it before he left.

The two men were watching her as she put down the letter and said:

273

"And you really think that the Bank will hand over such a large sum without making further enquiries?"

"Why not?" Lane asked. "Your life's worth a great deal more, Your Ladyship, but we're being sensible and asking for a sum that'll not make them suspicious."

"If you ask me," Matthews said before Carmela could speak, "we should demand a great deal more. Make it twenty thousand pounds, Arthur. We can do with it."

Lane shook his head.

"No! They would think it strange that the young lady would want so much in cash. They may think that anyway."

"You told me ten thousand was safe!" Matthews argued aggressively.

"Nothing's safe," Lane answered. "But I thought, seeing how wealthy Her Ladyship is, they'll think she's buying horses or jewellery and will not query the letter or the cheque."

"If you're wrong, I'll murder you!" Matthews said. "Well, get on with it!"

Lane looked towards Carmela and pointed with his finger to the bottom of the page.

"Sign your name here, M'Lady."

Carmela was debating whether she should sign the letter in a passable imitation of Felicity's writing, or make it so different that the Bank would instantly be suspicious and refuse to give the two men any money.

For a moment she thought this was a brilliant idea and they would get the punishment they richly deserved.

Then she thought that on the first sign of hesitation by the Bank they would run away, and it might be some time before Coutts could get in touch with her to tell her what had occurred.

All that time she would be imprisoned here in the wooden hut which she supposed had been erected by wood-cutters.

If the Earl did not find her in the meantime, she could be a prisoner for days or weeks with no chance of escape.

She thought that in fact her only chance for freedom would be to bargain with the men who were threatening her.

She did not pick up the pen but merely said:

"If I sign this and you receive the money, will you then come back and set me free?"

Matthews hesitated, and she knew his instinct was to say that she could rot here for all he cared.

Then a crafty look came into his eyes as he replied:

"Of course, M'Lady! That'd be only fair, wouldn't it, as you're being fair to us?"

He was lying, and Carmela knew he had no intention of returning to release her. The moment they had the money, he and Lane would go abroad.

'I will sign Felicity's name in my own writing,' she decided.

Then as if he read her thoughts Lane said:

"If you try to trick us, M'Lady, you'll be sorry!"

"What do you mean, trick us?" Matthews asked. "What're you thinking she might do?"

"She could sign in such a way that the Bank wouldn't honour the cheque," Lane replied, "and that's what I suspect she's thinking of doing."

Matthews gave a snarl of rage that was like that of a wild animal.

"You dare!" he said to Carmela. "If you do anything like that, I'll bash your face in! I've had enough from His Lordship without any more from you!"

Carmela felt as if her heart contracted in fear, and she said hesitatingly:

"I . . . I will sign it as you . . . want me to do."

"You'd better!" Matthews said menacingly.

He turned to Lane to ask:

"Do you know what her signature looks like?"

"How should I know?"

"Then we'll have to trust her."

"I agree," Lane said, "and you've promised her that once we have the money we'll come back and set her free."

He spoke with a note in his voice which was intended to warn Matthews that that was the one way they could be certain she would sign as they wanted, but Matthews, stupid with drink, did not understand.

"I'm not coming back to this da . . ."

He realised as he was about to swear that Lane was making a signal to him behind Carmela's back, and with difficulty he prevented the words from leaving his lips.

"All right," he said. "Have it your own way. "We'll come back."

Carmela thought with a little sigh that it was hopeless.

They had no intention of returning, but she was too afraid to trick them in case they avenged themselves on her physically.

Without saying anything more, she dipped the quill-pen into the ink-well, and then slowly, because she had to be careful how she forged Felicity's name, she signed the letter.

Then Lane produced the cheque for her.

It had been printed for another Bank and he had carefully crossed out the name of it and instead had written under it: *Coutts and Company.*"

As Carmela looked at it she thought how much ten thousand pounds would have meant to her father and mother and how they had often to pinch and scrape along on a few pounds a month when her father was unable to sell one of his pictures.

Then she told herself that although it seemed an enormous sum to her, Felicity's fortune was so large that if Matthews and Lane did get away with it, the loss would not matter greatly.

She therefore signed Felicity's name without saying anything further, and as she did so, both Matthews and Lane were watching every movement of the pen.

Then as Lane sanded the cheque, Matthews said:

"Now then, let's see how quickly those horses you've hired can get us to London."

"We'll be there before the Bank opens," Lane replied.

He put the cheque and the letter in his pocket, screwed down the ink-well, and put it and the pens back into the bag.

"I hope you'll be comfortable, M'Lady," Matthews said mockingly. "And while you're here you can meditate on the old adage: 'He laughs longer who laughs last.' "

As he spoke he walked towards the door and bent his head to pass through it, and was followed by Lane carrying the lantern.

"Please, do not leave me here in the dark!" Carmela cried.

But by this time they were outside the hut, and the only answer was a creak of the door as they pressed it into place.

Then she heard the bolt slammed down and knew she was a prisoner, for the door could not be opened except from the outside.

She was now in complete darkness, and she knew there was no window in the hut, since otherwise she would have seen the light from the lantern as they walked away through the trees.

She was still sitting on the rough piece of wood that she had used as a seat, and the box was in front of her.

She put her hands together and tried to think how long it would be before there was any chance of her being rescued.

Now she was aware that she was shivering not only from fear but from cold, and the foot without a shoe was beginning to feel numb.

"I must be sensible," Carmela told herself, "and wait until it is daylight, then I shall have some idea if there is any means by which I can escape."

However, she had the feeling that it was going to be impossible.

She had seen the huts that the wood-cutters made in which to keep their tools and where they sat when the weather was too wet for work.

She knew they were usually constructed of tree-trunks split down the middle and hammered deep into the ground. The roof would be made in the same way and covered with something to make it rain-proof.

Because tools were valuable, no wood-cutter would wish to lose his saw or his axe, and therefore the huts were usually solidly constructed and impervious to thieves.

'Perhaps I shall never be found,' Carmela thought dismally. 'I will die of starvation and all that will remain will be my bones.'

Then she told herself that it was wrong to think of anything so depressing.

She had to believe that God would look after her and that He would hear her prayers.

Being really rather frightened, she thought she would be wise to sit down on the ground with her back against the wall and perhaps in a little while she would be able to sleep.

She groped her way along the side of the hut and sat down in a corner, covering her feet as best she could with her dressing-gown.

As she touched it she thought she should be grateful to Suzy for having chosen something so warm, then she knew as she thought about it that Suzy was obviously in league with Matthews and Lane.

'How angry that will make the Earl,' she thought, 'that another of his staff has deceived him! And Suzy is a servant in the house.'

She could almost feel sorry for him, until she remembered that she too was lying, she too was deceiving him.

Yet, she felt sure that when he learnt that she was

missing he would use all his perception and all his determination to find her and bring her back.

The earliest time he could know about it would be when she was not there to breakfast with him at eight o'clock in the morning, as they had planned.

Then he would know that something was wrong. He would hardly believe that she had run away when she had taken no clothes from the house except for her dressing-gown. The elderly maid would be able to inform him of that.

'He will find me . . . I know he will . . . find me!' Carmela thought.

She knew it would be a long time until he did so, but she felt as if the idea lifted her heart like a light in the darkness.

She leant back against the wall and listened, and now in the silence of the hut she could hear faintly the sounds of the wood outside.

Far away in the distance there was the bark of a fox, and an owl hooted overhead, and although she could not be certain, she thought there was the scamper of tiny feet.

She knew that if she were outside she would not be afraid.

The wood was very much a part of the fairy-stories her father had told her when she was a child.

Now she wished that the goblins that burrowed under the trees would come up through the floor of the hut to help her, or perhaps the birds would carry a message to the Earl to wake him and tell him of the danger she was in.

Because she could not send a bird, she felt as if instead she sent her thoughts winging their way across the trees towards the great house.

"Help me! Help me!" she called.

But she thought that although the Earl might be perceptive in some ways, they were not so closely attuned to each other that he would understand her need.

Then she remembered the way he had kissed her hand when they had said good-night to each other, and she thought she could still feel his lips warm and somehow possessive on her skin.

"Help me! Help me!"

She felt again as if her vibrations flew like birds from her prison towards the only person who could save her.

Then as her whole mind and body yearned for him, she knew as if forked lightning flashed through her that she loved him.

The Earl awoke with a feeling of satisfaction because something enjoyable lay ahead.

He remembered the plans he had made with Felicity for an expedition on horse-back, and he thought it was something he would enjoy enormously, besides bringing him a new knowledge of his Estate.

He stretched out his arms as he yawned, then he remembered that he had woken in the night, feeling that something was perturbing him, although he could not think what it could be.

He had in fact lain awake for some time and found himself thinking of how attractive and how unexpectedly intelligent Felicity was.

'She could never bore me,' he thought, 'but brains are wasted on a woman.'

He knew that when he had a son he would want him to be clever as well as athletic, but he had never thought that necessary for any daughters he might have.

Now he told himself that while it might be a dangerous precedent for a woman to have a brain, it certainly made her more interesting to her husband.

'The Prince will not be bored very quickly with Felicity,' he thought.

Then he wondered if the Prince's brain would equal hers.

"I expect what will happen soon or later is that she will rule Horngelstein," he told himself, "and there will be nothing Frederich can do to prevent it."

He thought that he himself would dislike a woman who bossed him because she was cleverer than he was.

Then he told himself that when he found this mythical wife to give him the children he needed to carry on the inheritance from father to son, she might as well be clever rather than stupid.

He remembered all the women with whom he had had tempestuous but short affairs, but he could not remember one who had talked to him on serious subjects or had stimulated his brain as Felicity had managed to do.

He knew that today when they stopped for luncheon at some country Inn she would amuse and tease him.

He enjoyed it when she looked at him from under her eye-lashes, which curled back like a child's. There would be a mischievous sparkle in her eyes which he had grown to recognise.

"Dammit all!" he told himself. "She is far too good for young Frederich! He will just be enamoured of her because she has a pretty face and will not appreciate the twists and turns of her exceptional brain."

As he thought about Felicity she seemed very vivid in his mind, in fact so vivid that she might have been standing beside the bed talking to him.

Then he turned over and forced himself to think of other things so that he could go to sleep again.

The Earl's valet came softly into the room to set down beside the bed a tray on which there was a pot of tea and a wafer-thin slice of bread and butter.

He then crossed to the windows to pull back the curtains and let in the morning sunshine.

"It is a nice day, Jarvis," the Earl remarked.

"Yes, M'Lord. Excuse me, M'Lord, but Mrs. Humphries is worried."

"Worried? What has she to be worried about?"

The Earl poured some tea into the cup as he spoke.

"She can't find Her Ladyship, M'Lord!"

The Earl looked surprised.

"What do you mean—she cannot find Her Ladyship?"

"Well, M'Lord, she's not in her room. She asked to be woken early so as to go riding with Your Lordship, but she doesn't appear to be anywhere else."

"She must have got up early and gone to the stables," the Earl suggested.

"No, M'Lord. Mrs. Humphries has already thought of that, and Her Ladyship's not dressed. In fact, the only thing missing from her wardrobe, Mrs. Humphries says, is a thick dressing-gown Her Ladyship hasn't worn since she has been here."

"It certainly sounds a mystery," the Earl said goodhumouredly, "but I expect there is a simple explanation."

As he spoke he thought that perhaps Felicity had gone up to the roof to see the dawn rising or into the Library to choose some particular book she wanted to read.

He always thought Mrs. Humphries was an old "fuss-pot," and this was a very good example of it.

There was a knock on the door and Jarvis went to open it.

He spoke to somebody outside and a minute later came back into the room.

"What is it?" the Earl asked, sipping his tea.

"Mrs. Humphries asked me to tell you, M'Lord, that one of the lower housemaids just found this outside the door that leads to the back driveway."

As Jarvis spoke he held out to the Earl a pale mauve satin slipper.

"You say this was found on the back drive?" the Earl asked.

"Yes, M'Lord, and Mr. Newman says there's signs of carriage wheels which he would swear weren't there yesterday evening when he came in that way."

The Earl put down his cup and got quickly out of bed.

He dressed hurriedly and went from his room to where Carmela had been sleeping.

As he expected, he found Mrs. Humphries wringing her hands.

"I'm glad you've come, Your Lordship, that I am! Her Ladyship's never been unpredictable ever since she's stayed here, and I've sent the maids searching everywhere and there's not a room in the house that they haven't looked in for her."

"I cannot understand it!" the Earl exclaimed.

"And Suzy's disappeared as well," Mrs. Humphries went on, "not that I can believe she's with Her Ladyship, being a feckless girl who I were thinking of dismissing anyway."

"Suzy?" the Earl questioned in an indifferent tone.

"Suzy Lane, M'Lord."

The Earl was suddenly very still.

"Did you say Suzy *Lane?*"

"Yes, M'Lord."

"Is she any relation to Arthur Lane, the Estate Accountant?"

"She's his niece, M'Lord," Mrs. Humphries replied. "He asked me to take her into the house, but although she's proved far from satisfactory, I gave her chance after chance, so as not to make trouble, so to speak."

"And you say she too is missing?" the Earl asked.

"Well, Emily, who sleeps with her, tells me that she must have left the room last night after she were asleep. She wasn't there this morning when Emily woke."

The Earl did not wait to hear any more. He hurried downstairs and went to the side-door to inspect the marks of the carriage wheels which Newman informed him over and over again were new.

"The marks was not there, M'Lord, when I walks along here just before dinner for a little 'constitutional' as one might say."

"Yes, yes!" the Earl said. "You are quite sure the marks were not there then?"

"I'm sure of it, M'Lord, being rather observant about such matters, and as Your Lordship can see, the vehicle was drawn by two horses."

The Earl was shown the exact place where Carmela's slipper had been found.

He then sent a few footmen running with a summons to the stables, the gardens, and the woodmen.

About twenty minutes later the men employed near the house were all gathered together outside the front door, where he addressed them.

He told them that Lady Felicity was missing and he wanted them all to search their own parts of the Estate and to make certain no bush or ditch or building was overlooked.

"Does Your Lordship think Her Ladyship might have been kidnapped, M'Lord?" the Head Groom asked.

"That is certainly a possibility," the Earl said briefly.

He was remembering only too clearly how much the Gale relatives had talked about Felicity's fortune, and like Carmela he was aware that all their servants would have known about it. The news would have spread like wild-fire over the Estate and in the villages where they lived.

'Blast the money!' he thought to himself. 'The only thing that matters is that Felicity is safe!'

When he finished giving the men instructions, he

swung himself into the saddle of his stallion and set off to search for her himself.

As he went, he felt an urgency to find her which was different from any emotion he had ever known before.

He suddenly had a terror that she might have been hurt, drugged, or injured by those who had carried her away.

Even if they had not hurt her physically, he was well aware how sensitive she was and that mentally anything unpleasant that happened would be a tremendous shock.

"I have to find her, and quickly!" the Earl said aloud.

Without really meaning to, he spurred his horse into a gallop.

CHAPTER SEVEN

*A*s the Earl drew in his reins he was feeling hot and his stallion was sweating.

He was now on the very edge of the Estate, and he thought despairingly that if Lane and Matthews had carried Felicity into another County, it would be almost impossible to find her.

All the time he had been searching for her, which was now over four hours, he had been aware that his feelings for her were growing and growing until he knew that she meant something very different in his life from anything he had ever known before.

At the same time, he had an almost uncontrollable impulse to murder the men who had abducted her, and he thought he had been remiss in not having had them convicted for their crimes as soon as he had discovered what was going on.

He looked round him and realised he was in a clearing in the wood in which the trees had been felled.

It suddenly struck him that as it was in connection with the sale of timber that he had first discovered that Matthews was stealing, he might, with his mind working in some twisted manner at an effort at revenge, have brought Felicity here, thinking it was the last place anyone would think of looking for her.

It was as if these thoughts came to him like an inspiration from a source outside himself, and now as he saw that there was a track between the tree-trunks, he urged his horse forward.

He was not really optimistic that this was where Felicity would be. At the same time, he had begun to feel despairingly that it was his last hope.

A few moments later he saw in front of him a heavily constructed wooden hut which he knew had been erected by the wood-cutters.

Carmela knew when dawn came, because faint streaks of light percolated through the narrow cracks between the tree-trunks with which the hut had been made.

The sound of the birds grew louder and she was conscious of feeling stiff and cold and even more frightened than she had been before.

This was because she was sensible enough to realise that her chances of being found were very slender.

She was sure that the wood in which she was

imprisoned was in a part of the Estate that was not visited frequently, and she had to face the fact that she might stay here for a very long time before the searchers, if there were any, found her.

She thought she heard a sound outside that was different from any she had heard before, and instantly she ran to the door, shouting as she did so:

"Help! Help!"

Immediately there was what she knew was the sound of an animal scampering away through the undergrowth, and she knew it was probably a deer which had attracted her attention.

She felt ashamed of the panic in her voice and went back to sit down where she had been all night, trying to calm the tumultuous beating of her heart and the breath that came quickly from between her lips.

"I am frightened!" she confessed to herself. "Very, very frightened!"

The light coming in small streaks through the cracks in the walls grew brighter, but as the hours passed nothing else happened.

Because she had hardly slept during the night, Carmela began to doze from sheer exhaustion.

Then, suddenly and unexpectedly, there was the sound of the bolt being raised on the door, and she sat up, alert and half-fearful for the moment that it might be Matthews or Lane returning.

Then as the sunlight flooded in she saw the outline of a man, large and broad-shouldered, silhouetted against the trees outside, and she gave a cry of joy that seemed to fill the hut with music.

Then the Earl was beside her, pulling her into his arms.

She held on to him, saying incoherently, her words falling over one another:

"You have . . . found . . . me! You have . . . found me! I . . . prayed that . . . you would . . . come! I was . . . so afraid . . . that I would . . . die before . . . you did."

287

"I have found you," the Earl said in a strange voice.

Then as tears of relief ran down Carmela's cheeks, his lips came down on hers and he held her mouth captive.

For a moment she was too bemused to think of anything except that he was there.

Then as she felt the pressure of his lips, she felt that everything faded away except for the feeling that she was safe, he was holding her close, and she loved him.

His kiss became more demanding, more insistent, and she felt as if he carried her up to the sun and her fears and terror were left behind, and there was only him, the closeness of his arms, and the pressure of his lips.

Then she felt as if the golden rays of sunlight seeped through her body, rising through her breasts and into her throat and up to her lips. The glory of it was his, too, and her love reached towards his heart.

The Earl's arms tightened, then he was kissing the tears from her cheeks, her eyes, her forehead, and again her lips, as she leant against him with a rapture that aroused feelings in her which she had never known before.

Only when she felt as though they had reached the zenith of ecstasy and it was too intense and too wonderful to be borne did Carmela with a little murmur hide her face against the Earl's neck.

But she was still holding on to him as if she was afraid that he might vanish and she would be left alone again.

"How could I have lost you?" the Earl asked in a voice that sounded hoarse and a little unsteady.

"I . . . I was afraid . . . you would . . . never find . . . me."

"I have found you, and I will never let this happen again!"

He put his fingers under her chin to turn her face up to his.

"I have been frantic, desperate!" he said almost as if he spoke to himself.

Then before she could answer he was kissing her, kissing her with slow, passionate kisses which made her feel as if her whole body merged with his and she was no longer herself but part of him.

Finally, when the rapture of his lips made her feel she must have died in the night and was in Heaven, the Earl said:

"I must take you home."

She lifted her head and said incoherently:

"I . . . love you! I . . . tried to call . . . you in the night and tell you . . . where I was . . . but I was . . . afraid that you . . . would not . . . hear me."

"I was awake, thinking about you," the Earl said, "and although it took me a little time to get your message, I am here now, and that is all that matters."

As if Carmela was suddenly aware that she had told the Earl she loved him and that he had kissed her, and they were both things that should not have happened, she moved from his arms, and he said:

"You told me you loved me, my darling, and I knew when I was searching for you that I not only loved you but could not live without you."

Carmela looked at him wide-eyed, and he said:

"We may be first cousins, but that is immaterial beside the fact that you are mine, and I will never let you go."

It was then that Carmela came back to reality, knowing that she would have to tell him the truth but that it was impossible to do so at this moment.

Because she suddenly felt weak, she put her head on his shoulder and frantically tried to think what she should do and how she could tell him that she had been deceiving him and acting a lie.

For the moment nothing seemed real except that she was close to him and he had said that he loved her.

The Earl picked her up in his arms.

"When you were missing," he said, "like 'Cinderella,' you left behind one of your slippers. I knew then that something terrible had happened to you."

"But you did not . . . know who had . . . taken me . . . away," Carmela asked in a low voice, "and carried me here into the . . . wood?"

"When I knew that Lane's niece had also disappeared," the Earl replied, "I was aware of what had happened. But we will talk of it later. You have been through enough for now. I must get you home."

As he spoke he lifted her onto the stallion's back, then untied the reins, which he had attached to a fallen tree.

He mounted behind Carmela, pulled her close against him, and started to ride back through the wood to the clearing.

Carmela shut her eyes.

For the moment she only wanted to think that she was safe and close to the Earl, and that she would confess her deception to him later, when she was feeling stronger.

When they neared the house the Earl asked:

"Did Matthews and Lane say what they were going to do about you? Did they intend to demand a ransom?"

"No," Carmela replied. "They made me sign a cheque for ten thousand pounds and also a letter to Coutts Bank saying they should cash it."

"Ten thousand pounds!" the Earl murmured.

"They said that as soon as they had it they were going abroad."

"I would have them brought to trial if I thought it was worth trying to do so," the Earl said, "but they are the type of criminals who will hang themselves sooner or later, and I would pay a thousand times more to have you safe."

His arms tightened, and as Carmela looked up at

him she knew that he wanted to kiss her, but they were now in sight of the house.

Only when the Earl carried her up the stairs to her bedroom, and the servants were all fussing over her because she had come back safely, did she feel that she was once again confronted by her lies.

Sooner or later she would have to explain them to the Earl, and she shivered because she was afraid of his anger.

The Earl was conscious of it.

"Are you cold?" he asked.

"No . . . no! Only . . . happy to be . . . back," Carmela said quickly.

"As I am happy to have you," he said in a low voice.

He carried her into her bedroom and put her down on the bed.

"Put Her Ladyship to bed," he said to Mrs. Humphries, who was clucking like an agitated hen. "Give her something to eat and let her sleep."

"Yes, M'Lord, of course, M'Lord," Mrs. Humphries replied, "and it's glad and thankful I am that Her Ladyship's returned safe and sound."

The Earl stared down at Carmela lying against the pillows, and there was a look on his face she had never seen before.

"We will talk later," he said quietly.

As he went from the room she wanted desperately to hold on to him to prevent him from leaving her.

Carmela slept, ate, and slept again. But after tea she insisted that she would get up for dinner.

"His Lordship said you were not to do so unless Your Ladyship really felt well enough," Mrs. Humphries argued.

"I am perfectly all right."

She knew she was still a little tired, but at the same time she could not stay away from the Earl any longer. She wanted to be near him, she wanted to talk to him, and she wanted him to kiss her again.

She felt a thrill run through her every time she

thought of the wonderful, magical kisses he had given her in the hut, and how she felt he had taken not only her heart but her soul from her body and made them his.

Then insidiously the thought came to her that when he knew the truth, he would not forgive her for pretending to be Felicity!

Perhaps he would be so angry that his love would die and she would never know it again.

She was so frightened that this would happen that she prayed fervently all the time she was dressing, and tried to reassure herself with the thought that she did not have to tell him the truth yet.

Felicity was not yet married, and therefore she could go on pretending to be her until the moment came when she could pretend no longer.

Even though she loved the Earl, her loyalty was still to Felicity, and she must keep her promise and continue to take her place until Jimmy's wife was dead.

Because she was torn between telling the truth to the man she loved and living for the moment with him in a "Fools' Paradise," she could not make up her mind which she wanted most.

Then she knew that if in his anger the Earl sent her away, life without him would be utterly and completely dark and pointless, and she would never again know any happiness.

"I love him! I love him! I love him!" she said on every step of the stairs as she went down to the Salon.

As she went in through the door and saw him standing at the end of the room in front of the mantelpiece, she stood still, thinking how handsome and magnificent he looked in his evening-clothes.

There was a smile on his lips, and as their eyes met the Earl held out his arms and she ran towards him with a little cry of happiness.

His arms encircled her, then he was kissing her, and his kisses were passionate and demanding, as if he had been frustrated in waiting so long until he could give them to her.

"I love you!" he said in a deep voice. "Now tell me what you told me this morning."

"I love . . . you!" Carmela said. "How could I . . . help it?"

"I have no wish for you to help it."

Then he was kissing her again.

Only when the Butler came in to announce that dinner was ready did they draw apart from each other.

When the Earl gave Carmela his arm and she put her hand on it, he covered it with his hand and felt her quiver at his touch.

He smiled at her, and somehow there was no need for words; they each knew what the other was feeling.

At dinner their lips said one thing and their eyes said another, and Carmela felt as if they were enveloped with a celestial light that came from the sky.

When the meal was over they walked back together to the Salon, and as she sat down on the sofa the Earl said:

"Now we have to make plans, my darling."

She was just about to reply that he should leave it until tomorrow when she could think more clearly, then the door opened and Newman came in with a silver salver in his hand.

"What is it, Newman?" the Earl asked in a tone that told Carmela he did not wish to be disturbed.

"The horses have just returned from Dover, M'Lord," Newman replied, "and the coachman brought with him this letter from His Royal Highness, which he wrote as soon as he boarded the yacht."

The Earl took the letter from the salver, and as the Butler left the room he started to open it, saying as he did so:

"I am afraid our Royal friend will have to look

elsewhere for a wife. I am sure together we can find him one."

There was a little pause. Then Carmela said hesitatingly:

"I . . . I do not . . . think the Prince will . . . mind losing me."

Even as she spoke she realised that the Earl was not listening but was staring down at the letter he held in his hand.

He was silent until because she was nervous Carmela asked:

"What is the matter? What has His Royal Highness . . . said to . . . you?"

"It is extraordinary!" the Earl replied. "I can hardly believe the strange things that happen are not part of a dream."

"What is it?" Carmela asked.

The Earl looked down at the letter in his hand before he said:

"Prince Frederich wrote the letter from the yacht just after he boarded it. He thanks me for my hospitality and says that he is extremely grateful for the use of my horses and my yacht. He sends his regards to you in most fulsome terms."

Carmela listened, puzzled because she could not understand why the Earl seemed to think that what he was saying was strange.

Then he continued:

"There is a post-script, which reads:

"*'As I stepped onto the Quay I met one of the Officials of our Embassy in London. He had just returned from Paris, and he handed me a newspaper, saying he had bought it that morning. I am sure the extract I am enclosing will surprise you as much as it surprised me!'*"

"An . . . extract?" Carmela enquired.

In answer the Earl handed her a small piece of

newspaper, and as she took it she knew what she would read before she actually did so.

For a moment the news-print seemed to dance in front of her eyes. Then she translated swiftly:

" *'Lord Salwick, a British Peer, was married yesterday at the British Embassy Church in the Rue du Faubourg St. Honoré to Lady Felicity Gale, daughter of the 6th Earl of Galeston. The happy couple are starting their honeymoon by staying at the Hotel de Fontainbleu in the Champs Elysées.'* "

Carmela read it to the end and knew as she did so that her hands were trembling.

Then without looking at the Earl she said in a frightened, breathless little voice:

"Forgive me . . . please forgive me . . . I was . . . going to . . . tell you . . . when it was . . . safe for me to do so."

"Are you saying that what is written in the newspaper is true?" the Earl asked incredulously.

Carmela could not reply and after a moment he asked:

"If you are not my cousin Felicity, then who are you?"

"I . . . I am her . . . friend . . . Carmela Lyndon."

The Earl rose to his feet to stand with his back to the mantelpiece, and she felt as if he towered over her.

"I am . . . sorry . . . so very . . . very sorry," she whispered, "but Felicity . . . was . . . in love with . . . Lord Salwick . . . and had been for . . . years."

"Then why did she not marry him before this?" the Earl asked in a puzzled voice.

"Because . . . His Lordship was . . . already married . . . very unhappily, but his wife was dying."

Although she did not look at him, Carmela thought that the Earl's lips tightened, and she went on:

"I . . . I agreed to come . . . here because it was the . . . only way that Felicity could be with . . . Lord Salwick . . . and . . . anyway . . . she did not want him to know about . . . her fortune."

"Why not?"

The Earl's question was abrupt and harsh. Carmela thought despairingly that he was angry and now she had lost him as Felicity might have lost Jimmy.

She knew he was waiting for her answer and after a moment she said:

"Felicity knew . . . because he was . . . proud, that he would refuse to marry a wife who was . . . so wealthy."

"So she was lying to her future husband as you were lying to me?"

"I . . . kn-know it sounds . . . terrible and . . . very reprehensible," Carmela said, "but they were . . . lies for love."

She drew in her breath before she went on:

"I know you think that . . . lies and deception are . . . always . . . wrong and never . . . excusable, but they are . . . sometimes right when they are used to . . . save somebody from suffering or from losing the . . . person they . . . love."

She spoke desperately, feeling as if she was fighting for everything that mattered to her.

Then, because she thought he did not understand, the tears came into her eyes and as they ran down her cheeks she clasped her hands together and said:

"Please . . . please . . . you may not believe it . . . but I love you with my whole heart . . . and soul . . . and if you send me away . . . I shall never . . . however long I live . . . ever love anybody else."

The Earl's eyes searched her face as if he were looking deep down into her soul.

Then as Carmela waited tensely, feeling as if there was no hope and he would repudiate her, he smiled.

His smile seemed to light the whole Salon and dim the candles.

"So you love me!" he said. "And as I love you, what are we to do about it, Carmela?"

She thought her name on his lips was the loveliest sound she had ever heard!

Because she could not help herself, she sprang to her feet and moved close to him, not touching him, only looking at him, fearful that she had misunderstood what he had said.

"I love you!" he said. "And because you are not my cousin and not my Ward, it actually makes things very much easier."

"Do you . . . mean that . . . do you . . . really mean it?"

"I mean it."

The Earl pulled her roughly against him. Then he was kissing her until the world whirled round them and Carmela's feet were no longer on the ground.

He carried her into the sky and placed the moon in her arms and strung the stars round her neck.

Only when she felt as if they were both part of God Himself did the Earl, holding her so closely that she could hardly breathe, ask:

"Have you any idea, my deceitful darling, how we are going to get out of the mess we are in without a scandal?"

She looked up at him apprehensively, and he explained:

"You are staying here with me unchaperoned, and the relatives you have met will think it extraordinary that you should suddenly be marrying under another name."

"Perhaps I ought to . . . go away . . . after all."

The Earl laughed and his arms tightened round her.

"Do you think I would let you? You will never

escape me, my lovely one, and what is more, you will never deceive me or lie to me again. I will make sure of that!"

"I have . . . no wish to do so . . . how could I lie to you . . . when I love you so overwhelmingly?"

"I will make certain I do not give you the opportunity," he said. "At the same time, I think we will both have to tell a few 'lies for love,' as you call them."

He put his lips against her forehead and Carmela knew he was thinking before he said:

"How much do you resemble the real Felicity?"

"We are very alike," Carmela replied, "but of course to look more like her I did my hair in the style she wears, and I am also wearing her clothes."

A thought struck her and she added quickly:

"I have not told you . . . but I have . . . no money, and my father and mother are dead. I had been . . . working in a Vicarage . . . looking after the children of the . . . local Vicar."

Her voice sounded worried and frightened, but the Earl only intensified the pressure of his lips against her skin as he said:

"You will have enough to do in the future, my precious one, looking after our own children, and I have plenty of money without needing yours or my cousin Felicity's."

Carmela gave a little sigh of relief and he went on:

"I have a plan, and I think we must act on it at once."

"What is . . . it?"

The Earl spoke slowly, as if he was thinking aloud as he did so.

"We will leave for Paris first thing in the morning. We will find Felicity and her bridegroom, then we will make sure that not only their marriage is reported in the English newspapers, especially *The London Gazette*, but also our own."

Carmela looked puzzled, and he explained:

"You have just told me that you made yourself look

like Felicity. Now I want you to look like your adorable self."

Carmela understood and she asked:

"Do you really think when we . . . return, the Gales will be deceived into thinking I am somebody . . . different? And that Felicity is the person they met before?"

"I think you will find," the Earl said, "that people see what they expect to see, and when you are dressed in Paris and have, my precious, a Parisian *chic,* I think together we can deceive them quite skilfully with 'lies for love.' "

"You are so clever!" Carmela cried. "I am sure that when they see Felicity, they may easily think that it was she they met when they came here yesterday."

"If not, we will convince them," the Earl said firmly. "But what is more important than anything else is that I want you as my wife."

The way he spoke made Carmela blush, and once again she hid her face against his shoulder.

"I want you!" the Earl said. "And I feel as if I have fought a very hard battle to win you."

"But . . . now you are . . . victorious!" Carmela whispered.

The Earl looked down at the love in her eyes, the flush on her cheeks, and her lips trembling a little from the traumatic emotions she had passed through.

Then he said very softly:

"I adore your face, your entrancing little brain, your graceful body, but most of all your love."

"They are all yours," Carmela said, "and everything . . . else that is . . . me. Tell me that you forgive me, because I want you to trust me and to know that never . . . never again will I . . . lie or . . . deceive you."

"I know that," the Earl said, "and I do trust you, my alluring one, not only because your honesty and goodness shine from you like a light, but also because

I am trusting you with my heart, which I have never given to anybody else."

Carmela gave a little cry.

"It is very precious, very wonderful, and I will treasure it for ever and ever!"

The Earl smiled at the happiness in her voice.

Then he pulled her against him and was kissing her again, kissing her until Carmela knew that everything he said was true, and that he had given her his heart as she had given him hers.

Whatever happened in the future, they would never lose each other because their love was true and would last for all eternity.

FROM HATE
TO LOVE

———— ❧ ————

Author's Note

The indissolubility of marriage was part of the doctrine of the Christian Church from early times, and it was held that all sexual activity outside marriage was suspect.

The first breach in this doctrine was made by the Protestant Reformers who regarded it as permissible for a man to repudiate an adulterous wife and, even if she was not put to death by the executioner, to marry again.

Sometime later, adultery by the husband if coupled with severe cruelty was recognised as grounds for a wife to seek the termination of a marriage.

In contrast to the non-Roman Catholic Churches in Scotland and on the Continent of Europe, the Church of England was less progressive and still upheld the doctrine of indissolubility. Eventually Parliament assumed the power to dissolve marriage. However, this was so expensive a procedure that the total number of divorces granted by Parliament between 1602 and 1859 was only 317.

In 1837, after heated debates it became lawful for a husband to obtain a judicial divorce from a wife guilty of adultery. But a wife had to prove that her husband's adultery was aggravated by cruelty or vice. This provision was not rescinded until 1923.

The power of the King's Proctor to intervene during the six-month period between the *decree nisi* and the *decree absolute* was very unpopular, but continued until the Divorce Reform Act of 1969.

Chapter One

1899

"*Y*ou're late! If you want something to eat, you'd better get it yourself! I'm not here to wait on you. I've got other things to do!"

As she spoke, the elderly woman, who was half-Spanish, half-Arab, walked out of the kitchen and slammed the door.

Atayla sighed, having expected this reaction.

Her first impulse was to go without food, but then her common sense told her that this would be a very stupid thing to do.

After she had been so ill with the wound in her shoulder, she knew that what she needed now was what any Doctor would call "building up" in order to regain her strength.

But this was difficult in a religious household where every other day seemed to be a Fast Day, and Mrs. Mansur, Housekeeper to Father Ignatius, was extremely hostile.

When Atayla had first been brought to the Mission in Tangiers, she was unconscious, and it was some time before she realised where she was or could re-member what had happened.

Then the whole horror of the sudden attack by the desert robbers upon herself and her father as they were making their way towards Tangiers seemed like a nightmare from which she could not awaken.

It seemed extraordinary, after Gordon Lindsay had travelled all over North Africa without coming to any harm, although there had been moments of danger, that when he was almost within sight of Tangiers at the end of his latest expedition, disaster had struck.

It might have been anticipated, Atayla thought now, as she remembered how few servants they had with them, because in the first place one of their camels had died and the other had been too weak to make the journey home, and secondly they could not afford to buy replacements.

The result was that she was now destitute.

Her father was dead and she was penniless, but she had to pull herself together and work out how she could get back to England, and once there find some of her father's relatives and hope they would look after her until she could find employment of some sort.

It was all too much of an effort!

She felt so weak and her head seemed to be stuffed full of cotton-wool, so that she felt unable to use her brain and think things out sensibly and clearly.

She looked round the airless, low-ceilinged kitchen and wondered what she should eat.

Last week, when she had first been able to get out of bed, she was aware that the Housekeeper not only grudged her every mouthful she ate, but was also wildly jealous because Father Ignatius, for whom she had an admiration that was almost idolatrous, talked to her.

An elderly man, kind and extremely sympathetic to all those who came to him in trouble, Father Ignatius ran the Mission.

It consisted of Catholic Missionaries who had training in medicine, and they went out to preach the Gospel to the Arab tribes, who in most cases had no wish to listen to them.

But the Missionaries' lives were dedicated to

converting the heathen, and if they suffered intolerable hardships and sometimes premature death in the process, they would undoubtedly be accepted in Heaven with open arms.

But such ideals apparently had not communicated themselves to the Housekeeper. Atayla knew that she must make plans to leave, and decided she would talk about it to Father Ignatius that evening after supper.

Because she would be eating with him, she would at least have something of a square meal, unless, of course, it was a Fast Day.

In the meantime, she was hungry, and she remembered that last night had been one of the evenings on which a long grace was said over two slices of coarse bread, and there had been nothing else for supper except a glass of water.

She opened the cupboards in the kitchen and found a very small egg, which, because it was pushed to the back behind some cups, she was sure Mrs. Mansur had deliberately hidden from her.

She put it on the kitchen-table, then found a loaf of stale bread, from which she cut herself a thick slice and toasted it in front of the range, in which the fire had almost died out.

It all took time, and by the time she had poached the egg and put it on the bread she was no longer hungry.

But because she had had much experience in coping with illness during her travels with her father, she forced herself to eat, and when the last crumb was finished she knew that she felt a little stronger.

"What I should really enjoy," she told herself, "is a fat chicken that has been roasted in the oven, some fresh vegetables from an English garden, and new potatoes."

Then she laughed at the idea. It seemed so out of keeping with the brilliant sunshine outside, which was really too hot at midday to be enjoyable.

She sat at the table with the empty plate in front of

her and told herself that now was the moment when she must plan her future.

There was just a chance that her father's publishers, if she could get in touch with them, would give her a small advance on the latest manuscript which her father had sent them only a month ago.

By the mercy of God, it had not been with them when the robbers had left them for dead and made off with everything they possessed.

They had even stripped her father of his clothing, Atayla subsequently learnt, but they did not touch her, apart from stabbing her in the shoulder, and had left her unconscious.

The horses they had been riding and the one camel they had left, which was worth at least a hundred pounds and had been carrying all their worldly possessions, had vanished.

Atayla was left with just what she "stood up in" and, as she said herself, not even a penny to bless herself with.

She started worrying that even if the publishers did give her a small advance, it would not be enough for her fare to England, and she would have to throw herself on the mercy of the British Consul.

But when she had suggested this to Father Ignatius, he had not been very optimistic.

From what he said, she gathered that there were far too many English people who found themselves stranded in North Africa because they had either been robbed or had lost their money through sheer carelessness, and the British Consul helped them back to their own country only under very extenuating circumstances.

Atayla considered that her father, having a fine reputation amongst scholars, might come into this category.

At the same time, every instinct in her body shied away from asking for charity and doubtless having to submit to an humiliating cross-examination as to why her father was not better off.

While scholars like himself, and explorers who acknowledged him to be an authority, would understand, it would be quite a different thing to explain to some Senior Clerk that her father had dedicated his life to research into the tribes of North Africa, especially the Berbers.

As very little was known about these people, and since so much about their history, their religion, and their habits was secret, Gordon Lindsay knew that he was contributing something of great importance to historical research.

'Perhaps when Papa's book is published,' Atayla thought, 'he will be acclaimed as he should have been in his lifetime.'

At the same time, she had the dismal idea that as in the case of other books he had written and articles he had contributed to the Royal Geographical Society and the *Société des Géographes,* only a chosen few would appreciate his discoveries, and his sales would be infinitesimal.

'I will have to rely on myself,' Atayla thought, and wondered what qualifications she had for earning money.

That she could speak Arabic and a number of African dialects was hardly a saleable ability if she returned to England.

At the same time, she knew it would be impossible for her to live alone in any part of Africa, and she had the uncomfortable feeling that if she stayed in the Mission, or in any other place that catered for unattached young women, she would come up against the same hostility that she was experiencing in the house of Father Ignatius.

Her mother, before she died, had said to her:

"You are going to be very lovely, my darling, just as Papa and I always thought you would be. But you will have to face the truth that a beautiful woman always pays a penalty for her looks."

Atayla had not understood, and her mother had smiled as she went on:

"There will be men who will pursue you, and women who will hate you. I can only hope, my dearest, that you will find a man who will make you as happy as I have been with your father."

"Have you really been happy, Mama," Atayla had asked, "without a proper home, always wandering, always moving from one place to another?"

Just for a moment there had been a radiant expression on her mother's face before she answered:

"I think it would be impossible for any woman to be as happy as I have been! Everything I have done with your father has been so exciting, and even when things have been desperate, uncomfortable, and dangerous, we have always managed to laugh."

That was true, Atayla thought, for when her mother had died it seemed as if the laughter had gone out of her father's life and hers.

She had tried desperately to take her mother's place in looking after him and seeing that he had proper meals, and making their journeys from place to place, sometimes across unknown, uncharted deserts, a happy adventure.

But while her father had loved her and she loved him, she had always known that he missed her mother desperately.

Although he still laughed, the spontaneity and the joy had been left behind in an unmarked grave in an Arab village that was so small it did not even have a name.

Once or twice during their married life her father and mother had returned to England, and she had been born there.

They had gone back six years ago, when her mother's father had died, and Atayla had met a number of relations, all of whom disapproved of her father and the life he led.

Because she had been only twelve at the time, it was hard to remember them at all clearly, but she was sure that they would not welcome her with any enthusiasm if she arrived orphaned and penniless on their doorstep.

Her father's relatives lived in the far North of England on the border of Scotland.

It was perhaps his Scottish blood which had made him an adventurer, and his North Country brain which had made him a writer.

Atayla remembered now that, although his parents were dead, he had a brother who was older than he was and from whom he had not heard for several years.

She had the uncomfortable feeling that he might be dead. There was also a sister who was married, but try as she would she could not remember her married name.

The only thing to do, she told herself practically, would be to go North and look for them.

Then she asked herself how she could find the money to do that.

It was depressing now to remember that her father, before they had set off on their last expedition, had drawn everything he possessed, which was only a few hundred pounds, out of the Bank in Tangiers.

He had spent most of it on the animals and servants they required for their journey, but when they were on the way back he reckoned that there was enough money left to keep them in comfort for a month or so when they reached Tangiers.

"What we will do," he said, "is rent ourselves a small house on the outskirts of the town, and the two articles I intend to write for the *Société des Géographes,* who are always interested in Africa, will bring in quite a good sum. Then we must decide, my dearest, what to do next."

Atayla had not worried. She was used to what her mother called "living from hand to mouth" and was content to accept her father's optimism that something would "turn up," as it invariably had.

But now her father was not there, and for the first time in her life she was really frightened about the future.

She had sat so long in thought at the kitchen-table that she started when she heard the front door open and knew it was Father Ignatius returning.

Quickly she jumped to her feet and put her plate in the sink, meaning to wash it up later, and went from the kitchen to speak to him.

A good-looking man of nearly sixty, with deep lines on his face and eyes tired from overwork, Atayla knew he found the sun too strong in the middle of the day, which was why he had returned to the Mission to rest in the small room he had fitted up as a Study.

As Atayla appeared, he smiled, put down his flat clerical hat with its wide brim, and said:

"Ah, there you are, my child. I want to talk to you."

"And I want to talk to you, Father, if you have the time."

"Then let us go into my Study," Father Ignatius suggested. "It will be cooler there."

"Can I get you something to drink?" Atayla asked.

"A glass of water would be very refreshing."

Atayla went into the kitchen and, having poured some water into a glass, found one withered lime in the wicker basket which should have contained fruit.

She sliced it and squeezed what little juice there was into the water, hoping it would at least give it a pleasant taste.

She knew it was what her father would have wanted, but she had the feeling that Father Ignatius, deep in his thoughts and prayers, would hardly have noticed if she had poured him a glass of champagne.

She took the water to where he was already seated

in one of the worn bamboo chairs that had seen better days, and he took the glass from her absentmind-
edly and drank a little as she sat down beside him.

"You are too tired to talk now," Atayla said. "I will
let you rest and come back in an hour."

"I think the person who should be resting is you,"
Father Ignatius replied. "How do you feel?"

"Better," Atayla answered, "and the wound on my
shoulder has healed, although it does not look very
pretty. But as no-one is likely to see it, it is of no
particular importance."

She spoke lightly, hoping that Father Ignatius
would smile, but he was staring ahead of him. Then,
as if he had not even heard what she said, he said:

"I have a proposition to put to you, Atayla, although I am not certain it is the right thing for me to
do."

Atayla was surprised by his tone of voice, and she
answered:

"If it is a proposition by which I can make some
money, Father, you know it is something I have to
consider. Everything Papa possessed was taken by the
robbers, and I can only be grateful that the manuscript of his last book was already on its way to England."

"We should certainly thank God that it is safe," Father Ignatius replied, "and that you, my child, did
not lose your life, which is a more precious possession
than anything else."

"I agree, Father," Atayla answered. "At the same
time, as you are well aware, I now have to keep myself, or at least make enough money so that I can
return to England and find Papa's relatives, if they
are still alive."

There was a little silence. Then Father Ignatius
said:

"That is what I want to tell you about. God indeed
often moves in mysterious ways."

Atayla waited, her eyes on his face, knowing he did

not like to be hurried when he had something to relate.

"Today," Father Ignatius began, "I received a request from a Doctor to visit a lady who is one of his patients, and who is very ill."

He spoke seriously, and as if he was choosing every word with care he went on:

"She lives in one of the fine Villas overlooking the bay, and when I saw her, she requested me to find her an Englishwoman who would take her child, a little girl, back to England."

Atayla, who had been leaning back in the bamboo chair in which she had seated herself, sat upright.

She could hardly believe she had heard what the Priest was saying, and it seemed already as if she saw a light at the end of a dark tunnel.

"This lady was very insistent," Father Ignatius went on, "that the person who should escort her child should be an Englishwoman, and as I talked to her I thought of you, realising that this could be the answer to your problem. It would enable you to return to your own country without it costing you anything."

Atayla drew in her breath.

"Father Ignatius, that is exactly what I want! How wonderful that you should have had such a request at this very moment!"

The Priest did not speak, and after a moment Atayla asked:

"What is worrying you? Why are you not pleased by the idea?"

Again Father Ignatius seemed to be feeling for words. Then he said:

"The lady in question calls herself the '*Comtesse* de Soisson,' but she was honest with me, although actually I was already aware of her circumstances. She is not, in fact, married to the *Comte* de Soisson, with whom she is living."

Atayla drew in her breath again.

She was aware that there were many people in

Tangiers who were not accepted by the Spanish, who dominated the social life of the town.

People of other nationalities, for personal reasons, made Tangiers their home because they found it convenient to live as they wished without incurring too much censure and condemnation.

There was a pause before she said:

"Is the lady's child, who is to return to England, English or French?"

"It is a little girl, and she is English."

"Then I shall be very willing to take her."

"I thought that was what you would say," Father Ignatius said. "At the same time, it is not right that you should come in contact with a woman who in the eyes of God and His Church is living a life of sin."

"Is this lady a Catholic?"

Father Ignatius shook his head.

"No, but the *Comte* is, and he has left his wife and family in France."

The way the Priest spoke told Atayla how deeply he deprecated such behaviour, but she could not help feeling that from her own point of view it was unimportant.

All that mattered was that she could take the lady's daughter back to England, which at least would be the first step in planning to fend for herself.

Because she thought the Priest was hesitating as to whether he would allow her to do such a thing, she bent forward to say eagerly:

"Please, Father, you must realise what this opportunity will mean to me. I have no other way of getting to England, unless I can find work of some sort in Tangiers. Even then it would take me a very long time to save up enough money for my fare, and I have nowhere to stay while I am working."

She saw the Priest's lips move to say that she could stay here with him, but it was quite unnecessary for either of them to say aloud what opposition there would be to this from Mrs. Mansur.

Father Ignatius was too astute and too used to dealing with every type and condition of person not to realise how deeply his Housekeeper resented Atayla being in the Mission.

Her antagonism seemed to vibrate through the small rooms, making not only Atayla but Father Ignatius himself feel that every word Mrs. Mansur uttered was like an unsheathed sword.

"Please, Father," Atayla pleaded. "Let me go and see this lady and tell her that I am willing to do what she wishes."

The Priest's lips tightened, then he said:

"I have prayed, Atayla. I have prayed all the time I was returning home that I should do the right thing. You are too young to come in contact with such wickedness, and yet, what is the alternative?"

"I promise you, Father, that this wickedness, as you call it, will not affect me. I shall be concerned only with the child, and when she and I leave Tangiers, she will be free of any bad influence her mother might have over her."

As she spoke, Atayla thought that the worry in the Priest's eyes cleared a little. Then he said:

"Now that your father and mother are with God, I feel that the responsibility for what you should do rests with me. That is why I am afraid for you, and yet I am aware that we are all in the hands of a Power greater than ourselves."

"I believe that too," Atayla said. "But you must be aware, Father, that because Papa and I went to such very strange places, and met tribes with many strange customs, I am not ignorant of life and people as I would be if I had just been brought up quietly in England."

This time the Priest smiled.

"I suppose that is true, and, as you say, the customs of some of the tribes would certainly shock many English people if they were aware of them."

"Therefore, Father," Atayla said quickly, "perhaps

it is God's will that I should have this chance to get to England, and I am sure that the child's relatives who will welcome her back live exemplary lives!"

The Priest sighed. Then, as if he was aware of Atayla's eagerness and there seemed to be no alternative, he said:

"Go and rest, my child, and when it is cooler I will take you to meet this lady. It is quite a walk and you must not overtire yourself after being so ill."

Atayla knew she had won, and her eyes lit up as she said:

"Thank you, thank you, Father! I feel sure you will never regret allowing me to do this, and I am more grateful than I can say that in this way I can reach England without worrying about how I can find the money."

The Priest did not speak, and Atayla sensed that he was praying he had made the right decision.

She went from the room, closing the door quietly behind her, and went up to her small bedroom, which was very hot at this time of the day.

She lay down on her bed, thinking that once again, as her father would have said, something had "turned up."

That there were difficulties and everything was not plain sailing was unimportant beside the fact that this was the means by which she could reach England.

She hoped that wherever she had to take the child, it would be somewhere in the North, from where she would have a shorter journey to Baronswell, where her father's family house was situated.

Because he had been so obsessed by his work in Africa, her father had very seldom talked of his life as a boy or of his family.

It was her mother who had described to Atayla the large grey brick house standing in its own grounds where her father had been born, and where she had been taken when they became engaged to meet his father and mother.

"They were rather awe-inspiring," her mother had said, "and Papa's brother disapproved of the marriage because he said we could not afford it."

Her mother had laughed as she had added:

"I think they were in fact very surprised that I had agreed to marry your father, and my own family were furious, having expected me to make a very much more advantageous match from a social point of view."

"Is that because you were so pretty, Mama?" Atayla had asked.

"Your father thought I was beautiful," her mother replied. "My father, who was a Baronet, was very proud of his family-tree, and as I was his only child and he was bitterly disappointed not to have a son, he expected great things of me."

"He did not approve of Papa?"

"He thought him delightful—how could he fail to do that?" her mother replied loyally. "But he had no money and was determined to go to Africa, and I was equally determined to go with him."

Her mother laughed as she said:

"I might as well have suggested flying to the moon or setting off for the North Pole. They all talked about Africa as if they were not certain such a place existed!"

"But you enjoyed it, Mama?"

"I have loved every moment of being with your father," her mother answered, "and actually I have become as interested as he is in the tribes and their strange evolution from their contacts with other nations."

As her mother spoke, Atayla knew that she was speaking of how the Berbers, with whom her father was particularly concerned, had mingled with their successive conquerors—the Phoenicians, the Romans, the Vandals, and the Arabs.

When her father had taken his family to the Riff mountains, where the majority of the Berbers lived, being known there as the "Rifft," she had begun to understand why he found them so interesting.

Then year after year as she grew older she began to learn the history of the people of North Africa, who seemed more complex and at the same time more fascinating than any others she read about in her history-books.

She followed the invasion of the Arabs who came from Arabia to the "lands of the farthest West" with "a sword in one hand, and a Koran in the other."

She studied the Moors, whose ancestors overran Spain in their endeavour to spread the Islamic faith, and her father taught her the code of that faith, which enabled its followers to decide what was good and noble in man.

There was so much to learn, so much to admire, and if there were aspects of it which seemed bestial and evil, they were not so important as what was good and fine in the peoples who had roamed over the desert for century upon century.

"What does it matter to me if the *Comtesse* is not really a *Comtesse* and is living with a man who has deserted his wife and family?" Atayla asked herself.

Then she knew how horrified Father Ignatius would be at the question.

"Of course it is wrong," she admitted. "At the same time, Papa never passed judgement on anyone unless they committed an act of cruelty. He believed that everybody had to find their own salvation for themselves, and that is what I want to believe too."

To think of her father brought the tears to her eyes and made her realise how much she missed him, and how difficult it would be to face the future without him.

Because she had been so ill when she had been picked up by some kindly travellers and brought unconscious to Father Ignatius in Tangiers, it had been a long time before the loss of her father had had its full impact upon her mind.

In her first moments of consciousness she had shrunk from acknowledging it even to herself because it was too painful to contemplate.

Then as the days went by and the dagger-wound in her body healed, when she realised that she was alone in the world with nobody to turn to or to help and guide her, she wished that the robbers had killed her as they had killed her father.

Then, because she was young and life was an irresistible force, she knew she had to face things as they were and not as she wanted them to be.

She could almost hear her father laughing at her for being a coward and being afraid.

"Do not worry, something will turn up," he was saying, and that was exactly what had happened!

Walking through the crowded streets with Father Ignatius, Atayla was too used to women in burnouses and yashmaks shuffling along in babouches and men wearing fezes to notice anything but the way Father Ignatius was leading her.

She was aware that they were leaving the flat-topped houses behind and were climbing a small hill behind the town. They had not gone far before he pointed to where there was a large white Villa surrounded by a high wall.

They went a little farther, and now the view over the sea was breathtaking. But the ground beneath their feet was stony, and there were a number of small goats grazing on the tufts of grass and flowers between the stones.

There were trees, the leaves of which were thick and dark in colour, and Atayla thought they were very beautiful silhouetted against the sky.

She wished she could share their loveliness with somebody but realised that the Priest walking beside her was deep in thought, or prayer, his rosary swinging from his waist with each movement of his sandalled feet.

Then in the centre of the wall was a large, imposing gate, and as soon as they approached, it was opened by a servant dressed in spotless white.

Father Ignatius spoke to him in his own language, and Atayla stared at green lawns, fountains, and a profusion of flowers.

Cypress trees, pointing like long fingers towards the sky, seemed completely in keeping with the Oriental architecture of the Villa.

Without speaking, Father Ignatius walked up to the front door, and it in its turn was opened by a smartly dressed servant, and they were shown into a large cool room from which there was a magnificent view over the bay.

It was furnished with deep sofas and armchairs that looked so comfortable that Atayla thought if once she sat down in one, it would be hard to get up again.

There were plants in china pots, and paintings which she knew must be of great value, besides some exquisite pieces of French furniture that were more beautiful than anything she had ever seen before.

There was a long wait while she and Father Ignatius sat on the edges of their armchairs in silence, until a maid came to his side and said something in Spanish.

Father Ignatius frowned. Then he said to Atayla:

"The maid says her mistress is very weak, and it would be best for her to see you alone. Go with her, my child."

Atayla was eager to do so, and only as she walked up the very elegant staircase did she wonder for the first time what the lady she was about to see would think of her.

It had never struck her until this moment that while she might have been very willing to take the so-called *Comtesse*'s child to England, there was also a decision to be made by the mother, who might not be impressed by her appearance.

The clothes she had been wearing when she was attacked were threadbare, and her blouse had been torn and stained from the dagger-thrust.

She had therefore been obliged to accept a dress from a collection of clothes at the Mission sent there from England by sewing-parties in Cheltenham, Bath, and other Provincial towns as an act of Charity.

Atayla had realised it was typical that the material chosen for what were called "the natives" was a coarse grey cotton of a particularly ugly hue, which looked drab and very out-of-place in the brilliant sunshine.

Only orphans and the poorest beggars would accept such hideous garments when instinctively they longed for the colour which they saw all round them.

The dress was full in places where it should have been tight, and tight where it should have been full, but Atayla had improved it by making a belt out of several handkerchiefs and converting one into a small white collar.

Even so, with a black bonnet on her head, she knew how unprepossessing she must look, and she was suddenly afraid that the child's mother would insist on looking for somebody better dressed and perhaps older to be in charge of her daughter.

"I should have thought of it before," Atayla told herself.

Then she realised that even if she had, there would have been little she could do about it.

In any other household there might have been a woman who would have lent her a slightly more attractive outfit to wear than the one she had on, but she well knew that Mrs. Mansur was only too glad if she looked ugly and would not have lifted a finger to lend her so much as a pair of gloves.

The maid had reached the top of the stairs and was opening the door of a room.

Because it seemed to be expected of her, Atayla

followed her into it, and saw that she was in one of the most beautiful bedrooms she had ever seen.

There was a bow-window looking out over the garden and to the sea beyond, there were sun-blinds to keep out the glare of the sun, and dominating the room was an enormous bed draped with white curtains which fell from a corona of gold angels suspended from the ceiling.

In the bed, propped against silk pillows trimmed with wide lace, was one of the loveliest women Atayla could imagine.

Because she had become so accustomed to the Arab women with their dark skin, in contrast the woman in the bed was even more sensational.

She had long golden hair the colour of a corn-field, and small classical features. However, she was very thin and pale, and it was obvious that she was delicate, or perhaps very ill.

Her eyes were closed, and her eye-lashes were dark against the pallor of her cheeks, but as the maid approached she looked up, and it was then that Atayla saw that her eyes were the blue of the sea and thought she was like a flower.

"The young lady's here to see you, *Señora*," the maid said, speaking with a broken accent.

"Yes, yes, of course," the lady in the bed said in little more than a whisper.

The maid moved to one side, motioned Atayla to go forward, and placed a chair for her so that she was as near as possible to the lady in the bed.

Then the maid left the room, and after what seemed a long pause the lady said:

"You have come from Father Ignatius?"

"Yes, *Madame*."

"You are English?"

"Yes, *Madame*."

"The Priest tells me your father was a famous writer."

"That is correct, *Madame*."

"And he is dead?"

"Yes, *Madame*."

There was a little silence, as if the lady was making an effort to remember what she had been told. Then she said:

"You are willing, I understand, to go to England."

"Yes, *Madame*."

"And you will take my daughter with you? I want her to go to her father."

"Her . . . father?"

Atayla could not help her voice sounding somewhat surprised.

"Yes, her father," the lady said. "Felicity should be with him. My—the *Comte*—does not want her here."

The way in which she spoke told Atayla more than her words, and she asked:

"How old is your daughter?"

"She is eight," the lady said, "and has been with me here in Tangiers for three years, but now she must go—home."

"Where am I to take her?" Atayla asked.

There was a pause, then almost as if the lady found it hard to say the words, she replied:

"To Roth Castle. Her father is the Earl of Rothwell, and she should be with him, where she belongs."

The lady's voice was suddenly hard. Then, as if she could not help herself, she said:

"I shall miss her! I shall miss her more than I can say, but I am not well, and if I die, the *Comte* might not let her go back."

Atayla could not think what to say to this, so she was silent until the lady went on:

"You must try to make Felicity understand that as she is English she must live in England. It will not be easy for her to return to a life she has forgotten, so you must help her. Promise me you will help her."

"Of course I will," Atayla replied. "I will do everything I can."

"It will be hard for her, very hard, but there is

nothing else I can do. I know that she will be forgiven and accepted, while I am damned forever!"

She spoke bitterly, and Atayla knew perceptively that she did not mean religiously but socially.

Then the lady went on:

"You must take her at once, before the *Comte* returns. He might try to stop her, and that would make things more difficult than they are already."

Atayla's eyes widened but she thought she should not ask questions, but merely take her orders.

The lady was silent for a moment. Then she said:

"I will give you money. It will be expensive to travel to England, and you must also have a salary."

Atayla was just about to say that she wanted nothing but her own fare. Then, seeing the beauty and luxury of the bedroom she was in, she thought she would be very silly if she did not accept what she was offered.

Somehow it went against her instincts, although she told herself she must be practical since she owned nothing and there were things she would need for the voyage.

"Thank you, *Madame*," she said aloud. "As I expect Father Ignatius told you, my father was killed by desert robbers, who also took literally everything we possessed. So if I am to travel to England with your daughter, I shall have to buy myself a few clothes."

The lady's eyes opened and she said:

"Clothes? But that will take time, and I want you to go at once, tomorrow, if possible."

"I am sure I could find the things I need in the Market," Atayla suggested vaguely.

"No, that is ridiculous!" the lady said. "I have clothes, masses of clothes, and as you are very slim I am sure mine will fit you."

She did not wait for Atayla to reply but reached out and picked up a little gold bell which stood on the table by her bed.

She rang it, and instantly, almost as if she had been listening outside the door, the Spanish maid came in.

"Listen, Mala," the lady said, "I have a trunk filled with clothes that have never been unpacked, since it was too hot to wear them here."

"*Si, señora.*"

"Have it brought downstairs and put in a carriage, and pack another trunk with all the things I do not need any more. There are some coming from Paris this week, and some which arrived last week. The rest I have finished with. Do you understand?"

"*Si, Señora.*"

"Then pack them, pack them quickly! They can go first thing tomorrow morning, or better still the carriage can go into Tangiers tonight and take them to this young lady at the Mission."

"Shall I pack some hats and bonnets, *Señora?*"

"Pack everything. This lady has no clothes at all. They were all stolen from her. She will require to be dressed from her head to her feet. Is that understood?"

"*Si, Señora.*"

"I have far too many clothes, and it is a good opportunity to dispose of them. Get the other maids to help you. There is no time to be lost!"

"But . . . *Madame* . . ." Atayla expostulated, "it is too much! I cannot possibly accept so many things."

"Do not be foolish," the lady said. "You need them and I have finished with them, and there is no time, I tell you, no time for you to buy anything."

She paused before she continued:

"Now that I think of it, I am making a mistake: you will take Felicity with you now—yes—that would be best—and the trunks will follow as soon as Mala has packed them."

As she spoke she rang the bell again in a feverish manner, and as the maid came hurrying back into the room, she said:

"Fetch Lady Felicity. Tell her I want her, and see

that her clothes are packed too, every one of them, you understand? Everything! Her toys, her dolls—everything she possesses!"

The lady spoke in a feverish, almost hysterical manner, and the maid rushed from the room. As soon as she had gone, the lady said, as if she was still making an effort to think of everything:

"I must give you some money!"

There was a little handbag lying on the bed beside her, and she opened it and took out a key.

"The safe is over there," she said, "on the floor under that table."

A little bewildered, Atayla took the key from her, and crossing the room, she saw that there was a large table covered by a cloth, to which the lady was pointing.

For a moment she thought she must be mistaken, then she told herself she should try to be intelligent about this, and raising the cloth she saw that underneath was a large, square safe.

She inserted the key into the lock, pressed down on the handle, and the safe door opened.

"There is a tray on the top shelf," the voice from the bed said, "bring it to me."

Atayla did as she was told, and saw that on the tray were packets of Moroccan francs done up with elastic-bands, and also two brown envelopes like those used in Banks which she was sure contained coins.

"I think I can give you about three hundred pounds," the lady said. "I have no more at the moment, but that will cover the cost of your fare and Felicity's. What is left over you may keep."

"I am sure it is too much," Atayla expostulated.

"I trust you, and I know you are honest. My child must travel First Class in reserved carriages, and in the best cabins of the ships. The train will take you to the Halt near Roth Castle in Yorkshire, and from there you must hire a carriage for the last three miles. I trust you to do what is right."

"I promise you I will do exactly what you have told me," Atayla replied.

The lady handed her the rolls of notes and two little brown envelopes, which were very heavy. Atayla held them in her hand, wondering what she should do with them, until the lady said:

"Of course, you have no handbag! There is one of mine in the chest-of-drawers over there. I will give it to you."

Even while she thought this could not be happening, Atayla went to the chest-of-drawers and took out a leather handbag which appeared to her to be very expensive and much finer than anything she had ever owned before.

She took it back to the bed, put the money inside it, and then on the lady's instructions put the tray back in the safe, locked it, and gave her back the key.

As she did so, the door opened, and without anybody announcing her a small girl came into the room.

One glance at her showed Atayla that she was not like her mother, except that her eyes were blue. Otherwise, her face was a different shape, her hair, which was thick and curly, was dark, and she was not delicately made, but rather sturdy.

She ran across the room eagerly, her expensive white dress of muslin and lace showing her bare, dimpled knees, white silk socks, and pretty buttoned shoes.

"Mama, Mama! You are better? Come and play in the garden with me."

"I cannot do that, dearest," her mother said, "and listen, Felicity, I have something to tell you."

"I have a lot to tell you, Mama. I rode my pony today and went very fast."

The lady held Felicity's hand in hers as she said:

"Sit on the bed, my precious, and listen carefully to what I have to tell you. You are going to England!"

"To England, Mama?"

"Yes, dearest, to your father."

"I do not want to go to Papa," Felicity said. "I want to stay here with you. England is cold and foggy, and *Mon Père* says it is not a nice place. He says he hates English people, and it is a pity I am not French."

"You are English, Felicity, and I want you to go to England and see it for yourself. This kind lady is going to take you there. Think how exciting it will be to travel in a big ship and by train."

Felicity put her head on one side and contemplated the idea. Then she asked:

"Can my pony come with me?"

"No, dearest, but your father has dozens of horses, and I am sure he will give you a pony as soon as you arrive."

"I love the pony I have here," Felicity said, "and *Mon Père* says that England is a bad place! Before he went away I knew he was cross with me, because he said I was behaving like an English girl."

The lady looked at Atayla, and she knew she was telling her without words what the *Comte* felt about Felicity.

She was sure he was finding her an encumbrance, and it was tiresome for him to have her in the house where he had installed her mother as his mistress.

It was almost as if somebody were relating a story to her. Atayla could understand that the *Comte* at times missed his own children and found it intolerable to have instead the child of an Englishman whom he disliked.

"What I want you to do now, Felicity darling," the lady said, "is to go and choose all the toys you want to go with you to England—your dolls and, of course, your Teddy Bear!"

She grasped her daughter's small hand in hers and went on:

"Help the maids to pack them carefully so that they are not uncomfortable on the journey, and I know they will find it very exciting to see the great big Castle in which your father lives."

Felicity looked indecisive, and her mother said:

"Go quickly, or they might be forgotten!"

The child gave a little cry, as if the idea frightened her, and without saying any more she jumped down from the bed and ran from the room.

Her mother looked at Atayla, who said:

"She is very attractive, and I am sure you will miss her very much."

"It will break my heart to part with her," the lady said, "but there is nothing I can do but send her away. The *Comte* does not really like her, and she is making things difficult for both of us. Besides, I realise there is no life for her here. When she grows older she must, as her father's daughter, take her proper place in Society."

"That is a long time ahead," Atayla said with a smile.

"She is beginning to notice things," the lady explained, almost as if she spoke to herself. "Yesterday she asked me why she had two fathers, Papa, whom she hardly remembers, and *Mon Père*, who lives with me here. What am I to tell her?"

"I know I seem rather stupid," Atayla said, "but I must get this straight. If your husband is the Earl of Rothwell, then you are the Countess of Rothwell!"

The lady nodded.

"But because it makes the *Comte* happy, I call myself '*La Comtesse* de Soisson,' and that is how I wish to be known by you and everyone. I am sorry you cannot meet him, because he is very, very charming, but his dislike of Felicity is increasing. If I live, it will be a mistake for her to be here, and if I . . . die . . ."

She ceased speaking, and there was a pause.

"I will take Felicity to England," Atayla said. "As you have said, it is where she belongs."

"Thank you."

The lady looked at Atayla as if she saw her for the first time and said:

"You are very pretty, and when you are well

dressed you will look prettier still. Let me beg you—
do not listen to your heart. If you do—then you will
do mad, crazy things—as I have done—and once you
have thrown your bonnet over the wind-mill, there is
no going back!"

CHAPTER TWO

When they left the Mission the next morning,
Atayla could hardly believe it was really happening.

She supposed it was because she was still weak from
her wound and the fever which had followed it that
she found it difficult to grasp that so much was taking
place so quickly.

And yet, she had thought afterwards that while she
was in the Villa she had been quite efficient.

After the *Comtesse* had given her orders for the
packing to be done and Felicity had left them, Atayla
had said hesitatingly:

"I think, *Madame,* I should go downstairs and tell
Father Ignatius that I am to leave him tomorrow, and
also that Lady Felicity will come back with me tonight
to the Mission."

"Yes, of course," the *Comtesse* agreed, "and while
you are away I will try to think of anything else you
will need."

"Thank you," Atayla said.

She hurried from the room and down the curved

white staircase to where Father Ignatius was sitting where she had left him.

He had obviously been looked after, for in front of him was a glass of the mint tea which every guest in Morocco is offered whether it is a private house he enters or a shop.

With it were the traditional sweetmeats, mostly of almonds and honey, and little cakes made with coconut.

As Atayla joined him, the servant who had let them in immediately brought her a glass of mint tea, and because she felt she needed sustenance she sipped it gratefully.

"Eat, my child," Father Ignatius said, pushing a plate of sweetmeats towards her, and after the very inadequate meal she had cooked for herself in the Mission, Atayla reached out towards them eagerly.

"There is so much I have to tell you," she said when she could get her breath, "and I hardly know where to begin."

Father Ignatius smiled.

"I imagine the *Comtesse* has asked you to leave as soon as possible for England with her daughter."

"That is right," Atayla replied.

"I think in case there is any difficulty with which she has not the strength to cope, she is anxious to get her away before the *Comte* returns," the Priest said.

"She wishes us to take Lady Felicity back with us now."

Father Ignatius nodded, as if that was what he had expected, and Atayla had the idea that he knew far more about the situation than he had told her.

"Also," Atayla said a little shyly, "*Madame* has been extremely kind in giving me a great quantity of clothes. I explained to her that all mine had been stolen by the robbers."

"That is generous and makes things much easier for you," Father Ignatius replied. "I am well aware that the clothes you are wearing at the moment would not be suitable for a journey to England or when you present yourself on arrival."

Atayla looked at him in surprise, then realised his eyes were twinkling.

She thought, as had occurred to her before since her arrival at the Mission, that Father Ignatius had a great deal of worldly knowledge in addition to spiritual.

Then she put down the sweetmeat she had been eating and said:

"I have just thought . . . the maids are packing the clothes the *Comtesse* has given me, but I shall have no time to unpack them and find something to wear for the journey. Shall I go ask the maid if she will kindly put out what I will need in a separate case?"

"That certainly seems a sensible thing to do," Father Ignatius replied.

Atayla rose to her feet and walked up the staircase again, hoping she would find Mala, the maid, without having to ask the *Comtesse* where she was.

When she reached the landing she heard voices, and two doors away from the *Comtesse*'s room she found Mala and three other maids busily taking gowns from several built-in wardrobes and packing them into large leather trunks.

Atayla could not believe they were all for her, but the maids looked up when she appeared and Mala said:

"You want me, *Señorita?*"

"Yes," Atayla replied. "I came to ask you if you would be very kind and put a gown and coat in which I could travel in a separate case from the other things. If the trunks are to arrive at the Mission tonight, there will be no time in which to unpack anything."

"*Si, si, Señorita,* I should have thought of it," Mala said crossly, as if her efficiency as a lady's-maid was in question.

She spoke quickly in Spanish to the other maids. Then to Atayla:

"Do not worry, *Señorita*, it will be arranged, and as you have nothing of your own, I will pack separately everything for the voyage so that you need not open the other trunks until after you reach your destination."

"Thank you very much," Atayla said. "It is very kind of you."

As she turned away, the maid gave a little cry.

"Wait, *Señorita*, wait!" she said. "There is the problem of shoes. Try on a pair belonging to the *Señora* and see if they fit you."

She snapped her fingers, and one of the other maids brought from the wardrobe a pair of very elegant kid shoes that were smarter than anything Atayla had ever seen, let alone owned.

She pulled off the worn, flat-heeled black leather shoes which were all the Mission could offer, and slipped her feet into the *Comtesse*'s.

They seemed a trifle tight, but that, she thought, was very likely owing to the fact that she had been wearing loose shoes, and also it was very hot.

Mala held up her hands in delight.

"That makes everything easy," she said. "I was afraid the *Señorita* would look very elegant on top, but have to go barefoot, as the *Señora* has very small feet."

"These are very lovely," Atayla said. "Thank you again for all you are doing for me."

She thought the maids seemed pleased by her gratitude. Then, feeling embarrassed at being given so much, she hurried down the stairs again to Father Ignatius.

"I have been thinking," he said as she sat down, "that if the *Comtesse* wishes to leave tomorrow, you will have to take the ship to Gibraltar. It leaves early and takes four hours for the crossing."

"The *Comtesse* insists that Lady Felicity has a cabin

on every ship in which we travel, and a reserved First Class carriage on every train."

"I will see what I can do about that," Father Ignatius promised. "I hope she has given you enough money for such extravagances."

"She has been very generous."

"You will find it expensive," the Priest said, "and you will doubtless have to stay in London before you can catch a train to the North."

Atayla looked worried.

"When I last stayed in London," she said, "it was with Mama and Papa in a private house. I do not know of an Hotel where I could take Lady Felicity."

"Leave this to me," Father Ignatius said. "I have a friend who deals with travellers who come to Tangiers and arranges their transport not only in Morocco but also in Europe."

Atayla gave a little sigh of relief and said:

"I have travelled so much with Papa that it should hold no fears for me. But, as you know, Father, I am more used to camels than trains, and dhows than steamships!"

Father Ignatius laughed.

"That is true, but you are a sensible girl, and I am sure you will soon adjust yourself to the difference."

"I hope so," Atayla said.

It had of course always been her father who had arranged the caravans in which they crossed the desert, and when they were not sleeping in their own tents, there was usually not much choice when it came to Hotels in native towns.

It was not until they were driving back in the *Comte*'s comfortable carriage that Atayla felt exhausted, and also apprehensive of what lay ahead.

There had been an emotional scene when the *Comtesse* had said good-bye to her daughter, and because she had wept and kissed the little girl over and over again, Felicity had cried too.

"You will not forget me, my darling, promise me you will not forget me," the *Comtesse* pleaded.

Even with the tears running down her cheeks and her blue eyes wet with them she still looked exceedingly beautiful.

But when Atayla finally took Felicity by the hand and drew her toward the door, she looked back to see the *Comtesse* lying with closed eyes against the pillows and seemingly on the point of collapse.

"I do not . . . want to leave . . . Mama," Felicity wept. "I want to . . . stay here with my . . . pony."

"You will have a pony in England," Atayla promised, "and think how exciting it will be tomorrow to go in a big ship on the sea!"

However, Felicity was not appeased, and all the way from the Villa to the Mission she cried and said she wished to stay with her mother.

Atayla thought wearily that they would doubtless go from one emotional upset to another, and Mrs. Mansur would be annoyed that Father Ignatius had brought another guest to stay at the Mission.

But Mrs. Mansur was so delighted to hear that Atayla was leaving the next morning that she hurriedly prepared a bed for Felicity, and the supper was more palatable than anything Atayla had eaten since she had become well enough to notice the food.

They had driven back without any luggage, as Mala had said it was not yet ready, and there was a great deal more packing yet to be done.

There was no sign of it when the evening meal was finished, and as Atayla rose from the table she was wondering what Felicity would think of having to go to bed in a shapeless, thick calico nightgown which was all that was obtainable at the Mission, when there was a knock on the door.

Mrs. Mansur went to open it and they heard her voice scream shrilly at what she saw outside.

Atayla looked across the table at Father Ignatius.

"I expect the luggage has arrived."

There was a faint smile on his lips as he replied:

"I am sure Mrs. Mansur will find it somewhat over-whelming. Take the child upstairs while I cope with it."

Atayla obeyed him, and as they went up the small, rickety staircase, she saw the *Comtesse*'s servants carry-ing in a number of huge leather trunks and thought they would be another responsibility for her on the voyage.

She had not been mistaken in this, for the next morning, after a restless night in which she found it difficult to sleep, she had gone downstairs to be ap-palled at the mountain of baggage.

It filled the small entrance-hall and spilt over into what was the Waiting-Room for those who wished to have an interview with Father Ignatius.

The leather trunks were all obviously expensive ones, some with carved tops, some with heavy straps.

There were also a number of hat-boxes, which Atayla looked at longingly, then she searched for the case in which Mala had promised to pack her clothes for the voyage.

She was far too nervous to ask Mrs. Mansur to have it brought up to her, so on rising she had put on her usual shapeless grey cotton gown.

Now she saw that there was in fact a smaller trunk, a very elegant one bearing an embossed coronet.

She knew instinctively that it was English and must have been part of the luggage which the *Comtesse* had brought with her when she left the Earl of Rothwell.

Atayla pulled it away from the heap of baggage and was just wondering how she was to get it upstairs, when one of the younger Priests who worked with Father Ignatius came from the Study.

He was a very earnest young man, of French na-tionality, and Atayla had the idea that whenever he saw her he looked the other way in case she should prove a temptation to him.

Then, before he could slip through the outside door, she said quickly:

"I wonder if you would be very kind and carry this trunk upstairs? I am afraid it is too heavy for me to manage alone, and I do not want to worry Father Ignatius if I can help it."

"No, of course not," the young Priest replied.

He lifted up the small trunk without any difficulty and hurried up the stairs, almost, Atayla thought with a faint smile, as if the Devil was at his heels.

She had already noticed that there was a label on the trunk on which was written FOR THE JOURNEY, and now she saw a similar label was attached to one of the small hat-boxes.

Carrying it in her hand, she climbed the stairs after the Priest.

He had already placed the trunk in her bedroom, and as he came from it he did not look at her but hurried down the stairs, and had almost reached the front door before she could thank him.

"Thank you, thank you!" she called.

He murmured something in too low a voice for her to hear it, then the Mission door slammed shut behind him.

Atayla laughed because it was difficult to believe she could be a temptation to anybody, looking as she did in the hideous gray cotton gown.

Then, excited as she had not been since her father died, she undid the straps of the small trunk and threw back the lid.

Five minutes later she looked at herself in the mirror and gasped. She could hardly believe she was the same person who had walked up to the Villa yesterday with Father Ignatius.

The *Comtesse*'s gown fitted her almost as if it had been made for her, and it was so exquisite and so elegant that Atayla felt that any woman seeing it would know that it came from Paris.

Of blue silk, the colour of the *Comtesse*'s eyes, it had

338

a neat little jacket ending at the waist to wear over it, and although she could hardly believe it, as she took it from the trunk she found a cape in the same material edged with sable that reached from her neck to the ground.

"How could she possibly part with anything so expensive?" Atayla questioned.

Then as she delved deeper into the trunk she found underclothes trimmed with lace that were more beautiful than anything she had ever imagined she might see, let alone own.

There was a silk petticoat that rustled like the wind in the trees when she put it on, there was a nightgown and a negligé, slippers trimmed with marabou, and quite a number of other small items that she had no time to inspect.

She was aware that time was passing and she must wake Felicity and get her dressed for the journey.

Felicity's travelling-case had been brought up to her room last night by Father Ignatius, and Atayla had appreciated that the nightgown and the pretty little dressing-gown trimmed with lace was laid on the top.

Beneath these was a coat that matched the dress the child had worn when she left the Villa and in which she was obviously intended to travel the next day.

Atayla then opened the hat-box and found a small, pretty toque in the same colour as her gown, trimmed only with veiling.

However, it was so smart that she felt despairingly that her hair was not worthy of such a crown to embellish it.

Hastily she brushed it back from her forehead, and coiled it at the back of her head in a more elegant chignon than she usually wore.

It did not seem to Atayla from what she could remember a very fashionable coiffure, and it was to be a long time before she realised that across the Atlantic,

Dana Gibson had introduced a new look for the American woman, which had also become the rage of England and France.

Anyway, as she looked at herself in the mirror she could not help feeling that she was viewing a complete stranger, somebody she had never met before, and who not only looked what her mother would have called a "Lady" but also was undoubtedly extremely attractive.

Then, because she knew she was loitering when she should be busy, Atayla hurried into the next room to wake Felicity.

They drove through the crowded streets down to the Quay with two hired carriages because it was impossible to get all the luggage into one.

A great number of people stared at them because vehicles on wheels were few and far between in Tangiers.

Atayla suddenly felt that she could not leave the land she knew so well and in which she had spent so many years of her life.

What did she know of England? She was familiar only with the desert and the tribes who roamed and lived in it.

The cities of Morocco, which her father had said with their packed streets and fortified walls, with gates which were shut at night, were more mediaeval than anything to be found in more civilised parts of the world.

"I shall be alien to everything in England, and I had much better stay here," Atayla told herself.

Then she remembered the hostility she had encountered from Mrs. Mansur and knew that without her father neither Morocco nor any other part of North Africa would welcome her as an unattached and unprotected woman, nor was there any work for her because she was so young.

'I am a Nomad, a wanderer without roots,' she thought a little bitterly.

Then she was ashamed because she knew she should be grateful that something had turned up at the last moment, when she had no money and little chance of earning any.

She put out her hand towards Father Ignatius.

"I want to thank you, Father," she said, "not only for your great kindness in nursing me back to health but for letting me stay with you, and of course for finding a very comfortable way for me to return to England."

"God answered my prayers," Father Ignatius said simply. "I know, my child, that it was meant that you should go back to your father's and mother's country, which is also yours, even though it may seem strange to you at first."

Atayla felt he had read her thoughts and been aware of the fear she was trying to hide from him.

'If the worst comes to the worst,' she thought, 'I can come back.'

At the same time, she knew that would not be a very practical move, and she would somehow have to adjust herself to England and to her father's relatives, if she could find them.

Then there was the bustle and the excitement of going aboard the ship, and because it was very crowded, it was a relief to find that Father Ignatius's friend had procured a private cabin for them.

He also had their First Class tickets for the train which would carry them from Gibraltar to Madrid, and from Madrid to Calais.

"You will have to change at Madrid," he told Atayla, "but when you get there go at once to the Ticket Office and ask them not only the times of the trains but for a reserved carriage, and they will advise you which is the quickest and best way to reach England."

"Thank you, I will do that," Atayla answered.

"It may mean," he went on, "taking a ship from Le Havre rather than Calais, but I do not have enough information here to help you."

Atayla thanked him again. At the same time, she hoped rather doubtfully that it would be as easy as he made it sound.

Then she told herself she was being ridiculous. If she and her father could find their way over miles and miles of sandy desert without getting lost, there was no reason why she should lose herself and Felicity when it was really a straightforward journey across Europe.

At the same time, it was hard to say good-bye to Father Ignatius.

He seemed to be her last contact with her old life, and she was setting out alone on an uncharted course without a guide and without even a compass.

"May God bless you, my child," Father Ignatius said, "and keep you safe. If you are in any difficulty, pray, and help will always come to you."

Then he had gone ashore, and Atayla and Felicity waved good-bye as the ship's engines began to turn, and they moved slowly away from the Quay.

Felicity wanted to run round the deck, but there were too many people crowded on it, and Atayla persuaded her to come into the cabin.

"We have a little house all to ourselves," she said. "Let us sit down and make ourselves comfortable, and if you would like something to eat or drink, I am sure I can find a steward to bring it to you."

The child was at first restless, then Atayla told her a story in which a dhow that she and her father were travelling in became becalmed in the centre of a huge lake and they did not know how they were to reach the shore.

Felicity listened, then asked for another story.

Atayla soon found that she was insatiable in her demands for them.

Although it was an excellent way of keeping her amused and quiet on what was to prove a very long and arduous journey, she herself became tired of her own voice, and longed to sleep, or at least to be able to think quietly.

The only thing, she knew later, which saved her from collapsing was the food she was able to buy at the different stations, and which, after the meagre fare provided by Mrs. Mansur, seemed delicious and was certainly sustaining.

As they passed through Spain there was plenty of fresh fruit to be bought, and when they crossed the frontier into France there were pies and pastries that were different from anything Atayla had eaten for a long time.

Felicity was, she discovered, an intelligent little girl who had moments of shrewdness that made her seem older than her age.

Soon after they started, she said to Atayla:

"When *Mon Père* comes home he'll be surprised to find me gone."

"I am sure he will," Atayla replied.

"He'll also be glad," Felicity said. "He does not like me. Why does he not like me?"

"I am sure you are mistaken," Atayla said quickly. "He loves you, but sometimes he had to reprove you if you did anything wrong."

Felicity shook her head, making her dark curls dance round her cheeks.

"No, he does not like me," she said, "and Mala says it is because he hates my Papa."

Atayla did not know what to say, and after a moment Felicity went on:

"I have two fathers! Most girls have only one father, but I have two."

"Then you are very lucky. My father is dead, so I have no father and I miss him very much."

Felicity's attention was diverted from herself.

"Why did your father die?"

Atayla told her the story of how they had been set upon by robbers in the desert, and the child listened with fascination.

"And they tried to kill you too?" she asked.

Atayla nodded.

"They thought I was dead," she said, "but God kept me alive, perhaps so that I should be useful in taking you to England."

Felicity pondered over this for a moment or two. Then she said:

"It seems a funny way to choose me a Governess. Mama says you're to be my Governess and teach me lots of things about England."

"That is what I hope to do," Atayla said, "but as I have not been to England for some time, perhaps you will have to teach me!"

Felicity laughed.

"I remember lots of things about England, so I will be able to teach you."

When they reached Calais, Atayla felt they had been travelling for weeks, because there had been a long wait for a train at Madrid.

As they had arrived late at night and would be leaving early in the morning, it was not worth going to an Hotel, and they had therefore slept rather uncomfortably in the Ladies' Waiting-Room.

Atayla's insistence on having reserved carriages ensured that they were treated with respect, and also, she thought, with some amusement at their impressive mountain of luggage.

Everywhere they changed there were a number of porters only too willing to carry it because it looked expensive.

The Channel crossing was fortunately fairly smooth, certainly not half as rough, Atayla thought with a smile, as riding on the back of a camel.

However, she persuaded Felicity to lie down in the

cabin in case she felt sick, and to her relief the child fell asleep.

Then there was a long train journey to London, and when they arrived, as Atayla had expected, they were told they had to change stations for the trains to the North.

As Felicity was tired and hungry, Atayla did not waste time in making enquiries about trains leaving late in the evening, but asked the Station Master, who stood resplendent in a tall hat on the platform, if he could recommend a quiet, respectable Hotel.

One look at the elegant way in which she was dressed made him reply with hardly a pause that he was quite certain she would be comfortable at Brown's Hotel in Dover Street.

Atayla took his advice and drove there, but when she received the bill the next morning she was horrified at how expensive it was.

The large tip she was obliged to give and the extravagant way they were travelling were fast swallowing up the money the *Comtesse* had given her.

She had also learnt that the Moroccan francs were priced very low against European currency.

However, she was confident that she had enough to reach Roth Castle, but it was obvious that there would be very little left over, and when the journey was finished she would be as penniless as she had been before it had begun.

But after a good and substantial breakfast at Brown's Hotel, she did not feel worried, and accepted the Manager's suggestion that as they had a long journey in front of them they should take a packed luncheon from the Hotel for the train, and augment it on the journey with hampers which would be supplied at the main stations at which they stopped.

It all sounded so comfortable that Atayla agreed instantly. At the same time, she was aware that this was yet another drain on the money in her handbag, which was dwindling away day by day.

The Manager of Brown's sent with them to the train a Commissionaire who obtained their reserved carriage for them and ordered their hampers, and of course he too had to be generously tipped.

When the train moved off, Felicity said:

"I'm tired of travelling. I want to ride my pony in the sunshine!"

Atayla thought that was what she too would like, but there was no sunshine, only dark clouds and scuds of rain which splattered against the window.

She remembered learning:

March winds and April showers
Bring forth May flowers.

It was not yet May and she was sure that April in England was really unpredictable, despite Browning's eulogy about it.

Ever since they had left Gibraltar she had been glad of her travelling-cloak, although every time she put it on she could hardly believe that she, Atayla, was wearing anything trimmed with sable.

She was certain it must have cost more money than her father could ever have earned from his writing.

Felicity's cloak was warmly lined and the collar and cuffs were of velvet. There was, however, in the bottom of her case a small tippet of white ermine with little black tails, and a muff to match.

When Atayla produced it, Felicity had exclaimed:

"I had that years and years ago when I was very little, but I have not wanted them in Tangiers."

"No, of course not," Atayla agreed, "it was much too hot. But you will find they will keep your fingers nice and warm in England, where it can be cold even in the spring."

"Is that what it is now?" Felicity enquired. *"Mon*

Père is right, it is dull and ugly, and I want to go home!"

Atayla thought that was what she would like too, but there was no point in saying so, and she merely tried to divert Felicity's attention to something else.

As they were in the Edinburgh Express, Atayla had learnt that they should reach the Halt for Roth Castle at about five o'clock in the evening.

However, this proved to be optimistic, for there were delays at two stations, and later when she asked the time she found the train was already an hour late.

It was no use complaining, and time seemed to drag by until finally when it was long after six o'clock the train came to a standstill at a very small platform on which was a Notice Board saying: HALT FOR ROTH CASTLE.

The Guard came hurrying to the door of the carriage and helped them to alight, and when they had done so the train had to move on quite a considerable way so that the van which contained their luggage was at the platform.

There was only one old Porter and he seemed to Atayla to take an endless time to get all their trunks out, and when finally this was achieved the old man stared at them helplessly.

"Ye goin' t' the Castle, Lady?" he asked Atayla. "There b'aint a carriage to meet ye."

"I would like to hire one," Atayla said.

The Porter pushed his cap back and scratched his head.

"It be too late fer that," he said, "an' we was given no instructions there was visitors arrivin'."

"We have to get there," Atayla said a little desperately, "and this little girl is very tired. It has been a long journey."

"'Is Lordship be expectin' ye?"

It was a question she had not anticipated, and because she thought it would be a mistake to say "no," Atayla replied:

"I hope so, unless the post has delayed my letter, which might have happened."

This seemed quite reasonable, and Atayla thought the Porter accepted it.

"Weel, sit ye down," he said, "an' Oi'll see wot Oi can do."

"I'm tired," Felicity complained. "I want to see the Castle."

"We just have to wait a little while," Atayla said, "while they find a carriage to take us there."

"Why is there no carriage waiting for us?"

Felicity spoke in an affronted manner, which made Atayla think with a smile that children soon grew used to luxury and took it as their right.

So that they could keep warm and be out of the bitter wind blowing over the countryside, they went into the tiny, box-like Waiting-Room, and Atayla managed to light the fire in the small grate.

There was only a newspaper and a few large sticks of wood with which to do so, but fortunately there was a box of matches on the mantelshelf, and it amused Felicity to watch Atayla getting it going.

Atayla could not help thinking that she was not correctly dressed for such a menial task, and she was very careful not to dirty the beautiful long suede gloves that Mala had put in with her travelling-clothes.

They were already rather creased and did not look as clean as they had when she had started out on the journey, but at least she felt they gave a finish to her whole appearance.

She hoped that in consequence the Earl would approve of her and allow her to remain at least for a little while as Felicity's Governess.

She had thought it over very carefully while they were travelling, and had decided that from her own point of view it would be wise until she could get her bearings to try to convince the Earl that, since she had been engaged as a Governess for Felicity, that was what she should remain.

She could not believe that he would find it easy to get somebody else very quickly.

An added complication was that when she had tipped the Porter and paid for the carriage to the Castle, there would not be much more than a pound or two left from the money the *Comtesse* had given her.

"I must earn something," she told herself firmly. "Then at least I shall be able to leave when I want to."

At the same time, she knew it was an uncomfortable position in which to be, and she only hoped that the Earl would accept her services and give her a generous salary.

The fire was going well and Felicity was warming her hands by it when the Porter returned.

"Oi've found a carriage for ye, Lady," he said, "but 'tis on'y 'cause ye be goin' to the Castle. Oi persuaded Jim Roberts to take ye there. 'E don't turn out as a rule after 'e's stabled 'is 'orse for the night."

"I am very grateful," Atayla said.

She realised that she would have to double what she had intended to give the Porter and was quite certain that Jim Roberts would expect a double fare as well.

When he did arrive, in a very old closed Brougham which smelt of hay, horse, and dry leather, he was appalled at the mountain of luggage.

"Oi can't take all that gear on this!" he said firmly.

"You could make two journeys," Atayla suggested, "and if some of the trunks can be locked up for the night, they can be left until tomorrow morning."

This seemed to appease Jim Roberts slightly, and he and the Porter piled up quite half of the luggage onto the front and the back of the Brougham, besides packing the hat-boxes inside on the small seat opposite Atayla and Felicity.

When they finally moved off, Atayla was almost

afraid the horses would find it impossible to pull them, but they managed it, and they left behind only four big trunks to be collected on the following day.

She was aware as they drove away that dusk was falling, and Jim Roberts had lit the candle-lanterns on either side of the carriage.

"Now you are going to show me the Castle, which, if you remember, I have never seen," Atayla said.

"I have forgotten! I have forgotten what it is like," the child replied crossly.

"But you have not forgotten your father?"

Felicity thought for some minutes. Then she said:

"Papa was very cross with Mama. He shouted at her and she cried."

Atayla was wondering what she should say to this when Felicity finished:

"Then Mama and I went away to *Mon Père*. He was very, very glad to see Mama, and he never shouted at her."

Atayla felt that this was uncomfortably revealing, and to divert Felicity's attention she said:

"Tell me about the Castle. Is it very old?"

"I'm cold," Felicity said. "I want to go back to the sun! I want Mama!"

At the warning note that she was about to cry, Atayla put her arms round her.

"Sit close to me," she said, "and keep warm, and I will tell you a story about how my father and I once saw a lake with lots of big crocodiles in it and how frightening they were."

The story lasted until Atayla was aware that they were passing through some huge stone-flanked gates with lodges on either side of them that had crenellated tops as if they were tiny Castles.

Then there was a long drive which was dark because of the trees on either side of it, and then in the far distance she saw lights which she was sure came from windows.

Suddenly the trees ended and she had her first glimpse of Roth Castle.

It was certainly very impressive, very large, with a huge round tower on one side and turrets that were silhouetted against the sky.

"We are here," Atayla said with a lilt in her voice, "and look how large and exciting your Castle is!"

As they drew nearer she thought perhaps "exciting" was the wrong word, for there was something heavy, dark, and menacing about the Castle that made her feel afraid.

Then she told herself she was being ridiculous; she was over-tired, it was getting late, and no building, however beautiful, looked its best in the dark.

When they drew nearer still, there seemed to be only two windows with any light in them, and just one light in the shape of a lantern over a huge stone Gothic-arched front door.

The tired horses came to a standstill, and Atayla made no effort to move, hoping the servants inside the Castle would be aware that somebody had arrived and the door would open.

But there was no movement, and Jim Roberts got down from the cab and walked slowly and heavily up the steps, stamping his feet as he did so as if they were cold.

He tugged at an iron bell beside the door and waited until what seemed to Atayla a very long time had passed before the door opened.

It was then she decided that it would be wise to alight, and opening the carriage door for herself she said to Felicity:

"Come along, dearest. Now you can go inside and get warm."

She climbed out as she spoke, and taking the child by the hand walked up the steps to where she saw an elderly Butler standing in the doorway, staring in astonishment at the luggage on the carriage below.

"Is the Earl of Rothwell at home?" Atayla asked.

Even as she asked the question it suddenly struck her how embarrassing it would be if he was away and in his absence the household refused to let them in.

But to her relief the Butler replied:

"His Lordship's in residence, Madam, but I don't think His Lordship's expecting visitors."

"No, but it is of great importance that I should see him," Atayla replied.

"His Lordship'll see you, Madam, only if you've an appoint . . ."

He could not go on, because Atayla interrupted him to say:

"Will you tell His Lordship that I have brought his daughter, Lady Felicity Roth, to him?"

The Butler stared at her, then stared down at Felicity in astonishment, before he said in a different tone:

"Well, Your Ladyship's grown a great deal since I last saw you!"

"I am eight," Felicity announced, "and I remember the flags."

As she spoke she pointed to where over the huge, mediaeval stone fireplace there were ancient flags jutting out from the wall.

"Of course you do," the Butler said. "Your Ladyship always wanted to play with them, but if you touch 'em they'll fall to bits."

"Why will they fall to bits?" Felicity enquired.

"Because they're old, very old, Your Ladyship," the Butler replied.

He looked at Atayla.

"Will you come this way, Madam, and I'll tell His Lordship of your arrival. He'll be surprised, very surprised to see Her Ladyship!"

Atayla did not reply, and the Butler led the way across the marble Hall, on which were laid some Persian rugs.

He opened a door, and as Atayla went in followed by Felicity he said:

"I'll see to your luggage, Madam. I presume Her Ladyship's staying here?"

"I hope so," Atayla replied. "We have nowhere else to go at this hour of the night."

Then as the Butler would have moved away she said:

"I must pay the cabman."

"Leave that to me, Madam," the Butler answered, and shut the door of the room.

It was a Sitting-Room and there were gas-lights on each side of the mantelpiece and a large oil-lamp on a table that was heaped with books.

As Atayla looked round she realised there were also a number of bookcases and a large, flat-topped writing-desk in front of what when the curtains were opened she was sure was a long window.

There were comfortable sofas and deep armchairs such as a man would enjoy, and as there was a fire burning brightly in the hearth, she was sure that this was the Earl's Private Room, where he sat when he was alone.

"Do you remember this room?" she asked Felicity.

The child was not interested. She had sat down on the sofa and put her head against the cushions.

"I'm tired," she said, "and I'm thirsty!"

"I will ask for a drink as soon as we can go upstairs," Atayla said, "but you must remember we have taken much longer to arrive here than we expected, because the train was delayed, and it may take us a little time to get all the things we want."

"I'm tired," Felicity said again.

She yawned, and because the round hat she wore on the back of her head was obviously making her uncomfortable, Atayla undid the ribbons under her chin and took it away from her.

She fluffed out her hair over her ears and thought she looked very pretty and attractive, and it would be impossible for the Earl not to appreciate his daughter.

Then she wondered a little apprehensively if he would resent their arrival so late at night unannounced and without his having any warning that his wife was returning his child to him.

She had in fact wondered once or twice on the journey if it was a wise thing to do, and she thought she should have asked the *Comtesse* to write to Felicity's father and perhaps explain to him why she could no longer keep the child with her.

But it had seemed not only far too intimate and personal for her to speak in such a way, but also, she thought, it was none of her business.

All she had done was to accept the job of taking Felicity back to the Earl, and there was no reason why she should be involved any deeper in the situation than that.

And yet, she thought a little uncomfortably, she was involved because she was here and the *Comtesse* was far away.

The door opened, and she looked up quickly and apprehensively, but it was only the Butler returning.

"His Lordship's having his dinner, Madam," he said. "When he's finished, I think he'll see you."

He did not wait for Atayla's reply, but closed the door again, and she thought she did not like the sound of "I *think* he will see you."

"What else can he do?" she asked herself.

Felicity was complaining again.

"I'm thirsty. Give me something to drink!"

Atayla looked quickly round the room, thinking perhaps there would be a grog-tray on which she would find some water or lemonade, but there was nothing there.

She was afraid that if she opened the door and looked outside into the Hall for the Butler, she might instead encounter the Earl coming from the Dining-Room, and he would think she was behaving in a strange manner in his house.

She was sure that the Butler and the footman were in fact waiting on him in the Dining-Room, and that was why there had been a long delay before the door-bell was answered.

"I am sorry, dearest," she said to Felicity. "I cannot get you anything at the moment, but it will not be long now, and we will ask for some nice milk like you had at the Hotel."

She had been amused at how delighted Felicity was with English milk, which was something she had not had in Tangiers and was not even obtainable in France.

Thick and creamy, she had drunk it down with relish and asked for more.

Vaguely Atayla remembered how much she had enjoyed milk when she was very small and when she had stayed in England for her grandfather's Funeral.

But she had grown so used to the lack of it in Africa that she had not missed it until she had tasted it again.

Time passed and she was conscious of the tick of the clock on the mantelpiece. Then as Felicity was very quiet she realised that the child was asleep.

Carefully, so as not to awaken her, she lifted her two little legs in their white socks up onto the sofa, then sat very stiff and still on the edge of it, waiting.

Suddenly the door opened and the Earl came in, and one look at him made her feel apprehensive.

He seemed very tall and overpowering. His hair was dark, as she had somehow expected it would be, like Felicity's.

His eyes were dark too, and he was scowling so deeply that his eye-brows seemed to meet over his straight, aristocratic nose, and as he walked towards her Atayla was aware that his mouth was set in a hard line.

His appearance was so frightening and indeed so awe-inspiring that she rose nervously to her feet, and

as he reached her he looked at her, then at the sleeping child, then back at her.

"Who are you?" he asked. "And what the hell are
you doing here?"

CHAPTER THREE

*T*he way he spoke, and the manner in which his
words appeared to vibrate round the room, took
Atayla's voice away.

Then as she remembered that he knew who Felicity
was and had been told that they both had arrived, she
said quietly:

"I have brought your daughter . . . home."

"On whose instructions?" the Earl enquired. "Or
need I ask? Well, you can go back to where you came
from!"

Atayla stared at him in sheer astonishment. Then
she said, and her voice sounded weak and feeble even
to herself:

"That . . . is impossible!"

"Nothing is impossible!" the Earl snapped. "You
can tell whoever sent you that I have no intention of
accepting any communication from her, except
through my Solicitors."

He turned and walked towards the door, and as he
reached it he said:

"Get out, and quickly!"

Because it was obvious that he meant to leave the

room, Atayla gave a little cry of sheer horror, and moving hastily towards him said:

"You cannot do . . . this! You cannot send us away now . . . at this time of the . . . night!"

"Why not?" the Earl asked. "I did not invite you here, and I am sure you can find a more appropriate place to stay."

The way he spoke was somehow insulting, but Atayla was too agitated to realise it.

Because she was frightened she pleaded:

"Please . . . we have been travelling for days and I cannot take Felicity . . . out again, even if I had anywhere to take her. She is very . . . tired."

"That is your business!"

"You . . . do not understand," Atayla said. "We have come all the way from Tangiers."

The Earl had once again turned towards the door and his hand was on the handle. Now he looked back.

"Tangiers?" he questioned. "I thought she would be in . . ."

Then he interrupted himself to say again harshly:

"It is none of my business! She has had the child with her for three years and now she can keep her!"

"You cannot say that," Atayla argued. "Felicity was not . . . happy where she . . . was, and her mother was insistent that she should come . . . home where she . . . belongs."

The Earl laughed, and it was a very unpleasant sound.

"Where she belongs! It is a bit late for that now! No! I will not accept the very belated return of what was once mine. Take the child back to her mother and be damned to you!"

Perhaps it was the swear-word more than anything else that made Atayla lose her temper.

She was frightened, at the same time she thought the Earl was being brutal to Felicity, and she hated him for his behaviour and for the cruel way in which he was speaking.

357

She had no idea how her grey eyes were flashing fire at him as she said:

"Very well, My Lord, if that is your last word, Felicity and I will leave. But as we have nowhere to go, we can perhaps sleep on your doorstep, or shelter in one of your barns for the night, as there could be no other accommodation for us at this late hour."

As she was speaking to him no less angrily than he had, the Earl seemed for the moment somewhat disconcerted. Then he said:

"You must have come here in a conveyance of some sort."

"We obtained a hired carriage from the Halt, where we left our luggage," Atayla said. "The man was willing to bring us, but I should imagine by this time he has returned home again."

As if the Earl accepted this as a reasonable statement, he walked away from the door to the fireplace.

He stood with his back to it, looking down at the sleeping child on the sofa.

The resemblance between them was, Atayla thought, very obvious, but the Earl's hard face did not seem to soften.

He merely looked at Felicity as if he hated her and bitterly resented their intrusion into the Castle.

Slowly Atayla retraced her steps from the door back to the sofa.

Then as she sat down on the end of it, where she had been sitting before, Felicity stirred and opened her eyes.

First she looked round her in surprise, as if she did not know where she was, then she saw the Earl.

She looked at him for one second before she said a little questioningly:

"Papa?"

"So you remember me, do you?" the Earl asked grimly.

"You are Papa!" Felicity said as if she had convinced

herself. "And Mama said you would give me a pony as you have lots of horses."

"Why should I give you anything?" the Earl asked sharply, as if he were speaking to a grown-up. "You ran away and left me."

"I've come back," Felicity replied, "and I'm very tired, and thirsty. I want a drink!"

Atayla looked at the Earl, and after a moment, grudgingly, as if he deeply resented having to give in, he said:

"I suppose you must stay here for tonight. I will tell Dawson to take you to my Housekeeper."

With that he walked from the room before Atayla could reply and shut the door sharply behind him.

Felicity yawned and said again:

"I want a drink. I'm very thirsty!"

"I am sure we will be able to have one in a few minutes," Atayla said comfortingly.

She felt as if she had fought a battle that had exhausted her both physically and mentally, and she knew now how frightened she had been that the Earl might carry out his threat and compel them to leave the Castle.

The Butler came hurrying in to take them upstairs to where an elderly Housekeeper in rustling black, and with a chatelaine at her waist, was waiting for them.

As she climbed the stairs Atayla said a prayer of thankfulness that they had not been turned away penniless and with nowhere to go.

"How can he be so horrible, so offensive, and so aggressive?" she asked herself.

When finally she got into bed, she found herself sympathising with the *Comtesse* for running away, although it was with a man who was already married.

Atayla remembered also the beauty of the white bedroom with its curtains falling from a gold corona, and she had a sneaking feeling that the *Comtesse* had every incentive for leaving both her husband and the Castle.

The bedroom into which they were shown by the Housekeeper, whose name, she learnt, was Mrs. Briercliffe, was certainly awe-inspiring, though at the same time it was comfortable.

The high ceiling, the long windows with curtains surmounted by carved pelmets, and the huge oak four-poster bed, all made Atayla feel that it was part of history, but perhaps not a particularly pleasant part.

"Tomorrow," Mrs. Briercliffe said, "I will open the Nurseries again. But tonight, as you are both tired, I don't expect you want to wait before putting Her Ladyship to bed."

"She is very tired," Atayla agreed. "We have travelled a very long way to come here."

"From Paris?" Mrs. Briercliffe asked, and Atayla knew that was what the Earl had been about to say.

"No, from Tangiers, in Morocco."

"Goodness me!" Mrs. Briercliffe exclaimed. "I never thought of Her Ladyship as being in such a heathen part of the world as that!"

Then, as if she felt embarrassed at having said too much, she busied herself giving orders to the housemaids who were unpacking the trunks which had come with them in the carriage.

Felicity had been appeased by being given milk and biscuits as soon as they got upstairs, but then she complained that her bed was too big.

"I want the room I used to sleep in," she said, as if she suddenly remembered it, "and where's my rocking-horse?"

"It's all upstairs, Your Ladyship," Mrs. Briercliffe replied, "and tomorrow I'll have the rooms dusted and aired for you. They're just as they were when you left them."

"I want my rocking-horse and a pony," Felicity whimpered.

Atayla, who was undressing her with the help of one of the housemaids, answered:

"I am sure you will be able to have those tomorrow, but now you must go to sleep in here, and when you wake up everything will seem different."

As she spoke, she only hoped that she was prophesying accurately.

She had not forgotten what the Earl had said, that they could stay for the night, and she had the uncomfortable feeling that tomorrow he might insist on their leaving.

Only when she had got Felicity into bed did she think of how tired she was herself, and as if Mrs. Briercliffe realised it without being told, she said:

"I'll send something upstairs for you to eat, Miss, and perhaps you will tell Jeannie what you'd like unpacked for you tonight. The rest can wait until tomorrow."

"Thank you, that will be best," Atayla agreed. "Like Her Ladyship, I too am very tired."

"You look done in, and that's a fact!" Mrs. Briercliffe said.

She gave sharp orders to Jeannie to hurry up and unpack the case Atayla indicated, then supervised the tray that was brought upstairs by a footman who arranged it on a table in her bedroom.

Because Atayla felt it would be embarrassing to eat before Jeannie had left, she waited until she was alone, then found that although what was waiting for her in covered dishes looked delicious, she could in fact manage very little of it.

She was so tired that she felt that if she sat down she would never get up again.

She was exhausted not only by the demands of the journey but by the Earl's behaviour and her terror that she and Felicity would be turned away with only enough money to go a few miles, let alone return to Tangiers.

"Why did I not anticipate that this might happen?" she asked herself.

She felt she had been very remiss in not suggesting to the *Comtesse* that the Earl might bitterly resent having his daughter returned to him without explanation or even notice of her arrival.

Finally, when Atayla got into bed, feeling that if she did not do so she would collapse on the floor, she asked herself apprehensively what tomorrow would bring.

She was finding it very difficult to think clearly, when almost as if he were beside her and speaking to her she heard Father Ignatius say:

"Pray if you need help, and it will come to you."

'I certainly need help now!' Atayla thought a little wryly, and she prayed until she fell asleep.

Atayla was awakened from a deep slumber by Felicity jumping onto her bed and saying:

"Wake up, Miss Lindsay, I want to go and look at my pony. Mama said Papa would give me a pony, and I looked out the window to see if he was running about on the grass."

With an effort, Atayla brought her mind back from her dream-world to reality.

"If there is a pony," she said, smiling, "I expect he is in the stable."

"Then let us go and find him!" Felicity insisted.

"I think we should have breakfast first."

She sat up in bed and waited for the sleep to clear from her eyes so that she could think clearly.

Then she remembered that Jeannie had said before she left the room the previous evening:

"If you want anything, Miss, ring the bell, and I'll be told you want me, although sometimes it takes a little time as the Castle's so big."

Now Atayla looked round for a bell and found a long embroidered bell-pull hanging beside the bed.

She gave it a tug and wondered how far the wires would have to go from the top before a bell rang which would summon Jeannie to her.

Felicity slipped off the bed to stand at the window where the curtains had not been pulled.

"I cannot see any horses," she said, "but there are little animals that look like goats."

Atayla pulled back the curtains.

"Those are deer!" she said.

"What are they?" Felicity asked.

"They live in the Park," Atayla said, "and they are very beautiful."

"Deer!" Felicity repeated to herself, and Atayla knew she was trying to remember whether she had seen them before.

When Jeannie arrived, apologising for being so long, Atayla asked where they would have breakfast.

"As the Nursery's not yet ready, Miss," Jeannie replied, "Mrs. Briercliffe thought you and Her Ladyship could have it downstairs in the Morning-Room. His Lordship breakfasts in the Dining-Room, but Mrs. Briercliffe thought he would not wish you to join him."

"No, no, of course not," Atayla said.

She thought that nothing would be more embarrassing than to breakfast with the Earl after his behavior of last night.

Because she was also nervous of meeting him, she hurried Felicity down the main staircase.

A footman who was on duty in the Hall escorted them along the passage hung with ancient armour into a comparatively small room, although the ceiling was very high, where breakfast was laid on a table in the centre of the room.

There were several dishes to choose from and a footman to wait on them.

Atayla could not help thinking with a secret smile

how very different this was from the discomfort and frugality of the Mission, where she was lucky to have anything to eat and usually was forced to cook it for herself.

Felicity, on the other hand, seemed quite at home, asked for a second helping of a dish she fancied, and finished with toast spread with Jersey butter and honey from the comb.

"I like this honey," she said. "It is nicer than the honey we had in Tangiers."

Atayla was glad she had found something of which to approve, for while she was being dressed she had complained that she had to wear so many clothes, and also that she was cold.

Atayla was hoping that there would be some warm dresses amongst her clothes that were not yet unpacked.

But she had the suspicion that because she had been in a warm climate, her gowns would all be like the one she had first seen her in, of muslin and lace, which would be very unsuitable in the North.

However, she thought, although she was not certain that it was comparatively warm for the time of year, and her travelling-gown with its little jacket seemed quite suitable, although she was hoping that when she finally unpacked she could find another gown to wear.

However, she was far too frightened to allow Jeannie to unpack anything before the Earl had made up his mind to whether they were to stay or leave.

She had known that Mrs. Briercliffe and Jeannie, thinking that the rooms they had slept in last night were to be changed for the Nurseries, had been glad when she said that everything should be left in their trunks until later in the day.

She had not forgotten that there was still some baggage at the Halt, and when she and Felicity came from the Morning-Room, Dawson came towards them down the passage from the Hall to say:

"Your other trunks have arrived, Miss, and I've thanked Roberts for bringing them. He's a difficult man to deal with and sometimes takes half the day to bring us anything left at the station."

"I would like to thank him myself," Atayla said, thinking she should tip him for his kindness of last night.

"He's gone now, Miss," Dawson replied, "but I paid him well for his services."

Atayla could not help a feeling of relief that at least that left her a little more money in her purse, but still, as she was well aware, it was not enough to take her and Felicity many miles from the Castle.

"I want to go and see my pony," Felicity was saying impatiently.

Then with an uncomfortable feeling of constriction Atayla saw the Earl walking towards them.

He was obviously coming from the Dining-Room, and there was a scowl on his forehead, very much as there had been last night.

Atayla held her breath, but Felicity released her hand and ran towards him.

"I want to see my pony, Papa," she said, "and Miss Lindsay says he'll be in the stable. Please, can I go and look at him now, this moment?"

The Earl looked down at her with what Atayla thought was an expression of dislike. Then he said to the Butler:

"Tell one of the footmen to take Her Ladyship to the stables, or better still go yourself. I wish to speak to the lady who brought her here."

He looked at Atayla with what she thought was an expression of even greater dislike.

For a moment she longed to tell the Earl that she had no intention to talking to him and would much prefer to go to the stables with Felicity.

But even as she thought it she knew it was something she could not do, and Dawson put out his hand to the small girl, saying:

"Come along, Your Ladyship, we'll go and look at His Lordship's horses, and very fine they be."

Felicity gave a little skip of excitement. Then when they were moving away Atayla said quickly:

"I think Her Ladyship should wear a coat in case she feels the cold. Perhaps somebody could fetch it for her?"

"I'll see to it, Miss," Dawson replied.

Then he and Felicity disappeared down the passage into the Hall, and Atayla looked up nervously at the Earl.

"Come with me!" he said sharply.

He walked ahead of her as he spoke, and she followed, feeling like a naughty School-girl who was about to be reprimanded for some misdemeanour.

As she walked a few paces behind him, she thought that it was a very Arabian attitude and she was in the place where every woman in North Africa would expect to be.

The Earl opened the door of a room, and as Atayla followed him in, she realised it was the Library and exactly what she thought a Library should look like in any Castle or great house in England.

Her father had often described the joys of being in the Libraries owned by the English nobility, where their collections of books accumulated over the centuries were housed more elaborately than anywhere else in the world.

As she looked at the thousands of books stretching from the floor to the ceiling of the room, which was encircled by a balcony which was reached by a small twisting stairway, she had a sudden longing for her father.

She knew how much he would have appreciated the room and more especially the books in it.

Just for a moment she forgot the Earl and the uncomfortable interview she was about to undergo, simply because she was thinking how fortunate he was to possess something her father had longed for when he was writing his books on the tribes of Africa.

"Goodness knows, it's impossible to do much re-search on this place," he had said in Algiers, Tunis, Tangiers, or any other place in which they stayed when he was writing down the information he had accumulated while they were travelling.

"Was your Library at home a very large one, Papa?" she had asked.

"It is certainly what I could do with at the mo-ment," her father had replied, "although actually my grandfather and my great-grandfather, who collected most of the books, were more interested in English literature than in anything that came from other countries."

Then he had laughed as he added:

"As you well know, there is very little written work available about my particular subject, otherwise I would not be considered an authority on it!"

"That is true, Papa," Atayla had answered, "and that is why your books are so important."

She was brought sharply back from the past as the Earl said:

"Sit down!"

As he spoke he indicated a chair on the other side of a large Georgian desk at which he sat himself.

It was flanked by high windows embellished at the top with quarterings of the Roth family on the glass.

Through the clear panes the sunshine poured in and brought out the red lights in Atayla's fair hair.

It was a very different colour from the *Comtesse*'s, which was the pale gold of unripened corn.

Without the light Atayla's hair just seemed fair, but when the sun touched it it revealed that there was red amongst the gold, which seemed to glow with a warmth that was otherwise missing.

Her eyes were grey and specked with gold. Because she was thin from her illness, they seemed enormous in her face, and her chin was a very sharp line against her long neck.

The Earl was staring at her and she thought as she had thought last night that there was something insulting in the way he regarded her, but it was difficult to put it into words.

"Now," he said sharply, "I want an explanation from you as to why you are here, and also why you should have assumed that I would accept my daughter, Felicity, after she was taken away from me three years ago."

Atayla's first impulse was to tell him that as she had heard of the *Comtesse* and Felicity only the day before they had left Tangiers, it was impossible for her to answer any questions.

Then it struck her that if she said anything like that, it would give the Earl a good excuse to dispense with her services, and if he kept Felicity and found a Governess for her of his own choosing, she would have nowhere to go.

Because she was very quick-brained, there was only a slight pause before she said:

"I was engaged, My Lord, as Governess to Lady Felicity, and I am here merely because my instructions were to bring her to you."

The Earl looked at her as if he did not believe what she had said. At the same time, it was difficult for him to contradict her.

"What you are saying, Miss Lindsay," he said, "and I think that is the name by which Felicity called you, is that you are here, as one might say, as a paid servant, and it is not your place to question your orders."

He was definitely being rude, and because it made her angry, Atayla looked down at her hands in case he should see by the expression in her eyes what she thought of him.

She told herself that all that mattered for the moment was that she should have a roof over her head and the chance to earn some money before she was dismissed.

"I think, My Lord," she said, "that is an accurate, if unflattering, description of my position."

"If I turn you away, as I intended to do last night, where would you go?"

"Quite frankly, I do not know," Atayla replied. "Although I presume Felicity has other relatives besides yourself, I have no idea where they are or how I could find them."

The Earl's lips tightened and Atayla knew she had been clever enough to put him in a position in which he would find it difficult to carry out his threat of turning her and Felicity out of the Castle.

There was a long pause before he said:

"If I keep Felicity here, are you prepared to stay with her?"

"That is what I hoped I would be asked to do, My Lord. But of course, it is entirely up to you as to how she is taught, and by whom."

As if he found it hard to know what to say, the Earl rose from the desk and walked across the room to stand with his back to the fireplace, in which a small fire was burning.

"I find this intolerable!" he said after a moment, almost as if he spoke to himself.

Atayla did not reply, as some inner reasoning advised her not to commiserate with him or try to solve his problems.

Then, as he was aware that she was sitting stiffly on the edge of her chair, her back very straight, he said angrily:

"For God's sake, what do you expect me to do? I have heard nothing from anybody about my child, and I had no idea where she was or that she would be arriving until she appeared last night."

"Now she has come home," Atayla said quietly.

"I am only surprised," the Earl said, "that the person who took her from me recognised that as being the truth. At the same time, if I did what I think I have the right to do, I would send the child back to Tangiers, or wherever it is you have come from."

Atayla was just about to say that if he did so, Felicity's mother might be dead when she returned. Then she told herself that would be a dangerous thing to say.

After all, if the *Comtesse* was ill, and Father Ignatius had said she was very ill, there was no reason to believe that she would not recover from whatever it was she was suffering from, and it was certainly unlikely that she would die.

Moreover, if she told the Earl his wife was ill, it might raise his hopes of being free.

'Perhaps there is somebody he would like to marry,' she thought, 'and he would therefore be extremely angry later if it turned out that there was nothing radically wrong with his wife, and I had merely repeated gossip that was not substantiated.'

She therefore said nothing, and after a moment the Earl asked:

"Surely you must have some opinion on this situation as it appears to you?"

"All I am concerned with, My Lord, is Lady Felicity," Atayla replied. "I understand she was not very happy in Tangiers, and that was the real reason for her being sent to Your Lordship."

"What do you mean, she was not happy?" the Earl asked sharply. "If that swine did not treat her properly, I swear I will kill him!"

He spoke so violently that Atayla stiffened and clasped her hands together.

She found the Earl very disturbing. Her heart was beating fiercely and she thought, as she had last night, that his manner was insufferable besides being frightening.

As if he was aware that she was frightened, the Earl said:

"I should not inflict on you my feelings in this

matter. At the same time, you do not look at me like an ordinary Governess would. I suppose there was some good reason that you were chosen for the position?"

"I think the only reason was that I also am English."

The Earl stared at her, and she thought this was something that had never crossed his mind.

Although he didn't say so, she was aware that he was thinking that perhaps it actually had been difficult in Tangiers to find an English Governess, and Felicity's mother, for reasons that were better not mentioned, had not wished her to have one who was French.

"What are you teaching Felicity?" he asked, as if he must assert himself in some way.

"It had not been possible to have ordinary lessons while we have been travelling," Atayla replied, "but I think the first thing she should have now are lessons about England and the English."

She paused, then went on, thinking it out for herself:

"That will be easier, because everything here is new to her, and she cannot remember very much of what she saw and heard when she was only five years old, three years ago."

As Atayla spoke, she thought that the same might almost be said of herself. She too had so much to learn, and she knew already that she was finding it strange, but very lovely, that England was so green and fertile.

After years of moving about the desert, to be able to look all round her and see everything green had a magic all its own.

All the way they had been travelling by train, and even when she was telling Felicity of her strange adventures in Africa, her eyes had been absorbing the landscape, which was so different, and yet, because a child's memory could be very vivid, it was somehow familiar.

"I see your point," the Earl said briefly, "and perhaps when Felicity has settled down we could discuss what subjects would be best for her to study with you, and those for which we must try to find suitable teachers."

Atayla gave an audible gasp, realising as she did so that she had won. They were not to be turned away, and she was to remain as Felicity's Governess.

With an effort she forced herself to reply calmly and quietly:

"I am sure that is the right thing to do, My Lord, and I think for the moment, at any rate, I can cover most subjects which are important for Felicity to study at her age."

As she spoke she rose to her feet, and added:

"Is there anything else Your Lordship wishes to talk to me about?"

"No, Miss Lindsay," the Earl replied. "You have made your position quite clear."

Somewhat belatedly, because she had forgotten it until now, Atayla dropped him a small curtsey.

"Thank you, My Lord."

She walked towards the door and had almost reached it when the Earl said:

"I presume you can ride?"

Atayla almost replied: "Anything on four legs, from a dromedary to a donkey," then decided that would sound frivolous and perhaps impertinent, and instead she answered:

"I have ridden all my life, My Lord."

"Then I will give orders that you can ride with Felicity," the Earl said, "but if my horses are too spirited and too strong for you, do not hesitate to say so."

"I think that is unlikely, My Lord."

She went from the Library, and once she was outside the door she felt like singing and dancing for joy.

She could stay! At least for the moment, she was safe and there was no need to be afraid either of starving or of having to beg the Earl to give her enough money to live until she could find her relatives.

She could not help thinking of how terribly embarrassing that would have been, and how humiliating after the way he had behaved.

"He is horrible and very frightening," she told herself.

At the same time, she had been clever enough to defeat him, and that was all that mattered.

Because she was so excited, she hurried to the stables just as she was, without going upstairs for a hat. Only when she had found Felicity, and saw the Butler's eyes look at her with a slight expression of surprise, did she realise she had been unconventional.

'I must be careful!' she thought. 'Governesses certainly do not walk about outside the Castle without being correctly dressed!'

Then she forgot herself, going from stall to stall, admiring the Earl's superlative horses and feeling wildly excited because she was allowed to ride them.

It suddenly occurred to her that perhaps amongst the clothes the *Comtesse* had given her there was no riding-habit.

For the moment she felt so disappointed that it was as if her spirits had dropped from the sky down to the earth with a heavy bang.

Then she tried to convince herself that amongst all the things the *Comtesse* had discarded there must be a habit, but she could not entirely banish her apprehension.

Only when they had looked at every horse in the stable and it was growing late in the morning did she take Felicity back into the Castle, where she found that their luggage had been taken upstairs to the Nurseries, which were now ready for them.

The Nurseries were on the third floor, as she had expected them to be. Vaguely at the back of her mind she could remember sleeping and living in a Nursery very like this one when she had stayed with her grandparents during one of her visits to England.

She had also heard her mother describe what her Nursery had looked like as a child.

There was a high guard in front of the fire, a screen which kept out the draught, covered in transfers pasted on it and then varnished, and a big dolls' house, which Felicity ran to with delight and kept saying she remembered.

There were dolls, too—Dutch dolls, patchwork dolls and golliwogs, and a Teddy Bear, a little smaller and older than the one which Felicity had in her trunk.

Now two maids under Mrs. Briercliffe's supervision were unpacking the trunks they had brought with them, and Atayla saw with relief that some of Felicity's dresses were plainer and of warmer materials than the ones she had worn in Tangiers.

However, she must have had them for some time, for they were too short and in some cases needed letting out round the waist.

But Mrs. Briercliffe said this was no problem as a seamstress always worked in the Castle and would soon alter them.

There was fortunately quite a number of coats, and when Atayla told the Housekeeper that she was afraid that the child might feel the chill after living in the heat of Tangiers, Mrs. Briercliffe gave strict instructions that there was always to be plenty of coal in the skuttle and a pile of logs.

Felicity's bed was a very pretty one with frilled muslin curtains decorating a brass bedstead, while in Atayla's room, which was next door, there was an extremely ornate one, again of brass.

"Her Ladyship chose these before His Lordship was born," Mrs. Briercliffe explained. "And that reminds me, Miss Lindsay—Her Ladyship will be expecting to see Lady Felicity before luncheon."

Atayla stared at her in surprise.

"Her Ladyship?" she questioned.

"His Lordship hasn't explained to you that his grandmother, the Dowager Lady Rothwell, is living here?"

"Do you mean she is Lady Felicity's great-grand-mother?"

"Yes, Miss Lindsay."

"I had no idea. The child has never mentioned her."

"I expect she has forgotten, Miss," Mrs. Briercliffe said. "Her Ladyship's very old, very old indeed, and you'll find her a little frightening. But, as we often say amongst ourselves, her bark's worse than her bite, although the younger maids are all terrified of her!"

Atayla thought it strange, although she was not quite certain why, that if there was a lady living in the Castle, nobody had ever mentioned it before.

She changed her gown, glad to have something fresh to wear, then a maid came hurrying up to the Nurseries to say that Lady Felicity and Miss Lindsay were to go to Her Ladyship's bedroom immediately.

"You are going to see your great-grandmother, dearest," Atayla said to Felicity. "Do you remember her?"

Felicity put her head to one side as she concentrated on the question.

"Grandmama," she said, as if she was trying to remember. "She made Mama cry."

As this did not sound very encouraging, Atayla said quickly:

"She wants to see you, and mind you are very polite and curtsey to her, and tell her how glad you are to see her again."

"I am not glad if she made Mama cry," Felicity said with unanswerable logic.

"That was a long time ago," Atayla replied. "It is always best to forget the unpleasant things that happened in the past, and think of the nice things that are to happen in the future."

"Like riding one of Papa's horses?" Felicity asked.

"Your father did not say you could ride one of his horses, and you may have to wait until he has a pony for you to ride."

"I shall ride a horse!" Felicity said firmly. "The man showed me one in the stable that he said would be quite all right for me."

"I hope you can do that," Atayla said, thinking that if Felicity could ride, she would be able to do so as well.

The child looked very attractive in a pretty dress that was skilfully smocked on the bodice, and which was worn over frilly lace petticoats, which made it look expensive and elegant, although it was quite plain.

There was a bow of pink satin ribbon in her dark hair, and because she was excited about the horses, her eyes were sparkling and she was smiling happily.

As they walked down the stairs and along the corridor, led by a footman who had waited for them, Felicity holding on to Atayla's hand was giving little skips of excitement.

"This afternoon we will ride for miles and miles," she said, "and very soon I'm going to learn to jump."

She was so thrilled by the idea that Atayla did not like to say that the Earl might not allow her to ride a horse, and she had not yet seen a pony in the stable.

'I shall have to speak to him,' she thought apprehensively. 'I can hardly take the responsibility of her riding anything that is too large for her.'

She was worrying about the horses, and only when the footman stopped outside a high mahogany door at what seemed to be the other side of the Castle did Atayla wonder what the Dowager Lady Rothwell was like.

An elderly maid with white hair and a lined face opened the door, and the footman said, rather unnecessarily as Atayla thought:

"Here's Lady Felicity."

"And about time!" the maid said. "You've not hurried yourself."

"I could only have come quicker if I'd flown," the footman said, "and God didn't give me wings!"

"That's enough from you!" the maid said sharply.

She opened the door wider so that she could look at Felicity.

"My word, Your Ladyship has grown!" she said in a different tone of voice. "Do you remember 'Ja-Ja,' as you used to call me?"

Felicity looked at her, then after a moment she said:

"I can remember my dolls' house."

The maid opened another door and said:

"Here's Her Ladyship, M'Lady, and grown into a big girl since you last saw her."

Because it seemed to be expected of her, Atayla followed Felicity into a bedroom which was very large and very impressive.

At the far end of it was a huge four-poster bed which reached almost to the ceiling, the posts carved to resemble the trunks of pine trees tipped with gold, and on each of the four corners of the canopy was a huge frond of ostrich feathers.

In the very centre of the bed, propped up with dozens of pillows, was the most extraordinary old woman Atayla had ever seen.

Her face was deeply lined, and her eyes were sunk in her head.

She wore what appeared to be a red wig, in which were stuck a number of combs with diamond-encrusted tops, while round her neck were innumerable necklaces of huge pearls, which hung over her shrunken chest onto the sheets in front of her.

Her hands with their swollen fingers and enlarged veins were weighted down with rings which flashed with every movement she made, and her wrists were encircled with diamond bracelets.

She looked so fantastic that Atayla knew that she

was gaping at her, and she quickly remembered to curtsey as Felicity advanced towards the bed.

"So, you are back!" the Dowager said to Felicity. "And why have you not come to see us before now?"

"I remember you!" Felicity exclaimed. "I remember all your pretty jewels. You used to let me play with them."

The Dowager seemed pleased, and there was something like a smile on her thin lips as she said:

"That is right! What woman of any age can resist diamonds? Here, put this ring on your finger."

She pulled one from her own hand and put it down on the bed, and Felicity picked it up and put it on her thumb, where it flashed in the light from the window.

"Mama has a bigger diamond than this!" she said.

There was a silence which made Atayla draw in her breath. Then, as if the Dowager knew what she was feeling, she looked at her for the first time.

"You are the Governess, I understand."

"Yes, My Lady, I am Felicity's Governess," Atayla confirmed.

"You do not look like a Governess to me!" the Dowager objected. "Too young, too pretty! What are you after—a husband? You are not likely to find one here."

Atayla stiffened.

She thought she had met some very strange people in her life, but Felicity's great-grandmother was certainly stranger than any of them.

"I am here, My Lady," she said quickly, "to teach Felicity her lessons, especially English."

"I suppose after living in a French household that is definitely a necessity," the Dowager snapped. "I wonder what else besides French she has learnt in the years she has been away?"

The innuendo in the question was unmistakable, and Atayla lifted her chin but did not reply.

Then, as if she wished to find fault, the Dowager said:

"I asked you a question, young woman, or perhaps you think the environment to which my great-grand-daughter has been exposed for the last three years is acceptable and something of which you approve."

Atayla thought the question was almost as uncomfortable as those asked by the Earl, and in a deliberately quiet voice she replied:

"I have always understood, My Lady, that one should be loyal to the person by whom one is employed, and that is certainly what I have tried to be."

"I am sure it is an effort," the Dowager remarked. "I am not saying your attitude is not correct, but in my opinion a Governess should look like a Governess!"

"I should have thought it was more important that she should behave like one," Atayla replied, then was sure it was a mistake to have answered back.

Surprisingly, the old woman chuckled.

"So you have a temper, have you? Well, I daresay you are none the worse for that!"

She pulled another ring from her finger and gave it to Felicity. It was a very large emerald, and she said as the child took it:

"Does that please you better? Is it big enough for you?"

"It is very pretty, and very big!" Felicity replied.

"Bigger than your mother's?"

Felicity shook her head.

"Mama does not like emeralds, she thinks they are unlucky."

The Dowager laughed.

"She should know, and I daresay she needs luck."

She put out her hand, which was almost like a claw.

"Give me back my jewels, child. You can play with them another time. Come and see me tonight and bring your Governess with you. I want to keep an eye on her."

"Why should you want to do that?" Felicity asked.

Atayla thought it was a question she would have liked to ask herself.

"People do not deceive me," the Dowager said, and she was not talking to her great-grandchild as she spoke. "I may be old and senile, but I can still see what is in front of my nose."

Felicity did not understand and was bored. She turned from the bed and slipped her hand into Atayla's.

"Come along, Miss Lindsay," she said. "Let us have our luncheon quickly. Then we can go riding."

"Say good-bye to your great-grandmother," Atayla said, "and curtsey as I have told you to do."

Obediently Felicity turned round.

"Good-bye, Grandmama," she said. "I want to play with all your jewels, and have as many rings on my fingers as you have."

"We will see about that," the Dowager answered.

Felicity was not listening.

Once again she had her hand in Atayla's and was pulling her across the room.

"Quickly, quickly!" she said. "I want to ride a big horse and show Papa I am not afraid."

Atayla opened the door and without looking back followed Felicity through it.

Only when they were outside did she think it was without exception the most extraordinary conversation that she had ever had with anybody, and the Earl's grandmother was an exceptionally frightening person.

"What did she mean by saying I do not look like a Governess?" she asked herself.

It could hardly be expected that a Governess should be easily identifiable like a common laborer or a navvy.

She could understand that she looked too young, and yet a Nursery Governess for somebody of Felicity's age could easily be no more than twenty-one or twenty-two, which Atayla had intended to say was her age if she was asked.

'I may be only eighteen,' she thought, 'but I have done so much and been in so many different places that I am older in my mind if not my body.'

They went up to the Nursery, and Atayla saw that there was a quarter-of-an-hour before luncheon was likely to be served.

"I want you to wait here, Felicity," she said. "I must go downstairs and ask your father if it is all right for you to ride the horse you saw this morning."

"No, do not ask him," Felicity said quickly. "He might say 'no.' "

"He might also say 'yes,' " Atayla replied, "in which case we do not have to worry any more."

"Try to persuade him," Felicity begged.

"I promise I will. So please be good until I come back."

"I will play with my dolls' house."

Atayla, with one quick glance to see that the fireguard was firmly in place, ran down the stairs.

She was nervous of approaching the Earl again. At the same time, she knew she could not take upon herself the responsibility of Felicity riding a horse that might throw her.

'If he refuses,' she thought, 'I can at least press him to get her a pony as quickly as possible.'

She reached the Hall and saw there were two footmen on duty.

"Will you tell me where His Lordship is?" she asked.

"In his Sitting-Room, Miss," one of them replied.

He went ahead of her to open the door, and as she followed him into the room where she had first met him, the Earl looked up from the desk at which he was writing.

Because Atayla was quite certain he would be frowning at seeing her, she felt shy.

She had met so many different people in her

journeyings with her father that shyness was something unnatural to her, and she could hardly believe the feeling that made her a little breathless, and it was hard to look at the Earl as she should do.

Then she heard the door shut behind her and knew they were alone, and she walked quickly to the desk.

He made no attempt to rise, and merely waited for her to speak.

For a moment it was impossible to form the words she wanted to say.

Then at last she heard her own voice, rather low and hesitant, begin:

"I apologise for . . . troubling Your Lordship again but Felicity has set her heart on riding one of your horses. Your Head Groom thinks it would be safe enough for her, but I felt I should . . . first ask . . . your . . . permission."

"Why?"

The monosyllable was disconcerting, and because she thought he was being rude it made Atayla's chin go up and it was no longer difficult to speak.

"Because, My Lord, Felicity is your responsibility, and while she has ridden a pony for some time, I need your approval before I take her riding on a horse."

"I should have thought it was something you could have decided for yourself without troubling me," the Earl replied. "Very well, Miss Lindsay, if she wishes to ride one of my horses, I see no reason to forbid her to do so. Remember that most people when they start riding have falls, and the best thing to do is to mount again as quickly as possible."

"I am aware of that, My Lord," Atayla said. "At the same time, Felicity is only eight, and I should have thought that however keen she is to ride and is apparently completely fearless at the moment, it would be better for her to have a pony of the right size."

She spoke firmly, and the Earl's eyes met hers as if

he challenged her, and for a moment it was as if there was a silent battle between them.

Then surprisingly he capitulated.

"Very well, Miss Lindsay, I will procure a pony for my daughter. In the meantime, if she rides a horse I am sure Jackson will put her on a very safe one, and either you or a groom can take her on a leading-rein."

"I am very glad to have your permission, My Lord."

She dropped him a small curtsey, then without looking at him again walked from the room.

Only when she shut the door very quietly behind her did she realise that once again she had won a battle.

'This time,' she thought, 'it was against an opponent who was fighting me because he dislikes me personally.'

CHAPTER FOUR

*G*oing upstairs from the Morning-Room, where they had had their luncheon because it was thought the Nursery was not quite ready, Felicity was in a wild state of excitement at the thought of riding.

"I am big enough to ride a horse!" she kept saying, and Atayla only hoped that a suitable animal could be found for her.

She had the uncomfortable feeling that if the child

had an accident, nobody would care except herself!
Then she thought such an idea was a mistake and
tried to put it out of her mind.

When they reached the top landing she was surprised to see the Dowager's lady's-maid, whose name
she had learnt was Jardine, coming from her bedroom.

When the elderly woman looked embarrassed and
hurried past her and down the stairs, Atayla wondered why she should be on the Nursery floor and
seemingly so surreptitious about it.

Then she walked into her own room and saw the
reason. The maids had unpacked her boxes but had
left the wardrobe doors open.

Her gowns were hanging so closely packed together that it was obvious there was not enough room
for them, and many were hanging on the sides of the
wardrobe.

To Atayla it was unbelievable that all these were
hers! Then Jeannie came into the room and said:

"I'm afraid, Miss, we couldn't get all your things in
here, so we've put some of them in the small room
next door, which isn't being used."

"Thank you," Atayla answered. "I do seem to have
rather a lot."

"I've never seen such lovely gowns, Miss," Jeannie
said, "and in such glorious colours!"

Because the maid seemed to expect it, Atayla
walked into the next room, which was smaller than
her own bedroom, and she imagined that in the past
it had been used by a Nursery-maid, or perhaps kept
for visiting children.

There was a large wardrobe against one wall and
that was also filled with gowns, with some more hanging on the outside of it.

On the bed there was, she saw, a profusion of bonnets and hats of all descriptions, and as she looked at
them she wanted to laugh.

Could it be possible that having had not one single

garment of her own to wear when she was in Tangiers, she now possessed what any bride would think was a very large and very expensive trousseau?

Even as she thought of it and was very grateful for the *Comtesse*'s generosity, she knew it would be a mistake while she was at the Castle to say who had originally owned the clothes.

"They had better think I was once rich but have come down in the world," she told herself.

That seemed to her quite a reasonable explanation, and she was sure that not only would the servants be shocked at her wearing the clothes that had belonged to the lady who in their opinion had behaved extremely badly, but that the Earl might make it an excuse to dismiss her.

'I must be very, very careful,' Atayla thought.

But when she had the time she wanted to examine every lovely gown and really believe that they would transform her from a very dowdy chrysalis into a brilliant butterfly.

However, there was no time for that at the moment, with Felicity saying:

"Where is my riding-habit? I want my riding-habit."

Atayla and Felicity went to the child's room, which opened out of the Nursery, and Jeannie followed them. As she went, Atayla asked over her shoulder:

"Is there a riding-habit amongst my things?"

"Oh, yes, Miss, and a riding-hat, which I left in the box as I didn't think you'd be wearing it."

"I shall want it," Atayla said firmly, "but first let us dress Her Ladyship."

She found that all Felicity's things also had been unpacked, and the child had several riding-habits.

While some were made of a thin, pretty piqué, which was suitable for Tangiers, others were in a slightly thicker material which had been bought to wear in cooler weather.

She hesitated as she looked at them. Then Jeannie said:

"There's one here, Miss, which seems newer than the rest, and looks like a skirt that's been divided in the middle."

"I can ride side-saddle now," Felicity said scornfully.

However, Atayla realised that if she was to ride a horse it would be far safer for the child to ride astride.

She persuaded Felicity to let Jeannie help her into it, then hurried to her own bedroom to find her own habit.

When she saw it she was very surprised.

She had somehow expected, because the *Comtesse* bought her clothes from Paris, that her riding-habits would be very elaborate and brightly coloured.

She could remember quite well when she was small that her mother's habit, which came from England, had been very plain, and she had said proudly that it had been made by the best habit-maker in the whole of London.

"There is nobody to touch Busvin," her mother had said, "but, alas, I have never been able to afford to go to him again."

By a strange coincidence, the habit Atayla lifted down from the wardrobe had been made by Busvin and was strictly tailored in a dark cloth that was almost black.

"At least on horseback I shall look conventional, as a Governess should look," Atayla told herself with a smile.

Then she thought it unlikely that the Earl would see her, and his grandmother, who was so critical of her appearance, would be the only person who would be interested in how she appeared.

She dressed herself in the beautifully cut habit, which seemed a little more worn than she had expected.

Then as she looked at herself in the mirror, noting how closely the coat fitted her and how small her waist appeared, she suddenly thought she had been stupid not to think of it before.

Of course the habit had been worn by the *Comtesse* when she was here at the Castle as the Earl's wife.

Atayla immediately felt that it might be recognised by somebody, then told herself such an idea was ridiculous.

One riding-habit looked much like another, and there was no reason for anybody to think that after three years abroad the *Comtesse* would keep anything that was connected with her former life in England.

It took Atayla a little time to tie the white stock round her neck, and she found there were several of them, which Jeannie had put in the drawer with her gloves and handkerchiefs.

She thought perhaps she had made somewhat of a mess of it, but that it did not really matter.

Then, hearing Felicity calling her, she looked round hurriedly for her hat, and as she did so Jeannie came into the room.

"Your riding hat's here, Miss," she said, bringing it to her.

Atayla saw that it was a top-hat which ladies wore out hunting.

She had already arranged her hair very neatly and securely with a number of hair-pins at the back of her head. Now as she put on the hat she thought that even in the hunting-field it would be difficult for any Englishwoman to criticise her appearance.

At the same time, she could not be certain, and she wished there was somebody she could ask.

"I am waiting, Miss Lindsay," Felicity was saying from the door. "Do hurry!"

"I am hurrying as quickly as I can," Atayla answered, and turned from the mirror.

Jeannie handed her a pair of gloves, and as Atayla

saw they were the right sort for riding, she wondered if she would have recognised them herself.

'But at least I have them,' she thought, 'and how very, very grateful I am that I can ride with Felicity and not have to watch her going off with a groom while I am left behind.'

Somebody, she supposed it was Dawson, had ordered the horses to come to the front door, and Felicity was helped into the saddle of a small, lightly built mare which Jackson had chosen for her.

Atayla had a black horse with a white star on his nose that was well trained and quiet.

With a little smile, she thought how amused people would be if they knew the extraordinary animals she had ridden in her years of travelling with her father.

The Arab horses that she preferred were often almost uncontrollable until she could make them realise that she was their master.

However, here she was on a horse, and it was a joy beyond words.

She took the leading-rein which the groom handed her, and as she did so he said:

"Mr. Jackson thinks it'd be a good idea if Oi came with ye, Miss, on your first day."

"I think that is a very good idea," Atayla answered, "and it is very important that Her Ladyship should enjoy her ride and not be afraid."

"I'm not afraid!" Felicity, who was listening, interrupted. "I'm a very, very good rider. *Mon Père* always said so, even though it annoyed him."

They were moving away as the child spoke, and because Atayla was curious she could not help asking:

"Why should it have annoyed him that you rode well?"

"Because I am English and because Mama said once that Papa was the best rider in England."

Atayla did not reply, she merely hoped that the child would not talk of the *Comte* in front of the Earl or the Dowager.

She settled herself comfortably in the saddle and thought that whatever her mount was like, she could not remember when she had ridden in such beautiful surroundings or in such comfort.

The groom, whose name was Jeb, informed Atayla that there was some flat meadowland where it was safe to gallop on the other side of the Park.

They therefore rode carefully through the Park, keeping clear of the low branches of the trees, and Felicity was thrilled at the sight of some small deer which ran away at their approach.

"I want to play with them," she said.

"They are shy and frightened of you at the moment," Atayla replied, "but perhaps when they grow used to you, you may be able to feed them."

"I would like that," Felicity said, "and I would like to have one of my own."

The way she spoke made Atayla realise that like all children she wanted to possess an animal and for it to be hers, and she wondered if it would be possible to ask the Earl if she could have a dog.

Then she thought it was far too soon to start asking for things, and they must, in fact, keep quiet and well out of his way in case he changed his mind and decided not to let them stay.

They reached the meadowland, which as the groom had said was flat and safe for the horses to gallop.

Atayla took Felicity first at a trot before she allowed her to gallop, and realised that the child had not exaggerated when she said she rode well.

'I suppose she really does take after her father,' she thought.

When they reached the end of the meadowland she asked:

"Would you like to try without the leading-rein?"

The child's eyes lit up, and Jeb jumped down to undo the leading-rein and put it in his pocket.

"Do not go too fast to start with," Atayla admonished, "and I will ride beside you."

"Shall we race?" Felicity suggested.

"Not until I am quite certain that you feel safe on your own."

"Of course I do," Felicity said. "I always rode on my own on my pony."

She did not wait to say any more but started off ahead of Atayla, who hastily caught up with her.

They rode to the end of the meadowland, and then as they turned back Atayla saw that Jeb, whom they had left at the other end of the gallop, was not alone.

She wondered at first if the Earl would be angry that Felicity was not on a leading-rein, but thought he could see for himself how well the child could ride, and that it was quite unnecessary for her to be led.

They galloped towards him, and as Felicity drew in her horse she shouted:

"Look, Papa, I can ride a big horse just as well as you!"

The Earl moved nearer to her, and Atayla thought that, however disagreeable he might be, he certainly looked magnificent on the huge black stallion he was riding and seemed very much part of the horse.

"You ride well," he said drily to Felicity, then turned his horse to look at Atayla and say:

"Surely the child is old enough to ride side-saddle? I disapprove of girls trying to pretend they are boys!"

The way he spoke and the note of rudeness in his voice made Atayla reply sharply:

"It is not a question of pretending, My Lord. I merely thought as Felicity was riding a horse for the first time, it was safer for her to ride astride. I also think the pummel on a lady's saddle would be too big for her."

"I have already instructed Jackson to buy a pony for her," the Earl said, "and in future see that she rides side-saddle. I have no use for modern ideas and innovations where women are concerned!"

He did not wait for Atayla to reply, but rode off, and she thought the manner in which he spoke was quite inexcusable.

However, she did not say anything, but when she rode to Felicity's side the child said:

"You are not crying! When Papa spoke to Mama like that, she used to cry!"

Atayla thought, as she had before, that the *Comtesse* doubtless had very good reason for running away from the Earl, but she merely said to Felicity:

"I think we ought to make our way back to the house, and perhaps Jeb will be able to suggest a different route from the one through the Park."

Jeb pointed out a ride through the wood which lay in front of them, which he said would bring them out at the bottom of the garden.

The wood was thick but, Atayla thought, very beautiful.

She began to feel that everything she saw seemed to make her heart respond to it as if it was a part of her childhood dreams, which, even though she had lived abroad for so long, she had never forgotten.

The songs of the birds, the sunshine percolating through the branches of the trees, and when they reached the garden, the flowers, the green lawns, and the trees just coming into blossom were all like a fairy-land after the barren desert, which had seemed to stretch away monotonously into infinity.

"It is so lovely," she said to herself, "and everybody ought to be happy here."

Then she looked at the Castle. It seemed strangely dark and menacing and to be scowling in the same way as its owner did.

As if the thought of the Earl was oppressive and somehow took the gold out of the sunshine, she told herself that all she was concerned with was Felicity, and if she was happy, then she had helped her as the *Comtesse* had asked her to do.

Although Jeb said he would take the horses when

they got to the front door, Atayla insisted on riding into the stables, where she told Felicity to thank Jackson for her ride.

"It was Papa who let me ride," Felicity argued.

"But it was Jackson who chose the horse for you, saddled him, and sent Jeb with us to show us the way," Atayla replied, "so you must thank him."

Felicity thought this over. Then she said:

"*Mon Père* did not thank the servants at the Villa. He said they were stupid and inefficient, and sometimes he was angry with them because they did not look after Mama properly."

"Most servants are very glad to be thanked," Atayla said. "If you do not thank people, you may find they do not look after you so willingly."

Felicity obviously thought this over, and when they arrived at the stables she thanked Jackson very prettily.

"Yer gettin' a pony of yer own, M'Lady," Jackson said, "an' Oi knows of one not far from 'ere. Oi'll try to get 'old o' 'im today or termorrow."

"I want a big pony," Felicity said firmly.

"'E be just the right size fer ye as ye are now," Jackson said, "an' a very pretty animal 'e be too."

He turned to Atayla and said:

"'Ow did ye get on, Miss? Oi can see ye're used to ridin'."

"I enjoyed myself very much, thank you," Atayla replied. "But, if it is possible, could I have something a little more spirited tomorrow? I promise you I will be able to manage him."

Jackson laughed.

"Oi can see that, Miss. Oi expects we'll 'ave ye 'untin' before we're finished!"

"I have never hunted," Atayla replied, "but it is something I think I would enjoy."

Then she told herself she was only dreaming. Long before the hunting-season she was quite certain the Earl would somehow have got rid of her.

The idea was depressing, but it persisted in her mind, and when they walked back and up the stairs she thought she must enjoy every moment and miss nothing while she was here.

The Castle might have come straight out of one of her fantasies which were inspired, as she knew, by the stories her mother had told her of life in England.

They went up to the Nursery, where tea was laid out on the round table in the centre of the room.

It was a very English tea, and Atayla could not help comparing the sandwiches, the cakes, the hot scones in a silver dish, and the several jams and honey that were available, with the meals she had had at the Mission.

Then she told herself firmly:

"Forget the past! The future is what should concern you, and making yourself indispensable so that you will not be sent away to starve."

She felt a little tremor of fear at the idea. Then as they finished tea she remembered that the Dowager Countess wanted to see Felicity.

The child had already been changed by Jeannie from her riding-habit into a very pretty and elaborate dress which the maid obviously thought suitable.

Atayla had not interfered, feeling that Jeannie knew better than she did what was expected at the Castle.

However, she found it difficult to select from her huge variety of clothes, which the *Comtesse* had given her, a garment that was plain and in which she hoped she looked correctly attired for a Governess.

The choice, she found, was very limited, for the *Comtesse*'s gowns were all obviously very expensive and, Atayla thought, elaborate, and although she knew she was no judge, they screamed "Paris!" as if it had been written all over them.

However, she found a gown of dark green satin that seemed plainer than the rest and had a bodice of

real Venetian lace over which there was a small bolero
in the same material as the skirt.

It was exceedingly becoming and made her skin
appear dazzlingly white, while it gave a green tinge to
her grey eyes.

She only hoped that the Dowager would not notice
her, and perhaps she would not be expected to accompany Felicity into her bedroom.

Such an idea, however, was soon dispelled, as Felicity ran into the bedroom crying:

"Can I play with your rings, Grandmama, as you
promised?"

The Dowager glanced at Atayla standing in the
doorway and said:

"Come here, young woman, I want to see what you
are wearing!"

Slowly, because she felt embarrassed, Atayla walked
towards the bed.

The Dowager pulled off several of her rings and
gave them to Felicity as if to keep the child quiet.
Then she exclaimed:

"Very elegant and cost a pretty penny! But who
paid for it? That is what I would like to know!"

At the innuendo in her voice Atayla stiffened, and
for the moment she could think of no reply. Then the
Dowager said:

"You can hardly blame me, living in the wilds of
Yorkshire, to be interested and curious as to how a
Governess earning a pittance—for who pays them
any more?—should be dressed by Worth of Paris!"

Atayla knew then why Jardine had been in her bedroom, and she said coldly:

"It is kind of Your Ladyship to interest herself in
me."

"You still have not answered my question."

It struck Atayla that if she said the clothes had been
a present from a friend they might guess the friend
had been the *Comtesse,* and her instinct warned her
once again that it would be very embarrassing to feel

that she was, as it were, impersonating the former mistress of the house.

Seeking frantically for some explanation which would conceal the truth, she said:

"I had the necessity of replenishing my wardrobe after being robbed, and fortunately was able to obtain what I required very cheaply."

It sounded to her a somewhat lame explanation, but she could think of nothing else on the spur of the moment.

She knew as she finished speaking that the Dowager did not believe her, but she merely said:

"You certainly 'pay for dressing,' Miss Lindsay, as the saying goes! I can only hope you find an appreciative audience for your appearance."

Atayla thought it wiser not to reply, and after a moment's silence she asked:

"Shall I leave Felicity with you, My Lady, and collect her in perhaps a quarter-of-an-hour?"

The Dowager chuckled.

"That is one way of avoiding answering questions," she said. "Very well, I shall look forward, Miss Lindsay, to seeing your gowns one by one, and I hope you will not disappoint me."

"I hope not, My Lady."

She made a small curtsey and went from the room.

"She is as disagreeable as her son," she told herself, and walked along the passage wondering how she could spend the quarter-of-an-hour until she must return for Felicity.

She thought what she would really love would be to look over the Castle, and she remembered that her mother had said that most ancestral houses had a Curator.

She therefore walked on until she reached the staircase into the Hall and hurried down it to ask Dawson, whom she saw was there:

"Do you have a Curator in the Castle?"

"Indeed we do, Miss. Do you want him?"

"I was hoping he could tell me," Atayla said on the spur of the moment, "where to find some books which would interest Her Ladyship and which could be part of her lessons."

"Will you come with me, Miss?" Dawson asked.

He led the way past the door into the Library to where, on the other side of the passage, Atayla saw as she entered what was an Office. There, an elderly man with white hair was sitting at a desk.

There were a number of bookcases in the room, and also maps of the Estate, which she thought would be interesting to study when she had the time.

"This is Mr. Osborne, Miss," Dawson said, "and you'll find he can tell you everything you wants to know."

Atayla shook hands with Mr. Osborne and explained to him that she wanted some books for Lady Felicity. Then, when Dawson had left them, she asked:

"Please, when you have the time, will you show me the Castle? When I tell you that I have come from abroad and have never seen a large English house or a Castle since I was very small, you can imagine how fascinating it is to me."

Mr. Osborne was delighted.

"I will show you everything, Miss Lindsay," he said, "as soon as you have the time. And, yes, I do have some picture-books which I am sure Her Ladyship would enjoy."

He went into the Library opposite and showed Atayla where on the balcony were some books on travel, many of them illustrated.

Atayla knew Felicity would love to see pictures of Tangiers and other parts of Morocco.

She also found picture-books of English houses, and one where there were illustrations of English birds and, what she was sure Felicity would like, stags of different species.

"These are exactly what I want," she said. "Please,

Mr. Osborne, look out for some more which will be suitable for Her Ladyship. You must remember that she has not been in England for so long that there is a great deal for her to learn."

"It's delightful to have her back, Miss Lindsay," Mr. Osborne said. "The place did not seem the same after Her Ladyship left."

Atayla knew he was referring to the *Comtesse,* and she said:

"It must have been very sad for you all."

"Especially for His Lordship," Mr. Osborne said in a low voice. "He's never been the same since he's been alone."

Then he added very quickly in a louder tone:

"I will find you just what you want, Miss, and have them sent up to the School-Room either tonight or tomorrow morning."

The change in the way he spoke made Atayla know instinctively without looking round that the Earl had come into the Library.

She could almost feel his dislike of her vibrating from him when he approached where she was standing with Mr. Osborne.

Then when he reached them she turned her head slowly and saw, as she had expected, that he was scowling.

"I hope you will not damage any books you take from here, Miss Lindsay," he said.

"I promise you that Felicity and I will be very careful with them," Atayla answered. "Apart from these, My Lord, I shall need a number of lesson-books, and of course crayons and pens and other things that are necessary for her lessons."

"You did not think to bring them with you?" he asked.

"No," Atayla replied briefly.

"Was that meanness or spite in the person who paid for them?" the Earl enquired. "Or was it merely your desire to make me responsible for my daughter in more ways than one?"

Once again he was being rude, and Atayla said sharply:

"To tell you the truth, My Lord, I did not think about it."

"Yet you brought a great deal of luggage with you," the Earl persisted, "and not a lesson-book amongst it! How very strange!"

Atayla thought he certainly had a way of finding the weakness in her defence, and for the moment she could not think of a reply.

Then, thinking that attack was the best form of tactics, she said:

"May I, with your permission, My Lord, give somebody a list of what I consider necessary for Felicity's education?"

As she spoke she looked at him defiantly, her chin up, and she thought the scowl between his eyes lightened and he looked almost amused.

"Of course, Miss Lindsay," he replied with exaggerated politeness. "How can I answer that question except in the affirmative?"

"Thank you, My Lord."

Then with an undoubted little flounce of her skirts she walked away from him, carrying the books that Mr. Osborne had given her.

When she went to collect Felicity from the Dowager's bedroom, the child had her hands and wrists covered with jewels, and as Atayla appeared she ran towards her, saying:

"See how beautiful I am! And very, very rich, with so many pretty jewels on my fingers!"

"Where do you think that will get you?" the Dowager asked in her sharp voice.

"I will sell them and buy lots and lots of horses!" Felicity replied.

The Dowager chuckled.

"You could not wear a horse on your fingers or round your wrists."

Felicity laughed.

"That would be funny! But I expect if I am pretty somebody will give me lots of rings and bracelets like these. *Mon Père* gave Mama lots and lots of jewels."

Atayla drew in her breath, and the Dowager said sarcastically:

"Just like her mother! You had better not let my son hear her talk like that."

Atayla was aware that the Dowager was deliberately taunting her with what Felicity had said.

She helped the child remove the jewels before taking her upstairs, and when they reached the Nursery she said quietly:

"Listen to me, Felicity, I want you to promise that you will not talk about the *Comte,* whom you call '*Mon Père,*' any more. Do not mention him to your Grandmama, your Papa, or to anybody else in the Castle. Do you understand?"

"Papa hates him," Felicity said. "I remember he called him a 'dirty Frenchman,' and *Mon Père* said that Papa was a pompous beast of an Englishman!"

"Felicity!" Atayla exclaimed. "You are not to repeat such things or think about them. What happened when you were in Tangiers is not important."

"Papa made Mama cry," Felicity said. "She cried and cried, then we ran away. It was nice in the sunshine, except that *Mon Père* did not like me."

Atayla thought as she had before that Felicity was too intelligent and too quick-brained not to remember what had happened.

To a stupid child it might have meant nothing, but she had the feeling, since in some ways Felicity was like herself, that everything that occurred was stored away in her mind until it was recalled, unfortunately at inconvenient moments.

"Promise me, Felicity," she said aloud, "promise

me that you will not mention *Mon Père* to anybody
here, and try not to think about him."

Felicity shrugged her shoulders, which was something, Atayla thought, that she must have picked up
from the *Comte* or perhaps from some of the French
servants he had employed.

"Mama would not let me talk about Papa to *Mon
Père*," she said, "and now I cannot talk about *Mon
Père* here! It is all very stupid!"

"I agree with you," Atayla said, "but if you want to
be happy here, and not make your Papa cross, let us
try to do things that will make people happy."

Felicity put her head on one side.

"Can I make people happy?" she asked.

"Of course you can," Atayla answered. "People are
unhappy when they do not have love. When you
loved your mother you made her happy, and now
you must try to love your Papa."

"He does not love me."

"I think he does, inside," Atayla said. "But people
are sometimes shy of showing their love for somebody and you have to dig it out of them."

"With a spade?" Felicity enquired.

"Not a real spade," Atayla said, "but you dig out by
smiling and saying nice things and paying them compliments, instead of snarling and being disagreeable."

Felicity laughed.

"That is funny!"

"We will make it a game," Atayla said. "You try to
make your father laugh and smile, then you will find
that he loves you. It is as easy as that!"

As she spoke she thought that it was going to be
very difficult for the Earl to accept the child.

At the same time, she suddenly realised that if the
Dowager, the Earl, and she went on fighting and
scrapping with one another, the person who would
suffer most would be Felicity.

'I would take the child away if I had the money to
do so,' she thought, 'but this is her home, and I

promised her mother I would help her. But it is not helping if she antagonises her father, and if I do the same.'

It suddenly seemed to her that Felicity was very small and vulnerable. She had been taken from one home to another where she was not wanted, and now she had been sent back, like a parcel, without any care, compassion, or understanding.

Atayla knelt down and put her arms round her.

"What is important, darling," she said, "is that you should be happy in this lovely Castle with all those splendid horses to ride. And if you are happy you will make lots of other people happy too."

Felicity looked at her, then quickly, as if it was an impulse that came from her heart, she put her arms round Atayla's neck.

"I love you," she said, "and I like your being with me. Promise you will never . . . never go away and leave me . . . alone."

It was a cry, Atayla knew, of a child who was unsure of herself, and whose sense of security has been disturbed not once but twice.

"I want to stay with you," she replied, "so we will have to try very, very hard to make your Papa like having us here."

CHAPTER FIVE

"*I*t's ever so exciting, Miss! What do you think's happening!"

As she spoke, Jeannie seemed to burst into the Nursery, and Atayla, who was reading Felicity a story, looked up in surprise.

"What is it?" she asked.

She did not think that anything which Jeannie called "exciting" was likely to happen, for the last six days at Roth Castle had been very quiet.

Unexpectedly the Earl had gone away, and the house in his absence seemed to settle down into a comatose state.

What was more, the servants seemed more relaxed and certainly much more pleasant to Felicity and to her.

The Chef sent up special little dishes to tempt Felicity's appetite, and Atayla thought that no-one could complain about the excellent suppers she had, with dishes which she had never tasted before but which she knew were French.

She wondered if the Chef had learnt them before the *Comtesse* had run away with the *Comte*.

She could not help being insatiably curious about the past, but she forced herself to ask no questions and to keep reminding Felicity not to talk about the *Comte* and if possible not about her mother.

She thought it was wrong that a child should be restricted in speaking of either of her parents, but at the same time she knew that mention of the *Comtesse* had an explosive quality which she was anxious to avoid.

She had the feeling that the Dowager was watching her, and she still made caustic remarks with innuendoes underlying them which at times were more amusing than unpleasant.

"What do you find to do with yourself, Miss Lindsay," she had asked yesterday, "when there are no gentlemen to admire your smart clothes?"

"Felicity and I have been very busy, My Lady," Atayla replied. "First we explored the Castle, then the gardens, and now we hope to ride all over the Estate."

She thought her soft answer to a rather impertinent question placated the old woman. At the same time, Atayla knew her sharp eyes took in and appraised every gown she wore.

In the same way, as she imagined Jardine had given the Dowager a graphic description of her evening-gowns hanging upstairs, she thought that as she was unlikely to have occasion to wear them, the Dowager would be prevented from making bitter comments and thereby would be disconcerted.

There was no doubt that the Dowager was beginning to grow very fond of Felicity.

The child went eagerly to her bedroom because she could play with her jewels, and to amuse her the Dowager made Jardine fetch and open her huge jewel-case, which Atayla thought was like Pandora's box.

Never had she seen such a profusion of emeralds, rubies, diamonds, and sapphires, besides diamond necklaces, long strings of enormous pearls, and bracelets and tiaras to match them.

To Felicity it was rather like being in an Aladdin's cave. She dressed herself in the necklaces, bracelets, and rings, and finally as a great concession was allowed to put on a tiara.

"Now I look like a Queen!" she said. "Perhaps one day I will sit on a Throne like Queen Victoria."

The Dowager laughed.

"You will have to find a King to marry you first."

Felicity considered this for a moment. Then she said:

"I think really it would be more exciting to live with a Sheikh in the desert, or a Bedouin Chieftain. Miss Lindsay says they have wonderful horses, and their followers either obey their orders or have their heads cut off!"

The Dowager looked at Atayla and said drily:

"A very enlightening history-lesson, Miss Lindsay, but I should have thought it advisable to keep to the more conventional Rulers."

Atayla did not reply that it had not been a history-lesson at which Felicity had learnt this, but part of the story she had told her about her journeys in North Africa.

Felicity was exceedingly curious about them, since while in Tangiers she had seen parts of the rough desert ground outside the city, and it was all very real to her.

However, Atayla thought that to explain this would be a mistake, and she merely said:

"I will certainly take your advice, My Lady."

Then she knew that her meekness made the Dowager look at her in surprise.

Apart from visits to the old lady's bedroom, there was nothing to interrupt the happy hours when she and Felicity rode in the Park, galloped over the meadowland, and took long rides to explore the Estate.

There were farmers by whom Felicity was greeted enthusiastically, and although Atayla knew that like everybody else they were intensely curious to know why the child had returned, they did not venture to ask any questions.

Because Atayla was having plenty of delicious food, went to bed early, and for the moment was not worried by the thought of being turned away, she slept well and knew that she looked very different from when she had first arrived.

She had put on weight, although she was still very slim, and her eyes and hair seemed to sparkle with a new brilliance.

The wound on her shoulder had healed, and she no longer had to bandage it, but there was still a tender and very ugly scar.

When she looked at it she hoped fervently that one day, as the Surgeon had promised her, it would fade away into just a thin white line.

She could not help remembering the horror of how it had happened, and how her father had died, but she tried very hard to put such thoughts behind her and, as she had told Felicity to do, to think only of the future.

Already she loved the child, although she had never expected to do so, and she knew that Felicity loved her.

She was aware that she was for the moment the one stable and secure factor in her young life, and only when Atayla was alone at night did she sometimes wonder apprehensively where she could go and what it would mean to Felicity if the Earl should dispense with her services.

Then she told herself that she was being needlessly apprehensive, and that although the Earl disliked her, there was no reason why he should not think of her as a competent Governess for his daughter.

Now at Jeannie's intrusion Atayla looked up with a smile and asked:

"What has happened?"

"You'll never believe it, Miss," Jeannie said, coming

farther into the Nursery, "but His Royal Highness the Prince of Wales is coming to dinner tomorrow night."

Atayla stared at her in astonishment.

"Can it be true?"

"Yes, Miss. His Lordship's just arrived back, and he's informed Mr. Dawson that there'll be a dinner-party of fourteen!"

Atayla listened in astonishment, and Jeannie went on:

"His Royal Highness, and of course Mrs. Keppel, are staying with the Marquis and Marchioness of Doncaster, and His Lordship told Mr. Dawson that His Royal Highness has said he wishes to see the Castle, as he's heard a great deal about it. So it's not to be a big party, and Mr. Osborne's to conduct them over the Castle after dinner!"

"Is the King coming here?" Felicity intervened.

"No, not a King, dearest," Atayla replied, "but the Prince of Wales, who will be King one day."

As she spoke, she thought that he had already waited a long time for that position, and Queen Victoria, who had recently celebrated her Diamond Jubilee, looked as if she would go on reigning for many years yet.

But Jeannie had not finished with her information.

"There will be three people staying in the house, Miss: the Marquis and Marchioness of Wick—she's ever so lovely, and she's been here before!—and another gentleman."

Atayla thought the whole thing was certainly surprising, and she had somehow got the impression since she had arrived that the Earl never entertained and was in some ways almost a hermit.

"You'll be able to have a peep at His Royal Highness, Miss," Jeannie went on, "if you come on to the landing when they're arriving. And we've all heard that Mrs. Keppel's very attractive."

Atayla thought she might be going to say something indiscreet about the Prince of Wales's favourite, and gave her a warning glance, but Jeannie was too excited to notice.

"I don't say that I wouldn't have rather seen Princess Alexandra," she said, "seeing how beautiful they say she is. But Mrs. Keppel's the next best thing. That's what the Prince thinks, anyhow!"

She laughed, and Atayla was well aware that the Prince's love-affairs were openly discussed in the Servants' Hall.

She was soon to learn what the Dowager thought about it when she took Felicity to see her great-grandmother after tea.

"I suppose you are all agog like the rest of the household," the Dowager said, "at the thought of seeing a real live Prince!"

"He will be a King one day, Grandmama," Felicity said.

"When he is too old to enjoy it!" the Dowager snapped. "But he has other ways of passing the time, and from what I hear, he is as infatuated with Mrs. Keppel as if he were a young man with his first love-affair."

Atayla thought this was not the sort of thing that should be said in front of Felicity, but fortunately the child was busy bedecking herself with her great-grandmother's jewels.

"Anyway, it will cheer up the gloom of this place," the Dowager said, "and do my grandson good to see a bit of life."

She paused, then as Atayla said nothing, she went on:

"Not that he doesn't do so when he is in London. I have my own way of hearing what he has been up to there."

"I think it is time we went upstairs, My Lady," Atayla said. "Give your Grandmama back her jewels, Felicity, and thank her for letting you play with them."

"Are you pretending to be shocked?" the Dowager

asked. "That sanctimonious look in your eye does not deceive me!"

She gave a little chuckle as she said:

"I expect, if the truth were known, you are sorry you cannot go downstairs and show them how alluring you can look in one of your Worth gowns."

"I shall be quite happy to hear about it afterwards," Atayla replied. "I am only sorry for you, My Lady, that you cannot act as hostess for His Lordship."

She spoke very pleasantly, but the Dowager was well aware that she was getting a little of her own back, and she laughed.

"I am too old to care," she said, "but I will wager you are well aware that you are wasting away in the Nursery, where there is nothing masculine to admire you except a Teddy Bear."

Atayla laughed because she could not help it.

"He is a very attractive one, My Lady!" she replied, and thought as she walked upstairs with Felicity that she had had the last word.

There was no doubt that the idea of the Prince of Wales coming to the Castle galvanised everybody in a way that Atayla found amusing.

When she came down the next morning after breakfast to take Felicity to the stables, so that they could go riding, the whole place seemed filled with people, polishing, brushing, dusting, and cleaning.

'It is like an ants' nest!' she thought, and remembered the huge ones she had seen in the Riff mountains and in other parts of Africa.

There had not been a sign of the Earl since his return, but she could not help feeling an awareness that he was in the house.

It was almost as if, because he was so strong a personality, he vibrated everywhere, and she thought that even if she had not been told he was at home she would have been aware of it.

Jackson greeted them when they reached the stables, and even he, Atayla thought, was thinking of the excitements that were to take place that evening and was not concentrating so much on Felicity's riding as he usually did.

Nevertheless, her new pony, which was a very attractive animal, was brought to the mounting-block and following it was *Rollo,* a horse to which Atayla had taken a great liking.

He was almost completely black except for one fetlock, and was young and inclined to be skittish. She enjoyed the tussles she had with him, knowing that however hard he tried to assert his independence, she could quickly get him under control.

"Oi'm not sendin' a groom wi' ye this morning, Miss," Jackson said, "an' Oi 'opes ye'll excuse us, but Jeb's got things to do tidyin' up the stables."

Atayla looked surprised because she thought there was no chance of His Royal Highness visiting the stables.

Then she remembered that the Earl had several guests staying in the house, and they would undoubtedly wish to see the horses.

"We shall be all right, Jackson," she replied, and she and Felicity rode off along their usual route across the Park.

"Are we going to have another race this morning?" Felicity asked.

"Yes, of course," Atayla replied, "but this time I will give you a little more of a start than I gave you yesterday."

As she spoke she remembered that she had great difficulty in holding back *Rollo* so as to allow the race to end in a dead heat.

"Today *Dragonfly* and I are going to win!" Felicity said firmly.

They reached the meadowland and were just getting into place when Atayla looked round and saw that they were not alone.

The Earl was coming through the wood on his favourite stallion.

Felicity saw him and gave a little cry.

"Come and join us, Papa!" she called. "I am racing Miss Lindsay, and I will race you too. *Dragonfly* is so fast that I am sure he will beat you!"

The Earl raised his eye-brows, then said to Atayla: "Is this a new idea?"

"Felicity wants to race, and she really rides very well, as might be expected."

For the first time since she had known him, the Earl smiled.

"Is that a compliment?"

"I think actually it is a fact," Atayla replied.

"Very well," the Earl said, "I will race you both."

Atayla looked at the stallion and said:

"Felicity will want a start, and so shall I."

The Earl instantly took over and sent Felicity some way ahead and Atayla halfway between the child and him. Then he counted and gave the command to go, and Felicity set off with a quickness and an expertise which Atayla felt the Earl could not help admiring.

She was so intent on watching Felicity and not letting *Rollo* pass her that they were nearly at the end of the gallop before she realised that the Earl was doing the same thing.

She flashed him a smile to show it was what she had hoped he would do, then as Felicity surged ahead, she deliberately rode a little faster, hoping that she would be able to beat the Earl.

Even as she tried to do so she knew it was hopeless and was aware that it would amuse him to know it.

When they finally drew in their horses, letting Felicity win by half a length, he said:

"One day, Miss Lindsay, I will challenge you without any handicaps."

"Thank you," Atayla replied. "In that case, My Lord, I would like to choose my mount."

"Are you really telling me that you could handle *Green Dragon?*" the Earl enquired.

Atayla knew he was referring to the stallion he was riding, and she said:

"I am quite certain I could."

She saw that the Earl did not believe her, and added:

"I have had the opportunity, My Lord, although you may not believe it, of riding Arabian mares, which I expect you know are always the best and fastest of the herd before they are broken in."

The Earl looked at her in astonishment. Then, before he could ask any questions, she had joined Felicity and they turned for home.

The Earl did not go with them, and as he rode off, Atayla wondered if he had been intrigued by what she had said, or if he merely thought she was showing off to impress him.

"It was nice of Papa to race with us, wasn't it?" Felicity remarked as they rode through the Park.

"Very nice," Atayla replied, "and you must ask him to race you again. If you see him this afternoon, say how pleased you are that he has come home."

"He has not come home to see me," Felicity replied, "but only because he is giving a party for the Prince of Wales."

The way she spoke made Atayla realise that the child wanted the attention of her father, and because Atayla had loved her own father so much, she knew how much the Earl could mean in his daughter's life if only he could forget how her mother had taken her away for three years.

It was a cruel thing to do, and yet in some ways Atayla could not help feeling, because she was so beautiful, so fragile, and obviously very sensitive, that in the Castle the *Comtesse* must have been like a songbird imprisoned in an iron cage.

Even if she had loved the Earl and he had loved her, it could have been a difficult and frustrating life for a very young girl.

Atayla wished she knew more of the truth about

their marriage, but she was too proud to ask questions of the servants even if they had wished to talk.

However, she was certain that as the Dowager obviously hated the Earl's wife, anything she could learn from her would be prejudiced.

"It is rather like reading a story in a book and coming in halfway to find all the characters reacting very strangely to what has happened," she told herself, "but the first chapters have somehow been lost."

She smiled at her own fantasy, then wondered whether Felicity missed her mother, and if the child ever lay at night, as she did, longing for her father with such intensity that it was a physical pain.

Everything at the Castle seemed as if a whirlwind was sweeping through it, and everybody was running about rather than walking.

Later in the afternoon, Atayla was aware that the Marquis and Marchioness of Wick had arrived, and when Jeannie came upstairs after tea, she apologised for not having helped Felicity as she usually did out of her outdoor clothes.

"They're a bit short-handed downstairs, Miss," she said to Atayla, "because Miss Jones has one of her headaches."

Jones was the elderly housemaid who worked under Mrs. Briercliffe, and her headaches were frequent and so intense that she had to lie down.

"It means I've got a lot more to do," Jeannie said, "and although Her Ladyship's brought her own maid with her, she's feeling poorly after being in the train, and we've all got to give a helping hand."

"Do not worry about us," Atayla said. "I know you want everything to go smoothly and be at its best for His Royal Highness."

"We do indeed!" Jeannie said. "And don't forget, Miss, I'll come and fetch you to see the Marchioness going down for dinner, and the Royal Party coming in through the front door."

"It all sounds very exciting," Atayla said.

She was aware, because her father had told her, that Royalty were always greeted by the host himself on the doorstep, and seen off in the same way.

"In England it is only Royalty who receive such attention," he said, "but in Arab countries, as you know, my dear, every host whether in a tent or a house meets his guests and speeds their departure with exquisite good manners."

Atayla knew this was true and was interested by the courtesy which Arab Chiefs always showed their guests.

She was aware that one had only to praise a possession of one's host, whether it was an *objet d'art* or a beautiful woman, for its owner to reply:

"It is yours!"

"Does one really take it away when leaving?" Atayla had asked.

Her father laughed.

"If that happened, I should have a numerous Harem by now! No, you accept the gift with gratitude, then conveniently forget it has been given to you."

'I shall watch the Earl receiving His Royal Highness,' Atayla thought, 'and see if he is as hospitable as a Bedouin Chieftain, or the Sheikh who entertained Papa and me with a huge feast at which we were expected to eat the special delicacy consisting of the eyes of the sheep which had been roasted for us.'

Then she told herself her mother would have been shocked at her peeping and peering, thinking it beneath her dignity.

"If I were a Lady, that would be true, Mama," she said, as if her mother was listening, "but I am merely a Governess and, as the Earl pointed out to me, a paid servant."

She put Felicity to bed, heard her prayers, and kissed her good-night.

"Do you think Papa will race with us tomorrow?" Felicity asked.

"He will probably have to look after his guests," Atayla replied, "but I am sure when they have gone he will be willing to race again, if you ask him nicely."

"I will do that," Felicity said, "but I think Papa would be very surprised if I kissed him as I kiss you."

"Try it and see," Atayla advised. "Perhaps he wants you to kiss him, but feels that he does not like to ask you, in case you don't want to."

Felicity thought this over for a moment, then she said:

"I would like to kiss Papa. The servants all think him very handsome, and so do I."

"Then you kiss him," Atayla advised.

She turned out the light and knew when she left Felicity's bedroom that she was almost asleep.

She undressed and had her bath as she did every night before dinner, and was just thinking of putting on one of the comfortable, loose tea-gowns which were amongst the clothes the *Comtesse* had given her, when there was a knock on her bedroom door.

When she called out: "Come in!" she saw to her surprise that it was Mrs. Briercliffe.

She had not expected that the Housekeeper when she was so busy would climb the stairs to the Third Floor.

"I've come to tell you, Miss," Mrs. Briercliffe began rather breathlessly, "that His Lordship's instructions are that you're to dine downstairs tonight."

"Dine downstairs?" Atayla repeated in astonishment.

"You'll have to hurry, Miss, because His Royal Highness'll be arriving in under an hour."

"I do not know what you are saying!" Atayla said.

"It's Lady Bellew, Miss, who was to be one of the

414

dinner-party. She lives only about two miles from here, and her husband's the High Sheriff."

Atayla looked bewildered as Mrs. Briercliffe went on:

"A groom has just come with a message to say that Her Ladyship's very sorry, but she's stricken down with such a bad cold that she's unable to dine to-night."

"Is her husband coming?"

"Yes, Miss," Mrs. Briercliffe replied, "but that makes the dinner-party thirteen, and it's quite impossible to get anybody else at such short notice."

Atayla gave a little laugh.

"Are you saying, Mrs. Briercliffe, that His Lordship has really asked me to dine with his guests?"

"Yes, Miss, and very pretty you'll look in one of them lovely gowns of yours, which I thought you would never have the chance of wearing."

"That is what I thought too," Atayla agreed.

It seemed so incredible that she should dine with the Prince of Wales and the Earl's other guests that she felt she must be dreaming or had not heard correctly what Mrs. Briercliffe had told her.

Then, because it was an excitement she had certainly never expected to happen, she jumped to her feet and said:

"The difficulty, Mrs. Briercliffe, will be to decide which gown I should wear! Can Jeannie come and help me? I am sure you are too busy."

"I am indeed, Miss, but when His Lordship told me to tell you to come downstairs, I thought it only right that I should come myself, to inform you that you were invited."

"And I am thrilled to hear it!" Atayla replied. "It is so utterly unexpected."

Mrs. Briercliffe smiled at her enthusiasm, then said:

"There will not be a lady at the table, Miss, as'll look prettier and smarter than you, and that's a fact!"

"Thank you."

Mrs. Briercliffe went towards the door.

"I'll send Jeannie to you, Miss, and don't you be late! The guests all have to be downstairs in the Drawing-Room before His Royal Highness arrives."

"I will not be late," Atayla promised, and started to brush her hair.

As she did so she was thinking how glad she was that she had washed it only the night before, and it was now soft, silky, and shining.

However, she thought it would be a mistake to try any new arrangement that she had not practised before, and therefore she swept it from her forehead and coiled it at the back of her head in a chignon.

She was just putting in the last hair-pins when Jeannie came hurrying into the room.

"Oh, Miss, I couldn't believe it when Mrs. Briercliffe told me you'll not only see the Prince but speak to him! It's ever so thrilling, it is really!"

"I have to choose the right gown to wear, Jeannie," Atayla said. "Which one do you think would be the most becoming?"

Jeannie thought for a moment. Then she said:

"I knows the one I'd like to see you in, Miss. I thought when I unpacked it that it was just like a bit of sunshine, and that's what's often wanted in this place!"

Because she had thought she would never wear them, Atayla had moved all the evening-gowns out of the wardrobe in her bedroom and into the smaller room next door.

Jeannie now disappeared into the next room and came back holding high in the air so that it did not touch the floor a gown that Atayla had, in fact, thought was one of the prettiest that the *Comtesse* had given her.

Of very pale gold, which actually was the colour of her hair, it was heavily embroidered round the hem, which was held out by frill upon frill of gauze, all of which sparkled with gold sequins.

The sequins made a pattern on the skirt and decorated the bodice, and the frills which encircled the décolletage formed small, puffed sleeves that covered her upper arms.

What was fortunate, Atayla thought, was that the gown was cut in such a way that it would hide completely the scar on her shoulder.

When Jeannie had buttoned her into it she saw she had been right in anticipating this, and also that the dress accentuated the tininess of her waist and gave her a grace she thought she had never had before.

It was certainly like a ray of sunshine, and because it was so skilfully embroidered, she felt she would not feel a lack of the profusion of jewels which every other lady in the party would be wearing in the Royal presence.

Somebody had told her, although Atayla could not remember who it was, that the Prince of Wales expected any woman with whom he dined to wear a tiara.

"Tonight he will be disappointed!" she told herself.

Then Jeannie exclaimed:

"Did you know, Miss, there's some little bunches of flowers made from the same material as this gown and embroidered with the same sequins?"

"No, I did not know," Atayla answered. "Where have you put them?"

Jeannie ran into the next room and came back with two tiny bunches which glittered and shone almost as if they were jewels.

She fixed them on each side of the chignon, and Atayla felt they gave a finish to her appearance that she had not had before.

There were long gloves to be worn that were of such a fine, delicate suede that they were unlike any gloves Atayla had ever seen.

Like the *Comtesse*'s shoes, they were a little tight, but

she knew it would be *lèse-majesté* to shake hands with
the Prince of Wales unless she was wearing gloves.

"You looks lovely, Miss, you really do!" Jeannie said
when she was dressed. "If Mrs. Keppel's jealous of
you, I'll not be a bit surprised!"

Atayla laughed.

"I think that is very unlikely."

At the same time, as she went down the Grand
Staircase she was aware that her heart was beating
tumultuously, and she felt excited in a way she had
never felt before.

She was to see for the first time the way of life that
her mother had described to her as being hers before
she had married her father.

Atayla had known, because there had often been a
wistful note in her mother's voice when she spoke of
the Balls she had attended and the parties her father
and mother had given for her, that she longed for
her own daughter to be part, as she had been, of the
Social World.

"I am afraid, dearest," she had said to Atayla, "that
it is something that will never happen, but I would
love to have presented you at Court and watched you
waltz at your first Ball with a lot of handsome young
men."

"I may not be doing that tonight, Mama," Atayla
said to her mother in her heart, "but I shall be meeting the Prince of Wales, and you must help me not to
make mistakes which would make you ashamed of
me."

Dawson was waiting at the bottom of the staircase,
and she knew as she saw the expression on his face
that he was very surprised at the way she looked, and
at the same time delighted.

"You're a sight for sore eyes, Miss!" he said, and
the way he spoke made Atayla laugh.

He went ahead of her across the Hall and opened
the door into the Drawing-Room.

It was a very impressive room, which Atayla had

briefly explored with Felicity, but now that the huge chandeliers were lit, it had a beauty she had not expected.

The austerity of it had been swept away because there was a profusion of flowers everywhere, and Atayla felt as if she were walking onto a stage!

The difficulty was that she was not certain what her role entailed.

There were two men at the far end of the room, and Dawson announced:

"Miss Lindsay, M'Lord!"

For a moment she felt so shy that everything seemed to swim in front of Atayla's eyes.

Then she realised that the Earl was walking towards her, and because it was the first time she had seen him in evening-clothes, she thought he looked not only most impressive wearing several decorations on his chest but even more awe-inspiring than usual.

As he reached her he said:

"I am very grateful to you, Miss Lindsay, for helping me out of what would otherwise have been a disastrous situation."

He must have been aware that she thought his description was somewhat exaggerated, for he explained:

"His Royal Highness has a horror of sitting down thirteen. In fact, he refuses to do so, and I should have found it very difficult to know who should be sent away from the door."

"I am very grateful to be allowed to be of use, My Lord," Atayla replied.

As they were talking they had walked towards the hearth-rug, and the Earl said:

"May I introduce Sir Christopher Hogarth, an old friend of mine? Christopher, this is Miss Lindsay, who has so obligingly saved the situation at only a few minutes' notice."

Sir Christopher, who was a good-looking man and, Atayla thought, a little older than the Earl, said:

"I can only imagine, Miss Lindsay, that you obliged our host by dropping down from a star in the sky, or perhaps you were the last ray of sun left behind at sunset!"

Atayla laughed, and the Earl said:

"You are very poetical, Christopher!"

He did not make it sound exactly a compliment, but before Sir Christopher could reply, the Butler announced:

"The Marquis and Marchioness of Wick, M'Lord!"

The Marquis was an elderly man, and the Marchioness was middle-aged but very attractive.

She was glittering with jewels and wore a diamond tiara, but Atayla thought that while her gown was extremely elaborate, it was not as sensational as her own.

They were introduced, then the Earl glanced at the clock and said:

"I had better take up my position in the Hall. I am sure Doncaster, who is extremely punctilious on the race-course, will get His Royal Highness here exactly on time."

"I will act as host until you return, Valor," Sir Christopher said, "and I cannot imagine a more pleasant task."

It was obvious that he knew the Marchioness well, and she talked to him animatedly, but Atayla was aware that even while he listened his eyes were on her.

It made her feel less shy and more sure of herself to know that at least one person in the party admired her, and she said a little prayer of thankfulness that the *Comtesse* had included evening-gowns amongst the other things she had given her.

She could not imagine anything more frustrating than if after the invitation to join the party she had had to reply that she could not accept as she had nothing to wear.

'That is something I will not be able to say for years and years,' she thought.

She felt as her gold sequins sparkled in the light of the candles that it was all like a dream, and she only hoped she would not wake up too soon.

The Prince of Wales was very stout, very genial, and obviously in a good temper.

A member of the party was the Portuguese Ambassador, the Marquis of Soveral, who, although Atayla was not aware of it, could always manage, because he was a great wit, to keep the Prince in a good mood, and was therefore included in almost every house-party to which His Royal Highness was invited.

Mrs. Keppel was a little stouter and a little older than Atayla had expected, but there was no doubt that, if not strictly beautiful, she had a fascinating face, and the Prince's eyes when he looked at her were very revealing.

There was champagne to drink before dinner, and Atayla thought it seemed to make everything that was said by the guests sparkle like the bubbles in the glasses, and when she was taken in to dinner on the arm of Sir Christopher, she said:

"This is very, very exciting for me!"

"Our host tells me you are Governess to his daughter, Felicity. Can that be true?"

"I do not know why you sound so surprised," Atayla answered. "I am actually a very proficient Governess!"

"I can picture you doing a great many other things rather better," Sir Christopher said. "And why have you chosen to bury yourself in a Castle that should exist only in one of Grimm's Fairy Tales?"

Atayla laughed.

"I like being here," she said, "and I am only afraid

that I will not be allowed to stay and will have to go elsewhere."

"Why should anybody want to turn you away," Sir Christopher enquired, "least of all your host?"

Atayla did not answer, and he said:

"As an old friend of Valor's, I gather it was a tremendous surprise when his daughter was returned to him after being kidnapped in that appalling manner three years ago."

"Kidnapped?"

"There is no other word for it," Sir Christopher said. "Nadine left and took the child with her without explanation or warning."

Atayla thought it best to say nothing, and after a moment Sir Christopher said:

"To look at, Nadine was one of the most beautiful women I have ever seen. Is she still as lovely?"

Again Atayla hesitated, and he said:

"There is no need to pretend to me, Miss Lindsay. Valor told me that you arrived completely unexpectedly and uninvited from Tangiers, and as the only person who would have sent the child back to her father was Nadine, presumably she engaged you as a very unlikely-looking Governess."

Atayla laughed.

"What exactly should a Governess look like?" she asked. "People always seem to be complaining about my appearance!"

"Are you surprised?" Sir Christopher enquired. "And dressed as you are now, no-one would suspect for one moment that you were anything but a Professional Beauty, and in exactly the right place, being at a party given for His Royal Highness."

Atayla had heard about the Professional Beauties whose post-cards sold in their thousands, and who, even though they were Society Ladies, were acclaimed as if they were actresses.

She supposed it was a compliment to be told that

she was one, but at the same time she was not quite sure.

"Well?" Sir Christopher said. "I am waiting for an answer to my question."

"I think it would be a mistake," Atayla replied in a low voice, "to talk about the past, which would obviously upset the Earl. So it is something on which I prefer to remain silent."

Sir Christopher smiled.

"That is very wise. At the same time, you might tell me what you were doing in Tangiers."

"I had not been there long, having in fact come there from Moulay Idriss."

Atayla was being deliberately provocative, thinking that Sir Christopher would never have heard of the Holy City in the Zerhoun Hills, and she was also trying to divert his mind from the *Comtesse*.

But to her astonishment he looked at her sharply and said:

"Lindsay! You cannot be any relation of Gordon Lindsay?"

"He . . . he was my . . . father!"

"I do not believe it!" Sir Christopher exclaimed. "Then how, of all places, have you landed up here?"

"You knew my father?"

"I have admired him and have read everything he has written. Moreover, although you may find it an amazing coincidence, my mother was a Lindsay!"

Atayla drew in her breath.

"She was . . . one of Papa's . . . relations?"

"A very distant one, but when she was alive she was an extremely well-read and well-educated woman. It was she who first showed me your father's books and the articles he wrote in the *Royal Geographical Magazine*."

"And you enjoyed them?"

"I was enthralled by them!" Sir Christopher replied.

"Papa had finished a book about the Berbers just before he died."

"He is dead?"

"He was murdered by robbers," Atayla replied. "We were on our way home to Tangiers, a very small caravan with few servants with us. The robbers swooped down from the hills and everybody was . . . killed except me."

"How did you survive?"

"They left me for dead, but I was carried by some kind people to Tangiers and nursed in the Mission."

"It is the most fascinating story I have ever heard!" Sir Christopher said.

Atayla looked towards the top of the table to where the Earl sat looking, she thought, almost as if he himself were Royal. Without asking herself why, she said to Sir Christopher:

"Please do not say anything to anybody here . . . will you promise me? . . . as to who I am and where I come from."

"Are you telling me our host does not know that your father was Gordon Lindsay?"

"He just thinks I am a Governess chosen by Felicity's mother," Atayla said, "and that is how I would like to leave it."

She did not know why she wanted to be secretive about it. But perhaps she was afraid that the Earl would think that she was therefore incompetent to teach Felicity in a civilised country, or perhaps he might disapprove of the life she must have led with her father.

"Please," she begged, "promise me you will say nothing."

"Of course," Sir Christopher answered, "but only on condition that you tell me what latest discoveries your father made and all about his new book, which I shall order immediately from the publishers."

"It is very, very interesting," Atayla said.

They went on talking, and it was only when dinner

424

had been in progress for quite a long time that Atayla remembered she should turn and talk to the gentleman on her other side.

With an effort, because she had found it fascinating to find anybody who was so interested in her father and knew so much about him, she turned to her left.

But she discovered that her other dinner-partner, an elderly Peer, was deep in conversation with the lady beside him, discussing the horses that were running in the Spring meeting at Doncaster.

As they obviously had no wish to be interrupted, she turned back to Sir Christopher, and he said with a smile:

"Fate has played into our hands, since the lady on my other side seems equally engrossed! So now we can continue what to me is one of the most exciting conversations I have had for a long time!"

They talked about her father's other books, of his latest discoveries regarding the Berbers, and of what he thought of the way the French had established themselves in Algeria after the Battle of Isly.

It was so long since she had talked of such things to anyone to whom they meant anything that Atayla's eyes were shining like stars.

More than one of the Earl's guests asked who she was with an inescapable expression of admiration in their eyes.

Only when the ladies retired to the Drawing-Room was Atayla aware that one or two of them were regarding her with somewhat hostile looks, until Mrs. Keppel asked her to sit down beside her.

"I hear you are looking after our host's daughter," she said. "Does she look like her mother? I remember seeing her some years ago and thought her very beautiful."

"Felicity more resembles her father."

"Nobody could be more handsome," Mrs. Keppel remarked, "but it is a pity the child is not a son."

"Why?" Atayla enquired.

425

"Because as things are," Mrs. Keppel replied, "there is no chance of his ever marrying again, although naturally, like every man, he wants an heir."

"Yes, of course," Atayla agreed. "I had not thought of that."

"But what could be a more delightful place in which to bring up children?" Mrs. Keppel said. "I am so looking forward to exploring the Castle after dinner, and His Royal Highness is particularly interested in seeing the Library."

As soon as the gentlemen joined the ladies, the Earl said that those who wished to see the Castle could come with him and meet Mr. Osborne, who was waiting in the Hall.

But, he added, anybody who preferred it could stay in the Drawing-Room, where card-tables had been erected for those who wanted to play games.

"Personally," Sir Christopher said, "I want to talk to you, Miss Lindsay."

"I am not quite certain," Atayla replied, "whether I am expected to stay or go."

"What do you mean by that?"

"I was only asked down to make up the fourteen at dinner, and no-one has told me what I should do now when there is no more necessity for my presence."

"There is every necessity as far as I am concerned," Sir Christopher said, "and I have no intention of letting you leave. So let us sit on the sofa while you go on telling me about your father's discoveries."

"Have you ever been to Africa?"

"Several times," he answered, "for big-game hunting and shooting, but not in the parts where you have been. Now tell me what your father thought about the Riff mountains."

There was so much to say that when the Royal Party returned from touring the Castle, Atayla thought they could only have been away for about five minutes.

However, the Marquis of Doncaster said:

"I think we should be leaving now, Valor. His Royal Highness is going back to London tomorrow, and we, as you know, will have to be at the race-course early in the morning."

They all shook hands, and as Atayla made a deep curtsey to the Prince, he said:

"You are very pretty, my dear, and if you ever come to London you will be a sensation! I shall certainly welcome you at Marlborough House."

"Thank you, Sir."

However, she felt as he turned away that that was something which would never happen. At the same time, she knew her mother would have been pleased at what the Prince had said.

Then as the Earl escorted the Royal Party to the front door, she thought it would be sensible for her to leave too.

"I am going to bed now," she said to Sir Christopher. "Please, keep your promise."

"I never break a promise," he answered, "and I shall look forward to seeing you tomorrow, when you can tell me more about your father. Besides, do you realise that, if somewhat distantly, we are related?"

"That means a great deal to me, because I have no idea where in England I have any relations," Atayla said.

Because she felt he would want to talk to her about it, she quickly said good-night to the Marquis and Marchioness of Wick, and hurried from the room before Sir Christopher could prevent her from doing so.

She did not go up the main staircase, where the Earl might have seen her. Instead, she slipped away down the passage which led to a secondary staircase, and there she climbed up to her own bedroom.

When she reached it, she thought it was the most exciting evening she had ever spent, and because she could not help expressing it in some way, she twirled round and round in the Nursery, swinging her skirts round her ankles.

"It was lovely, lovely, lovely!" she said aloud. "Thank You, God, for letting it happen!"

CHAPTER SIX

*A*tayla was fast asleep when she was awakened by the sound of the door opening, and she thought to her surprise that it must be time for her to be called.

Then she heard Jeannie's voice saying:

"Sorry to disturb you, Miss!"

She opened her eyes to see Jeannie standing just inside the door with a candle in her hand, fully dressed but rather untidily, with her white cap crooked on her head.

"What is the matter?" she asked.

"I came to ask, Miss, if I could borrow your bandages," Jeannie replied.

It struck Atayla that something might have happened to Felicity, and she sat up quickly.

"What is it? Who has been hurt?"

"It's the Marchioness, Miss. She's cut her hand, and as I knew you had some bandages, I thought it'd be quicker to come to you than to wake Mrs. Briercliffe."

"Yes, of course," Atayla said.

"Can I get them, Miss? I think they're in a drawer over there."

Jeannie walked across the room, and Atayla asked: "How did the Marchioness cut herself?"

"With a glass, Miss, an' her hand's bleeding badly."

"You will have to wash it before you bandage . . ." Atayla began, then stopped. "I had better come and do it."

She remembered how many people she had bandaged when she was travelling with her father, and she knew she would be far more skilful than Jeannie.

The maid gave a sigh of relief and said:

"I'd be ever so grateful, Miss, but I don't like to trouble you."

"It is no trouble," Atayla replied.

She got out of bed and put on over the diaphanous nightgown which the *Comtesse* had given her a loose negligé of chiffon and lace.

She thought when she wore it that she would have to get something thicker before the winter, but that did not concern her now, and without bothering to look in the mirror she followed Jeannie to the door.

"The quickest way," the maid said, "is along the top of the house and down another staircase."

"I will follow you," Atayla replied, and without saying any more Jeannie set off quickly, the candle flickering in her hand.

Atayla realised that they were walking along the top floor of the Castle, where she thought the maid-servants slept. Then, after going a long way, they descended a narrow staircase which on the next floor gave way to a wider one, which was thickly carpeted.

When they reached the end of that staircase, Atayla realised they were in the corridor which led to the bedrooms where she and Felicity had slept their first night at the Castle.

She had the idea that at the end of it, not far from the staircase by which they had descended, there was the Master Suite of rooms where the Earl slept.

However, she had little time to think of anything but keeping up with Jeannie, and now it was easier to see where they were, as there were a few gas-lights left burning in the corridor.

Jeannie walked on, knocked at a door and then opened it, and Atayla realised that the Marchioness was sleeping in the room which Felicity had occupied and which contained a large four-poster bed.

She was alone, and Atayla suspected that the Marquis was sleeping in the next room, which she had occupied.

The Marchioness was sitting up in bed with a hand-towel wrapped round her hand, and it was already deeply stained with blood.

"I've brought Miss Lindsay, M'Lady," Jeannie said. "I'm sure she'll bandage you better than I can."

"It is very kind of you, Miss Lindsay," the Marchioness said gratefully. "I understand my lady's-maid took a sleeping-potion before she retired to bed, and it is impossible to wake her."

"I am very experienced at bandaging," Atayla said. "How did you hurt your hand?"

The Marchioness explained that reaching out in the darkness for the glass of water which stood beside her bed, she had knocked it against a heavy candlestick and the glass had broken in her hand.

She undid the linen hand-towel as she spoke, and Atayla saw that she had cut several of her fingers on the inside, and also the base of the thumb.

She was sure they were only surface wounds, but, at the same time, they were bleeding profusely.

She sent Jeannie to fetch a basin of water, and washed the Marchioness's hand very carefully before she put a pad of lint and cotton-wool on it to stop any further bleeding.

Then she bandaged it with a skill which could only have come from having done the same thing many times in the past.

"You have done that beautifully, Miss Lindsay!" the Marchioness exclaimed when she had finished. "Just as good as any Nurse!"

"I am afraid it will hurt you a little," Atayla said, "but try not to move it too much and start it bleeding again. You had better see a Doctor in the morning."

The Marchioness sighed.

"How could I have been so careless?" she asked. "But that is what everybody asks after an accident has happened."

Jeannie emptied the water into a china pail beneath the wash-hand-stand and picked up the pieces of broken glass very carefully. Then she collected the bandages and was obviously anxious to return to her bed.

"Try to sleep," Atayla said to the Marchioness, "or perhaps you would like a drink first, as you were prevented from having one."

"I am rather thirsty," the Marchioness admitted.

Atayla looked at Jeannie.

"Go back to bed," she said. "I know you have to get up early."

"Thank you, Miss," Jeannie answered. "I'll leave the candle at the bottom of the stairs."

She slipped away, obviously glad to be released, and Atayla walked to the wash-hand-stand, found another glass, and filled it with water from a glass bottle.

She took it to the Marchioness, who drank it thirstily.

"I suppose," Atayla said, "I ought really to get you a cup of tea or something warm to drink, after what has been a shock, but I am afraid I should never find my way about the Castle as I would in an ordinary house."

The Marchioness gave a little laugh.

"No, indeed," she agreed, "but I am quite all right now. Just angry at my own stupidity."

"You will feel better in the morning," Atayla said consolingly.

She took the empty glass from the Marchioness and put it back on the wash-hand-stand in case she should knock it over again. Then she blew out the candle by the bedside, and by the light from the passage outside found her way to the open door.

"Good-night, My Lady."

"Good-night, Miss Lindsay, and thank you for being so very kind," the Marchioness replied.

Atayla realised that all the time she was in her room, the Marchioness had spoken in a low voice, and she was certain she was doing so because she did not wish to disturb her husband in the next room.

She started to walk along the passage the way she had come with Jeannie, thinking as she did so of some of the accidents that had happened to their servants when she was travelling with her father.

Only his expert knowledge and hers had prevented their wounds, from either a weapon or the thorns on many of the desert shrubs, from becoming gangrenous or deeply infected.

She had almost reached the bottom of the staircase when a door just in front of her opened, and she felt her heart give a leap as silhouetted against the light behind him she saw the Earl.

He was wearing a long robe that reached to the floor, and she realised he must have been awakened.

As Atayla walked towards him, she thought he was staring at her incredulously. Then he asked, and his voice was harsh:

"What is going on? What are you doing here, Miss Lindsay?"

She parted her lips to explain to him, but he added furiously:

"Need I ask? I saw the way you were behaving at dinner and afterwards, but I could not believe you could be so easily side-tracked from your main objective."

Atayla looked at him in astonishment, having no idea what he was talking about.

Then, as if he suddenly lost control of his temper, he reached out and, taking her by her arm, pulled her through the open doorway into his bedroom.

She had a quick glimpse of a huge room with a light burning beside an enormous four-poster bed, but she could only think of the Earl's fingers, which hurt her, while the furious expression on his face was frightening.

Never had she seen a man looking so angry, and before she could speak, before she could think or ask what he was doing, he said:

"I am well aware of why you came here, Miss Lindsay, and why my wife sent you to seduce me into giving her the divorce she needs. But I did not expect you to behave like a prostitute with one of my guests."

"What are you . . . saying? How . . . dare you say such . . . things to . . . me?"

She could get no further, for the Earl went on in a voice that was almost a shout:

"Do you suppose I was deceived by my wife's sudden change of heart in returning my daughter to me? Do you suppose I am such a fool that I did not realise why she sent you and what your real mission was?"

He laughed mockingly.

"Only a man who was blind and deaf would believe you to be a Governess! Who ever heard of a Governess wearing Worth gowns, any one of which would have cost more than treble her year's salary?"

"I can . . . explain . . ." Atayla tried to say.

"There is nothing to explain," the Earl retorted. "You can go back to my wife and tell her that you have been unable to carry out your instructions. And, as far as I am concerned, you can take Felicity with you!"

"No! No!" Atayla cried. "I cannot do . . . that!"

"Why not?" the Earl asked. "Are you so anxious to stay?"

He looked down at her, and his eyes were hard as he went on:

"How boring you must have found it when I was not here for you to captivate! But you have certainly made up for it tonight, and I hope you have enjoyed yourself!"

"You must . . . listen to . . . me," Atayla pleaded. "Please . . . please . . . let me . . . explain!"

"I have no intention of listening to your lies," the Earl replied, "and you will, I am sure, try to make them more convincing than your very poor impersonation of a Governess."

He almost spat the words at her. Then, as if he was suddenly aware that she was trembling because she was frightened, that her eyes, which were looking up at him, were large in her small face, and her hair shimmering in the light of the candles was flecked with gold, he said in a very different tone:

"Perhaps it is cruel of me to send you away without anything to report. You came for one reason, and one reason only, and I would not wish you to be disappointed, unless of course you have had enough love-making for one night."

The words seemed to vibrate from him with a violence that he could not control.

As he finished speaking, his arms went round her, he pulled her against him, and his lips came down on hers.

He kissed her roughly and brutally, and although she tried to struggle against him, she was completely helpless in his arms.

As she tried with all her strength to push him away from her, she realised that he not only held her captive with his lips, but his arms were like bands of steel.

Suddenly he picked her up, and as she gave a cry of sheer terror he threw her down on the bed.

For a moment she could hardly believe what was happening. Then frantically she pleaded:

"Please . . . please . . . you are . . . frightening me! You . . . cannot do this . . . please . . . please . . . let me . . . go."

Her hands were free and she pushed violently

against him and struggled to get up. Then as she gave another little scream of terror, he flung himself upon her and forced her backwards.

As he did so, he gripped her shoulder, his fingers digging into the wound she had received from the robber's dagger.

The pain of it struck through her body as if she had been stabbed again. She gave one little muffled scream at the agony of it, and knew nothing more. . . .

Atayla came back to consciousness from a darkness that seemed to envelop her, and not only was she unable to move but it was impossible to think.

Then she remembered that she was afraid, and made an inarticulate murmur of fear.

Something terrifying was happening, and she did not know what it was. She knew only that she was desperately frightened.

Then a deep voice which for the moment she could not recognise said:

"It is all right, nothing will hurt you now. Go to sleep."

Because it was a command and was easier to obey than refuse, she shut her eyes and slipped away into unconsciousness.

When Atayla woke again, she was aware that somebody was pulling back the curtains and the sunshine was coming in through the windows.

All she was aware of was a great disinclination to come back to reality, and she kept her eyes closed until she heard Jeannie moving about the room.

Then the maid asked in surprise:

"Are you all right, Miss? You didn't get into bed when you came back last night."

Atayla opened her eyes, and she could see Jeannie staring at her and realised she was lying on top of her bed, still wearing her negligé.

Everything that had happened came back like a flood-tide, but her memory stopped at the point when the agony of the Earl touching her wound had made her scream with pain.

What had happened after that was a blank.

Then she realised that she had not walked upstairs to her own room and the Earl must have carried her there, and she supposed she must have fainted and therefore not been aware of what was happening.

She knew Jeannie was waiting for an answer, and after a moment she said hesitatingly and in a voice that did not sound like her own:

"I was tired . . . when I got . . . back upstairs . . . and it was very . . . hot."

Jeannie turned from the bed.

"I were sorry to have to wake you, Miss, but I couldn't have bandaged Her Ladyship anything like as good as you did."

She put a brass can into the basin on the wash-hand-stand and covered it with a Turkish towel to keep it warm.

"You don't want to hurry to get up after such a disturbed night, Miss. I'll see to Her Ladyship."

"Thank you . . . Jeannie."

When Atayla was alone, she put her hand to her shoulder.

As she did so, she was aware that a frill of lace was slightly torn, and it must have happened when the Earl gripped her shoulder.

Then she remembered how he had kissed her and the things he had said, which still seemed wildly incomprehensible, until gradually as she thought back over what had happened they began to make sense.

Vaguely at the back of her mind she remembered

that either her mother or her father had told her that
for a woman to obtain a divorce in England, which
was thought very reprehensible, however justified,
she had to prove both infidelity on the part of her
husband and, in addition, cruelty.

As the thought came to Atayla, she drew in her
breath sharply, and understood why the Earl had insulted and raged at her.

"How could he . . . think such a . . . thing of
. . . me?" she asked herself indignantly.

Then she supposed that it was her clothes, the
beautiful gowns that the *Comtesse* had given her,
which had made him believe she had been sent there
to trap him into an act of immorality.

"It is . . . impossible!" she said aloud. "How could
anybody believe . . . such a thing?"

Then, almost as if it were a picture in front of her
eyes, she saw her reflection in the mirror and knew
that last night, in the expensive, sequinned and embroidered gown of pale gold, she had looked, as Sir
Christopher had said, like a ray of sunlight left over
from the sunset.

Even so, no-one but the Earl, with his suspicions,
his hatred, and his violence, could possibly believe
her father's daughter could stoop to doing anything
so utterly and completely despicable.

Then she remembered that to him she was not her
father's daughter, but just an unknown woman who
had arrived unexpectedly with a little girl who had
been kidnapped by her mother.

It all seemed a tangled nightmare of horror from
which it was impossible to extricate herself.

Suddenly she sat up in bed from sheer shock.

She remembered that when he had raged at her he
had told her to leave.

After that, he had kissed her before throwing her
down on the bed and frightening her to the point
where she thought it would be impossible to escape
from him.

She had to leave, but where could she go? And, what was more, she had no money.

The whole horror of it seemed to sweep over her like a wave that was drowning her, and it was impossible to breathe, impossible to survive.

Slowly, she got out of bed, knew that she was trembling, and found that she was unsteady on her legs.

She was not sure whether it was a result of last night's shock or because she now had a new and different terror to face.

It flashed through her mind that she might ask Sir Christopher for help.

Then she knew that after what the Earl had accused her of, she would rather die than approach his friend, even though they were, as he had said, distantly related.

"If I ask him for help, then the Earl will be more convinced than he is already that I am a wicked and immoral woman," she told herself.

It was difficult to believe that anybody would think such a thing of her!

Yet, with some intelligent part of her brain, she began to understand how the Earl had reasoned it out from what she had to admit was circumstantial evidence, of a sort, against her.

He already suspected that she had come to the Castle to seduce him, and she had certainly allowed Sir Christopher to monopolise her all evening. The Earl had some grounds for being suspicious when he found her on the floor where his friend's bedroom was situated.

Atayla gave a little cry.

"It is horrible, beastly, degrading!" she told herself.

Yet, she felt despairingly she could in no way convince him that everything he believed was untrue.

'No wonder he hates me,' she thought, but she wondered why the Earl should think the *Comtesse* wanted a divorce when the *Comte,* according to Father Ignatius, was married with a wife in France.

It was all too complicated for Atayla to understand, and she went to the window, feeling in need of air because she felt shaky and as if she might faint again.

Then she told herself that she must get up and give Felicity breakfast.

With the greatest difficulty she managed to dress, thinking all the time that she would have to leave the Castle and not knowing how she could do so.

"You look done in, Miss!" Jeannie said when she came up to the Nursery. "Why don't you go and have a lie-down, and I'll look after Her Ladyship?"

"I am all right," Atayla replied. "But I wonder if you could arrange for Her Ladyship to ride with Jeb this morning? I have some things to do for myself."

"Yes, of course," Jeannie said. "I'll send one of the footmen to the stables now."

"I want to ride with you, Miss Lindsay," Felicity cried, looking up from her plate. "It is much more fun with you."

"Yes, I know, dearest," Atayla replied, "but I have a headache. So go with Jeb this morning, and perhaps when I feel better we can ride again this afternoon."

"That would be lovely!" Felicity said. "And I need not do any lessons?"

"Not this morning."

Atayla wanted to add: "And never with me again," but she knew it would upset the child, and she felt tears come into her eyes at the thought.

She did not want to leave the Castle, she wanted to stay, not only because it was a roof over her head but because she loved Felicity, and because everything about it had been exciting and different from anything she had ever known before.

She drank a cup of tea and felt a little better, but she knew it would be impossible to eat anything.

It was Jeannie who put Felicity's velvet riding-cap on her head, helped her into her jacket, and found her whip and gloves.

"I'll take her downstairs, Miss," she said, "and if

you take my advice, you'll go to sleep for the next hour or two. No-one'll disturb you."

"Thank you," Atayla said weakly.

Felicity held up her face to be kissed.

"I will tell you all about it when I come back, Miss Lindsay, but it will not be such fun riding with Jeb as it would be racing with you."

"Do as Jeb tells you," Atayla admonished, "and be careful not to fall off, because that would worry me."

"I am a very good rider, like Papa," Felicity answered.

Then she was hurrying down the stairs with Jeannie, and Atayla went to her own bedroom.

She stood for a moment looking at the wardrobe that was overflowing with gowns and wondered how she would be able to pack everything and, when she was ready to leave the Castle, how far her money would take her.

Because she was trying to be practical, she took her handbag from the drawer and, opening it, found the purse which contained all the money that was left.

She emptied it out onto the white cover of the bed, which had been made while they were having breakfast, and counted it.

There were three pound notes, two half-sovereigns, and three shillings. That was all that remained of the money which the *Comtesse* had given her in Tangiers.

Atayla stared at it despairingly, wondering how far away from the Castle it would take her and how she could live until she found work of some sort.

Now she wished she had made enquiries since she had been there as to how far away Baronswell in Northumberland was.

'Perhaps,' she thought, 'there will be some of Papa's relatives still living there.'

Because she had no idea of their names or ages, or even if they were still alive, she knew it would be much more difficult to arrive unannounced and unexpected in what had once been her grandfather's house than it had been to arrive at the Castle.

"What can I do? Where can I go?"

The questions seemed to be repeated tauntingly in the air round her, and she felt despairingly that she could not cope with life on her own. It would have been far better if the robber's dagger had killed her as the Arab had intended it should.

Then, as if she knew she had to do something, she opened a cupboard where she knew Jeannie had put some of the trunks, and found the smallest one, in which the things she had wanted for the journey from Tangiers had been packed.

She pulled it into the centre of the bedroom and opened it.

Then as she looked at the wardrobe packed with pretty gowns, and remembered that as many more were hanging up in the room next door, she knelt down on the floor beside the trunk, knowing it would be absurd to try to take everything with her, and she must pack just enough for her needs.

Yet, she had no idea what her needs would be, and she supposed it was because she was still feeling weak and shaken from the events of the night before that as the helplessness of her position once again swept over her, tears gathered in her eyes.

She fought against them, but slowly, one by one, they began to run down her cheeks, and it was too much of an effort even to wipe them away.

She heard somebody come into the Nursery next door and thought it was Jeannie returning from taking Felicity to the stables.

She did not move, thinking the maid would not disturb her, but as she stared through her tears at the empty trunk in front of her, the door of her bedroom opened.

She felt for her handkerchief, not wanting Jeannie to ask why she was crying, then heard a deep voice ask:

"What are you doing?"

For a moment she thought she must be dreaming.

Then as she raised her eyes she saw not Jeannie standing just inside the room, but the Earl.

He shut the door behind him and moved towards her to stand looking down at her kneeling beside the trunk, the tears on her cheeks.

"Why are you crying?" he asked.

She had the feeling that it was not what he had intended to say, but because there seemed to be no point in not answering him, she merely replied:

"I . . . I am . . . going . . . away."

As she spoke, she again felt in her belt for a handkerchief. She did not seem to have one, and the Earl took a handkerchief from his breast-pocket and held it out to her.

After a moment she took it from him and wiped her cheeks and eyes, wondering why he had come to her bedroom and feeling that perhaps he was still as angry as he had been the night before.

If he was, she felt it would be impossible to answer his accusations, and yet she longed to tell him that he had been mistaken.

He waited until she put the handkerchief into her lap. Then he said:

"I have come to apologise."

It was not what she had expected him to say, and her eyes widened as he went on:

"I learnt from Elizabeth Wick what you did for her last night. She is very grateful to you, and asks if before she leaves you will go and say good-bye to her."

"Y-yes . . . of course," Atayla managed to say.

"I have no excuse for the way I behaved," the Earl said, "except that you drove me mad with jealousy!"

Atayla felt she could not have heard him aright, and as she looked at him enquiringly, he said harshly:

"You have made me suffer in a million different ways ever since you came here, and last night, when I thought you had been with Hogarth, I could bear it no longer!"

"I . . . I do not think . . . understand," Atayla stammered.

Unexpectedly, the Earl smiled.

"Nor do I," he said. "It is something I have never experienced before, and I cannot explain it now."

He drew in his breath as he said:

"I suppose really I should ask you to tell me about yourself, and why you look as you do, and why you are dressed from Paris. Instead, I can only say that you have frightened me ever since you arrived."

"F-frightened you?" Atayla questioned in a little voice that seemed to come from very far away.

She was not certain what was happening.

She only knew that just as last night seemed a terrifying, dark nightmare, so now she seemed to have stepped into a dream that filled the room with sunshine and made her heart beat in a very strange and incomprehensible manner.

"If you really are, as I accused you last night, working on behalf of my wife, to incriminate me so that she can obtain a divorce, I know now that it does not matter. Whoever you are, whatever you are doing here, you are still you, and that is something from which I cannot escape."

"What . . . what are you . . . saying to me?" Atayla asked in a whisper.

The Earl drew in his breath.

"I am saying," he said, "that strangely, unpredictably, and completely incomprehensibly, I have fallen in love with you, and although I can hardly believe it myself, there is nothing I can do about it!"

"It . . . cannot be . . . true!"

"It is true!" he said. "And that is my only excuse for the way I treated you and the things I said."

He smiled, and it was very beguiling.

"I now come back to my original question—will you forgive me?"

443

A little unsteadily Atayla rose to her feet.

As she did so, she found it impossible to take her eyes from the Earl's, and she stood in front of him, looking up at him, as she said:

"I do not think I am . . . hearing what you are saying to me. Perhaps I am just . . . dreaming . . . and this is not . . . real."

The Earl moved a little nearer to her.

"It is very real," he said, "so real that nothing else matters, except that you are here. If you think I will let you leave, you are very much mistaken!"

"Y-you told me to . . . go," Atayla said childishly.

"Only because you tortured me until I could bear it no longer!" he answered. "Can you imagine what I felt when I saw you walking down the corridor? I believed . . ."

"How . . . could you . . . believe such wicked things of me?" Atayla interrupted.

"I asked myself the same question when I learnt where in fact you had been," the Earl admitted. "At the same time, I have been trying to hate and despise you ever since you first arrived, but have found it impossible."

Atayla looked at him wide-eyed, trying to realise exactly what he was saying to her. Then in a different tone of voice the Earl said:

"Help me, make me understand, tell me exactly why you came here with Felicity."

"I . . . wanted to tell you . . . last night . . . but you would not listen."

"I know," the Earl said, "and when I carried you back here unconscious and I saw the wound in your shoulder, I found it impossible to go on believing you were anything but as pure, sweet, and honest as you look."

He put out his hand to Atayla and said:

"Trust me. Tell me the truth, and whatever it may be, I know it will not prevent me from continuing to love you."

Without thinking, because his hands were out-stretched towards her, Atayla put her fingers in his, and as she touched him she felt as if a streak of sun-shine swept through her body.

She knew it was because he thrilled her, and al-though she had tried to hate him as he had tried to hate her, what she felt for him now was very differ-ent.

It was not only that he was handsome, magnificent, and she liked to look at him even when he was scowl-ing at her, but also that when he had gone away from the Castle it had seemed empty.

Although she would not admit it to herself, she had missed him and longed for his return.

Last night, even while she had been talking to Sir Christopher about her father, she had been vividly conscious of the Earl seated at the top of the table.

She had thought he looked Royal, but more than that he had looked a man she could admire because he was indeed a man, and she could feel the vibra-tions from him even when she was not looking at him.

Now as her fingers tightened on his, she was so vividly conscious of him that she felt they were joined together by some invisible link, and there was no ne-cessity for explanations.

She belonged to him, but how, she did not dare to think even to herself. She just knew, because he was touching her, that she was a part of him.

Then as she raised her eyes, she knew that he was thinking the same thing.

He took his hands from hers, and very slowly, as if he was afraid to frighten her, he put his arms round her and drew her closer to him.

"There is really no need to say anything," he said. "All I know is that I love you very much, my darling, and you are mine, and nothing else is of any impor-tance."

His voice was very deep and moving as he spoke. Then, still slowly and gently, his lips found hers.

He kissed her in a very different way from the way he had the night before, and as she felt the tenderness of his kiss, her heart seemed to turn over in her breast.

She knew this was love as she had wanted to find it, the love that her father had had for her mother, and which was the only treasure that was of any importance.

The Earl drew her closer still, and his lips became more demanding, more insistent, and very possessive, and yet he was still very gentle, and because it was so wonderful, Atayla felt once again the tears come into her eyes and run down her cheeks.

He raised his head.

"My darling, you must not cry. The goblins are all gone, and they will not frighten you again."

She tried to smile at what he had said. Then, because it was too much to bear, she hid her face against his shoulder.

"I . . . I thought I should . . . have to go away and . . . l-leave you!" she whispered.

His arms tightened.

"That is something you will never do. I was crazy last night when I told you to go, when I knew I could not live without you."

Suddenly he stiffened and said:

"You know, much as I love you, my precious one, I cannot, at the moment, ask you to marry me. But I will give Nadine the divorce she wants."

Atayla raised her head.

"You do not . . . really believe I came here with such wicked . . . intentions?"

"Why did you come?"

"It is so much less . . . complicated than what you have been . . . thinking," Atayla replied. "The *Comtesse,* for that is what she is called in Tangiers, asked Father Ignatius, at whose Mission I was staying, if he knew of an Englishwoman who would take Felicity safely to England."

She saw that the Earl was listening intently, but his arms were still holding her.

"I had been very ill," Atayla continued, "after desert robbers had swooped on our caravan . . . killed my father . . . and stabbed . . . me."

"So that is how you received that terrible wound on your shoulder!" the Earl exclaimed. "When I saw it last night, I understood why you fainted when I touched it."

"It had only just healed," Atayla replied. "As I had no money and could not stay at the Mission indefinitely, Father Ignatius took me to the Villa where Felicity's mother was living, and the very next day we started our journey to England."

"But why—why did my wife suddenly decide to return the child to me after taking her away in that cruel and heartless manner?" the Earl enquired.

"The *Comtesse* is very ill," Atayla replied, "and she said that Felicity was upsetting her relationship with the *Comte*. Moreover, the child herself was not . . . happy with him."

She felt the Earl stiffen and was afraid he might abuse the *Comte* as he had before, but he did not speak, and she went on:

"I agreed because I wanted to get back to England and try to find my relations, and it was a wonderful opportunity to have everything paid."

She looked towards the bed as she said:

"When we arrived, we had spent everything that I was given for the journey, and that is all I have left."

The Earl gave a little laugh that was very tender.

"And you really thought, my precious, that you could leave me and manage on your own with only that much between you and starvation?"

"I . . . I was frightened," Atayla confessed.

"You will never be frightened again," he promised. "Now I understand, and again I beg you to forgive me for thinking you had an ulterior motive when you arrived here looking so exquisitely beautiful, and of course so unsuitably dressed."

He paused before he said:

"I can guess now, and it was extremely stupid of me not to have thought of it before, but of course it was my wife who gave you the clothes you have been wearing."

Atayla nodded.

"The robbers took literally everything Papa and I possessed. All I had to wear was a Mission dress of grey cotton, which was so ugly that I am sure nobody would have looked at me except in horror!"

The Earl laughed.

"However ugly your dress, it would not hide your hair, your eyes, your adorable little nose, or your lips, my precious one, which were made for my kisses."

He kissed her again, demandingly, passionately. Then he asked:

"How many men have kissed you in the past?"

"None," Atayla replied, "and actually . . . I have never . . . met a man like . . . you before."

"I shall try to prevent you from meeting any men like me again," the Earl said. "But what on earth were you talking about to Christopher last night when I imagined he was making love to you?"

Atayla laughed.

"He knew all about Papa, and had read his books and the articles he wrote for the *Royal Geographical Magazine*."

The Earl looked down at her in surprise. Then he said:

"Are you telling me that your father was Gordon Lindsay?"

"Yes, but I never thought you would have heard of him."

"I have heard of him," the Earl said, "because I happen to be the President of the Royal Geographical

448

Society, and naturally I read the magazine whenever it is published."

"How could I have imagined . . . how could I have guessed that you would have . . . heard of Papa?"

"I found his articles extremely interesting and exciting," the Earl said, "but not as interesting and exciting as I find his daughter!"

Then he was kissing her again, kissing her with long, slow kisses which seemed to Atayla to take her heart from between her lips and make it his.

Because everything was suddenly so wonderful and so perfect, she moved a little closer to him, and he kissed her for a long time before he said:

"Now, as this is the first time you have been kissed and I am the only man to do so, tell me what you feel."

"It is wonderful! There are no . . . words," Atayla replied. "Your kisses are like the stars over the desert when they seem to fill not only the sky but the Universe and the sunshine coming up over the horizon. It is happiness I cannot possibly express . . . except perhaps in music."

The rapture and the touch of passion in her voice made the Earl draw in his breath.

Then he was kissing her until the room seemed to swing dizzily round them and he was lifting her into the sky, where there was only sunshine, and it seemed to burn in them both until it became a fire.

"I love you . . . I love you!" Atayla said first in her heart, then out loud.

"And I love you, my darling," he said, "but there is a great deal to do before I can make you my wife."

"I am not quite . . . sure that you should . . . marry me."

"I am quite sure, and I intend to marry you!" the Earl said firmly. "Nothing and nobody shall stop me, but as you must be aware, my precious one, a divorce takes time, and it also causes a scandal, which is extremely regrettable from the point of view of the family, but there is nothing we can do about that."

Because she loved him, Atayla heard the note of regret in his voice, and knew how much he would hate his private affairs to be dragged through the mud.

Then, as if he told himself that nothing mattered except their love, he swept her into his arms and was kissing her again.

It was impossible to think, but only to feel that un-expectedly, miraculously, they had reached a Heaven where there were no problems but only love.

CHAPTER SEVEN

*H*aving gone through the day still in the dream-world into which the Earl had taken her, all the time she was with Felicity Atayla was counting the hours, the minutes, and the seconds until she could be with him again.

After having lost time and space with the wonder of their love, the Earl had said in a voice that sounded strange and unsteady:

"I must leave you, my darling. The Wicks are leaving after luncheon and so is Hogarth. Although I know now I need not be jealous of him, I still do not want you to see him again."

"When can we be . . . together?" Atayla asked.

"I think it would be best after tea," the Earl said. "I

am sure you can leave somebody to amuse Felicity and come down to my Sitting-Room, where we can make plans."

She smiled at him, and he thought that the whole room was lit from the wonder in her eyes.

"I have a great deal to tell you," he said in a deep voice. "At the same time, all that matters is that you love me and I will never lose you."

He kissed her quickly, as if he knew that if he lingered he would never be able to go. Then he had gone from her bedroom, shutting the door behind him.

For the moment Atayla could not move, then she ran to the window, as if only by looking up at the sky could she be certain that the darkness had gone, she was no longer afraid, and could thank God for her happiness.

When Felicity returned from riding, they had luncheon, and afterwards, because Atayla knew she had to fill the afternoon, she made Felicity lie on the sofa and read to her one of the books she had brought up from the Library.

It was about Africa, but soon Atayla felt that she could explain to Felicity what she knew about it so much better in her own words.

So she told stories of the desert, the Arab tribes, and the strange towns, like Fez and Marrakesh, which had remained practically unchanged through the centuries.

Because she was so happy where she was now, the past seemed to Atayla to be receding into the distance, and the only things that were real were the Earl and the Castle.

At three o'clock she took Felicity riding again, and as she did not want the child to be tired, they did not gallop or race, but only rode round the Park and in the orchards.

Because of her love, Atayla felt the grounds were even more beautiful than they had been before and meant something so precious that it was part of her heart and her mind.

As if the child knew perceptively what she was thinking, Felicity asked:

"You like the Castle, do you not, Miss Lindsay?"

"It is the most beautiful place I have ever seen," Atayla answered, "and you and I are going to try to make it as beautiful inside as it is outside."

Felicity put her head on one side, as if she was thinking. Then she said:

"Do you mean with love?"

"Yes," Atayla answered, "with love. Then it will be perfect!"

When Felicity had had tea, Atayla felt her heart beating more quickly because it was now only a question of minutes before she would see the Earl.

She started to play a game with the little girl, with her dolls' house, and they rearranged the rooms and the small dolls which fitted inside it, and she told her a story about each one of them, so that they became like real people.

When at five o'clock Jeannie came to the Nursery as Atayla had asked her to do, she said:

"Here I am, Miss, and as I guessed Her Ladyship would be playing with the dolls' house, Chef has made some tiny little dishes which can be put inside for the dolls to eat."

Felicity was entranced at this idea, and while she and Jeannie were arranging them, Atayla slipped away.

She paused just for a moment in her own bedroom to look at herself in the mirror and wonder if the gown she was wearing was one of her most becoming.

But she knew as she looked at her reflection that it was the radiance in her eyes that the Earl would see, and the softness of her lips.

She blushed as she thought of him kissing her, and she knew it was something she wanted more than anything else in the world.

Because she was in such a hurry to be with him, she ran down the stairs, along the corridor, and down the Grand Staircase to the Hall.

The footman on duty moved towards her, but without waiting Atayla ran on towards the Earl's private Sitting-Room and opened the door herself.

As she expected, he was waiting for her, standing with his back to the mantelpiece, and as she entered their eyes met, and for the moment it was impossible for either of them to move.

Atayla felt as if her whole being vibrated towards him, and as if he felt the same he held out his arms and she ran to him.

He held her very close against him but he did not kiss her, and after a moment he said in a very deep voice:

"Before I tell you how much I love you, my precious one, I think we should talk. There are a great many things you must know and many explanations to be made."

Because his arms were round her and she could feel his heart beating against hers, it was hard to listen to what he was saying.

Yet, her mind told her that he was being sensible and she must do as he asked.

He pressed his lips for a moment against her forehead, then drew her to the sofa. They sat down side by side and he took her hand in his.

"This is the room in which I first saw you," he said, "and because you were so beautiful, I was sure you were dangerous, and I fought not only against you but against my own instinct."

"I can understand that now," Atayla said, "but you were very . . . intimidating."

"I swear that I will never frighten you again! And try to understand that if you were frightened, so was I!"

She looked up at him, and with a smile he said:

"After all I had been through, I had sworn that

never again would I give any woman my heart—
never again would I be such a fool as to fall in love."

Because Atayla knew that his first love had been the
Comtesse, she felt a little stab of jealousy, and looked
down so that he would not be aware of what she was
feeling.

He gave a little laugh that was very tender as he
said:

"Yes, I was in love with Nadine, but it was not in
the least, my precious one, what I feel now for you. I
thought I loved her because she was so beautiful, and
also because her parents told me she wished to marry
me. When I asked her, she said the same thing."

He paused, but Atayla did not speak, and he
went on:

"It is difficult now to realise how trusting I was, and
perhaps conceited enough to think that while I was
what is called a 'Matrimonial Catch,' Nadine really
loved me as a man."

There was a bitter note in his voice which made
Atayla tighten her fingers on his.

"Why did she not love you?"

Even as she asked the question she thought it extraordinary that anybody as handsome, wealthy, and
important as the Earl would not arouse love in a
young girl who could not have had much experience
of men.

Once again he read her thoughts and said:

"When she married me, Nadine was already passionately in love with the *Comte* de Soisson!"

"Oh . . . no!" Atayla exclaimed. "Why then did
she not marry him?"

"He was already married," the Earl answered,
"and had been for some years. The French marry
young. It was an arranged marriage, and his wife has
an equally distinguished lineage as that of the de Sois-
sons."

"And you did not know?"

"I had not the slightest idea she had even met the

man," the Earl answered, "until after we were married, when we encountered him by chance at a party in London."

There was silence for a few moments, as if he was looking back over the past. Then he said:

"Only a complacent man, or an idiot, would not have been aware that the moment my wife saw de Soisson she seemed to come alive, and the expression on their faces as they looked at each other was very revealing."

"It must have been very hurtful for you."

"I was hurt because, although I knew by that time that Nadine did not love me, she was at least pleasant and complacent and did everything I asked of her. She was also carrying our child."

There was silence until Atayla asked:

"What happened?"

"Nothing then," the Earl replied. "I asked my wife to tell me the truth, and she finally admitted that she was in love with the *Comte*. After a great deal of prevarication and lies, she told me that she had loved him ever since she was seventeen, and that he had seduced her when she was in Paris with her parents."

Atayla gave a little cry of horror, and the Earl went on:

"The *Comte* had then withdrawn from what he knew was an explosive situation and told Nadine he would not see her again. But soon after Felicity was born I became aware that they were writing to each other and meeting secretly whenever he came to London."

"What did you do . . . about it?"

"I threatened to kill him, and he was wise enough to keep out of my way. But Nadine made it very clear where her affections lay, and we became more and more estranged, until we saw as little as possible of each other, except on public occasions or when we had guests staying in the Castle."

Because she could not bear to think of him being unhappy, Atayla murmured softly:

"It must have been very . . . hard for . . . you."

"I told myself I did not care," the Earl answered, "and actually I no longer loved Nadine. But she was my wife, and I was determined that there would be no scandal which would hurt the family and damage our name, which has been respected for centuries."

"I can understand how that sort of life must have made you very . . . very . . . unhappy."

"I suppose I grew bitter and cynical," the Earl said, "and I told myself that all women were untrustworthy and promiscuous."

Atayla shivered, and the Earl said:

"All that is now forgotten, my precious. I know you are different, so very, very different, and are everything I wanted to find in the woman I loved but I was sure did not exist."

Because what he had said moved her and the note of passion in his voice made her yearn for his kisses, Atayla turned her face up to his and thought he would take her in his arms.

Then, with what seemed a superhuman effort, he looked away from her as he said:

"I must go on telling you everything that happened so that you will understand."

"I do . . . understand," Atayla said. "At the same time . . . I am . . . listening."

"Three years ago," the Earl said, "I learnt that the *Comte* was in England and Nadine was seeing him, and I was quite certain they were lovers even though she deceived me so cleverly that I could not prove it."

His lips tightened before he said:

"We had some flaming rows, then one day, quite unexpectedly, when I was out hunting, she left the Castle early in the morning, and it was not until I returned just before dinner that I learnt that she had gone and had taken Felicity with her."

"It was a . . . cruel thing to do."

"I am sure it was the *Comte*'s idea, because he hated me and wanted to hurt me," the Earl said simply. "It was not surprising, as I had said some very unpleasant things about him to Nadine, which she doubtless repeated to him."

"What did you do?"

"When I realised she and the *Comte* had left England together and gone to Paris, I did nothing."

"Nothing?"

"At first I pretended that she had gone on a holiday with the child and would soon be returning. Then, as the months passed and people began to talk, I refused to discuss it, and left them to think what they wished."

"And you did not hear from . . . your wife?"

"I heard nothing," the Earl replied, "until about ten months ago. Then a letter arrived from some French Solicitors, informing me that the *Comte*'s wife was dead, and asking me to divorce my wife so that she and de Soisson could be married."

"So the *Comte*'s wife is dead!" Atayla exclaimed in surprise. "Father Ignatius was not aware of that."

"Yes, he was free to marry, but Nadine was still tied to me."

"And you would not divorce her?"

"Why should I?" the Earl asked. "A divorce, whoever is at fault, causes a scandal, and what is a private affair between two people then becomes public and is reported in the newspapers for every Tom, Dick, and Harry to read."

"So you refused."

"I refused categorically, and had no wish whatever to remarry, until, my darling, I saw you."

"How could I have guessed . . . how could I have thought for one moment that you could ever love me," Atayla asked, "when all I could see was hate in your eyes?"

"I was hating you because you disturbed and upset

me; because every time I looked at you, my heart seemed to turn a dozen somersaults."

He smiled before he went on:

"I was convinced that you were a temptress, a serpent, who had been sent to blackmail me into giving Nadine a divorce."

"I do not think I . . . understand," Atayla said.

"It is quite simple," the Earl answered. "If she could obtain evidence against me of infidelity, and since we had so many rows before she left she could call the servants as witnesses to my cruelty towards her, she would definitely have a case against me."

He paused for a moment, then went on:

"Actually, I thought that she would more probably insist that I divorce her, citing the *Comte*. The case would then go through much more quickly and with less publicity."

"I . . . understand," Atayla said, "but will you . . . now divorce her . . . as she . . . wants?"

"I have already draughted a letter to my Solicitors in London," the Earl replied, "telling them to go ahead immediately and to inform my wife that she will be free as quickly as it can be arranged."

As he finished speaking, he released Atayla's hand and put his arms round her.

"Then, my precious love," he said, "I will be able to ask you to do me the honour of becoming my wife."

"You know it will be the most . . . wonderful thing that could ever . . . happen to . . . me," Atayla said.

"I swear I will make you happy! I do not think either of us doubts that. But, my darling, it means that you will have to leave here immediately."

Atayla stiffened and looked at him in astonishment.

"Leave?" she asked. "But . . . why?"

"Because, my sweet, if I am to be what is called the innocent party, it would be a great mistake for you to stay here, even with Grandmama as a Chaperone."

"But . . . why? Why?" Atayla asked again.

"Because in England we have a faceless official called 'The Queen's Proctor,' and whoever brings a case for divorce has to lead a blameless life until the case has been heard and a further six months have passed."

"Six months!" Atayla exclaimed, with a little cry of dismay.

"It will be hard, very hard, but then we will be together for the rest of our lives."

"I cannot . . . lose you," Atayla said. "I cannot bear to . . . leave you!"

"Oh, my darling, if you only knew what it means to me to hear you say that," the Earl replied. "But it is something that has to be done, first because I must protect you not only against any scandal and gossip but also against myself, and secondly, I must be free!"

He gave a little laugh as he added:

"Do you really think I could be here with you every day in the Castle without making everybody aware how much I love you and how desperately I want you?"

Atayla knew he was speaking sense. At the same time, she was afraid to leave him.

"Suppose," she said, "if it takes all that long . . . time for you to be . . . free, you find when it is . . . all over that you do not . . . love me?"

"That will never happen," the Earl answered. "I love you, adore you, and worship you. I also know unmistakably that we not only belong to each other but that nothing and nobody will ever come between us."

As if he thought he was being too confident, he put his fingers under Atayla's chin and turned her face up to his.

"Swear to me," he said, "that you love me as I love you, and that no other man will ever mean anything to you."

"There is . . . no other man in the whole world but you," Atayla replied, "and it is only because I love you so desperately with all my heart and soul that I am afraid of losing you."

The Earl pulled her closer and his lips were on hers.

Then as she surrendered herself to the insistent demand of his kisses, she knew he was right when he said they could never be parted and they belonged to each other.

Once again she felt as if the sunshine swept through her, lighting her whole body and kindling a fire within her which answered the fire she felt burning within the Earl.

It was in the beat of their hearts, in the touch of their lips, and in every breath they drew.

Only as he carried her up into the sky and they touched the wings of ecstasy did she say a little incoherently:

"I love you . . . I love you . . . and when you kiss me there is . . . nothing but love . . . and you in the whole world!"

The Earl kissed her again, and she knew they were no longer human but part of the stars, the moon, and the sun, and it would be impossible ever to come back to earth.

"I love you!" the Earl said a long time later, and his voice was deep and unsteady, "but, my precious, I have to tell you what plans I am making for you."

"What are . . . they?" Atayla asked, and now she was afraid because his voice was serious.

"I have an aunt who lives about five miles from here. She is a widow and a very kind woman given to good works. I know she is lonely, because she has no children, and that she would welcome both you and Felicity if you went to live with her."

"I shall be . . . able to see . . . you?" Atayla asked.

The Earl smiled.

"You may be quite certain of that. I will ride across the fields and we will meet several times a week, and naturally you will bring Felicity here to see her great-grandmother."

"You are . . . quite sure you will . . . come?" Atayla asked in a small voice.

"You may be sure of it!" the Earl replied. "At the same time, it will be hard, my darling, as you are well aware, not to be with you every moment of the day and night. But we have to wait. Then when finally we are together, we shall be able to forget the discomfort and misery we must endure so that we can be married."

"You are . . . certain that is really the . . . quickest way of doing it?"

"It is the only way," the Earl replied. "In fact, if my wife brought a divorce case against me, because she has already left me and is living in what the world calls 'sin,' she would probably not be successful in the Courts, and we would have to remain married for the rest of our lives."

Atayla gave a cry of horror, and the Earl went on:

"Do not be afraid—that is not going to happen! But because I am fighting in every way for our future happiness, we have to observe the proprieties and be very, very careful."

"I will do whatever you tell me to do."

The Earl looked down at her and his eyes were very tender.

"You are so sweet, my lovely one," he said, "and one day, when you are my wife, I shall be able to tell you how much you mean to me, and give you all the things I long for you to have."

"All I want are . . . your kisses."

As she spoke she saw the fire in the Earl's eyes, and he kissed her until they were both breathless.

Only when it was possible to speak again did she ask:

"How soon . . . are Felicity and I to . . . leave?"

"I shall arrange everything tomorrow," he said, "and I anticipate that my aunt will be ready to receive you the following day."

He saw the unhappiness in Atayla's eyes and said:

"That gives us two nights and a day together, my precious love. Will you dine with me tonight?"

"Can I do that?"

"Nobody as yet knows of our plans, and although perhaps some of the staff will be surprised that a Governess should come downstairs to the Dining-Room, I think if anyone asks questions in the future, they will be loyal to us. Besides, as I have already said, you are chaperoned by my grandmother."

"You are going to tell her about us?"

"I will not have to tell her," the Earl replied. "I do not mind betting a very large sum that she already knows what is happening."

He saw the consternation in Atayla's face and laughed.

"Do not worry! Grandmama will be so delighted that I am to be married again and have an heir that she will welcome any woman, and especially you, my precious one."

"Why should you think that?"

"Because she already admires you, and although she is suspicious that you are not the Governess you pretend to be, she will, I know, be very impressed when she learns who your father was."

"Are you saying that she will have heard of Papa?"

"Why does that seem so surprising to you? I am only astonished that she has not discovered it already!" the Earl said. "Grandmama visited North Africa several times with my grandfather, who was an inveterate traveller and insatiably curious about the strange customs of the Moslem and Arab world."

Atayla gave a little cry.

"It is so extraordinary! Papa had no idea anybody

ever read his books except some elderly Dons in Universities and a few younger students who study the subject in Schools. And yet, here, where I least expected it, I find that not only you and Sir Christopher but also your grandmother have heard of him!"

"Which is the most important?" the Earl asked.

"You, of course!" Atayla answered, resting her cheek against his shoulder. "I am so thrilled, and so proud that you realise how clever Papa was, and how valuable in the future his research on African tribes will be to those who really want to know about that almost-unknown Continent."

"I will make sure that your father's books are known, and when I next go to London I will persuade his publishers to take such steps that the sales will be much larger than they anticipate."

"That is the most wonderful present you could give me!" Atayla cried. "Thank you . . . thank you for being so . . . understanding."

The Earl did not answer. He only kissed her again.

Then as she realised that the time they had been together had flown and she should go upstairs and say good-night to Felicity, Atayla rose to her feet.

"I may really dine with you this evening?"

"I have no intention of sitting in the Dining-Room alone," the Earl said, "and also, my precious, we have a great deal to say to each other after dinner, only perhaps it will not all be in words."

His eyes were on her lips, and she felt as if he kissed them again.

Then, because she wanted to stay but knew she should go, she smiled at him and went from the room before he could prevent her from doing so.

As she went upstairs, she was saying over and over again in her heart a prayer of gratitude and thankfulness for the happiness she had found so unexpectedly at a moment when she had been feeling nothing but fear and misery.

Felicity had had her supper and was undressed and ready for bed when Atayla came into the Nursery.

"You are back!" Felicity cried. "I have so much to tell you! Jeannie and I put the dishes in the dolls' house and they had such a big supper that we think they will all have tummy-aches."

"I hope that is something that will not happen to you," Atayla said.

"No, of course not," Felicity replied. "I must not have a tummy-ache because tomorrow you promised to race me on my pony. Did you ask Papa if he would race too?"

"I am sure he will want to," Atayla answered, and Felicity gave a little shout of joy.

"I love Papa when he is racing with me," she said, "and when those silly people have gone away, perhaps he will race every day."

Atayla felt a little constriction of her heart at the thought that the Earl would not be with them and she and Felicity would be living in a strange house.

However, she did not want to spoil the evening by thinking about it, so she heard Felicity's prayers and kissed her good-night.

Felicity put her arms round her neck and kissed her.

"I love you, Miss Lindsay," she said, "and I am loving everybody like you told me to do."

She thought for a moment, then she said:

"I love you, and Papa, and Grandmama because she lets me play with her jewellery, and Jeannie and Jackson, and of course *Dragonfly* but not quite as much as I love you."

Atayla laughed.

"Thank you, darling, that is a very big compliment."

Felicity kissed her again. Then Atayla tucked her up and said:

"Good-night, dearest. God keep you, and His angels watch over you."

It was something her mother had said to her as a child, and as she left Felicity's room she thought that God had watched over her and sent His angels to protect her and help her.

Now never again in her whole life would she doubt that help was always there if one prayed for it.

Jeannie had her bath ready for her, and they had a long discussion as to which gown would be most suitable for her to wear as she was dining downstairs.

Because she thought the Earl would think it wise, Atayla told Jeannie for the first time about her father and how he had written articles for the *Royal Geographical Magazine* and how the Earl had read them because he was President of the Society.

"You can understand," she said, "that it is very exciting for me to find here in the Castle somebody who understands the work my father was doing in Africa."

"Well, whatever the reason, I think it's ever so nice for you, Miss, to be dining downstairs, which is where you ought to be. We were all saying in the Housekeeper's room that you looked prettier than any of the other ladies who came to the party."

"Thank you," Atayla said with a smile.

The gown they decided on was white and silver and made her look very young, which was how she felt the Earl would want her to look, young and untouched by anybody except himself.

When she was ready, she stood for a moment looking in the mirror. Her eyes were shining with excitement, and she thought perhaps the Earl was wise in sending her away.

It would have been impossible for anybody who saw them together not to be aware that they were in love.

"I love him, I love him!" she told her reflection, then walked excitedly to the door.

Only as she reached it did Jeannie, who was gathering up her things, say:

"Oh, by the way, Miss, I nearly forgot, there's a letter come for you by the afternoon post. I put it on the mantelpiece so you'd see it when you came up to the Nursery."

"A letter?" Atayla questioned.

"Yes, Miss, with a foreign stamp on it, but you went straight into Her Ladyship's bedroom, so I expects you missed it."

Atayla did not speak, but she went into the Nursery and found the letter where Jeannie had put it on the mantelpiece propped up against the clock.

She looked at it and saw as she had expected that it had come from Tangiers, and she wondered if it was from the *Comtesse*.

Just for a moment she thought it might be a mistake to open it. Perhaps something she might read there would spoil her evening with the Earl.

Then she knew she could not go down to him and be wondering all the time whether there was news of his wife which was important to them both.

Slowly, because her fingers were trembling, she opened the envelope.

There was only a very thin sheet of writing-paper inside, and as she drew it out she read the signature and was aware that it was not from the *Comtesse* but from Father Ignatius.

She thought it was kind of him to write, and started to read what he had written in his upright, well-formed hand.

My dear Atayla,

I am praying that God has brought you safely to the end of your journey and that you are now installed in Roth Castle and the Earl has been pleased to see his daughter again and have her with him.

I am writing to give you the very sad news that the Comtesse died yesterday and her Funeral will take place tomorrow.

She had, as the Doctors suspected, a deeply infected lung, and there was no chance of her ever recovering from the Tuberculosis which, alas, takes the lives of so many people, and for which there is no known cure.

I am hoping you will break the news of her mother's death to Felicity as gently as possible, who we know loved her and was loved by her. But she is now with her father, and I think God, in his wisdom, directed that she should reach England in safety before this tragedy happened.

Write to me when you have the time. You know that I pray for you daily, that God is looking after you, and His love never fails.

I remain, my dear Atayla,
Yours in Christ Jesus,
Father Ignatius

Atayla reread the letter and for a moment she could hardly believe that what she had read was not just a figment of her imagination and her hopes.

To make sure, she read it again.

Then as she put it back into the envelope, she knew that Father Ignatius was right: God had looked after her and the future was filled with sunshine.

The Earl looked down at Atayla and said gently:
"I think, my darling, we should leave now."

"Yes, of course," Atayla answered.

As she spoke she found it difficult to believe that she was the Earl's wife and they were leaving the Castle to join the private train that was waiting for them at the Halt.

They had been married in the little Church in the

Park, and the only other person there had been a wildly excited Felicity, who had been allowed to be a bridesmaid and hold Atayla's bouquet when the Earl put the ring on her finger.

It was a very simple, very quiet little Service, but the sincerity of it seemed to Atayla to join with the music that vibrated from her heart to the Earl's and was the song of the angels in a special Heaven into which he was taking her.

"How could I have known, how could I have guessed," she asked, "when I came here frightened and with no money, that I was stepping into Paradise? Or that the Earl of Rothwell, who threatened to throw Felicity and me out into the night, was the man I would love with all my heart and soul?"

As soon as the Earl read Father Ignatius's letter, he had taken control of the situation. He insisted that they should be married at once, secretly and without any fuss.

The explanation of what had happened to Nadine, he said, could be given after they returned from their honeymoon.

"Will people not think it very . . . strange that you should marry me?" Atayla asked.

"Some of my friends and relations will obviously ask questions," the Earl said, "but as far as the Social World is concerned, Nadine has not been heard of or mentioned for three years. They will, I expect, assume that she died before Felicity came back to the Castle, and as a free man I can obviously do what I like."

He gave a laugh before he said:

"And what I like, my precious one, is that you should be my wife and we will be together now, at this moment, and forever!"

He kissed from her lips any further questions she might ask, and she knew that all she wanted was to be in his arms and not have to worry ever again about the future.

The Dowager, as the Earl had expected, had been delighted.

"You are certainly full of surprises, my child," she had said to Atayla, "but I was always convinced you were not the Governess you pretended to be."

"I only wish you could have met Papa before he died," Atayla replied. "I am sure he would have interested and amused you far better than I can."

"I am just staying alive now," the Dowager said, "to see Valor's son running about the Castle, and then I can give half my jewellery to him, and half to Felicity."

"It would be a great mistake for you to spoil them," the Earl replied, "and you must keep alive so that your great-grandson can enjoy you just as I always have done."

The Dowager was delighted.

"I thought I was growing too old for compliments," she said, "but I am hoping to hear some more before I finally sink into the grave."

They had laughed, then she had kissed Atayla and the Earl and said:

"Go off and enjoy yourselves. I will look after the Castle until you come back."

"And I will look after you, Grandmama," Felicity said. "I am going to be very, very good, so as not to worry my new Mama, whom I love very much."

Because she was so moved by what the child said, Atayla felt the tears come into her eyes, and, as if the Earl understood, he put his arm round her.

"We are not going to worry about anything," he said, "and Felicity is going to look after the horses for us, are you not, my poppet?"

He picked her up in his arms as he spoke, and Felicity hugged him and said:

"I'll look after them and see that Jackson exercises them properly so that you'll be pleased when you come back."

"I will be very, very pleased," the Earl said with a smile, and kissed her.

As he did so, Atayla thought it was the first time she had seen him kiss his daughter, and the love he gave Felicity would be the same as the love he would give their children.

"I was right," she told herself. "All the Castle needed was love, and now it will be perfect!"

The household was waiting on the steps to wave them off, and Atayla and the Earl, having said good-bye to Mr. Osborne and Dawson, walked down the steps to where the carriage was waiting.

Felicity threw the first rose-petals at them. Then there was a shower of petals and also some rice, which Atayla remembered symbolised fertility.

There were cheers as the carriage drove down the drive, and Atayla slipped her hand into the Earl's.

"Did you enjoy your wedding, my precious?" he asked. "To me it was exactly the ceremony I wanted to have with somebody I love, and the Church seemed to be filled with love."

"That is . . . what I felt too."

He lifted her hand to his lips as he said:

"I knew that was what you were feeling! I think I know everything about you, and while I read your thoughts, I know they are my thoughts too."

"Oh, darling, you must always be like that!" Atayla said. "And I love you until I can only think, dream, and speak of love!"

Later that night, when the Earl's private train had drawn into a siding so that they could sleep without being disturbed, they lay close in a large bedstead which almost filled the sleeping-compartment, and Atayla said:

"I love you so much . . . and what you have made me feel is so wonderful . . . so perfect . . . so glorious that neither French nor Arabic, which are the only two languages I speak besides English, have . . . words to express it."

"Why should we need words?" the Earl asked in his deep voice. "But, my darling, tell me if I made you happy."

"So happy that I am still . . . flying in the . . . sky," Atayla answered passionately.

"I should be very frightened if that were true," the Earl said. "But I am holding you here safely in my arms, and I will never lose you, never let you go."

He drew a deep breath which was almost a sigh before he said:

"God certainly moves in a mysterious way! How could I have guessed that you would walk into my life so unexpectedly and change it so that I am not even sure if I am myself?"

"I want you just as you are," Atayla said. "No man could be more wonderful."

"You did not think that when you first met me."

"You frightened me," Atayla said. "At the same time, I thought no man could be so handsome, so distinguished . . . or so . . . masculine."

She paused before she added:

"When I came down to dinner when the Prince of Wales was there, I thought you were the one who looked Royal."

"You are flattering me!" the Earl exclaimed. "But I knew even then that you had turned my whole life upside-down, and although I was afraid to admit it, you were the Queen of my heart."

"Now you are flattering me!" Atayla whispered. "I have never presumed to be a Queen, but only to occupy the most important post in the world—that of your wife!"

The way she spoke made the Earl's lips seek hers, and for a moment as he touched them it was just a kiss of love and adoration.

Then as he felt her quiver against him and as her

lips clung to his, their softness and innocence aroused an emotion in him different from anything he had ever known before.

He drew her closer still, and the fire within him leapt into flame.

To Atayla the love he had already given her was so perfect and so incredibly rapturous that she felt as if they were indivisibly one person and had no identity apart from each other.

While she knew their love was sacred, she was aware that at the same time he was teaching her about a love that invaded her like shafts of sunshine and vibrated through her until it was as if a light blazed from them both and grew and intensified with every breath they drew.

As he kissed her and his hands were touching her body, she could feel the strange sensations he had given her, which were unlike anything she had ever known existed, grow and intensify.

The fire on his lips was answered by the flames she felt within her, rising and rising until the Earl was lifting her into the sky and they were part of the blazing centre of the sun itself.

"You are mine!" she heard him say hoarsely, and his voice seemed very far away. "You are mine, my darling, from now until eternity, and I will never lose you."

"I am . . . yours!" Atayla replied. "Love me . . . please . . . love me . . . I am yours . . . all yours forever . . . and ever . . ."

Then the fires within them joined, and it was impossible to think.

The glory and wonder of it blinded their eyes, and there was only the radiance of the sun and the song of the angels.

About the Author

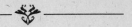

DAME BARBARA CARTLAND, the world's best known and bestselling author of romantic fiction, is also an historian, playwright, lecturer, political speaker and television personality. She has now written over six hundred and thirty-four books and has the distinction of holding *The Guinness Book of Records* title of the world's bestselling author, having sold over six hundred and fifty million copies of her books all over the world.

Barbara Cartland was invested by Her Majesty The Queen as a Dame of the Order of the British Empire in 1991, is a Dame of Grace of St. John of Jerusalem, and was one of the first women in one thousand years ever to be admitted to the Chapter General. She is President of the Hertfordshire Branch of The Royal College of Midwives, and is President and Founder in 1964 of the National Association for Health.

Miss Cartland lives in England at Camfield Place, Hatfield, Hertfordshire.